NIGHTMARE'S
R E A L M
NEW TALES OF THE WEIRD AND FANTASTIC

EDITED BY S. T. JOSHI

DARK REGIONS PRESS
—2017—

Nightmare's Realm: New Tales of The Weird and Fantastic
© 2017 Dark Regions Press LLC.

Introduction © 2017 by S. T. Joshi
Prologue: To a Dreamer © 1920 by H. P. Lovecraft
The Dreamed © 2017 by Ramsey Campbell
A Predicament © 2017 by Darrell Schweitzer
Kafkaesque © 2017 by Jason V Brock
Beneath the Veil © 2017 by David Barker
Dreams Downstream © 2017 by John Shirley
Death-Dreaming © 2017 by Nancy Kilpatrick
Cast Lots © 2017 by Richard Gavin
The Wake © 2017 by Steve Rasnic Tem
Dead Letter Office © 2017 by Caitlín R. Kiernan
The Art of Memory © 2017 by Donald Tyson
What You Do Not Bring Forth © 2017 by John Langan
The Barrier Between © 2017 by W. H. Pugmire
Sleep Hygiene © 2017 by Gemma Files
Purging Mom © 2017 by Jonathan Thomas
The Fifth Stone © 2017 by Simon Strantzas
In the City of Sharp Edges © 2017 by Stephen Woodworth
An Actor's Nightmare © 2017 by Reggie Oliver
Epilogue: Dream-Land by Edgar Allan Poe
(first published in the June 1844 issue of *Graham's Magazine*)

Dark Regions Press, LLC
P.O. Box 31022
Portland, OR 97231
United States of America
www.darkregions.com

Edited by S. T. Joshi
Cover image © 2015 by Samuel Araya
Interior design by Cyrus Wraith Walker

Trade Paperback Edition

ISBN: 978-1-62641-246-0

CONTENTS

Introduction *by S. T. Joshi* 4

Prologue: To a Dreamer *by H. P. Lovecraft* 9

The Dreamed *by Ramsey Campbell* 11
A Predicament *by Darrell Schweitzer* 38
Kafkaesque *by Jason V Brock* 45
Beneath the Veil *by David Barker* 70
Dreams Downstream *by John Shirley* 79
Death-Dreaming *by Nancy Kilpatrick* 106
Cast Lots *by Richard Gavin* 116
The Wake *by Steve Rasnic Tem* 131
Dead Letter Office *by Caitlín R. Kiernan* 143
The Art of Memory *by Donald Tyson* 161
What You Do Not Bring Forth *by John Langan* 179
The Barrier Between *by W. H. Pugmire* 189
Sleep Hygiene *by Gemma Files* 199
Purging Mom *by Jonathan Thomas* 222
The Fifth Stone *by Simon Strantzas* 243
In the City of Sharp Edges *by Stephen Woodworth* 259
An Actor's Nightmare *by Reggie Oliver* 279

Epilogue: Dream-Land *by Edgar Allan Poe* 314

Notes on Contributors 317

INTRODUCTION

The now hackneyed Shakespearean dictum "There are more things in heaven and earth, Horatio, / Than are dreamt of in your philosophy" (*Hamlet* 1.5.166–67) could serve as an encapsulated motto for the entire realm of weird fiction, which is devoted to revealing exactly what those "more things" might be, whether they be in the external world or in the depths of our tortured minds. The central tenet of supernatural fiction is the implicit assertion that the events depicted in a story are *not* a dream but actually exist in the objectively "real" world—but the matter is rarely as clear-cut as that. Could the phenomena in question be "just a dream" (in which case the story becomes one of psychological, rather than supernatural, horror)? Or is there some nebulous middle ground where dream, hallucination, and reality mingle inextricably, with only terror as the result?

The linkage of dreams and weird fiction can be traced all the way back to the very dawn of literary history, if the prophetic dreams in the *Epic of Gilgamesh* (c. 1700 B.C.E.) are any testimony. Dreams figure in Shakespeare's two strangest plays, *Hamlet* (does Hamlet really see the ghost of his father, or is it merely a dream?) and *Macbeth.* And it seems obligatory to cite the dream that Horace Walpole maintained—several months after the novel was published—inspired *The Castle of Otranto* (1764), a book that laid the foundations for the entire genre of weird fiction:

> I waked one morning in the beginning of last June from a dream, of which all I could recover was, that I had thought myself in an ancient castle (a very natural dream for a head filled like mine with Gothic story) and that on the uppermost bannister of a great staircase I saw a gigantic hand in armour. In the evening I sat down and began to write, without knowing in the least what I intended to say or relate. The work grew on my hands, and I grew fond of it . . . (Letter to William Cole, 9 March 1765)

The "it was all a dream" trope, now the butt of such deserved ridicule, can be found as early as William Makepeace Thackeray's "The Painter's Bargain" (1838), and the terrifying reality of dreams on a disturbed consciousness figure largely in the novels of Charles Brockden Brown.

Ambrose Bierce wrote a scintillating essay, "Visions of the Night" (1887), in which he outlined the bizarre dreams that inspired some of his greatest tales, including "The Death of Halpin Frayser," in which the hapless protagonist dreams that he is being pursued by the ghost of his own mother. Arthur Machen's *The Hill of Dreams* (1907) may only be on the borderline of the weird, but its mesmerizing account of the protagonist's dream of living a life in ancient Rome is one of its most compelling features. And who can forget that, in the invented cosmology of Lord Dunsany in *The Gods of Pegāna* (1905), the entire universe and all its inhabitants are merely the dreams of the god Māna-Yood-Sushāī? Dunsany, let us recall, also wrote a volume frankly titled *A Dreamer's Tales* (1910).

Franz Kafka's "The Metamorphosis" (1912) opens strikingly: "As Gregor Samsa awoke one morning from uneasy dreams he found himself transformed in his bed into a gigantic insect." But if we are tempted to regard the entire narrative as a dream, Kafka bluntly rejects that notion by stating "It was no dream." Kafka is, however, clearly intent on incorporating the imagery of nightmare into his narrative, as he does in much of his other work, especially his three novels.

H. P. Lovecraft was haunted by bizarre dreams from childhood. At the age of five he had horrible nightmares of winged, faceless creatures that he labeled "night-gaunts." "Beyond the Wall of Sleep" (1919) opens with a veritable manifesto on the relation of dreams and reality:

> I have frequently wondered if the majority of mankind ever pause to reflect upon the occasionally titanic significance of dreams, and of the obscure world to which they belong. Whilst the greater number of our nocturnal visions are perhaps no more than faint and fantastic reflections of our waking experiences—Freud to the contrary with his puerile symbolism—there are still a certain remainder whose immundane and ethereal character permits of no ordinary interpretation, and whose vaguely exciting and disquieting effect suggests possible minute glimpses into a sphere of mental existence no less important than physical life, yet separated from that life by an all but impassable barrier. From my experience I cannot doubt but that man, when lost to terrestrial consciousness, is indeed sojourning in another and uncorporeal life of far different nature

from the life we know; and of which only the slightest and most indistinct memories linger after waking. From those blurred and fragmentary memories we may infer much, yet prove little. We may guess that in dreams life, matter, and vitality, as the earth knows such things, are not necessarily constant; and that time and space do not exist as our waking selves comprehend them. Sometimes I believe that this less material life is our truer life, and that our vain presence on the terraqueous globe is itself the secondary or merely virtual phenomenon.

All this, let us recall, is written in the context of a short story, and the views expressed here cannot be regarded as reflecting Lovecraft's own philosophical thought. But throughout his work he emphasizes the tenuousness of the distinction between the dream world and the real world. The mere fact that such a figure as Richard Upton Pickman, the human painter in "Pickman's Model" (1926), can find himself a king of the ghouls in *The Dream-Quest of Unknown Kadath* (1926–27) shows how permeable these realms are.

The dream theme is a dominant one in twentieth-century weird fiction, if such works as Fritz Leiber's "The Dreams of Albert Moreland" (1945), Ray Bradbury's "Fever Dream" (1948), and Charles Beaumont's "Perchance to Dream" (1958) are any guide. Ramsey Campbell's pioneering volume *Demons by Daylight* (1973) is a rich feast of dream-imagery, and he returned to the theme in one of his best novels, *Incarnate* (1983), where a character makes the provocative utterance: "Dreaming isn't a state of mind . . . it's a state of being." It is a sentiment that Thomas Ligotti in *Songs of a Dead Dreamer* (1989) would no doubt endorse.

The stories in this volume probe the relation of dreams

to the real world, and to the human mind, in ways that are baffling, intriguing, terrifying, and poignant. Are we dreaming or are we awake? Can dreams create a kind of quasi-reality and affect the workings of the real world? Can technology enhance or even create a dream-realm? The stories in this book make no claims to provide definitive answers to these questions, but they all seem to underscore that plangent utterance we find in one of Poe's last poems: "*All* that we see or seem / Is but a dream within a dream."

—S. T. Joshi

PROLOGUE:
TO A DREAMER

H. P. LOVECRAFT

I scan thy features, calm and white
Beneath the single taper's light;
Thy dark-fring'd lids, behind whose screen
Are eyes that view not earth's demesne.

And as I look, I fain would know
The paths whereon thy dream-steps go;
The spectral realms that thou canst see
With eyes veil'd from the world and me.

For I have likewise gaz'd in sleep
On things my mem'ry scarce can keep,
And from half-knowing long to spy
Again the scenes before thine eye.

To a Dreamer

I, too, have known the peaks of Thok;
The vales of Pnath, where dream-shapes flock;
The vaults of Zin—and well I trow
Why thou demand'st that taper's glow.

But what is this that subtly slips
Over thy face and bearded lips?
What fear distracts thy mind and heart,
That drops must from thy forehead start?

Old visions wake—thine op'ning eyes
Gleam black with clouds of other skies,
And as from some daemoniac sight
I flee into the haunted night.

THE DREAMED

RAMSEY CAMPBELL

By the time Don reached the Sea Panorama apartments he felt ready to sleep for a week. He hadn't been able to doze on the plane to the Greek island, and he'd been afraid to do so on the coach in case he missed his destination; Estelle from the travel company had stayed at the airport, promising her clients she would see them tomorrow. Just the same, he must have nodded off, because when the driver's voice roused him he found he was the sole remaining passenger. "Sleep in an armour," the driver said.

He was announcing the apartments outside which the bus had stopped, of course. He lugged Don's suitcase out of the belly of the bus and drove away without another word. Don hauled the case up the ramp to Reception, a large space in which straight chairs that put him in mind of a waiting-room were lined up beside a bookcase full of tipsy books. The indirect yellowish light was so subdued that he could have fancied it was meant to aid slumber. The trundling of his luggage brought a broad swarthy woman with an unashamed moustache out of the office behind the counter. "You are leaving," she told him.

"I certainly hope not," Don said and laughed as much as seemed polite. "I've only just arrived."

"Ah, you are another." By way of explanation she flourished a passport before laying it on the counter. "Passport," she declared—requested, rather.

Don fumbled in his jacket, which felt weighed down by the sultry humid midnight. The cover of his passport was tacky with traces of stickers. She peered at the photograph and blinked at him. "Mr Johns," she said.

"Well, really Jones."

"Yes, Johns."

"Jones," Don said with as much amusement as he could summon. "Donald Jones, but everybody calls me Don."

"Don." Apparently this signified some kind of acceptance. "You are two," she said as she made for the office, returning with a key that bore the number on a metal tag. Along with it she gave him an envelope printed with the logo of the travel company but otherwise blank. "Go round," she said, scooping at the air to indicate his route, but his luggage was only leading him back down the ramp when she called "You are finished."

She was holding out the passport. When he took it she pointed out his way around the corner of the building, along a flagged path. Half-buried lights illuminated the roots of bushes in front of two-storey concrete apartment blocks. Don's apartment was almost at the far end of the path. As he unlocked the door he heard a faint hiss of waves on a beach. He dropped the metal tag into the holder on the wall and switched on the lights in the room.

Two single beds nestled together for company opposite a dressing-table and an equally basic wardrobe, inside which Don found a safe. He'd get the key later. He opened the envelope to find he was invited to a welcome meeting at eleven, though not by name. He rummaged in his suitcase for toothpaste and brush, then stumbled to the bathroom that occupied a quarter of the apartment. His eyes were so eager for sleep that he could scarcely make out his reflection, not that he would have taken much pleasure in the sight of his untanned roundish freckled face thatched with red hair. He only just remembered to hide his wallet and passport and mobile phone under the pillow before slumping into bed.

Despite if not because of his exhaustion, he found it hard to fall asleep. He wouldn't have expected the night to be so oppressively hot in October. He tried not to feel that sleeping by himself was bothering him, but he couldn't help recalling how he and Louise had split up. Traits they'd found charming at the start had amplified themselves into irritations—her habit of tugging at a lock of hair to nibble as an aid to pondering, his murmuring "Never mind" under his breath to avoid arguments . . . All the disagreements they'd suppressed had erupted in a shouting competition before they'd very eventually calmed down and settled on parting as friends. Booking this last-minute holiday had been a bid to celebrate being free once more rather than yet again by himself. Louise hadn't liked hot places, which made Don even more determined to enjoy the week.

All at once his thoughts had gone, until light penetrated his eyelids—sunshine through the flimsy whitish curtains beside the bed. He disentangled his arm from the single clammy sheet to squint at his watch. It was well past ten o'clock, and later still before he managed to recollect why it should concern him. By the time he'd used the toilet and the shower, which was on its way to growing warm, he had just a few minutes to unpack. He found swimming trunks and a short-sleeved shirt and sandals, and stuffed passport and wallet and phone into his pockets as he raced his headless self past the dressing-table mirror.

Reception was deserted, but as Don sat on a straight chair to await the welcome meeting, the moustached woman came out of the office. "You want anything," she said.

"Air conditioning, thanks, and a key to the safe."

"How long are you?"

"Here, a week."

"Your two are sixty."

Her phrases kept making him feel not entirely awake. When her meaning reached him he counted out the notes, and she handed him a key and a remote control. As he sat down again she said "You wait for more?"

"The welcome," Don said and waved the envelope.

"Not here now. Gone."

"How can she have? I was here on time. It's still only—" Don raised his fist while he consulted his watch, and then his conviction failed him. "Oh," he said, "you fool."

"Who do you say?"

"Never mind," Don muttered and hurried away, too embarrassed to admit he'd neglected to move his watch forward two hours. "Why couldn't someone wake me?" he complained once he was sure she wouldn't hear.

He was in his room before he realised he had yet to see the view. The ground-floor balcony was occupied by a frame for drying clothes beside a small round table and two chairs of the same white plastic. Beyond the balcony a field of parched earth bare except for clumps of weeds stretched several hundred yards towards the sea, the near edge of which was hidden by a low ridge. The card in the travel agent's window had offered a sea view, and Don supposed he was seeing a version of that. "Never mind," he murmured, shutting the window so that he could trigger the air conditioning on his way to the safe.

He took a hundred euros from his wallet before stowing it away. He thought of wiping the traces of stickers off the cover of his passport, but apparently there was no need. Had he cleaned it in the night and forgotten? The idea made him feel unsure of himself. Or had the woman at Reception cleaned it up? One of them had bent the corner of a page, a detail Don had previously been too fatigued to notice. He opened the passport to smooth out the page, and the humid heat swarmed through the whole of him. The page bore an entry stamp for Turkey, where he had never been in his life.

The passport belonged to a blond-haired man called Eno Knoft, whose pale rounded face was bare of freckles. Don strode to Reception so fast that he almost forgot to lock the safe and the door. "Hello?" he called into the office. "Hello?"

The moustached woman emerged at less than half the speed his words had. "It takes time," she informed him.

He felt almost too bewildered to be furious. "What does?"

"Your conditioning."

"I don't know what on earth you mean."

"In your room."

"The air conditioning." He had no time to laugh at his mistake. "I'm not here about that," he said and opened the passport to brandish the photograph. "You gave me this."

"Yes, you keep it now."

"I most certainly don't," Don said, raising his voice as she began to turn away. "Look again. This isn't me."

She glanced over her shoulder before the rest of her swung towards him. "So that is it," she said, sounding no more apologetic than surprised. "He went when you came."

"How can he have? He won't have this."

"He goes to other islands."

Don clutched at the only hopeful thought he had. "He won't be able to leave Greece. They'll take my passport off him."

"Maybe they bring it if they know you are here."

"Why wouldn't they?" As more panic overtook him Don said "Do you know when he's going home?"

"He stays here one night."

"That's not what I'm asking. Will he try and leave before I have to?"

"He goes after the night here."

"You're saying he's coming back here."

"Yes, for night."

Don couldn't feel reassured yet. "Which one?"

"No need to say. Plenty of rooms. This week."

Her halting language made him feel not quite awake. "You're sure it's definitely this week," he persisted, "before I go home myself."

"I say."

"Will you let me know as soon as he arrives and keep my passport?"

She met this with a frown. "You want him to keep."

"No, that isn't what I said." He could have thought his own words were growing unfamiliar. "I asked you to keep it," he insisted. "Keep it safe for me."

"Safe," she said as if this might have been the solitary word she understood, and shut her eyes while she gave him a heavy nod.

"And please do tell me as soon as you have. Leave a note in my room if I'm not here."

She inclined her head further without opening her eyes, which Don had to take for assent and, with luck, reassurance. He mustn't let anxiety spoil his week, and he wasn't going to loiter in his room until his passport came back. He finished unpacking and hung up his clothes while his body tramped back and forth in the dressing-table mirror. He was about to consign Knoft's passport to the safe when he slipped it into his pocket—best to have it where he would be surest of it and be able to exchange it for his own the instant that he could. His credit card joined it, and he donned his hat on the way out of the room.

To the right of the courtyard a path led from the road towards the beach. Cicadas dodged from tree to tree, trailing silence, as he crossed the cracked dry field. When he reached the ridge he saw that the beach was no wider than the narrow promenade, by no means the image in the travel brochure. As he gazed in dismay at it, two young women with minimal swimsuits under their sundresses came abreast of him. "Looking for the beach?" one said.

"The tides were so high this year it all got swept away," her friend told him. "Walk where we're going and you'll find one."

Presumably it was beyond the headland against which waves were shattering. Don set about exploring the resort, such as it proved to be. A few tavernas and apartment complexes faced the sea, and he saw a fairground in the opposite direction from the headland. The main road was lined with supermarkets and tavernas, together with Hindustani Barney's restaurant and the British Bulldog pub. The Grecian Experience was a travel agency outside which boards advertised trips off the island, and Don made for it at once.

In a room where even the floor was white a burly man not much less bearded than a Greek priest sat behind a desk. A large fan turned back and forth, ruffling brochures in wooden racks. The man clasped his hands with an audible chafing of flesh and advanced an inviting smile. "What do we do for you today?"

"I'd like to go on some of your outings."

The man pushed a folder full of brochures across the desk. "How long you are here now?"

"All this week."

"You may find some things go away."

"Not your excursions, I hope." Celluloid pockets squeaked under Don's nails as he leafed through the folder. "I'd like both your trips off the island," he said, "and the tour of the island as well."

"Those are going." The man reached for a pad of vouchers. "Where do you stay?" he said.

"The Sea Panorama." Since the man had commenced writing, Don said "Room number two."

"Yes, that is it. I should know."

"Know what, sorry?"

"I should know you, Mr Knoft."

"Excuse me." When this didn't make the man look up, Don said louder "Excuse me, I'm not him."

"You are not?" The man's head rose as if it had been snagged by its frown. "Well, I see," he said with limited conviction.

"I assure you I'm not. I've only just got here. The name's Jones, Don Jones."

The man gazed at the passport that was peeking out of Don's breast pocket. How much would Don have to explain when he shouldn't need to prove anything about himself? He was close to speaking, whatever he might say, when the man tore off the voucher and the carbon copy to crumple them and drop the wad with a flat dead sound in a metal bin. "Mr Jones," he said and wrote. "I give you some islands tomorrow and the rest two days after. And two days more, our island."

"That'll do for me. I can go to the beach in between."

Rather than reply, the man seemed to prefer to write, and

Don took out his credit card. For a grotesque moment that left him feeling less than adequately awake, he forgot how to recall the code. Of course, it was 1514, the letters that his name repeated. Once he'd typed the digits the card reader emitted an electronic squeak and a receipt, which the man handed him along with the tour voucher. "Come back when you come back tomorrow."

"I imagine I will. Excuse me, you mean. . ."

"Come back and find if you are on the other boat."

"But I've already paid," Don protested, only to see that he'd been charged just for tomorrow's excursion. How unaware was he? "Why can't I pay for them all now?" he was determined to learn.

"We see how many you are."

Don supposed he had to be content with this. "Where will they pick me up tomorrow?"

"At apartments as usual."

As Don left the office he saw the man's head droop while the fan set his beard twitching. The white buildings and the relentlessly blue sky glared in Don's eyes, and he had to make an effort not to squeeze them shut. When had he last eaten? He ought to dine close to the Sea Panorama, just in case he caught Eno Knoft coming back. Every Greek resort seemed to have a taverna called Zorba's, and the one opposite the apartments had the film soundtrack on a tape to help it confirm its identity. Don found a table beside the road and ordered keftedes and kleftiko together with a tin carafe of red wine from the barrel. Perhaps his nervous vigilance was distracting him, since he felt unable to taste the food as much as he should. He wasn't to blame if the dishes were bland. Perhaps next time he would dine next door.

Could Knoft have returned while Don was at the travel

agency? He paid for the meal and crossed the road so fast that his sandals kicked up dust. As he strode into Reception a fleshy balding man with chest hairs poking through the gaps between the buttons of his shirt emerged from the office. "Did your colleague tell you about my passport?" Don said.

The man's large dark eyes winced as if they were about to close. "What do you ask?"

"I'm wondering if you know the lady gave someone else my passport."

The man jabbed a stubby finger at Don's pocket. "You have there."

"That's not mine. It belongs to the chap she gave mine."

The man turned his hand over, cupping the fingers. "You give."

"She's letting me look after it till he comes back."

The hand didn't move. "Not yours, you give."

"I'll keep it safe, don't worry. She obviously thinks I will. It'll make sure he gives me mine." When the man didn't alter his posture Don took a step back. "Just let me know if he shows up," he said. "The name's Knoft, Eno Knoft. I'll be in the room. I won't be going anywhere."

He could have fancied that the man was going nowhere either—that the words had frozen him in his expectant pose. Don made for the bookcase, where many of the titles on the cracked concave spines weren't in English. A lopsided copy of *War and Peace* was, and he'd often felt he should read the novel, though he never had the energy after a day of trying to find people jobs, especially when he brought home all the weight of their frustration and his own. He grasped the massive paperback and took it to his room.

On the balcony he found he couldn't read much. By the time he reached the third chapter the night was rising from the sea. He watched light drain from the sky as the sun was erased somewhere behind him. When stars began to glimmer he felt oddly like a child who'd been allowed to stay up late. He would need to rise early for the excursion, and he took himself to bed.

The air conditioning uttered a rattle whenever he was close to drifting off, and when he slept at last he kept dreaming that Knoft had returned unexpectedly but was about to leave once more. "Bring my face back," Don heard himself trying to plead in not much of a voice. Every time his struggles to speak wakened him he had to grope under the pillow to confirm that the passport was still there. The alarm on his phone sent him to use the bathroom, where his reflection looked unconvinced it was awake, and then he went to meet the dawn. "Out for the day now," he called into Reception. "Get my passport if Mr Knoft comes back. Tell him I'll give him his once I've got mine."

Before anyone emerged from the office, a coach came into view on the road. "Jones," Don said when the guide barely glanced at the voucher. He murmured mornings to his fellow passengers, and the coach picked up a few more on the way to the harbour. A crewman at the gangplank of the boat waved a dismissive hand at the passport in Don's pocket and told him "No need." By the time another coach brought rather less than a coachload of voyagers, the rocking of the boat had lulled Don close to slumber. Half an hour of open sea didn't rouse him much, but he prised his eyes wide when the first island came in sight. The boat was almost there when the guide with the microphone announced they wouldn't be visiting the island.

At once Don wondered if Knoft was on it. He could see a fishing village had attracted tourists, and he wished he had binoculars to help him make them out, but none of the passengers up here on the top deck had a pair he could borrow. "Never mind," he muttered, though the words felt as if they scarcely came from him.

The rest of the hour took them to the next island, where the guide led her party alongside the harbour, past a multitude of sponges to a factory full of nothing else. As she described the process of preparing them Don sidled to the door to watch the street, but saw nobody he was anxious to see. By the time the tour reached the third island he supposed he was ready for lunch, but he grew so preoccupied with scrutinising every face that passed the taverna by the wharf that he was barely able to taste how fresh the catch of the day was. He still had an hour to explore the town—to search it, rather.

Apartments were scattered through the narrow haphazard streets, and now and then he recognised a face, but always someone from the cruise. However far he ventured from the harbour, he seemed unable to avoid a pale plump couple apparently competing at how floral their dress or in the man's case shirt could be. He was sidestepping them yet again, and producing an increasingly dutiful grin, when he glanced past them and imagined he was looking in a mirror.

The man at the end of the sloping street turned away at once as if he hadn't seen him. Don dodged past the couple so hastily that his elbow jangled a mobile made of strings of shells dangling outside a shop. "Mr Knoft," he shouted.

Before the man's name was out, he wasn't there. Don felt forsaken by reality until he saw that Knoft must have darted into a side lane, and then a glimpse caught up with him. Hadn't the man's face stiffened at the sight of him? If he'd recognised Don, this could only mean he knew he had Don's passport, and his behaviour suggested he wasn't eager to return it. Don sprinted to the lane and saw the man disappearing at speed around a corner. "Mr Knoft," he yelled and dashed to the corner in time to see the man turning left yet again. If he did that once more, wouldn't they be back where they started? But when Don reached the corner, the side street was deserted, though it came to a dead end ahead.

Knoft must have gone into a house, even if Don hadn't heard a door shut. Presumably Knoft was lodging here, though neither house in the stark dusty sun-bleached street showed any sign of inviting tourists. Don strode to the door on the left and pounded on the hot scaly wood, and when this brought no response he did the same across the road. The doors might have been mutual reflections, and the sets of knocks virtually echoed each other, producing an identical silence. "Knoft," Don shouted and pressed his face against the veiled window of the left-hand house, and felt the window-frame begin to crumble under his fingers. He stalked across the street to peer through the dingy embroidered curtains inside the other window. Both houses were derelict, little more than frontages like sets on a stage.

He was struggling to open either of the doors—Knoft must have used one of them, blocking it from inside—when the blare of a horn resounded through the town. The boat was summoning passengers back. Don gave each door a final desperate thump with his shoulder, but neither door budged an inch. "You'll have to come back," he vowed under his breath and dashed through the devious streets to the harbour.

When the coach brought him to the apartments at last—a final break in the cruise to let people swim had felt as prolonged as a sleepless night—he hurried into Reception. "I'm back," he called. "Jones. Back."

So was the moustached woman, who blinked at him from the doorway of the office. "Knoft?" Don hoped aloud.

"You said Jones."

"Not me, him. Is he back?"

"Just you."

Don felt as if they were vying to keep their words terse, but it occurred to him to ask "Do you know what he does?"

"Travels."

"In life, I mean."

"Travels," she repeated with a somnolent shut-eyed nod.

While she was unlikely to know if Knoft was involved in any questionable activity, Don could have taken the word for a euphemism. He changed in his room once he'd showered, and then looked in at Reception. "I'm across the road," he called. "Taste of Greece."

Either the taverna failed to live up to its name or his senses were elsewhere. The empty courtyard across the sparsely populated road seemed more present than the food in his mouth. He finished off the slab of moussaka, not just since he supposed he needed to eat but because he was one of a very few diners, and then he went back to Reception. "Just going to Grecian Experience," he called into the office.

The bearded man might have been dozing, but he raised his head as Don approached the desk. "Mr Knoft," he said, then widened his eyes as though to rouse his mind. "No, you don't call yourself."

"I don't because it's not my name."

"You are—" The man levelled a hand at him to fend off any help. "You are number two at Panorama."

"I'm Jones." At half that speed Don said "Don Jones."

"That is name in there."

The hand was pointing at the passport now. "That's Donald," Don admitted, "except this isn't mine."

The man stared at it so hard that Don felt he wasn't being seen. "Who then?"

Don didn't think he had the energy to describe the situation yet again. "I'm holding it for someone else."

"Well, so you come back for more."

Incomprehension made Don nervous until he thought to say "The other cruise, you mean. Yes, if it's going."

"You are just enough."

He must have all the bookings in mind, not only Don. He set about filling in the voucher as Don typed his code on the card reader. Once the voucher was completed the man gazed at him. "Something is wrong?"

Don keyed in the digits again, only to be told a second time that they were incorrect. He shut his eyes as if this might erase whatever mistake he'd made and counted the values of the letters from his name once more, and then his eyes sprang open. "Oh, you fool," he muttered, feeling worse than that, since he'd somehow remembered the letters out of order. "There you are. That's me."

"Jones," he called into Reception, "I'm in my room," and made his way to the safe in the wardrobe, only to wonder nervously where he'd left his credit card. Of course, it was inside Knoft's passport, and there were the receipts from the Grecian Experience as well. He locked them in the safe and stared at the passport photograph. It couldn't have developed freckles, and the blond hair hadn't darkened except with ink from the receipts, which had also speckled the face. Don rubbed the picture with a tissue but desisted before he was entirely convinced that he'd restored its appearance. Knoft could deal with his own image once he'd brought Don's passport back. Surely he wasn't using it for anything illegal, though perhaps Don should establish that he hadn't before returning Knoft's passport to him.

As he watched the evening light dwindle into stars he grew aware how the days were shrinking. In bed he kept being wakened by the thought of a knock at the door—by the absence of a knock. At least he needn't rise early, but when he left his bed well after dawn he felt as if he'd hardly slept at all. He loaded his beach bag—book, towel, sun cream, a creaking plastic bottle of water—before heading for Reception. "Going to the beach."

The balding man glanced not much more than blankly at him. "Beach."

"Yes, beach. I'm told you've still got one."

The man looked indifferent if not unconvinced. "You have passport."

"Not yet. This is still his."

The man shoved his lower lip forward. "Police not like."

"You've told them, have you? Maybe you should tell them you give people the wrong passports. I think they might like that a good deal less."

The man's lip protruded further, and Don hoped he hadn't antagonised him. Perhaps he hadn't spoken to the police at all. "I'll stay as close as I can," Don said. "I'll be there if I'm needed."

From the promenade he saw lorries bearing sections of demolished rides away from the fairground. Absurdly, the sight left him feeling as if his holiday had been brought to a premature end. He made for the headland, which proved to be more distant than it looked. Beyond it was an expanse of sand across which a deserted taverna and a dozen unoccupied sun loungers faced a small bay. Don dragged a lounger close to the sea and opened the standing umbrella he'd reached, and contorted himself over trying to cover his body with sun cream without mixing it with sand.

Since he couldn't recall what he'd previously read, he started *War and Peace* again. His lack of sleep must be in the way, because he found it hard to grasp the prose even after it ceased to be French. Before long he closed his eyes, only to feel that the waves were washing away his consciousness. He tried to cling to it, but it was gone until an impression of a presence close by wakened him—somebody like him, no doubt, unless they'd come for payment for the lounger. He stretched his eyes wide and stared around him, then behind him. He wasn't just alone on the beach. His was the only lounger.

If someone had removed the loungers, why had they left him asleep? He could only think it had been meant as some kind of concession, but it made him feel worse than isolated. Suppose the staff from the apartments couldn't find him when they needed to? He stuffed all his beach items into the bag and strode, then ran as fast as the sand would let him, across the beach.

"Back again," he called, adding that he'd be at the Aegean Flavour. This fell as short of his palate as the other meals had, perhaps because he was ready for a nap in his room. On his way he replaced *War and Peace* with a thriller by an author whose name was as monosyllabic as most of his prose. "In my room now," he shouted into the office.

He couldn't doze for attempting to read, and the opposite happened as well. He must be too exhausted to cope with even the simplest prose or to sleep. He sat on the balcony, urging the sunset to bring Knoft, only to feel as if his mind was shrinking with the light. In bed he kept being wakened by a silence that should have been a knock, unless it had just been one. More than once he stumbled to the door and gazed along the deserted path, until eventually he saw the lights beside it had been ousted by the dawn. Though his alarm hadn't roused him, the coach was outside on the road.

"I'm here," he yelled, or at least "Mere" if not just "Me." He dashed back into the apartment and raced out as soon as decency permitted, buttoning the shirt in which he found

Knoft's passport, having apparently been too tired to remember it belonged under his pillow. "Jones," he assured the guide, and wondered if anyone else had failed to waken, since there were so few passengers on the coach. Even when more coaches joined it at the harbour, they left the boat nowhere near full.

Don was watching the sea shrink the harbour when a woman said "You're back with us again."

He imagined she was talking about his awareness until he recognised her and her equally pale plump partner. Their floral clothes made them resemble mutual reflections more than ever. "Third trip in a week," the man told him.

"Not for me."

"Then somebody was putting on a good act," the woman said with a laugh too terse for mirth.

For a moment Don felt utterly disoriented, and then he fumbled out Knoft's passport to show them the photograph. "Are you thinking of him?"

This time it was the man who laughed, although not much. "We can see that's you, chum. What's the joke?"

"I promise you it's not." Don rubbed the photograph with his thumb in a bid to dislodge the speckles and lighten the hair. "They gave me this at my apartments by mistake."

"How could you let them do that?" the woman protested. "Were you asleep?"

"I'm not the one who's asleep round here." Don saw them take this as a gibe, which it imprecisely was, and tried to keep them talking. "The fellow you say was me," he said. "What was he like?"

"A charmer." Just as much like a rebuke the woman said "We were looking forward to talking to him again."

"He talked funny English," the man said. "It was part of his charm."

"Nothing funny with mine, is there?" As their gazes grew blank as unconsciousness Don said "Did he say what he was?"

"Some kind of performer, we think," the man said.

"We thought he might let us see him put on a show."

Don was almost certain they meant him. Before he could respond the woman said "If you're honestly saying that's not you, who have you told?"

"The staff where I'm staying, of course."

"Haven't you let your rep know?" When Don barely shook his head the man persisted "The embassy, how about them?"

"He's coming back before I have to go home. He can't leave if I can't, so that'll make him."

Had exhaustion put the embassy and Estelle out of his mind? He couldn't call either just now, since his phone had no signal. Sea and more sea, islands that seemed to take something like a lifetime to crawl closer, harbours, beaches . . . He was willing the cruise to end so that he could resume his vigil at the apartments—that was all his head contained as he trudged back to the boat after visiting a monastery from which tourists appeared to have driven all the monks—when he saw Knoft staring landwards from the gangplank.

Before Don could tell whether the fellow was looking for him, Knoft turned away and was lost to sight. Don sprinted to the gangplank and panted at a crewman "Who just came on board?"

The man shrugged without smiling. "You did."

Don hadn't time to argue. He was about to search the boat when he saw that might let Knoft escape. He loitered by the gangplank until it was raised and the boat had left the harbour, and then he set about searching, peering into every face he couldn't immediately see. Before long he encountered the plump couple on the upper deck. "Have you seen him?"

They looked as if they might have hoped not to encounter Don again. "Who?" the woman said.

"Him." Don thumped his breast pocket fiercely enough to be trying to revive a heart. "Him."

"We're seeing you," the man said.

Don stalked around the upper deck before returning to the lower one and patrolling the saloon. Was Knoft hiding in a toilet? There were several on each deck, and whenever an occupant proved not to be Knoft, Don had to conclude the man was on the other level. Don was waiting by the gangplank long before the boat docked, and scrutinised every face that passed him. He was the last to go ashore, and yet he hadn't seen Knoft disembark.

Had the man disguised himself somehow or contrived to stay on board? As Don backed towards the coach he kept both eyes on the boat, but nobody except crewmen had left it by the time it receded out of sight. Could Knoft have posed as a member of the crew? Was that the kind of performance he put on? As soon as the coach brought him back to the apartments, Don marched into Reception. "I think Mr Knoft is back," he shouted into the office. "Just going to Grecian Experience."

The bearded man opened his eyes as he lifted his head. "Ah, Mr Not."

"No, not at all. Anybody but. I've told you twice, I'm—"

"I say that," the man declared with a hopeful grin. "Mr Not Him."

"Not Knoft, that's me, but was he on your boat today by any chance?"

"Just you from here. Not him from anywhere."

"Excuse me, but how can you be sure?"

"I have seen the names." The man rapped the screen of his computer with a knuckle, and Don imagined someone knocking on the apartment door—in fact, he had to remind himself that wasn't the sound he was hearing. "Are you here for book?" the man said.

"Which book?"

"Your last day. Can only be tomorrow."

At first Don felt he should stay in his apartment—the talk of a book made him feel he was already there—and then he grew furious. He wasn't going to let Knoft rob him of the last chance of a tour. "I'll book it," he said and slipped his card into the reader to type his code. "No, that's not right," he complained, which sounded like agreeing with the machine. He typed the digits again with a pause after each one, only to be told they were still incorrect. Was he so exhausted that he was entering them out of order? He keyed the values of the pair of letters the other way around and was immediately convinced this was wrong, but the machine confirmed the code and stuck out a paper tongue at him. "One of us is wrong," he muttered for nobody else to hear.

As he left the sleepy sluggish fan behind he folded the voucher and receipt around the card and slipped them behind the passport so as to keep ink away from Knoft's photograph. Now that he thought Knoft was on the island he seemed unable to think of anything else, and he hadn't noticed that the tavernas closest to the apartments had shut, leaving all their menu boards as blank as frames awaiting photographs. "Never," he mumbled, and eventually thought to add "Mind." The only restaurant still open that gave him a view of the courtyard was Hindustani Barney's. Perhaps at least he would taste that food. "Jones again," he called into the office. "Be across the road. Barney's Indian."

The flavours of a chilli chicken starter and a prawn jalfrezi stayed remote. He might have been trying to recall them or to taste them on somebody else's behalf. Were his thoughts being kept away from him as well? He'd forgotten to call Estelle or the embassy. He tramped back to his room, having told whoever was in Reception that he was there, and found the number on the welcome letter. His phone located only a meagre signal, signified by a solitary trembling bar on the display, and he reached nothing but a voicemail, both for Estelle and the embassy. "Jones," he pleaded with each of them. "Don Jones. That's Donald if you need the rest. Please call me back."

He sat with his book on the balcony, but long before dusk blurred the words he found he couldn't concentrate. He might have fancied he was losing his ability to read even the simplest English. He lay in bed with Knoft's passport in one fist and, so that he wouldn't miss the alarm, his phone in the other. Whenever he dozed he dreamed that Knoft had been disposed of by his criminal associates, and what had they done with Don's passport? The twitching of his fingers jerked him awake, or movement in his fists did. Knoft's passport couldn't be stirring as it underwent some transformation, but Don had to switch on the light more than once to reassure himself that the photograph wasn't too familiar – that it hadn't grown more red-haired and freckled. Every time he wakened, listening for the absent knock held him back from slumber. As he realised he was a chrysalis that sleep was about to transmute into someone else, the contents of his fist began to vibrate with the first stage of the process. It was the alarm, and he was more than glad to leave the dream.

"Jones. Out for day now. Coach tour." There was no response from the office, and he wondered when he'd last heard one. "You there?" he shouted louder.

"We hear you."

The voice was higher than he liked, given that it proved to

belong to the balding man. Presumably impatience had raised its pitch. Don plodded to meet the coach as it pulled up. "Jones again," he told the guide and then the plump couple he kept meeting. "Just Jones. Don Jones."

The flowered fellow gazed at him. "Funnier than that," he said.

"Quite a performance," said his wife.

After that Don didn't speak to them or anyone. The ancient ruined city that was the first stop on the tour felt like the state of his mind rendered solid, though he had a fleeting sense that somebody he used to know would have liked the site. Olive oil at a factory slipped down his throat without leaving a taste, and lunch at a taverna stayed just as distant from his palate. The wines and spirits offered at a village vineyard only made him feel in danger of losing all awareness, and he wandered into the street. He was gazing at a cloud like a wintry omen of night above the mountain across the valley that the village overlooked when rapid footsteps made him glance around. A man was vanishing past a bend in the road.

Wasn't that how Knoft had been dressed yesterday—a pale blue short-sleeved shirt, baggy brown knee-length shorts, grey sandals? Don raced to the bend and saw the man hurrying down a lane. "Knoft," he shouted and dashed to the lane, by which time the man was out of sight once more. The descent was so steep that Don almost lost his footing and had to grab the rough stone walls of houses for support. He was nearly at the bottom when he saw the man along a side lane. The fellow swung around to grin up at a noise on the main road, then turned away before Don could make out his face. Then how had Don glimpsed his expression? The question distracted him from recognising the sound on the road at once. The coach was moving off.

"Wait," he yelled at the top of his voice, though he hardly knew whether he meant it for the man in the lane or the driver. The man disappeared around the corner of the lane, and Don wasn't even sure the fellow had been Knoft. He mustn't be left behind, and he dashed up the slope towards the road. Long before he reached it he was no longer running but panting so hard that it overwhelmed his senses. He hadn't heard the coach drive away, but it was nowhere to be seen.

He felt as though he'd been lured away deliberately. He might even have imagined that the day of the excursion had been changed so that he wouldn't be at the Sea Panorama when Knoft came back. As he snatched out his phone he was afraid it would have no coverage, but it exhibited a single faltering bar, and then took minutes to find the number for the Grecian Experience. "Jones," he said like a curse. "Don Jones."

"I am sorry, who?"

"Jones. I was on your coach. It's gone and left me."

He heard static or the rustling of paper. "I am sorry," the bearded man said again. "That is nobody on there."

"That's right, I'm not," Don said through his teeth. "I'm in the road where I've been left."

"We do not leave anyone. The guide always counts."

"I know she does, but not this time," Don protested, and then suspicion overtook him. "Have you got a man called Knoft on it?"

Paper rustled, or the connection did. "Eno Knoft, yes."

"He's got my place. I need to get back." Don felt as if his mind was shrinking along with his words. "How will I?" he demanded.

"Take a taxi and come here."

"Can't I charge—" Don blurted, but even the rustling had gone.

By the time he trudged to the end of the village he was afraid of not finding a taxi. A hut with a goat tethered outside turned out to represent one, and ten minutes after the aged man dozing on a skimpy wooden chair used his vintage mobile, the decrepit vehicle showed up. It took most of an hour to bring Don back to the resort via a series of side roads through a wilderness too rocky for houses or even for vegetation above the size of stunted dusty bushes, a region suggesting the desolateness of a local winter. At last buildings sprouted from the horizon, and the sea rose up beyond them. In its own time the taxi reached the main street, and Don sprang his seatbelt free as soon as he saw the Grecian Experience. "Stop there," he said and only just remembered "Please."

No boards stood outside to advertise excursions. The window and the door were blinded. Don rattled the door until the blind flapped against the glass, and then he tried phoning. A shrill bell in the office belatedly echoed the version at his ear, and both of them might have been mocking him. He had just enough cash to pay for the taxi ride, and saw it fall short of pleasing the driver. Don tramped to the Sea Panorama and waited for the balding man to appear from the office. "Is he here?"

The man fingered his upper lip, which had grown unshaven. "Just you."

"Where's the trip man gone? Coach went and left me. Had to pay for a cab."

"Gone now." The man scowled as if he thought Don was imitating his rudimentary language. "Gone for winter."

"Gone." Putting all his rage into the syllable failed to help. "I won't be," Don vowed. "I'll be in the room."

He would stay there tomorrow if he had to. He wouldn't be tricked again, whoever tried. He might bring in food from the supermarket, though couldn't he survive without it for a couple of days? Leaving the apartments even so briefly felt like too much of a risk. When he sat on the balcony he left the window open so as not to miss any knock. He hadn't brought the book out with him, preferring not to learn how little of it he might be able to read. The sky had begun to rust above the sea when he remembered he had yet to hear from Estelle or the embassy. They were still represented by voicemails so anonymous that he could have thought he was hearing a single familiar voice. "Jones again," he repeated, "still Jones," and felt as if he was trying to reassure himself.

He stayed outside until it was too dark to see into the room. He had a sense that the night must resolve his situation. "Can't go," he told Knoft, wherever he was. "Got to come to me." In bed he clutched the passport in his clasped hands. Before he was ready the dark filled his skull.

The thought of wakening roused him. He could have fancied it wasn't his. Somebody needed to waken, but who? "I'm not the one who's asleep round here . . ." He felt as if he was recalling someone else's words, but all at once he was convinced the nightmare he'd been living wasn't his. Something besides the thoughts had wakened him—the absence of a sound. The air conditioning had shut down, though the room felt colder than it had. In the breathless silence he heard a tapping at the door.

It sounded tentative, close to surreptitious. He fumbled to turn on the light, but the room stayed dark. He floundered out of bed, gripping the passport in his fist, and stumbled to the door. Nobody was outside—just an onslaught of rain that had flooded the path and drowned the vegetation, apparently dousing the lights as well. Despite the gloom, his watch showed that it was almost noon.

He donned swimming trunks and sandals and hurried

to Reception, but the door was locked. "Where are you?" he cried, but this brought him nobody, even when he tramped shouting through the deserted waterlogged streets. All the apartments and shops and tavernas were vacant now. Even the houses were, as though the first storm of winter had washed away the populace. A chill wind flung the downpour at him as black waves spilled across the promenade like vanguards of the impatient night, and he retreated to his room.

He'd left his phone there out of the rain, but it was as dead as the resort if not the entire island. He stared at it until he felt its blankness was spreading to his mind. When he opened the passport he had the grotesque notion that he was turning to the only companionship he still had. Raindrops trickled over Eno Knoft's freckled red-haired photograph, and perhaps that was why the face appeared to start to grin at him. He slapped the passport shut as if to crush an insect, and thought there were words he should murmur—but he had no words, not even much breath. He threw his sodden trunks in the bath and dropped his grey sandals under the chair on which the rest of yesterday's outfit was crumpled, the pale blue short-sleeved shirt, the baggy brown knee-length shorts. After that he could only huddle in bed, clenching his whole body around the passport in his hands, and wait for the light to return, if it ever did—to waken whoever was doing all this to him.

A PREDICAMENT

DARRELL SCHWEITZER

In the dream I knew that I had done some dreadful thing. Of my guilt, there could be no question. Worse yet, I had been found out. The accusation came in a document, delivered into my hand by a cloaked messenger. I read the paper several times, carefully to the end, futilely turning it over in hope there might be some forgiveness on the back, but there was not. There was no denying its logic.

Even so, I thought I could get away. The first thing I did was burn the paper in a candle flame, tossing away the last bit as the flame touched me.

Then I put on my own dark cloak and a peculiar top hat—not my usual costume, but in the dream what was customarily worn—and I stole out, making my way along cobblestoned streets, beneath dripping arches, sometimes groping in utter darkness, sometimes stooping to conceal myself as I passed below candlelit windows.

This was not my native place, nor any city I knew, but in my haste to escape I convinced myself that it did not matter where I was, as long as I remained undetected. For that I could still hope.

Even as a wind rose, whistling through empty alleys and moaning over chimney pots, the sound gradually forming itself, in my ears at least, into language, into murmurous words; even as one after another dark shape detached itself from doorways or from out of narrow streets and began to follow me, to swarm around me, until I was an anonymous part of a great throng, with phantoms, with ghosts, with half-glimpsed forms jostling me from every side; even then I could hope to remain unknown, unnoticed.

Wherever I turned, I couldn't see any faces. A hooded cloak obscured my view. A broad-brimmed hat was drawn down in concealment, an almost skeletal wrist and gloved hand holding it in place against the wind. I made my way onward, one more shadow among the shadows.

I did not speak. I wanted to ask where we were going, but I dared not give myself away. I thought only of escape. I still *hoped* to escape.

Was this, then, indescribable folly?

I let myself be carried, a part of the great mass, all of us like ashes on that vigorous wind, out of the narrow streets, into a palatial square, past an empty fountain and some huge statue I couldn't quite make out, but which frightened me. I fancied it the figure of an executioner. But, as I say, I could not see it clearly.

Now a light appeared: an opening vast and curved like the entrance to a cathedral, lit from within, growing steadily brighter, like a mouth, into which all of us, the great whispering throng along with myself, were drawn, as if some giant were drinking us down.

Yet I could only follow, and a long journey up marble

steps ensued; and as we went, the appearances of some of my companions became more distinct: here, a tall, majestic man bearing a silver cane; there an old woman, gnarled and bent, leaning on a barefoot, half-naked child that seemed little more than an animate bundle of sticks in its emaciation; here again a soldier in armor, and so forth, but still there were no faces, the tall man's concealed by his hat, the old woman's by her unruly hair, the child's lost in her filthy skirt, the armored soldier's visor down; these followed by great multitudes of anonymous others.

We came at last to what might have been a courtroom, and we all stood trembling before faceless judges seated high above us—faceless because each of the judges wore a featureless mask, a plain covering of what might have been white cardboard. The only light came from little candles placed here and there on a long table.

A herald called us all to order. The court was in session. Clerks read out a list of charges, describing in excruciating detail numberless atrocities. The prosecutors thundered from behind their masks, while the judges sat impassively. If there was any defense, I never heard it. I couldn't think of any basis for one.

But, I told myself, it hardly mattered if I did or didn't, because this wasn't about me. I was just part of the crowd, a witness to these tumultuous events. There were witnesses wailing; others stood still and wordless, yet they were given close attention. So it went on and on, until I almost fell into a kind of swoon. I lost track of what was going on—the motions, the objections, the cries, the gasps from the horrifying testimony. It was so remote, so abstract. It began to fade from my hearing. I hadn't been discovered after all, had I?

From out of darkness and distance there suddenly came in a voice like a thunderclap. I snapped to attention. The verdict was guilty. Guilty of every crime, every impossible evil. The mass of folk around me fell to their knees, some of them fainting, some with their hands clapped desperately to their ears while blood oozed through their fingers. The sentence was also pronounced, too horrible to be repeated in words. It was like a blow.

I felt buffeted about, as if by winds.

But no one laid any hand on me. It was as if I were not there at all. I had been completely overlooked. I wept with enormous relief, in exhaustion at the unexpected mercy of my escape.

They must have convicted *someone else.* It had to be that.

I could barely restrain myself from laughing.

Then the dream shifted, and somehow we all came to be seated at the long table that stretched the length of the room, and by the light of those little candles I saw that banquet was in progress. There was laughter and music and, I think, even dancing, there in that shadow-filled, high vaulted room. I began to relax. The guests all around me—for surely we were all guests here, myself among them, no different from the rest, entertained by some gracious lord—spoke of pleasant things, such as I could make out any of their words at all. We were at ease. We were merry. All was right with the world. I drank deep of delicious liquor of some kind—how exquisite, how peculiar, that one could *taste* in a dream, and become intoxicated—and pondered how ironic it was that one could lose one's judgment, or common sense, or any and all caution by getting drunk on dream-liquor in a dream—which is exactly what I did when, laughing at last, I nudged the guest next to me, who happened to be the unkempt old woman. Nodding in the general direction of the judges' high bench, I said, "Well, I'm glad *that's* over with!"

And with this, there was absolute silence, every motion ceased, every heartbeat stilled.

The woman next to me shook her head, and I saw her face clearly. I saw the rictus of her terror as she shrieked out in a voice far too loud to have come from a human throat, *"It's him! It's him!"*

In an instant, everyone was screaming, "It's him! It's him!" I saw the crowd melting away in all directions, as there strode toward me a band of tall men in black cloaks and strange, tall hats, members of an ancient ritual order to which I myself belonged and which I had betrayed. How, I didn't know. I was weak on the details. In this dream, the most maddening thing was that, for all I understood the irrefutable logic of my guilt and there was clearly no escaping the consequences of my misdeeds, *I did not actually know the nature of my crime.* The testimony I'd heard, I had forgotten. It escaped from my memory like sand from between limp fingers. But everyone else knew. It was taken for granted by the screaming crowds around me, by the tall men in the cloaks and tall hats who laid hands on me and dragged me like a sack of rubbish in front of the chief judge, who leaned down in his high seat above us like a god out of heaven, pointed a great, pale finger at me, and spoke in a voice that made my ears gush with blood, saying only the single word, *"Thou."*

Now as I cringed before him, my hands were burning. There was a flame, and a document, which was *reconstituting itself* out of the fire, as if the whole process of combustion were occurring backwards, and in an instant I could see by its light that what I held was a *confession in my own handwriting,* but I didn't have a chance to read more than the first line or two before it fell from my grasp. Useless. I could only remember how I'd felt alarm, then terror, then false hope and false relief, then terror again— now followed by an angry, petulant sense that *it wasn't fair.*

Did any of that matter?

Will you say, then, that I was suffering only from some fantastic spasm of the brain that had produced this very dream?

I could only wish as much.

And the dream shifted one last time, and those I had wronged, those I betrayed, lifted me up and placed me in a coffin, which had a design in high relief on its lid, part like a deformed insect, part . . . I don't know. There was an oval opening where my face would show through, to give me the identity of that caricatured monstrosity, whatever it was. I was trapped inside as they screwed the lid into place. I tried to argue, to negotiate, to make excuses. "Can't we talk about this?" and "Hey, everybody has their faults." But grimly they finished their work, the screws screeching through the wood. I was loaded into the back of a hearse with glass panels. A procession followed, over sere hills and black valleys, beneath a dark sky and pale, unfamiliar stars. The multitude followed, bearing tiny candles flickering in the wind.

Only gradually did I became aware of a light ahead and heat from the same source. I could not see where we were going. I had been placed in the hearse head first, slightly tilted upward, so I could see behind me, the trailing procession, but not ahead. I thought it a sunrise. The sky lightened. The stars faded, as if a huge reddish sun rose over that desolate land.

It was only as they unloaded me and turned me around that I saw that we had not come into a sunrise at all. An immense, fiery furnace gaped, above which my bearers began to swing me from side to side with a heave and a ho—

I tried to reason with them. It was no good. I tried to bargain. Nothing. I pleaded, but they made no answer.

I screamed then, and in my final desperation I cried out, "Stop! Stop! This is a dream! I want to wake up! Please! *I want to wake up!*"

I banged on the inside of the coffin. I clawed at the wood, oblivious of the pain as my fingernails ripped off.

They hurled me through the air.

"I want to wake up! Please, let me wake up!"

But I couldn't wake up, even though all this was truly a dream, *because I was not the dreamer*, and the dream itself was someone else's act of inexorable vengeance.

KAFKAESQUE

JASON V BROCK

—REALITY—

It was a few years ago during a period of great stress in your life. You had to deal with an unexpected financial hardship, and as a result you were having trouble staying asleep; *getting* to sleep was not a problem, but you would invariably wake up around three A.M., the burdens of the day racing through the gauzy shreds of your semi-conscious mind. You were continually plagued in these lonely hours by the notion that some bill collector or other was going to sue you, or try to repossess your car, or something worse—perhaps you might lose your home to foreclosure before you could set the finances right again. It was a very tough time.

Typically, after you had suddenly awakened in your dark bedroom, you felt disoriented, the blankets sweaty and knotted around you; ominous thoughts would crowd your head as you lay there trying to catch your breath—the heaviness of the night was palpable, as though you were stranded in the inner vestibule of a sunken ship, running out of air as trillions of gallons of seawater pressed down on you, trapping you in a watery grave miles below the stormy ocean surface. Soon you would be completely awake, a free-floating anxiety ebbing and flowing through the core of your being. After a couple of hours, you were usually able to drift back to a fitful sleep.

Important to note: You are normally not one of those people who retain much about their dreams. As a writer, you would certainly *like* to remember them—you even keep a notebook by your bedside to jot down recollections and impressions— but you always seemed to forget the details within just a few moments of waking up. The fact is, you dream a great deal, and about many things: as a musician, you have dreamt entire songs, which you were somehow able to jot down, even when half-asleep. You have gained insights to problems at work—and solutions about concerns at home—which initially presented themselves out of dreams. And your dreams are always in vivid color, though your memories are most often in black-and-white. It seems you are able to wring answers and retain inspiration from dreams, but are seldom able to recall the "plots," as it were, of these reveries. Sometimes you can evoke the *dramatis personae,* but that was typically where the remembrance ended.

As it would happen, it was during one of these nocturnal disturbances that you met the writer Franz Kafka; it is the only time you would ever meet, but once would be enough. Even in the moment, you somehow understood that this was not a dream; this happened, was rooted in a certain reality-space.

—BLACKSTAR—

You remember a gradual awareness of walking out of thick fog and onto a long, dark road. The air is dry and bitterly cold; your breath condenses in the gusty breeze. Crickets and frogs murmur in the background, giving way to a gentle wash of noise as the wind blusters, ruffling your bangs against your forehead. You have on a black long-sleeve T-shirt with an abstract lightning bolt design on the chest, jeans and a belt, and ankle boots. Your nose, fingers, toes, and ears are slowly going numb. In the distance, at the other side of a wide, moon-silvered river, there is a massive, sharply gabled construction crouching on a hill silhouetted against the night. It reminds you of a great castle. As you watch, you can see the bastion is slowly expanding and contracting, alternately elongating and squatting, warping and shifting—as though it is alive and somehow trying to uproot itself. Around you, everything begins to seep into color. Before, you now realize, the world had been monochromatic; as you approach the fortress, the world seems to become more vivid— first turning a gentle sepia, then a collection of desaturated hues, and finally a rich, even surreal, amalgamation of deep pigments vying for attention: bluish night air, green-tinted wisps of fast-moving clouds, multicolored pinpoints of starlight in a black velvet sky. The crunchy ground, comprised of frozen slush and mud, is a contrast of brown and dirty white, like the lace of some ancient wedding dress, now soiled.

You have one goal: to reach the weird, gently morphing structure stationed on the denuded hilltop. The bloated moon looks down, fatly gibbous and yellow, casting stark, long shadows after you. You notice Spanish moss hanging in thick drapes from huge, ancient trees in the shadowed woods all around, the inky bulk of which feel slashed into the nocturnal landscape as though by the deranged pen strokes of some mad artist's crosshatching. The entire atmosphere has more the characteristic of a mixed-media painting come to life than any form of experience you ever recall having. In spite of this—

or perhaps because of it—you feel a sort of calm detachment, though this is gradually being countered by a mounting edge of expectancy, even dread. Just ahead, through billows of gossamer fog rising off the river, you make out the murky shape of a bridge; the span is old, its rustic majesty in crumbling, mildew-slicked ruin. As the night deepens, flickering lights begin to wink on from the many windows in the looming edifice, giving the impression of some great beast stirring to life and awareness. The place is at once melancholy and malevolent, though you are driven forward by the possibility of warmth and protection from the elements for the remainder of the evening. Purple lightning flashes on the horizon; in the forest behind you, there is gentle hissing that now overlays the pink noise from before as frozen drizzle begins to fall, bouncing on your cheeks and catching in your eyelashes. A cascade of meteorites shoots across the raven-dark firmament, trailing stardust; the largest of these reminds you of some self-eclipsing black star, some symbol that tickles in the subconscious, a harbinger. A warning, perhaps.

Crossing the bridge, the castle appears to swell and distend in size; you feel small, insignificant; the doors are fifty or sixty feet tall, jagged and imperfectly rendered. The strange perspectives and bizarre, nonlinear angles remind you of Expressionist paintings or films: Edvard Munch, *Nosferatu*, Francis Bacon, *Der Golem*. It is alarming and confusing; you feel an impulse to turn and run back, but to what? You realize that the only way out is through. You lift one of the great iron door knockers at your eye level and batter it against the door.

Time shifts after the door slowly swings open. You swallow anxiously, and the smell coming from inside the foyer is sickly and sweet—it reminds you of a favorite childhood dessert, the name of which eludes you. The backlit figure on the inside is knobby and stooped, impossibly tall and gangly, sloppily enfolded head-to-toe in elaborate maroon and cerulean strips of thick linen. Not tightly, as with a mummy, but more loosely, giving the impression of a striated, multilayered cloak swathing the body. It gestures for you to enter; as the door closes after you, the sound is final. In the distance, at the darkened end of a plain, dimly lit hallway, you believe you hear sounds—voices, screams, howls. The figure stiffly points a covered arm in the direction of the disturbance—indicating that you are to proceed. You comply, the hairs on the nape of your neck now standing on end, your mouth dry.

You walk for what seems like hours. The hall slopes and turns and winds, and though there is very little illumination, you are able to see well enough. On the walls are paintings from all eras of history, some of which you recognize. There are closed doors all along the way, and they muffle horrendous noises—barking dogs, screaming women, maniacal laughter, pitiful weeping. You are afraid, your heart beating thickly in your chest as sweat collects on your forehead and trickles down your back. At a few places along the route there are grimy windows barred from the outside; strangely, there are people in gowns congregated around them, appearing to stare outward, but they are rigid, unmoving. They look frozen, like those posed for a particularly unflattering photograph—stuck in time—their faces contorted in shock or surprise into the semblance of a masklike rictus, their arms and hands caught in mid-gesture. From what you can glimpse out of the windows as you move past, they are looking at similarly static events from each of their corresponding perspectives: a few watch a harrowing vista of New York City on 9/11; others observe the gruesome assassination of President Kennedy; some witness the disastrous sinking of the RMS *Titanic,* while still others stare at crowds huddled on an ominous yet innocuous-appearing train station platform in Auschwitz, and so on. When you look away and back again, it appears as though some of the images and people have incrementally changed, both the observers and the observed; they are slightly different somehow, but you cannot be sure of this—perhaps it is nothing more than a trick of the faint illumination. It bothers you, though, and that is when it occurs to you that you have no idea where the bandaged thing that let you in went, and you are not sure you want to know, though you have sensed an alien presence hovering just behind you this entire time.

At last, after what feels like years, you reach a door in the hallway that is half-open. Over the threshold is a sign that reads: SANATORIUM. And below that: *Opustit všechny naděje, vy, kteří sem vstoupit.* Though you hesitate, something within you understands that this is where you are supposed to be; at this instant in time, and in this life—everything good and bad that has ever happened in all human history has been leading to now.

You enter the room.

—SUBTERRANEANS—

The place is grungy, unclean. The chilly air reeks sharply of ammonia and despair. From a high, narrow window near the top of the room you can see the bright moon as it crosses the sky, its cold light bearing down on the scene within, motes of dust floating in the beams. There are no nurses, no doctors. Only patients.

As you walk across the threshold your throat tightens reflexively, gagging from the stench. The tiled floor is stained, covered with dirt and old newspapers. The chamber is large and boxy, with high ceilings. Beds with rotten linens are arranged haphazardly throughout the room. In the beds you can see some of the patients have been strapped down—a few for so long that they have died and dissolved into their mattresses—blackened, skeletonized faces agape with frozen, silent screams. Still other inmates, naked and malnourished, writhe and groan about on their creaking beds, engaged in all manner of perverse sexual acts with one another, oblivious to your trespassing through their *Caligari*-inflected warren. You try not to look at them, feeling disgust and shame as you move to the back of the room, drawn to a darkened corner; in it is a solitary bed, well away from the others, its sole inhabitant sitting up. The person watches you approach, their eyes gleaming in the night.

"Ignore them," the figure says. "They are vile creatures. Unrefined." Despite the fact that he is speaking a mixture of Czech and German, you are inexplicably able to understand him, though his accent is heavy.

"Who are you?" you ask after a pause, already knowing the answer. Your Czech is perfect, though it feels strange to your tongue.

The man laughs, leaning forward into a shaft of moonlight; his clean-shaven face is angular, gaunt, pale, his dark hair thin and short. His gown is ragged but still white. His clear eyes sparkle over deep circles. "I am Kafka." He gestures grandly around the room. "Welcome to my domain. I dwell in the subconscious, my friend. Do not come any closer, please; I'm sick . . . I have consumption."

You smile. "That's fine. I'm dreaming all this. You can't catch diseases in a dream—"

Kafka laughs again, louder, and clasps his delicate hands together excitedly. "Yes! Now, from my deathbed, I understand that from a certain point onward there is no longer any turning back, no? That is the point that must be reached. Do you, my friend, regret actions that have not happened yet? Future transgressions? Of course not. So you *almost* understand, correct?"

You feel confused. "What . . . what do you mean?"

Kafka nods, rising unsteadily from his bed. His body is fragile, too thin. He moves over to a scarred end table and pulls out a shirt with much effort, which he dons over his gown. He then steps into a pair of trousers and tucks in the tails of the garment before slipping tattered loafers on. "What I mean, dear friend, is that I'm afraid you are *incorrect.*" Looking into a cracked mirror that seems to hover in the air above the table, he drags a comb across his head before turning to face you again. "It is *I* who am dreaming *you!* You are in *my* dream, not I in yours. I have called you here to help me. As I say, he who seeks does not find, but he who *does not* seek *will* be found! I must have you write something down—something about you, and about me. You are the conduit that I need to document the final tale of Franz Kafka—greater than 'The Metamorphosis,' or 'In the Penal Colony.' I chose you because of your nocturnal habits, your ability to traverse the veil of sleep . . . This will be the *greatest* fiction ever written by a dead Jewish insurance company employee!" Kafka laughs again, amused by the predicament. "In fact, we are already *in* the story."

You are surprised by this turn of events. Kafka motions you toward him.

"I shall be your guide and protector, my friend. But hear me—we must try and avoid too much in the way of metadiegetic displays, you know?" He pauses, stroking his chin in thought. "However, there is *one* hold-up. . . . I have written the story down, of course, even completed revisions—but we must retrieve it. You see, I had to leave it in another part of the castle for safekeeping, away from these . . . *degenerates.* So we have to go get it. Then you may read the piece, and, when you awaken, simply write it down." He makes a scribbling gesture with his hand, then winks at you before continuing: "That is to say, I *would* give it to you . . . though you might have a difficult time taking it back!" He glances around, lowering his voice and licking his lips before finally searching your face with his gaze. "Simply know this: It is *quite dangerous* down here. . . . But then, nothing worthwhile or attainable is ever realized by declaring how impossible it may be to accomplish, no?" He becomes more serious, placing a frail hand on your shoulder, squeezing it with a surprising strength; he looks you directly in the eyes with frigid intensity. "And understand—this isn't a poem; I'm not the Virgil to your Dante, and this is not some extended metaphor. This is reality! There are things here that will *shock* you . . . *excite* you . . . *disturb* you. Things . . . things more exotic than the all the whores, more chilling than all the graves, of Praha . . . You have been warned."

He grows quiet, letting you ingest this; after a time—the grunting and screaming of the others in the room filling the silence between you—Kafka laughs once again. Detecting your nervousness perhaps, he adds: "But isn't it always the case that people want what isn't meant for them?"

—BLACKOUT—

You follow Kafka back into the terrible, long corridor you emerged from originally. You can sense that the hallway is gently sloping downward as you make your way through its turns and convolutions; the walls and windows expand and contract in time to your own breathing—the very essence of the bizarre architecture grows more active as you penetrate into its depths. The walls are sweating moisture here, breaking down in a kind of cracked, elegant decay, the air heavy with humidity and mold; you pass more motionless souls, trapped forever in their personal limbos.

Finally, you reach a giant doorway. Through a shattered stained-glass window as large as a coffin, you vaguely make out the dimensions of a cavernous chamber. "The cafeteria," Kafka informs you in a whisper. "We mustn't linger here—it is far too perilous."

As you swiftly cross the room, you witness what Kafka means. At first you see what appears to be several hundred people eating at large tables; as you draw closer, it becomes clear that they are engaged in much more than a ritual dining experience. Between continuous rounds of vomiting and gorging on anything that they can stuff into their bloody mouths, whether the flesh of their tablemates, the utensils, wine glasses, or even parts of the furnishings of the room, from chair legs to tablecloths, they are participants in a nauseating and boisterous repast, a kind of narcissistic feeding frenzy that fills you with terror. Alarmed, you see one table where a toast is being made over a disemboweled, headless child about to be consumed by Gilles de Rais, Muhammad, Hitler, and Rasputin . . . Elsewhere, Caligula, stuffing fistfuls of food into his mouth, moans in ecstasy as he is fellated by a garter-belted Marilyn Monroe, who is in turn being soundly fucked doggy-style by Oscar Wilde, himself about to be decapitated by Yukio Mishima . . . At yet another place setting, William S. Burroughs, a trinity of heroin syringes hanging from his bony arm, pontificates to a visibly bored H. P. Lovecraft over piles of rotten cheese as Winston Churchill, cigar jutting from his bulldog countenance and wreathed in smoke, fondles the defiled skull of John the Baptist.

Making your way through the ravenous, mutilated throng,

you exit into the gloomy kitchen, grateful that you cannot see all that is happening in the shadows.

—CANDIDATE—

"Kafka!"

The great mouth bellows grotty laughter, and the hot stink of its breath burns your skin.

"It is I, I cannot lie," Kafka answers. He looks at you, and you see in his eyes, for the first time, that he is nervous.

The being in front of you is in the process of *becoming*. *What*, exactly, it is hard to tell. You stumble into it as you leave the kitchen. As you follow Kafka into the adjoining corridor to continue your journey through this labyrinth, the doorway in front of you presents itself as a veiny, glistening mound of pulsating, saggy flesh. Wispy threads of fluid ooze upward from the thing's throbbing black base, which has large protuberances pushing outward in flowerings of layered skin; beneath these, ropy purple appendages extend into the hall, burrowing under the floorboards. The entity blocks the entire door, growing lighter and speckled in complexion as it rises to the ceiling. At the top of the doorframe, the cloudy liquid collects and drips slowly down like honey. The entity appears to have no eyes or nose, but there *is* the enormous mouth—a jagged vertical gash splitting the beast from top to bottom, crammed with yellowy dentition, its thin blue lips beslimed and quivering. As you watch, the creature strains against its confines, belching and spewing an orange effluent from its horrid maw, growing increasingly agitated at your presence as it tries to reach for you, its trunk bowing in your direction. Gradually, this liminal being appears to be morphing into either a huge, scabbed demi-frog, or perhaps some mantis hybrid, glazed in brown sludge.

Once again it noisily croaks: *"Kafka!"* With that, its slender black tongue flops at your feet, studded with dozens of red-irised eyeballs staring up at the two of you. The foul air coming off the beast is overwhelming—a mixture of hot asphalt and rotten food.

Kafka: "This we call Candidate—former custodians of the sanatorium. The inmates forcibly selected two men and a woman, the dullest and most attractive ones, to become the guardians of the castle's inner sanctum, which is where we must travel."

You stare at Kafka, dimly aware of the tongue wetly retracting back to its owner. "What . . . *happened?*"

Kafka shrugs. "It is this place. It destroys minds, hearts, bodies. Hell is personal to each of us . . . we make it up. Yours is not the same as mine, my friend; what *I* see is not what *you* see, necessarily, and vice versa. But, to answer you, the chosen ones were fused together by the *hate* in this place . . . by the self-loathing, the egotism and avarice; they were mashed together, their humanity extracted, their identities squeezed out of them . . . and into something altogether new and ever-changing. We named the result 'Candidate the Warden.' It guards the entry to the depths below, yearning for anything, demanding everything."

You nod your head in comprehension, even though you do not completely understand the meaning or rationale of the dream logic.

"You don't have to know a man to understand his heart, no?" Kafka shakes his head, regarding you, then Candidate. "In the end, evil is whatever distracts—"

He is interrupted by the shrilling of the creature in front of you. You recognize that the only way forward is to get past

Candidate.

Kafka nods once, resolute. "Prepare yourself, my friend, to be reborn."

—RICOCHET—

You have no memory of what happened, only that you have sustained a collection of deep lacerations on your face and hands and your clothes are torn. There is a dull ache at the center of your head, but otherwise you are intact. Kafka is fretfully hovering over you, his spindly hands wringing nervously.

"I thought you were dead, my friend! All the others died in their sleep after their encounter with Candidate. Such a despicable . . . *beast*." Kafka's eyes widen; his face seems to float just above you, its edges blurry, indistinct. "But," he continues, "I had a suspicion you would be the one; I have been trying to get this last tale out for *so long*. . . . Many have tried to help, but none have succeeded. Of course, they promised much! I see that *you* have *not* promised me anything, however, and this is good." Kafka helps you stand. Though shaky at first, you feel better than you did prostrate on the ground, which has the soft, moist feel of the antechamber of an enormous heart.

"There are only two things," Kafka informs you. "Truth and lies. Truth is indivisible, hence it cannot recognize itself; anyone who wants to recognize it has to be a lie."

You ponder this as the two of you continue forward. The only light in the place is from far above and behind you, a mere pinpoint, but it provides enough illumination to see by. You intuit that the light is emanating from the strange doorway from before—the gate guarded by Candidate—which seems tens of miles distant now, part of some faraway planetarium-curved emptiness. It is as though you have both fallen to the very center of an alien world. The space you walk through now is warm, though not unpleasant; it appears to be a type of organic subway system, and smells vaguely of latex and sterility.

At last, after seemingly hours of silence and miles of trudging ahead, you turn to Kafka and ask: "I was thinking about what you said. What did you mean about truth and lies?"

Kafka, as he is wont to do, laughs, his brittle frame shaking in amusement. You both pause to rest, and you notice that Kafka is standing in front of a portal that has a flight of stairs receding upward into a pitch-black stairwell. "It is simple," he replies. "*You*, my friend, are truth; *I* am a lie. You are a magnificent *monolith*. Here am I—Kafka the great *recognizer*, my role in my own life! I see you as you are, which is what you *cannot* do for yourself as the *completer*, the bringer of truth—"

Without warning, a shade erupts from the stairwell and envelops Kafka on its way to you. You scream as you are overtaken: every nerve fiber shreds in your encounter with what feels to you a galactic evil. As your liberated mind spreads through the cosmos—dismantled molecule by molecule, axons and dendrites smearing into the un/nothing vibrations of subatomic particle shells—you see Kafka's visage disturbingly extended to become an Yves Tanguy–like infinitely featureless vanishing point, an oblivion. There, Kafka resides in curdling n-dimensional space, in discrete brane subdivisions. You reach for him, but your rendered hands, alternately corporeal and ethereal like something from a poorly constructed Cubist assemblage, elongate and diffuse into hazy remnants that merge with the air, blending into Kafka's deconstructed face before trailing brilliant, polychromatic streamers of fragmented memories, crumpled sorrows, broken dreams. Your existence has become at once past and future in an eternal present. This is a convergence point of spacetime, you realize—a personal event horizon, a private Mandelbrot set loop of reality. Beneath it all, you feel the cold undertow of death and nonexistence.

There is an anger in you now. You have been placed here to do a service, and you feel a surge of rage that culminates in a spasm at your rapidly evaporating interior, what some might deem your soul. The pain this causes is unable to be described or even fathomed; through an effort of your fading will, you are able to snag the last vestiges of whatever it is that defines your humanity and reassemble them.

As suddenly as it happens, the incident is dispersed: you are standing beside Kafka, both of you trembling in shock and pain.

Kafka looks at you, his face drawn. "You were tested, and you pass. Through pain are we transformed—it morphs us into our true selves, my friend."

This time *you* smile.

Together, you ascend the stairs.

—HEATHEN—

As you climb the flight of steps, disembodied voices become loud, then dissipate. Some whisper promises, others scream threats, still more extol assurances and confidences. You gather that these are not in your head, but are individuals you cannot see stuck somehow in the claustrophobic stairwell. Perhaps they are the people Kafka mentioned who died before and are now trapped here, unable to leave, held in a sort of interdimensional prison. The thought drives you on.

"Almost there, my friend. Do not listen to these utterances; they say what they say, these great liars and blasphemers, but their intentions don't matter, only their actions, just like the rest of us. . . . So here they are, only expressions without throats or tongues. I assure you—these are not folks who shall be acting on *any* impulse for quite some time."

You relax, believing Kafka speaks the truth, even if he is a lie himself.

—REPETITION—

When you both arrive at the top of the stairs, you feel as though you have conquered a mountain, but you are not winded or tired. Quite the opposite, in fact. The staircase terminates into another enormous corridor; you can see ahead that there are more individuals fixed in their perpetual grief as they gawk from the barred windows along the perimeter; more paintings appear and disappear along the way, fading into and out of perception, which is everything. The hallway is hot, bordering on uncomfortable.

Kafka clucks his tongue in sympathy and gestures at the poor lost souls in the hallway. "It isn't, dear friend, that they are so different from us. Actually, the problem is that they are too much like what we are." You nod in understanding.

As you approach the first cluster of onlookers, they unexpectedly turn on you. Kafka has vanished. The spectators, their eyes mere hollows in doughy, stringy faces, say nothing, but they tear at your clothes and slap you in the face repeatedly. You call out in fear and desperation as the mob pummels you. After several long minutes of this beating, you are hoisted aloft and carried to one of the windows. From your exhausted, upside-down perspective, the world outside seems strangely frenetic and watery.

The crowd flings you through the glass; after smashing past it, your body is sliced into several meaty chunks by the bars on the exterior. Still conscious, you plunge miles to the castle's stony plaza below. Hitting the ground, the ragged sections of your body burst apart in showers of offal, like so many overripe pumpkins. Before you can react to the pain, you instantly reconsolidate. Eyelids closed, you breathe deeply, calming yourself.

Slowly you open your eyes; the attack and fall was all an illusion. You hear Kafka laughing out of view: his strange, lilting laugh, his knowing laugh. You never left the passage; the onlookers are still in their unmoving positions congregated around the windows. Perhaps Kafka is challenging you, testing whether you are worthy of his gift, his story.

"Is it a trick? When we are so very close now? Who can tell, no?" he asks, shrugging in his way as he strolls up next to you. Gradually, his laughter is replaced by violent coughing and wheezing. The coughing becomes a fit, his face turning cyanotic as he pulls a clotted handkerchief from his pants pocket. He deposits a bolus of bloody sputum into the cloth before addressing you once more. "Consumption. We will see my doctor now; he has much to share."

—DEAD MAN WALKING—

The physician is only partly human: The rest is an unsettling composite of reptile, arachnid, wolf. He looks at Kafka with his shiny instruments, sharp and cruel, studying his frail features with a practiced and oversized compound eye. While Dr. Gefort goes over a chart of Kafka's vital statistics in the cramped, poorly lit examination room, you feel more as if you are in a stifling, filthy embalming area than a doctor's office.

"Kafka, dying soon, correct this," Dr. Gefort says, his voice reedy, mottled. He smiles, then looks at you. "For you, the story have I." He waves one of his numerous malformed pincers in the air before dipping it into a cabinet. After fishing around, he offers you a loose stack of dingy manuscripts pages. As Kafka smiles, you gingerly take them into your hands.

You read the story; it is a wondrous tale of existential angst and self-loathing. Pure Kafka.

"I love this. I have it in my mind and feel ready to go back to consciousness, Kafka."

Once you look up, you see that Kafka is strapped to a surgical table, nude and lying on crisp white sheets; he beams as the organs of his vivisected body—heaving, rosy lungs, fluttering veined heart, trembling solid liver—lustrously pulsate from the examination table. Dr. Gefort glances up from his work, nodding his semi-reptilian head in agreement at your assessment of the story.

"Thank you, my friend," Kafka gasps, his brow dotted with sweat and blood droplets. He grimaces as Dr. Gefort continues his awful prodding into Kafka's viscera, observing finally: "Soul-searching excursions are the worst, no?"

As you watch, stunned, the dim ambiance of the room gradually changes into a hazy blacklight, causing the gory sheets to glow brightly as the blood on the bedclothes darken from deep red to a series of black stripes. A few dull-blue loops of small intestine slide out of the cavity the doctor has opened in your companion's torso, limply hanging nearly to the floor as the physician sifts through Kafka. The other organs fluoresce garishly: sunny yellow nerves, hot pink muscle tissue, luminous green gallbladder.

"Best one of, Kafka," the good doctor intones. Looking up at his eviscerated patient, he tells him: "Nothing is found within."

Kafka smiles through his pain. "I just wanted to check again, Dr. Gefort." He looks over to you. "Regarding the story, well . . . as the old saying goes, three can keep a secret if two are dead, so I have entrusted it to you. The doctor and I can tell no one, but with you it shall be a secret no more!"

You muster a shocked half-smile in return, nervously rolling the pages together.

"My friend, would you mind waiting outside while Dr. Gefort sews me back together?"

—SOME ARE—

You are anxiously twitching your feet as you sit in the stuffy waiting room. The place is old, decrepit. Kafka has been in the operating theatre for years. Everyone in the room with you has died, their bodies mummified and covered in inches of gray dust, like the fallout of remembrance. The shapely nurse seated at the reception desk, her face little more than a blank effigy, seems to regard you suspiciously, but you cannot be certain. The crinkly manuscript sleeves are silky to your fingers, and you feel ill, not like yourself, removed from life and emotion. It is a most foreboding and disheartening anomie.

"Good as new!" Kafka exclaims as he appears beside you. He is attired in the outfit he donned when you first set out on your quest and seems no worse for wear. You are pleased to see him.

"Is this truly you, my friend? I was in there for a long time," Kafka says as you stand. "Might you be an identical-looking imposter? It is possible. My lover has been replaced with someone who looks the same, acts the same, but—I *know* that she is someone different. Even though she is a *perfect* imitation, I can *sense* it. . . . There are strange things in the world, my friend, so strange. After all, I myself am absolutely dead, and was born that way."

You are confused. In your own research, you recall reading

about these types of mental conditions. It sounds as though Kafka is asserting that he suffers from Cotard's Delusion, where someone is convinced that he is *literally* a walking corpse. Of course, he *is* dead at this point, and is talking with you in a dream of his own conjuration, so he alleges, though you know better. And the impostor idea—perhaps he also has Capgras Syndrome, where an individual believes that everyone around him has been replaced by exact replicas. How can you argue the truth against such a notion—the truth being that you are, in fact, *yourself?*

"And did you know that dreams are how we, the dead, return to the living? It is how we communicate to you from beyond death—to family members, friends, even to strangers to whom we wish to impart wisdom, just as I did with you . . . before you were replaced, that is."

You shake your head, mulling this over. Finally you answer: "Well, that's fascinating, I'll admit. I know *I'm* alive, otherwise you wouldn't entrust me with the manuscript, so how could we *both* be dead? We're even discussing the conundrum, so that proves we can't be!" Kafka strokes his chin thoughtfully at this. You both start walking out of the reception area as you go on speaking: "And how could I be an impostor? To what end? I know every detail of our trip together, and I've read your fine last novella, *Das Denkmal*. Really, even if I *am* an exact copy and not myself, does it matter? That still means my goals are the same, which is to recreate your story for the world once I wake up."

This gives Kafka pause. "Ah, very true. I see you still have the pages, too." He looks askance at you, wary. "Of course, this is not something that can be easily resolved, though you *are* persuasive! Understand that one cannot always hear with one's mouth open; and though I have heard what you are telling me, perhaps what I hear is not what you are saying? It is a complex thing . . . I must be cautious. Even Atlas was permitted the opinion that he was at liberty, if he wished, to drop the Earth and creep away; but this opinion was all that he was permitted."

After a few minutes, Kafka places a hand on your shoulder and smiles. "We press ahead, my friend. I will have to trust in this process. Understand, no one has made it this far before. It is hard for me to believe it's happening now, no?"

The lights go out.

Your eyes snap open in the darkness. You are in your bed at home, the sheets drenched in sweat, your hair plastered to your forehead. After catching your breath, you glance over at the clock: *3:01 A.M.* You rub your eyes, then stare at the ceiling.

"Jesus, how weird was *that?*" After a few minutes, you realize your bladder is full and sit up. The floor is cold. You reach for your glasses on the nightstand and see something strange: a group of papers is next to your water glass. You snatch them off the table, bringing the pages closer to your face. There, handwritten on the first page:

Das Denkmal
von Franz Kafka

Your mind reels: *But . . . how could I have brought this back? That's impossible!*

The icy fingers on your shoulder cause you to scream in the darkened room.

"Bitte, mein Freund! Ich entschuldige mich!" It is Kafka's voice.

You spin around on the bed, and the environment changes. The two of you are in a wooded area near the castle, which has exploded into a massive fortress of pliable mortar and elastic stone many times the size of the original structure; it threatens to swallow you, to engulf the planet, to devour all temporal existence. As the fog parts, you realize that you are in a graveyard adjacent to the obscenely expansive monstrosity; the entire hilltop around the castle is a wasteland, as though it has been pummeled by heavy mortar fire in the past. Above, your bedroom ceiling has dissolved away to expose the clear night sky. The moon, ochre-red from the singularity of a total lunar eclipse, provides a gloomy luminance to the proceedings. It is then you see that you are both standing next to a massive black obelisk. Like some great phallus it stabs upward, and the moonlight reveals a strange blue-green iridescence—almost holographic in appearance—dancing subtly on the polished surface of the pillar.

"I am terribly sorry for the fright, my friend," Kafka says as he walks forward to stand next to you. "It was necessary to create a false awakening to get us out of Dr. Gefort's place. Otherwise, we would have had to go back as we entered and face the same perils once again." Kafka smiles. "He is a fine country doctor, though . . . from what country, I never bothered to ask. Perhaps it's better not to know!" Kafka laughs and you relax, realizing you still have the manuscript pages in your hand.

Kafka speaks again: "I brought us here so that you could remember the story better. *Das Denkmal—The Monument.* I assumed the column would help you recall the details of the tale later." He looks up the length of the great tower. "Why is it that such monuments are always to the past, and so rarely to the future?"

With that, other huge, and in some cases impossible, shapes—Necker cubes, Penrose triangles, blivets—begin to erupt violently from the fog-shrouded ground all around you, accompanied by a deep, penetrating hum that fills your awareness. The earth splits open between you and Kafka, allowing a hellish red light to stream upward, surreally underlighting the scene; soon, a spectrum of irrational colors—familiar and alien alike—begins to radiate from under the ground, spreading into the cold night air all around the castle environs. Kafka is thrown off balance; you instinctively reach for him, but your grasp slips and you both tumble away into opposite sides of the void. From the great fissure that has opened between you, uncanny and terrifying beings of enormous size and variety explode into the world all around the ever-expanding fortress, engaging one another and advancing on the place itself with willowy, Dalí-esque limbs.

As you watch, the colors gradually become more muted, cooler. You begin to feel drowsy, lethargic. In the distance, you can see that Kafka, screaming in terror, is being dragged back to the castle by one of the great beasts; the whole alarming tableau flares again as the things infiltrate the citadel's walls. Storming the castle, the situation becomes ever more bleak and destructive. You lose sight of Kafka in the riotous turmoil.

An abrupt silence then engulfs everything; slowly, the colors diminish until they are no longer perceptible.

At last there is only a total and gently pulsing blackness—

—OUTSIDE—

Your eyes snap open in the darkness. You are in your bed at home, the sheets drenched in sweat, your hair plastered to your forehead. After catching your breath, you glance over at the clock: *3:01 A.M.* You rub your eyes, then stare at the ceiling.

"Jesus, how weird was *that?*" After a few minutes, you realize your bladder is full and sit up. The floor is cold. You reach for your glasses on the nightstand and see something strange: a group of papers is next to your water glass. You snatch them off the table, bringing the pages closer to your face. There, handwritten on the first page:

Das Denkmal
von Franz Kafka

Your mind reels: *But . . . how could I have brought this back? That's impossible!*

You rifle through the pages: all blank. You drop your shoulders.

"I must have written the title down in my sleep, I guess."

You return from the bathroom and snap on the light next to your bed. Going to a fresh page, you understand what has happened: you have just experienced Kafka's final tale. You begin to transcribe what you remember of the account.

Touching your forehead in recollection, you are surprised to feel a series of fresh cuts there—similar to the ones you now notice on your hands. These you recall obtaining in the dream. *But how? It was a dream, nothing more. . . .* Confused, you decide to ignore your injuries for the moment and write down the story, before the memory of what you read in Kafka's manuscript fades away:

"People waste their lives running from things they can't escape," LaXarus said. *"A bad childhood, poor decisions, perceived slights, honest mistakes. They should instead focus on what they can have an impact on in the present. . . . The past is dead and gone, and the future is unwritten."*

He looked over at his wife, Magu. She rolled half-mirrored eyes at him, her complex mouthparts working the steel into a metallic paste. Spitting the molten mixture onto a luminous disc to keep its temperature constant, she regarded her husband for a moment. "The sooner we finish the monument," she finally said, "the sooner we can return."

He nodded. Time was short, this LaXarus knew to be true. His wife was wise, but he was anxious to reclaim to his old life, to be redeemed by the ancient ways.. . .

—*To the memory of Melanie Tem,*
who loved the idea

BENEATH THE VEIL

DAVID BARKER

He awakened in a darkened chamber in a tangle of sweat-drenched bedclothes, his mind empty of any shred of personal history or even disconnected traces of memory, except for two distinct episodes of recollected consciousness—those being separated by an interminable period of deep, dreamless sleep in the form of a profoundly blank oblivion. Given what seemed to him the obvious incompatibility of this enigmatic pair of memories, he suspected that one must be a purely physical event that had taken place in real life—something that had actually happened to him—while the other had to be either a hallucination or a dream, for given the conditions prevailing in either episode, the other one could not be true. But which was the dream and which was reality? In what he suspected must surely be a highly bizarre situation, he really did not know. If the first of the two sets of mental impressions he held in his mind was based on fact, then life was very good, it was fully worth living. But if the second set of impressions proved to be the greater reality, then life was nothing less than unending horror, and he did not wish to continue living it.

The dreadfulness of the latter possibility so terrorized him that for the present he could not find the inner strength to rise from the bed. He lay there motionless for what seemed like hours, reviewing the two sets of memories in as much detail as he had retained, hoping to discover a clue in either narrative that might reveal the true nature of one or the other.

The first memory — for their relative order in time was clearly fixed in his mind — took place in a modern-looking church in a small city. The quiet austerity of the building's décor led him to believe that it served some variety of Protestant assembly, although he could not determine the exact denomination. He was the groom at his own wedding, standing proudly on the chancel steps, nervously awaiting the imminent entrance of his young bride. Beside him stood his best man, the image of strength and confidence, with hands crossed gracefully before him, while seated throughout the church were his numerous friends and family, young and old, all of them happy to be sharing this life-changing occasion with him.

The organist began with a subdued prelude that seemed to go on for quite a while until finally, at the far end of the hall, the doors swung open and in came the flower girls carrying baskets overflowing with yellow blossoms. With an air of high seriousness they marched up the aisle toward the altar. As they reached the chancel area and began to peel off alternately to the right or left and took their places on the steps, the organist suddenly launched into the wedding march, its deep bass notes resonating throughout the length of the nave, making the walls and floors vibrate. A moment later the bride and her father entered the church, arm in arm, and slowly proceeded up the center aisle, each step made in time with the slow, plodding beat of the music.

With delight-filled satisfaction the groom watched the

guests all turn in unison upon the bride's appearance, captivated by her vitality and feminine allure on this, her wedding day. Members of the audience clapped softly at first sight of her, while some gasped audibly. He was a lucky man indeed to be joined together in holy matrimony with a woman of such innate charm, innocence, and goodness. He had chosen his bride well, and looked forward to a lifetime of countless joys and blessings.

Following the bride and her father up the aisle were the bridesmaids, who busied themselves with tending to her carefully coiffed hair, the gauzy white veil covering her face, and the train of her long white gown. The gown, sewn from the finest satin, shimmered in ways that displayed to great advantage a figure that was both as slender as a girl's and as voluptuous as a woman's.

After that, the time-honored steps of the ceremony passed by in rapid succession, with the arrival of the smiling cleric in his formal robes, the delivery of his sonorous incantations from an ancient book of sacred writings, the utterance of hallowed vows by the awestruck couple, and their solemn exchange of golden rings. All through these proceedings, the impatient groom yearned to see the bride's face without the impediment of the veil; for the translucent nature of its fabric and the fact that a strong ray of amber light was shining directly on it from a nearby stained glass window prevented him from seeing clearly through the material and confirming that underneath it lay the cherished physiognomy of his betrothed, and not the malign visage of some interloping creature of wickedness and shadow.

But why, he wondered as he lay there in the darkened chamber remembering what should have been a joyous moment, would he fear that some inhuman monstrosity had been substituted for his beloved? The perversity of such a thought was in strong disharmony with the joy of the occasion. And yet, that's what he had thought as he stared at the practically glowing veil—that he detected some semblance of a dark, hideous face below its fabric that spoke more of the grave than of the wedding bower, and at the same moment he thought that he detected from her direction a whiff of rotten stench when he should have been inhaling her delicious womanly scent.

Thankfully, these pernicious doubts were scattered to the four winds the very second the cleric pronounced them husband and wife, and the groom lifted his bride's veil and kissed her passionately on her honey-sweet, all too human lips.

Thereafter flowed the many delights large and small of a happy wedding party: inscribing their names in the huge, leather-clad register volume kept by the cleric in a private room behind the altar; warmly greeting the many guests in a receiving line at the back of the church; a sumptuous feast of rare meats, delicate wines, and exotic fruits in the lantern-strewn tent set up behind the church; a lively band of musicians playing festive tunes; dancing by the adults while the children ran and played; the simple pleasures of talking and laughter and watching others from across the room; and the one moment that all the single girls waited for when the new bride threw her bouquet into the air behind her and some lucky young woman caught it with the unspoken promise that she would be the next one to be chosen as a wife.

At some point during that leisurely summer evening before the sun went down behind the hills, the two of them slipped out unnoticed and escaped to start their married life together. As simple as that. That's how he recalled this first set of memories. It could easily be a real part of his waking life, aside from that disturbing idea he had entertained about what her face might look like, hidden beneath the veil—a thought that had almost ruined the ceremony for him. And if this first set of memories was the reality, then the second set of memories that followed it must only be a nightmare, and not something worse.

He recalled nothing of what transpired after they had left the church. A vast sea of dreamless sleep had engulfed and obliterated all memory of his wedding night. Did they make love, or did they simply collapse in each other's arms, too tired for sensual pleasures? He did not know. Now he lay awake in what might be their honeymoon suite, and she could return at any moment to rejoin him in their common bed. Surely she would, if that first set of mental impressions had been reality.

He recalled the wedding in the church with a melancholy yearning that was so poignant it was almost repellent, and that odd combination of positive and negative emotions made him wonder if it were only a wistful dream of what might have been, and not a recollection of something that was real.

He could not judge nor even guess at the duration of the period of dreamless oblivion he had then experienced, after they fled the wedding party. He might have slept for an hour, or an infinity of epochs may have passed by. There was no way he could take measure of its length, nor sound the mysteries of its depths. All he knew was that it formed a total break from all that had come before it—the degree of forgetfulness it provided was complete and perfect, and for that he felt a great mercy had been bestowed upon him.

The second memory, or set of impressions, that occupied his mind had as its setting the site of a ruined temple. He and a few others were gathered on an expanse of weathered stone slab under a drab gray sky. Through the action of long ages and the effects of earthquakes and volcanism, the slab had become tilted and sat at a pronounced angle, so that when he endeavored to cross it he was unsteady on his feet and feared he might stumble and fall. As before, he was an apprehensive groom, but this time at what seemed to be an occult matrimonial ceremony, and this was no sanctified church; it was a pagan enclave in a vast region of chaotic destruction and desolation. No organ played; the only sound was the mournful sighing of the wind across broken stone surfaces.

He stood facing the ritual's observers, keenly searching their eyes for an explanation as to why they were witnesses to this blasphemous rite, but could read nothing in their expressions. A raggedly attired urchin girl climbed up on the far edge of the slab and shuffled lethargically toward him, a cluster of wilted flowers drooping from her dirty hand. She was followed by another, then several more beggarly children—the decadent flower girls of this obscene mockery of a wedding.

Then he saw *her*—shambling alone toward him without the escort of a father figure—his bride to be. She had clambered over the jagged edge of the stone slab, in the process creating a long rent in the stained gown that covered her body from neck to ankle. The hole exposed one shriveled breast with a blackened nipple and a patch of gaunt belly mottled with blue bruises. A bevy of filthy bridesmaids soon emerged from out of the shadows of the surrounding piles of rubble and fell to accompanying her, some of them picking fitfully at her tattered garment, while others pulled small twigs and pale worms from her straggly hair. One of these waifish harpies, half naked with emaciated limbs caked in dried mud, clawed eagerly at the bride's veil of sackcloth while chattering incoherently, but was not successful in yanking it away. Had she done so, he wondered, what would the exposed face have resembled? A sultry demon? A dusky angel?

Her head awkwardly slumped downward with the chin resting against her sunken bosom, spindly arms hanging limply at her sides, his betrothed fitfully shuffled forward one laborious step at a time, pausing after each movement so as to gather her strength. It was not the way a vibrant young woman carried herself. This could not be the woman he loved! She was a pale sham of a bride—a cadaverous substitute for the woman he yearned to marry.

She shuffled ever closer, one terrible step at a time, until she stood immediately before him, the veil over her unknown aspect only inches from his eyes. She lifted her head until her eyes—could he detect them—would have been level with his own, and he sensed that she was staring directly at him through the density of the soiled covering. A dusty exhalation made the veil puff out, and he smelled the stench of her breath, rich with vile nuances of decay and foulness.

He would have turned and fled the temple ruin, would have abandoned this desiccated hag, had it not been for the dissuading presence of the evil priest in flowing crimson robes who began to chant unholy verses from an ancient book that he held spread open before the couple. Fearing both priest and bride, the groom dumbly repeated the vows read to him, ignoring their import, knowing full well he would not abide by them, could not keep nor honor them. It was all a profane lie, the babbling of devils, and he blocked the words and what they might mean from his consciousness, waiting only for the ceremony to end so that he might still make his escape. This was followed by the sacral exchange of rings, in which he slid a dented and twisted golden band formed in the likeness of a coiled snake onto her withered finger, and she, with great exertion, placed a band of hammered silver onto his left hand. At that juncture, the priest commanded in a frenzied tone, "Embrace the pristine consort!" and only with a tremendous effort of will power was the groom able to lift the soiled veil and gaze upon her face.

What he saw came as no surprise, but the sight nonetheless shocked and horrified him: hers was the face of a corpse, one long buried and lately exhumed. The skin was dried and yellowed, a parchment-like relic that had split in places, revealing brown stretches of underlying bone. The lips were largely gone, with only crumbling remnants of tissue remaining around her mouth, partly concealing the lengths of ivory-hued teeth. The nostrils were reduced to black crusted holes. All this and more one might anticipate when viewing the face of a cadaver. What was wholly unforeseen was the unnaturally glowing crimson eyes whose intense stare penetrated deep into his mind and soul.

At this final outrage he ought to have been completely panicked and repulsed; however, he was not. For within him now began to stir a strange desire, a perverse carnal lust that not only defied all reason but actually seemed to be driven by the horrors to which he was being exposed. It was sheer madness, but he craved an obscene physical union with the loathsome atrocity now lewdly pressing against him, wished to join her forever and eternally partake of the infinite corruption in which she reveled in the company of these lowly others, her begrimed followers.

That was the remarkable conclusion of the second set of memories. He could not imagine what might have followed the hideous climax to the ceremony. Immediately after staring upon the visage of his spurious bride, he was plunged into the blackest, emptiest space conceivable, as if he had ceased to live, had in fact never existed at all. Lying there in the darkened chamber, he wondered if perhaps he had died from mental shock at that instant; but if so, how could he have later awakened? It was all an unfathomable mystery.

One set of mental impressions must be a dream, and the

other must be a reality. No, that was not entirely true. It was possible both were dreams, and for some reason his real life had come to be completely hidden from him. He supposed it was also remotely possible that both sets of impressions were real, but there was no way he could rationally reconcile the two if that were the case. Well, he would soon know the answer to this mystery, for he would rise from the bed, exit the chamber, and see what kind of a world awaited him outside this dark, neutral space.

But before that could happen, a slender shadow suddenly appeared in the chamber's open doorway. Silhouetted against the moonlight was a female figure garbed in a long, pale dress. She was his bride, and this, their wedding night—but from which memory? The figure remained motionless for several long seconds, and then it began to shamble torpidly toward him.

DREAMS DOWNSTREAM

John Shirley

Monday

When the Cloud Shroud switched on in Feeney Valley, Josh noticed nothing special. He detected not even a flutter in the satellite TV transmission. The morning show proceeded without a pause in its soothing flow of inanity.

He finished breakfast, put the plate and cup in the dishwasher, and walked out of his house to the small hybrid car in his driveway; he glanced at the street, not sure what he expected to see. There had been obscure and ambiguous rumors. But it was the same suburban street, same lines of middle-class cars along the wide curving streets, same mix of split-level and ranch-style tract homes; the occasional palm tree, the eternal loom of enigmatic yellow hills overlooking the Southern California valley under the cloudless September sky.

Still, as he got in the car, backed out of the drive, and turned on the radio, Josh felt a kind of chill—an extended cold shudder. But that was something internal, perhaps a response to an allergy pill he'd taken that morning.

Josh started his long drive, passing the street where the hospice was; listening to talk radio to try to keep from thinking about his father and what it was like for him in the hospice. The shock jock on the radio wasn't much help, and Josh still had an hour-long commute to Globule Productions, and to the clammy, computer-animated grip of Rigby, Piggy, Wulf, and Smarm, the four MutiePets.

Not quite sunset.

"No, I swear, there's a guy out here in his underwear that looks like my Uncle Timmy," Ava said. She was sitting on the front step, her feet on the sidewalk, because she always felt as if her mom was listening to her talking on the cell when she was in the house.

"What?" said Kaylee in her ear. "Like your uncle? No way."

"Yeah, he . . . really does look just like him, and I thought he was wearing shorts, but—I swear he's in like tighty-whitey *undies* out here. . ." Eva was raptly watching the portly man coming up the sidewalk toward her; he was wearing a too-small ratty T-shirt and white briefs and nothing else. She couldn't see his face very well because the sun, easing to the hilly horizon, was glaring redly at her between the houses. But as he got closer. . .

"Oh my *God*, Kaylee. He *so* looks like my Uncle Timmy. . ." She broke off as the man came closer, stopping to talk to that Muslim lady who lived two houses down. The Muslim lady who always wore a hijab was backing away from the guy, was turning away and running into her house. His face. . .

"That's so creepy. Why don't you call the cops if he's running around in his—?"

"I'm going to. I'm. . ." She hung up. She stood and looked again.

It was really her Uncle Timmy. It *was.* Hr uncle who'd come to take care of her and Mom after Dad got convicted on that insurance fraud thing.

He was looking after the retreating Muslim lady, vaguely puzzled. Her uncle always made a point of being nice to the Muslim family.

Her uncle shook his head and turned to see his niece staring at him. He waved and smiled at Ava.

Uncle Timmy's eyes looked kind of vacant. *A stroke or something?*

She looked down at his underwear—and his feet. He had on two tattered tennis shoes and no socks.

He followed her gaze and looked down at himself. "Where my damn pants gone?" he said. His voice sounded as if his mouth was full of marbles.

Ava felt dizzy. She couldn't call the cops. It was her uncle. Her mom wasn't home yet. What should she do? "Timmy, you better get in the house."

Then a car came down the street, and she looked nervously at it. It was someone else who would see her uncle like this and call the cops, if that Muslim lady didn't.

But then she recognized the car. And the silhouette of the man in it. Wasn't that her Uncle Timmy driving the car?

It was. He was still a ways off, but she recognized his vanity plate, *RubrMan,* because he was a district manager for Goodyear.

She looked back at the man on the sidewalk—but that was definitely her Uncle Timmy . . . too. Only he was blurry now. He was transparent.

Then—the Uncle Timmy on the sidewalk . . . blinked out. He was simply *gone.*

Eva gaped. The man in his underwear had just vanished,

right there on the street.

And a few moments later her Uncle Timmy, wearing his blue suit, pulled into the driveway.

Tuesday

Josh blew his nose and said, "I don't know about this Cloud Shroud thing." He tossed the bunched tissue neatly into the little wastepaper basket. "Nobody asked me if it should be transmitted all over my damn neighborhood—the whole town really. Might screw up this entertainment system I spent like eight grand putting together."

"We haven't got that Cloud Shroud thing in Burbank yet," Choo said. Harry Choo was manager of MutiePets development; twelve years younger than Josh and eighty thousand dollars a year better paid.

They were sitting in the conference room, toying with their coffee mugs and scones, waiting for the rest of the Season Three team; trying to put off thinking about purple animated television heroes for as long as possible.

Josh sipped a little coffee. His stomach didn't like it. "Cloud Shroud's supposed to provide the 'Internet of things' or something. And, what, instant medical diagnosis if you get sick and whisper in your ear if you need to pay a bill. But you have to buy some interfacer thing to really use it. Expensive item."

Harry snorted. "I remember when that Cloud Shroud thing was a start-up: seems like ten minutes ago. *Boom,* now it's installed all over the place."

"Follow the money."

Harry nodded. "My cousin's neighborhood has it, he claims it makes him sick. Headaches and bad dreams. But he's always been pretty paranoid about stuff."

"Not feeling that great myself." Josh had a mild headache,

a twingeing stomach.

"Hey—you get that preliminary script outline done?"

Josh snorted. Any outline was going to be preliminary. "I can't outline when we haven't agreed on premises," Josh said. "And we can't do that until we decide if we're going to bring in the new characters for diversity as per notes . . . I mean, these are mutated animals, not people, so I can't really see the point but—"

"Well, they have human friends."

"They already have black human friends, brown human friends, they can be any color. I'm not sure what they want at network."

"I don't either. Muslim? Gay? They like to send notes so they cover their asses."

Josh wanted to say, *Their fat asses are too big to cover with notes,* but he knew Harry didn't like anyone going quite that far dissing the television network, even as a joke; probably he was hoping for a job there.

"Give them a Muslim gay friend then, I don't care. But after we do it I bet network says no to it."

The door opened and the rest of the team started filtering in, balancing coffee cups and pastries, and Josh resigned himself to the meeting.

§

"I shouldn't be bitching about my job," Josh said on the hands-free phone as he drove down the highway into Feeney Valley. It was four in the afternoon—he'd decided his vague sickliness was a good excuse to "work at home."

"No, you shouldn't be bitching," Marianne agreed, her voice sounding almost as far away as she was. Marianne was in South Carolina, ostensibly trying to complete a doctorate in digital media. He hadn't seen her in months. Supposedly she was still his girlfriend. But even now she had that clipped tone that hinted she wanted to go but didn't just want to hang up on him. Maybe she wasn't alone there.

"Lot of people would love to have a job working in animation, Josh, especially at your level. You could quit and end up waiting on tables or something. Then you'd appreciate the animation work."

"Yeah. I know."

"I've got to go to the library. There's stuff there I have to dig up—it's just not in the database."

"Okay. Well, I miss you, kiddo."

"I miss you too." Relief in her voice at saying goodbye.

Then she hung up.

Josh sighed. *Not going at all well.*

The curvy two-lane highway followed the ridge on the northeast side and looked down over the gridwork of ranch homes and split-levels and the occasional hulking, shiny-new McMansion. The grid was broken up by palm trees and ornamental plum trees and bottlebrush and what was left of the old oak groves. This had been all old oak growth once; a few gnarled silvery green oaks survived the razing, lonely sentinels that seemed, to Josh, forever waiting for some mysterious inevitability.

He slowed behind a ponderous RV that had to edge around the next curve, and took the moment to glance back at the valley.

A glimmering membrane appeared over it, an arching gleam that came and went and came back, all in split seconds, and it seemed to be swarming with two-dimensional pictures of people, crying people, running people, confused people looking desperately around for something. . .

Josh almost drove the car into the oncoming lane, had to swerve, heart thudding, to stay on his side of the road.

He steadied, glanced back at the valley. The glimmer was no longer there. The valley looked normal.

My imagination working with some atmospheric effect. . .

§

The guy who worked on the MutiePets TV show was pulling into his driveway a few houses down from where Eva sat on the step. Her mom had told her about him and the show, as if she would be interested; it was the new version of MutiePets. She'd watched the old version for a min-min or two when she was a little kid of, like, eight.

He was a doughy-faced guy, tall, with long black hair that looked as if he'd had it done in a man-perm. He had on a leather jacket shaped like a blazer, over a T-shirt displaying a picture of Godzilla. He had one of those tiny beards, she noticed.

Hipster, she decided. But he was probably a corporate hipster—that's what Rainy would say.

Eva was sitting here, with her phone in her lap, waiting to see if they came again. First she'd seen that half-naked ghost of her uncle, and then it had gone away, and getting out of his car Uncle Timmy asked her about the guy in the shorts she was talking to, and she'd had to tell him she wasn't talking to him, and anyway . . . he was gone now. She didn't know who he was. "Yeah, he was wearing some kind of, um, swimming suit and he ran off or something."

Couldn't say, *It was you in your underwear, Uncle Timmy, and you vanished.*

But she'd felt an enormous relief when he'd asked her about him. That meant he'd seen him too.

And later she saw something else: a big split-level house bursting into an intense fire down the street, flames blasting out second-story windows and licking up at the roof; terrified people scurrying out of the house.

Then the fire had just gone away—no smoke, nothing. The frantic people were gone too. The house was there, but quiet, windows intact.

The fire had only been there about ten seconds, but as Eva watched, a gangly old woman in a housecoat walked across the street and stared at the house. So Eva had gone up there and the old lady turned to her and asked Eva if she'd seen a fire. . .

And Eva had said, "I thought I did, but it must've been, um, an illusion or some . . . thing."

The lady smoothed her white hair back with a gnarled hand. "I was about to call the fire department, but then it . . . well, I'll call them anyway. But there's no one living there. It's so funny—I dreamed of a fire in that house last night."

The old woman turned away and went back to her own house.

Walking home, Eva felt a little sick and wondered if one of Rainy's older stoner friends had dosed her somehow. But she hadn't eaten anything for hours before then.

The fire department sent a couple of trucks right away, going to the house where the flames had come licking out. The firemen milled around in puzzlement, seemed disappointed as they interviewed the old lady, and finally went away.

That was yesterday. And Eva knew it wasn't over. There was weird shit going on, and she *felt* weird, so she was going to wait here on the front step and see if it happened again. She'd get pictures of it with her cell phone. It could be ghosts or something. She'd always wanted to see ghosts.

Eva waited. She kept looking up and down the street.

Nothing yet. But it wasn't that time of day exactly yet. It seemed as if it happened around dusk.

Rainy sent her a text asking if she could meet her at Kaylee's house, they were going to play GTA: *A Woman's Revenge* on X-BoxOne.

Eva replied, **No, chasing ghosts, explain later.**

A police car was cruising slowly down the street, a young cop in it, his hair cut flat-top, unnecessary dark glasses in this shaded street clapped on his head; a scowl on his face. Eva knew him a little—Officer Olberta, liked to seem gruff and tough but cried with happiness at his sister's wedding, or so Kaylee said.

Eva watched Olberta drive past; he nodded at her, she nodded back. He peered up the street . . . and stopped his cruiser, so abruptly Eva could hear the tires squeal.

A big woman was running down the street, a few steps from the sidewalk. She was a stout woman, barefoot, wearing tight jeans and a long white blouse, and her long brown hair was streaming behind; her face, Eva saw, was contorted like a baby about to squall.

A man, or something like a man, was pursuing her; a hulking man in colorless rags; he had a Neanderthal face, and tusks; he had hands instead of feet, and sometimes he was running on all fours, other times on his hind legs, loping clumsily along.

The sight paralyzed Eva for several long moments. Finally she stood up, her cell phone clattering from her lap.

Olberta was getting out of his cruiser, just about thirty feet from Eva; he was drawing his gun. "What the hell!" he muttered. He spoke into the little phone clipped to his shoulder. "This is Olberta 17, we have some guy in a costume chasing a woman here on Perry Avenue, 3329—"

"Help me!" the woman screamed hoarsely, running toward the police car. Her bare feet were bleeding.

"Oh God," Eva said. She scooped up the phone. The glass was cracked, but it seemed to be still working. She fumbled to set up a photo.

The blubbering barefoot woman was crouched down against the police car, on the other side from Olberta, her face turned toward it, as if she wanted to hide under the golden badge painted on the door.

Olberta hurried around the car, stepping between the woman and the loper. He had his Glock nine out, extended with both hands on it, aiming at the loper. "Stop right there!"

The loping thing rushed toward him.

"Stop!"

The loper was a few lopes away when Olberta fired—and Eva took a picture, and another—

The loping thing leapt over Officer Olberta and the crouching woman; it landed on the roof of the car—making no sound, no dent, and then spun around . . . and flickered out. It was gone.

Olberta turned, staring at the place where the loper should have been. His mouth was hanging open. He lowered his sidearm and looked around.

"You see where it went?" he asked Eva.

She shook her head.

"You saw it, didn't you?" he asked, blinking.

She nodded.

"Okay. You better go in the house."

She nodded again but she just stood there, looking into her cell phone's cracked screen.

Sirens were approaching. The blubbering lady was still crouching and crying. Olberta bent to help her.

The photos in Eva's cell phone showed the woman running and behind it, a blur, something like the loper.

But the picture was unclear; unconvincing.

§

Deep into the afternoon Josh fell asleep curled up on the mussed bed with his cat.

He immediately dreamt of his father in the hospice, his half-shriveled dad twisting and turning in the sheets, muttering. Then he saw something else in the room with his father: his older brother, whom he did such a good job of not thinking about, naked and covered in blood from his slashed wrists . . . floating horizontally, the same position as when Dad found him in the bathtub already bled to death, mouth and eyelids drooping.

Josh remembered coming home and finding Dad crying on the carpeted steps. . .

His father had regular nightmares about Roland's death. And it was as if Josh could see his father in his deathbed room and see the nightmare of his brother all bloody in the same room where his dad was dying and then his father sat up and looked right at Josh watching from his own dream. . .

The sirens warbling up the street woke Josh. He lay there a moment, his whole sight taken up with the close-up face of his black cat, who was on the pillow next to Josh's head, gazing unblinkingly at him with its golden-green eyes open wide open like a Halloween decoration.

"What you looking at, Panther Boy?" Josh asked him, scratching the cat's head.

Josh swung his legs to the side of the bed and sat up. His head throbbed. The dream was still close by, though invisible; he could almost smell Roland's blood in the room.

He made himself pick up the iPhone and call his dad's hospice. The lady with the Vietnamese accent answered, and he told her who he was and what he wanted.

"I don't think he can come to the phone now," she said.

"They had to sedate him. He had some kind of nightmare and he was trying to get out of bed and he fell down and hurt his knee. . ."

"What? Did he break anything?"

"No . . . I'm not sure. I don't think so. Just a cut."

"Okay. I'll . . . I'll come and see him. Soon."

"He'll be glad to hear that."

Josh winced. He could hear the judgment in the woman's voice. He hadn't been to see his father in almost two months.

He hung up and put on his shoes, went to see what all the noise outside was about.

But the police just told him to go back in and not to come out again tonight unless it was an emergency. Feeling muddled, tired, vaguely angry, Josh did as he was told.

He fed his cat, then went to his bedroom, took off his shoes, crawled under the covers, and found the television remote. He watched an old Anthony Mann western with Jimmy Stewart for an hour. . .

It was dark outside when he heard the loud, theatrical chortling outside the door. Chortling, gleeful chuckling, chattering; familiar voices. Someone must be pranking him with a recording. Should not have let the neighbors know where he worked.

He got up and went to the front door, looked through the peephole—and saw the MutiePets staring back at him. They were looking right at the peephole; amazingly good masks. They seemed flexible, innately expressive . . . glowingly purple. . .

He opened the door to shout at the pranksters . . . and the shout died on his lips.

It was them. The glittering eyes of Rigby; the slobber dripping from Piggy's snout; Wulf dancing about in exactly the impossible Wulf fashion, usually a few inches over the ground, a dance only an animation could do. Smarm, giggling and tilting his head, was spouting his catchphrase, "I'm faster 'n' I'm smarter, fartier, uglier, and buglier than YOU!"

They were human-sized bipedal caricatures of animals; they were standing on green-booted feet; and Rigby hissed, "You've written me *stupid* and I hatie hate *hate* you!" Then Wulf slashed at Josh's face with his ninja-star embedded paws, and—Josh could feel it, as the paw struck him. But it was like feeling a dash of cold water.

The MutiePets seemed to shimmer and melted away, leaving purple mist on the empty front porch.

Josh slammed and locked the door and fled to his bedroom.

Wednesday

I don't think they're ghosts, Eva texted, as she sat crosslegged on the plush white rug. That one you saw—a naked man flying over you . . . You said he was your neighbor. . .

It was so gross! Rainy texted back. **He was yelling about how we were stupid because we couldn't see he could fly . . . School was canceled though, Mrs. Gindy had a heart attack or something. . ."**

"Eva!" It was her uncle calling from outside the door of her bedroom. He knocked on the doorjamb. "We're going to have dinner, and right now! You're not eating in your room tonight!"

"Whatever! I'll be there in a min-min."

"Right now!"

G2G, Unc Tim hammering on door, she texted and shut the phone.

She left the bedroom just in time to hear her mom say, in her slightly Tagalog-inflected accent, "If there's something in the water then we should be evacuated, shouldn't we?"

Uncle Tim gave out an exasperated sigh. "They're not

evacuating people, they're just saying. . ." Something else Eva couldn't make out.

Eva found them in the kitchen, her uncle sitting at the little maplewood table, her small Filipino mother, still wearing her hospital tech uniform, dishing some *kalderata* onto a plate for Eva.

"They're just saying *what?*" Eva asked.

"That there might be some kind of hallucinogen in the water. They're going to see how it goes tomorrow, they're canvassing the hospitals, people seem to be. . ."

"Who's they?"

"State health authorities. We using bottled water to make the food. Just sit and eat, Eva."

Eva sat, but she had no appetite

§

Josh was in a sickly daze most of the day. Sleeping. Watching old movies. Not answering his phone. He'd called in sick and they'd just have to wait. It wasn't as if they had notes approval on the preliminary outline yet.

He felt a kind of throbbing lassitude, thudding in his head, hanging on him like lead weights, and he shouldn't have startled easily, but when the doorbell rang at six he almost fell off the bed.

"Fuck."

Pantherboy jumped off the bed and ran into the bedroom closet. Not a usual place for him to take refuge.

Josh got up, aware that he hadn't showered or changed his clothes in a couple of days. Maybe it was knowing Marianne had written him off. Maybe it was because he had pretty much written his father off. Maybe it was. . .

The doorbell rang again. He walked toward the front door, reached for the knob—and then stopped dead. What if it were the hallucinations again? What if it were the MutiePets?

He looked through the peephole. There was a thin pale man with a carefully sculpted short beard, pinched face, yellow-lensed retro sunglasses, and a suit without a tie.

A salesman, probably. Josh really felt like snarling at someone. He was ashamed to have the feeling, but he gave in to it and opened the door.

"Hi, I'm from Cloud Shroud," said the man in a piping, practiced voice. "My name's Simmons. I've got something free for you—"

"Not interested in any bullshit today," Josh said with barely muted savagery. "Not pretend-free stuff, free stuff till it costs money later, nothing."

"No, I'm really not selling anything. We're giving the interfacers out free so we can prevent, ah, interference, hereabouts. . ."

He held up a transparent clamshell package with a six-sided metal and black-plastic device in it. "It hooks onto your router or—"

"Just cut to the bad news."

The pinch-faced man licked his lips. "I just want to hand you this and I'll leave. I won't take any information from you, I won't call you about it, no one will. We're giving them away free in this area because of—complications of . . . Anyway, it has all the directions."

This Simmons was no salesman, Josh realized. He had no prepared sales talk. He had what looked like expensive Italian shoes.

"You're not some hired guy, you're pretty high up in the Cloud Shroud thing, aren't you, Simmons?" Josh asked, holding the man's gaze with his.

Simmons cleared his throat. "I'm not *high up*, as you put it, I'm . . . a junior executive, I guess you'd say. We want to keep this whole repercussion, whatever you want to call it, just between us and our subscribers—"

"I'm not a subscriber."

"Right, right, but—everyone here is affected and we're . . . You'll never have to officially subscribe."

"You're trying to keep the lid on this thing. Okay, you want this 'interfacer' installed, you come in and do it. Or it doesn't get installed and I call the . . . the local media."

"It's already on the media, but we just don't want it to—" He broke off, sighing. "I don't have time to install it myself, dude, I have a van-full of interfacers to give out—"

"Look, the neighborhood is practically about to riot, and I'm going to tell them to talk to you personally. Unless."

Simmons took a long slow breath. "Yeah, fine, okay, where's your router?"

§

Eva had to sneak out the back door of the house and slip around the side to the gate to get to the front—either that or fight with her mom and Uncle Timmy. She didn't want to fight with them again if she could avoid it, not after being in the back seat of the car that Amy Pressler had crashed into someone's garage, because Amy had been drinking and hitting bongs. . .

It was just about sunset; the sky was gripped by long luminous red fingers of cloud. She thought of Cloud Shroud, and how her dad had refused to get the interfacer, and how frustrating that was. Her friends were already using it to project screens onto the walls anywhere and. . .

What was that? Was that one of the dream ghosts, sitting in the grass over there?

Everyone knew they had to do with dreams. Some people recognized them from their dreams. That big lady, Geri Benfew, said the loping thing chasing her was from a nightmare; and Rainy said that she'd seen those bullying senior girls from school in her closet, jeering at her . . . and her mom had seen them too.

That one sitting in the grass—it looked like the retired black fireman who lived across the street, sitting in his own lawn, pulling weeds in with both hands, and the weeds were growing up around him, and he pulled them, and they grew quickly back . . . and he yelled something incoherent. . .

He suddenly had mud on himself, all over himself; he hadn't had any mud before, but now it was instantly all over him. Beetles scurried in the mud, she saw, recoiling. The fireman irritably brushed them off.

Eva took a picture of the dream ghost with her cell phone, but she knew it would come out as a blur, like the others.

Eva looked around and felt, again, the subtle but troubling pressure on her head, and her eyes—like thumbs pressing gently into her eyesockets—and when she looked at the sky there was a faint greenish tint to it, and the tint sometimes squeezed itself into faces, and odd shapes . . . and they would slip away into nothing.

She looked back at the street and saw two people walking toward her, their feet not quite touching the sidewalk. One of them was a teenaged Asian-American girl wearing no blouse, her small breasts bare; the other one was an older man who was stamping his feet and saying something about her homework, her homework, her homework, and the girl was shaking her head and crying without tears . . . and they slipped off into nothing too.

"Eva!" her mom snapped from the front door. "Get in here!"

"It's not any safer inside," Eva said. But she went in.

"And stay off the Internet," her mom said. "It seems like it makes things . . . worse."

"It's not really working anyway," Eva said, going down the hall toward her bedroom. "Not hardly working."

You couldn't really see anything definite on the Internet right now. Texting was possible on a cell phone; everything else was a blur of faces, most of them weeping.

§

"You know, a cop fired a bunch of shots at one of these 'image accidents' of yours," Josh said. He was standing over Simmons, who was kneeling behind Josh's desk, which Josh had pulled out from the wall so they could get at the router. "Real shots, right here on this street. And someone got a bullet hole through the window from one of those shots. People could've been killed. There were two car accidents on this street since this started. Two that I know of."

Simmons looked up at him nervously, licking his lips. "Yeah, there's no proof that it was—"

"Oh, it was your fucking tech," Josh snapped. He was well aware that he was being physically intimidating, looming over Simmons. That was the idea. Pressure this start-up parvenu to spill the goods. "Otherwise why are you here?"

Simmons finished hooking up the device, then sat back, leaning against the wall. "You're downstream," he said grudgingly. He winced, as if realizing it was just a non sequitur that might provoke Josh further. "From the spillover from the psychic reservoir. Would you mind moving so I can get up?"

"What the hell do you mean, psychic reservoir," Josh told him. "I saw some stuff that. . ." He shook his head. He couldn't explain why the MutiePets had seemed so frightening to him. They were just images of animated characters. But they had scared him to the bone.

Simmons made a gesture of helplessness. "We don't really understand fully but . . . it appears that without enough of the interfacing technology in the vicinity, the Cloud Shroud picks up on something that's . . . well, it's always there. We all put out some kind of transmissions, electromagnetic stuff, from our brains, and it's really powerful when we dream. Usually it's just lost, breaks up in the atmosphere, but the Shroud gives it some kind of protection, holds it in place, lets it *pool* there. And then it kinda overflows, in a direction that follows the local electromagnetics. There's a definite stream to it. So in some places where Cloud Shroud is pulsing—yesterday's dreams, they build up . . . and flow in the path of least resistance I guess, and they end up . . . downstream. Which is here. You got to have the right topography, the right electromagnetic profile . . . and your neighborhood does."

"But—they're not like just recordings of dreams. These things react to what's around them."

"Yeah, they seem to have some connection to the original mind, and, you know, part of your brain is always doing something you don't know about."

A thought struck Josh. "You guys knew something about this dream effect in your tech before now—or you wouldn't have this figured out already!"

Simmons rubbed his lips with a finger. "Could I, uh, have a glass of water?"

"Just answer the question first, dammit! You guys *knew?*"

"It came up when we were developing the Shroud, yeah.

We could see dreams before they seeped away—see 'em with our monitoring gear. We thought maybe it was a side benefit we could use as a data source, to market stuff to people—"

Josh stared. "Dreams . . . to market things to people."

"See, the Internet is almost like people dreaming awake, and people use the Internet to follow your preferences, all that, so . . . Anyway, we see didn't this big overflow effect coming, that people would start to see dreams on the street. And we want to correct that. The interfacer will be a kind of lightning rod to drain away that buildup."

"Somebody could've been killed! Christ—why don't you just switch the whole system off?"

"Switch off the Cloud Shroud itself?" Simmons frowned, as if it had never occurred to him. "I don't have the authority. And anyway—"

"And even if you could do it you wouldn't, right? You have stock options, you're betting on this company, and if you have to switch it off the stock will sink out of sight and you guys don't care who gets hurt."

"There are—fiscal considerations, sure. But if you just switch it off, you might get some kind of weird repercussions. I wouldn't want to be responsible."

"You people are *already* responsible!"

Simmons grimaced. "Look—I'm just small potatoes. It's not up to me. Just . . . let me show you this." Simmons bent over the interfacer again and pressed a small button on the side. A green light flicked on and, almost immediately, Josh felt a little better, as if a heavy atmospheric pressure had suddenly been lifted.

"Can I have that water now?" Simmons asked, looking plaintively up at him. "And—I need to go get some more of these out to people. Otherwise I'm going to have to slug you in the nuts or something."

Josh shrugged and stepped out of his way.

Dreamday Eve

"It just stopped last night, after those guys went around the neighborhood." Eva was talking to Rainy on Skype. She looked out the window. "And . . . I heard they're going to turn off the whole system."

"Really? The whole thing? I was just using the Cloud Shroud. That would suck."

Eva looked at the time in the corner of her laptop screen. "It's switching off . . . God, in about a minute! Less than that!"

"What about those pics you took?"

"I'm going to upload everything to YouTube, but you can't see that much, everyone'll say they're fake. . ."

Eva saw a movement at the corners of her eyes. She looked— and saw the walls quivering, just faintly. Then the windows shivered. The floor sighed.

A wispy sound, and something like fingers snapping—and Eva's laptop crashed. It just snapped off. Rainy's face was gone, snapped into digital nowhere.

Then the lights went—her bedroom was instantly in darkness except for a little moonlight at the window.

Eva swore and got up, immediately barking her shin on the corner of the bookshelf. "Ow, *shit!*"

A car's tires squealed down the street, and then she stiffened at the clanging crash of an impact—the unmistakable counterpoint of breaking glass.

Mom was calling to her uncle. *"Where's Eva?"*

No, sorry, no way. Mom was going to make her hang out in the living room with candles. Something was happening; something was unraveling.

Eva had to know. She had to *see.*

She grabbed her cell phone and climbed out the bedroom window.

It was dark except for a few spearing flashlight beams, people calling to one another; some laughing nervously, others afraid.

She couldn't see the car that had crashed—unless that was it, that black hulk at the corner half-bent around a light pole. There was a flashlight headed there.

She turned on her cell phone and walked toward the nearer flashlight. She recognized the MutiePets guy, with one of those extra big Everbrights in his hand. What was his name? Josh something. His hair was mussed; he was unshaven, wearing a jacket over pajamas and slippers. He looked pretty grubby.

He flicked his light briefly over her—she covered her eyes with a hand and he dropped the beam to point at the asphalt. "Hey," he said, "you should get out of the street, people are crashing cars."

"You're on the street," she pointed out.

"Well, I'm not going to be. I just wanted to see if I could help. . . . Oh, here come the cops."

A couple of police cars, then a third, whipped around the corner, their headlights working, their lightbars strobing as they pulled up. The third one cruised up the street toward Eva and Josh.

Officer Olberta stopped his patrol car and got out. "You folks want to go in, we've got cars losing control out there—some people are seeing things again. Not safe out here."

"I thought that was supposed to end when they switched off the Cloud Shroud," Josh said.

"That's when it started again, way I heard it. Go on home, please, I—" He broke off, looking upward.

Vivid colors flared from the sky, in a line from horizon to

horizon—it was like the lurid hues of a stained-glass window. They all gaped up at it. Then the colors seemed to focus, converging at the far end of the street, where it dead-ended at the hills. It was as if the sky was putting colored spotlights on that end of the Perry Avenue.

"He told me something might happen," Josh muttered.

"What?" Olberta turned sharply to him. "Who?"

"The guy from Cloud Shroud. He said there could be consequences."

"Like what?"

"I don't know. Maybe it's like a dam bursting, the psychic pool all coming out at once—look!"

He broke off, pointing. A great multicolored wave was surging toward them from the dead end of the avenue.

Eva had been almost, *almost* expecting this. As if she was part of a crowd of people standing on a frozen lake surface, and the ice had been creaking, crackling, cracking, and they were all trying to find their way to shore, when suddenly—

At first the dream flood looked like slow-motion liquid; then it took on more definition and became a roiling conglomeration of people and things writhing toward them, random objects and syntheses of objects charging at them in a thick front of chaos: a thirty-foot-high refrigerator opening to show rows of yellow teeth. And coming beside it was a big truck sliding along on two huge boa constrictors instead of wheels; twined round them were trees with hysterically laughing mouths worked into their gnarls. Looming from the glowing morass, twenty-foot-tall shrieking PE teachers blew giant whistles louder than air-raid sirens, and men with guns for heads rode hospital beds like surfboards; clacking birds made of cell phones and giant squirrels chased small terrified dogs, and just behind them toy store action-figures fired entrails from hand-held cannons and ugly four-armed old men pursued sobbing children, all amidst cascades of credit card bills. Angry people shouted from onrushing television screens and shrieking infants flailed at eyeless cats digging into their skulls with wicked claws as just beneath them crinkling, humped-up lawns exploded with bursting pipes. It was all one entangled mass coming right at them in a murky wave of imagery . . . coming closer, rearing above . . . and falling over them with a crash.

Eva screamed as it struck them—as it swirled around them, transparent but inescapable, touching them all with intrusive fingers of static electricity. . .

A lightning-flash of transition—and Eva was suddenly standing in her school's hallway, looking at her locker. It burst open and jeering teen faces spat at her, covering her with thick saliva. She tried to run—and couldn't move. Until someone grabbed her arm. It was Josh. . .

She turned, and the school hallway vanished. She was back on the street, in the flood of nightmare and dreams, and Josh was holding her arm.

"Where's your house?" he shouted, barely audible over the ambient noise, the shouts and laughter and endless murmurs of the dream flood.

Gasping for breath, Eva looked around for her house and saw only the torrent of tumultuous shapes. Mixed randomly amongst the trappings of nightmare were dancing people, children driving cars and passenger jets and swimming with friendly golden retrievers—there were good dreams too. . .

And then she felt Josh let go of her arm—she saw enormous purple MutiePets capering around him. But Josh was ignoring them, pointing at Officer Olberta, who was aiming his gun at a middle-aged black man in a T-shirt and sweat pants. That was Mira's dad, Mr. Kregg.

And then she saw that Mr. Kregg was encased in another image, a figure that flickered and solidified: another, much larger man with a double-sized AK-47 in his hand. He had an oversized red hoodie on. His howling face, twice too big for his body, was tattooed with gang signs. He was snarling and began firing his translucent assault rifle—the bullets streaking visibly around Officer Olberta.

The gangster apparition was completely enclosing Mr Kregg now . . . a fantasy gangster, something from a nightmare—she guessed it was Olberta's nightmare.

Backing up in twitching fear, Olberta shouted a warning— and then he fired, again and again, at the gangster apparition until it dissolved. And Mr. Kregg, a middle-aged African-American electrician, collapsed on the street. Blood gushed from his wounds, thick and red as cherry syrup.

"Oh, no," Josh muttered.

The dream flood was quieting, diminishing . . . the MutiePets had gone. . .

Gun extended, Officer Olberta was walking stiffly toward Mr. Kregg, who writhed slowly on the ground. As if he was considering firing again.

Eva ran to Olberta, tried to pull on his arm. He turned to her, reacting, and the gun went off.

She felt the wind as the bullet slashed by her head, so close it clipped a hank of her hair away.

"Missed me, you bastard!" she yelled, out of sheer hysteria.

She burst into tears.

Josh dragged her back from Olberta. "Officer!" he said sharply. "Hold your fire, for God's sake!"

Eva heard herself say, "Where's my house? Where's my mom?"

Josh patted her shoulder. "I think it's going away, most of it."

Sobbing, Eva felt a change around them, a palpable reduction of pressure.

The clamor of the cascading shapes muted; the dream ghosts were almost gone, sinking away, receding floodwaters into drains. The storm of dreams was ending.

A few dream images remained like flotsam, the space of ten heartbeats. Josh stared at one of them—and walked toward it. It was the dream ghost of an elderly old gent, kneeling in some other place and hugging a lifeless, bloody naked young man to him—and weeping inconsolably. On the right forearm of the young man was a Marine Corps tattoo.

"Dad . . . Dad. . ." Josh croaked.

Then the dream flotsam faded. And the streetlights came back on.

Eva turned dazedly, looking toward the place where Mr. Kregg had fallen, hoping it had all been a dream phantasm.

But he was still there, bleeding to death. And beside him knelt Olberta, crying, trying to staunch the wounds he'd made himself.

Sirens. Warbling sirens.

Friday

"Yeah, I got her into the house, and she was fine, Dad," Josh said. He was sitting in a cushioned chair, close by his father's hospital bed. "Just this neighbor girl, but I felt like I had to—to make sure she was okay. Her mom was panicking trying to find her. Kregg, though. . ." He let out a long sigh. "Mr. Kregg is in the hospital, and he's in critical condition. Probably he'll survive. Anyway—I know you guys had your episodes here from all this. . ." And he knew his dad came out of it sicker than before. Dying quickly now. "So—that's what happened, more or less."

Josh wasn't sure if his father was listening to him. He just felt he should be talking. His dad was lying there, eyes closed, in a hospital gown, with oxygen tubes in his nose, an IV plugged into an arm, emaciated, chest rising and falling with excruciating slowness. But after a moment the papery eyelids fluttered open, and he looked at Josh.

"Roland," Dad said hoarsely.

Josh had to swallow hard to keep the emotion in check. "Yeah. Roland. We all should have done more for him. The bomb in Kabul, all those guys blown to hell. I couldn't have dealt with that as long as he did. PTSD, sounds like—a disease you can give someone a shot for, or something but . . . not really. He wouldn't do the meds. He . . . felt like he should've gone with 'em, I guess."

His dad nodded, just faintly.

Josh took his father's cold, thin hand. "I should have been here, too. Should have come to see you every day. Maybe I had to see it like you saw it." He closed his eyes and thought, *Don't make excuses.* "There's no excuse. I should have been here before."

His dad squeezed his hand and closed his eyes.

At least he knows I'm here now, Josh thought. *That's something.*

There was a flicker at the edge of his vision. He glanced over—and thought he saw Roland there, his brother, looking young and strong in his uniform; unbloodied, his face solemn, holding his father's other hand.

Maybe it was just dream residue. Flotsam from the flood.

And after a moment Roland was gone. . .

But Josh stayed, right there, sitting quietly in the chair next to his father.

DEATH-DREAMING

NANCY KILPATRICK

I dreamed you were dead. That's not so unusual. People dream others are dead all the time, people they love, people they hate, people they don't even know or care about. And they dream that they themselves are dead, mostly when they freefall— that's a classic. Death is the end of life, so it's human nature to think about this, both waking and sleeping. And to worry. That's all normal; at least Dr. Howard believes it is.

I dream often that you're dead—well, *dying*, right at the brink of death, ready to tip. Once a week I dream this; if I'm being really truthful, sometimes more than that.

The first time I dreamt you were dying was just after Julie passed. Dr. Howard said her death triggered it and assured me that's not uncommon. I can still see you hanging by your fingertips from the marquee over the entrance to the Trump Tower Hotel in NYC where we stayed the week of the funeral. You had your head turned and tilted, gazing down at the sidewalk, at me. It wasn't a long drop to the ground—maybe twenty-five feet—and I wondered if such a fall would end in death or just a few broken bones. Maybe lifelong paralysis? For those reasons, I didn't take the remarkably ridiculous situation seriously at all, that first dream. As always in these dreams, as I would come to experience them, I stared at you as you pleaded with your eyes, begging me for help. For me, it was/is a dilemma. I never know if you're asking me to rescue you from the jaws of death or to shove you into the Grim Reaper's maw and get it over with. You've always had a sense of humor, and I laughed.

That first dream, I turned and walked away. And then jolted awake, as if something in my head had exploded. I sat up in the darkness, trembling, heart pounding, head throbbing, the dreamworld still vivid and immediate, my guilt palatable—I'd let you down. Again.

Since then, whenever I've dreamed of your death, I have not turned away early. I've stayed to watch until the end, as if it's a movie and I just have to see how it will conclude. But I always wake just before the finale.

I've realized that it's better to watch, wait, see if one of us will come to a decision. I wait. You wait. That long pause is always fraught with tension, and I know if either of us moves, something will happen. One of us will snap. Maybe both of us.

Over the last year I've dreamt so many different scenarios of your demise and in truth, despite the horror, it's kind of fun and invigorating every night as I go to sleep anticipating, wondering if I'll dream about your death again, wondering what it will be like *this* time. The big picture is always the same, but the details are unique.

Once, you held a gun to your temple. It was a big handgun, the kind cowboys regularly aimed at one another in the westerns we watched on TV as kids. A Colt .45, if I remember my *Trivial Pursuit* answers correctly from when we used to play the game with Julie. A romantic gun, because of actors like John Wayne. In the dream, the TV was on in the background and the old movie *Rio Grande* played, the sound muted. The radio in the next room blared out current insta-news, something about the Middle East. Your features were etched with grief and fear, maybe for the refugees of the most recent conflict, but probably not. You probably didn't care about the refugees, or about cowboys, or even about the grief I saw reflected in your eyes. Your hand shook, but your finger was steady and clearly poised over the trigger. All the while you stared at me, that pleading look. Should I stop you or should I wait to catch the final shootout? I waited to see what would happen. And then I woke up.

Another time it was a knife, a large one, the kind they use in abattoirs, the religious ones that still manually slit the throats of food animals. A knife also good for boning, I imagine, very sharp. In that dream you wore a chef's apron and the white hat, and I thought you looked absurd with copper-bottomed pots and pans hanging over your head and the array of culinary tools pegged to a board behind you. Absurd because you *never* liked to cook. Which was why it came as no surprise that you dropped out of the one cooking class you enrolled in.

You held the blade of the big knife to your throat, as if you were a bovine about to be slaughtered, then rendered and eventually appearing on a dinner table. You eyes seemed large in that dream, liquid-filled, conscious cow eyes, so unlike your hazel eyes, but still familiar. Eyes imploring. For what? I waited, but then I woke up without ever knowing what you wanted, what I could do, what you would do.

There are many more mundane dreams, all familiar means of dispatch: strangulation, hanging, drowning, gassing, even disease in the final stages. Nothing spectacular or unusual.

Some of the weapons were a bit more interesting than others, even amusing: the $200 goosedown 500-thread Egyptian cotton pillow you bought on a whim two years ago and which Julie joked might suffocate you while you slept—positioned over your nose and mouth in the dream; the taser you pressed against your cheek as lightning zapped through the air Tesla-style, waiting for a bolt to hit the gun and amp up the voltage; the axe that you used to chop wood against a tree stump during that god-awful ice-storm winter when you lived in a century-old farmhouse you rented, ostensibly to paint, yet produced only one painting—of the chipmunk you claimed you 'accidentally' axe-murdered. Oh, and there were those silly nunchucks and throwing stars you played with in your last year of high school, the matching set in black, red and silver, etched and highly ornate, the stars extremely sharp. You never did get the hang of these Oriental weapons and many times bashed your skull with one of the wooden handles, or sliced into your fingertips with the razor-stars.

All these and many other weapons made it into my dreams of your death. Bits and pieces of a life, scattered like ripped-up photographs littering the ground, fragments of memories with no rhyme or reason, no connections made except to someone who knows you well, and that someone is, unfortunately, me.

For that reason alone, I think my favorite dream involved poison. Nothing icky like an insect or snake or arachnid bite— although there *was* the Black Widow dream, but I digress. No, this poison was one of the no-mess powders or liquids that dissolve in food or drink and leave little or no trace. Poisons have always been a joint interest of ours, and we've explored the idea of ingesting a substance so lethal that life comes to an end before the toxin makes it to the stomach. Quick. Or slow. Agony or ecstasy. In that dream, next to you on the round mahogany table sat Julie's Brown Betty teapot you inherited, and a china cup and saucer (the set with the silver around the rim), a wedge of lemon on the saucer, the way you prefer tea. Oh so Agatha Christie, Julie used to laugh! Also on the small table was a tiny, opaque bottle, as brown as the teapot, its yellowing label hand-scripted with the word 'Poison' carefully lettered above the stereotypical skull-and-crossbones. The bottle struck me as from the late nineteenth century and looked very much like the one we found in Portobello Market on a trip to London. Its contents might have been laudanum, but that couldn't be right because you wouldn't die from a teaspoon's worth of laudanum in your tea, which is all that small bottle would have held. Besides, laudanum is only one percent morphine, after all, and you didn't look drugged, at least not drugged in the euphoric sense. I suspect that little bottle crying out 'Poison' contained something more lethal. Arsenic? Too 'old lace,' and not quick enough. Potassium cyanide? I did not smell bitter almond—the dreams have always been multi-sensory. Besides, you would already be dead. An overdose of digitalis, then? But where is the foxglove? And clearly you are not suffering a heart attack. Perhaps ricin from the flowering *Ricinus Communis* depicted in the painting on the wall behind you that you created one year ago in Julie's garden. The seeds within the gorgeous red, spiky-fuzzy balls of the castor oil plant produce ricin; and in this death scene your teacup is empty but for leaves, the tea already drunk, and now you will be gone in no time, or the usual amount of time. In this dream, I tried hard to decipher what you're asking for, and if I'm willing to give it, but I could not.

I don't mind the variations on the types of death; at least I'm not bored in my sleep. It's really that baffling look in your eyes, always the same, always open to interpretation. Are you begging to be left alone to die in misery or in peace, or are you asking for the antidote, or rejecting it? You've always been like this, caught between things, between life and death, and consequently waiting for someone else either to rescue you or to harm you. But then, so have I. Decisions are difficult and exhausting. Choices confusing. We were not taught how or encouraged to make decisions, and passivity reigned in our upbringing. You know that truth as well as I do.

So what does my therapist say about all this? *Dr. Howie*, as he prefers to be called, takes a Freudian interpretation one week, a Jungian slant the next, and throws in a bit of biofeedback to go with the anti-depressants he prescribes. Here's what he has said:

- You are worried about your own impending demise. (*obvious*)
- You are searching for spiritual answers, a way to make sense of life and death. (*sure*)
- You have unresolved issues around Julie's death. (*no kidding!*)
- You seem (*insert emotion: angry; sad; jealous; happy; in mourning*)

The dreams have become more frequent. Last night's drama was the third this week, and it was a doozie. You were in the far North, the Yukon perhaps, a place we always wanted to visit, the temperature sub-zero, both Celsius and Fahrenheit. The scene was a bit Jack London, a white wasteland, bitter, cutting wind, ice crystals layered on eyebrows and eyelashes, your down-filled coat warm but not warm enough. I expected to see sled dogs murdered for their fur, hands thrust into their entrails for warmth. Or wolves circling, sniffing out prey. But it was only you, propped against the lone, barren tree, slowly becoming buried beneath the relentlessly falling snow as the wind howled like a banshee. And yet I could only think: the air is so crisp and glacially clean!

You wore fleece mitts and in one of them clutched the largest icicle I'd ever seen, the length and thickness of a long, fat dagger or short sword. Death by icicle! I laughed and then saw that look in your eyes and knew I had to take this seriously. You were so bundled up, though, I couldn't imagine how you could dispatch yourself until, suddenly, I realized you wore no goggles. It was a horrifying thought, but I also wondered if the icicle would melt before a decision had to be made, one way or the other. Probably not in this extreme temperature. No, the cold was like the frigidity of our lives, we, the perpetually frozen Charlottes, in stasis, unable to move. And so I waited. You waited. And then I awoke.

Today, Dr. Howie said:

- A perfect murder weapon, ice. (*the world ends in fire or. . .*)
- Rather far-fetched. (*you think?*)
- The metaphor, the symbolism, that what's important. (*the symbolic cold reflects the real-life cold. did I get that right, doc?*)

This afternoon I had a sudden recall of that childhood summer we spent by the seashore in Wildwood. It was a peculiar apartment the adults rented, three bedrooms in a row, railroad boarding-house style, a kitchen and bathroom at the back.

The colors made the apartment a curiosity. The first room was completely pink, pink as a sunburn, everything, the carpet, the walls, the bedspread and lampshades and chair seats . . . The second blue as the cool Atlantic Ocean, the same, everything in the room blue . . . The third bedroom was yellow, blindingly so, resembling the landscape as the glaring sun beat down on us. . .

Our summer abode was situated on the narrow street across from the beach, and we were drawn to the water daily, with Julie, from morning until the sun began to set. The adults were happy to be left alone, a routine check periodically, a command to use sunscreen, not to go too far into the ocean because there might be an undertow that would drag us out to sea. I always wondered what it would be like to be dragged out to sea. Would it be painful to die engulfed and then drawn down into the murky depths with the jellyfish and flounders, caught by seaweed, a victim of the powerful salt water? What would be the last experience?

That day, I stepped out of my childhood comfort zone and verbalized my thoughts, only to be met with silence. And what was there to say? Then? Now?

In my mind I can still hear the waves crashing as they broke. I loved watching the white crests form, from the right, from the left, meeting in the middle, the momentum forcing the fracture, salty water rushing to our ankles, up our legs, sucking us into the sand as it retreated.

The sand back then was clean all the time, a beige non-color, crystalline and bright beneath the brilliant sun that cooked Julie's skin pink and then red. Her pale, fragile flesh did not tan, just burned, then blistered painfully, the nights permeated by the scent of Noxzema, and her sobs. But she would not leave the sunshine. She refused to leave us.

We of hardier stock, skin like a rhino's, prone to darkening, the sun our friend to the extent it was Julie's enemy. We did not even think about sending her to safety.

"Curious," Dr. Howie ventured when I conveyed this memory. (*perhaps*)

"I believe Julie died of melanoma. Damage from childhood exposure?" (i *get it!*)

"How do you feel about that?" (*helpless, of course. always helpless*)

"I think we are getting somewhere with the connections." (*do you? is it such a mystery?*)

I left his office in defeat and called after hours when I knew he would be gone to leave a message cancelling my follow-up appointment. For once I crawled into bed battling neither dread nor anticipation. My mind felt unclouded, my heart unburdened. What would be would be, and, as always, events were beyond my feeble control.

§

I close my eyes to sleep. I dream. But you are not in the dream, just a plethora of the various scenes, weapons a slide-show. Heat and chill on my flesh, scent of sweet fragrances and foul odors, sounds of waves and blaring horns and desperate, painful cries. I am trapped in a revolving sensory mosaic with snatches from all the dreams of your death, and suddenly I am afraid.

Frantically I search for you, fearful I will not find you, my stress escalating, the pressure in my chest and my head expanding at a dangerous rate. . .

And then, there you are!

The past-dream fragments give way to a locale that is not exotic, and it is not a place I recognize from where we have been or have wanted to go. It is visually sharp, like the setting in a movie, a picture from a travel brochure. You stand in a field of kelly-green grass on a midsummer's day, the cap of azure above strewn with pristine clouds, gilded sunlight glinting off your hair and forming a body aura, your hazel eyes intense, as always.

There are no weapons visible. Nothing and no one stands beyond you or between us. You stare at me, the familiar intimacy in your eyes pulling me toward you, pushing me away; the unspoken plea.

And in a split second it comes to me, psychically knocking me over as would physically a powerful wave, a ferocious wind, the blast of a handgun fired point-blank. Finally, *finally,* I get it!

We have grown so close, you and I, co-joined. Close enough to become as one. I believed that one night I would understand what you wanted. What you needed. What you have always needed. And now I do.

In this moment of luminosity you realize that I am certain now, and the look in your eyes alters. You can see with clarity what I've been seeing all along.

We wait. We watch. We tremble.

You are morphing into the vivid colors, the pungent scents, the reverberating sounds from dreams. To my utter joy and stark horror, impacted by eternal grief, before me is what I have always feared: evolution in a world of death-dreaming leads to evanescence. I watch you disappear. . .

CAST LOTS

RICHARD GAVIN

"I'm the clerk, I'm the scribe, at the hearings of what
cause I know not."

—SAMUEL BECKETT, "Texts for Nothing"

*She finds herself inside a tilting cottage. Gales test the twisted nails
that hold the planks of this most humble abode consecutive, firm. The
wooden walls creak, as does the bowing cot she rests upon.*

*The winds are cold and smell of yeast. They insinuate themselves
between the slats, snuffing out the low-burning kerosene lamp. There
is no moon.*

*Shifting in a strange bed, with its prodding springs and coarse
blankets, the woman is suddenly alerted to . . . what, a premonition,
a memory?*

*Knowledge. Knowledge that a great peril is encroaching; growing
keener, vaster, nearer.*

*The certainty of this danger rouses in the woman an all-consuming
terror, one that reaches a critical mass once she hears the bleating*

sound that begins to weave through the rumbling wind. These cries come rhythmically, penetrating the cottage as surely as a spear.

Flinging back the bedclothes, she charges for the door. She is thoughtless in her panic, but is intent only on fleeing, on racing down the first causeway she encounters.

She freezes mere paces outside her door.

There are no roads to tread, for this tiny cottage stands upon a tiny island. The mainland is clearly visible, its dunes baptized in a strange kind of manufactured light, but a raging channel stretches between it and the woman. She studies the choppy surface with its whitish peaks. It is like a horde of ghosts floating past her, endlessly.

Out here the bleating sound is that much louder, that much closer. Peering out across the roiling divide, she pinpoints the source of the noise. Standing on the far shore, planted in the sand like an incongruous tree, is a payphone. Fixed to a stout wooden pillar, the phone is of a style the woman has not seen in years. The metallic clang of its bell is painful, panicked, like the mechanized scream of a maimed creature. . .

§

Joyce Felton lifted her eyelids slowly, then immediately closed them again. Though the dream had dissolved, its significance lingered, spiting the dawn-light that had only just begun to brighten the blinds. Tears slipped from the corners of her eyes. Breathing had become a chore. Joyce knew she had to muster sufficient courage in order to face whatever changes might have been wrought during her sleep. She also knew that there were questions, difficult and delicate questions that needed to be asked.

She sat up quickly and forced herself to see.

The bedroom was as she had left it, complete with the half-drained water glass and an overfilled ashtray on the nightstand. Though these sights might have on any other morning reassured her, Joyce could not ignore the fact that she had endured a disturbing dream, a nightmare where every detail seemed to sweat menace, to shine with fell purpose.

She rose and began to walk, to scrutinize, to hunt for signs of transition.

In the hallway, pale carpet met smartly with moulding. Walls ran upright. All the light fixtures were functioning.

The number of steps on the main stairway had neither swelled nor diminished. The mums in the vase on the foyer stand had not withered.

A cursory check of the kitchen proved that the milk remained white in its container and that the water still drained clockwise in the sink.

Joyce had almost managed to convince herself that her lot in life had survived this most recent experience in the nightmare's realm, but her confidence crumbled when she chanced a glimpse through the laundry-room window that looked out into the back yard.

The lawn was strewn with the bodies of birds—crows, thrushes, sparrows.

At first Joyce was struck by the awful scenario of the creatures suffering some epidemic that stole their lives. But this theory was usurped by the worse reality once Joyce noticed that many of the birds were stirring and twitching. Their feathers were fluffed, bills were tucked under wings, tiny eyes were closed.

The knowledge, such as she had undergone in her nightmare, was flushing through her now, in the heatless light of the waking state.

This was how the change always came: creeping like a

Creator's hand of death passing over those it had cursed. In Joyce's case, for reasons she could never ascertain, the change had always staked its claim through slumber. It rode in like a horseman on a mare as dark as its namesake, spectral and marauding and unyielding in its wild run.

Sleep's reach, Joyce had learned, was vast. Though this was the first time she had ever seen evidence of it pulling birds from the sky and stunning them into an almost unshakable rest, she was not shocked by this development. Her past experiences had left her utterly consumed by the mounting unreality of oneiric shifting. It grew around her like a rising tide, dragging in any sentient creature that happened to be anywhere near Joyce's prostrate form. Anything lost in this undertow either floundered or, if they survived, awoke inside a wholly different world.

Joyce hoped, *prayed*, that these winged creatures were too slight and frail to impact her to any degree.

But she then discovered that the birds were not the only creatures to have been sucked into this dream-mire: a man must have been passing by her yard at some point in the night. Had he been trying to break in, Joyce wondered? No matter, for his punishment was to become a mere pawn in an enterprise that was beyond the ken of anyone.

The man was floating face up in her swimming pool.

All strength drained from Joyce's legs. She slipped down between the laundry tub and the dryer, which, she noticed, needlessly and inopportunely, had a thin scab of rust at its base. It was not fear that buckled her, but an exhaustion that is specific to this faint undying torture. It was happening so soon after last time. Had it ever truly ceased? Even its respites seemed somehow to be punishments.

Pulling herself erect, Joyce childishly hoped that the man

on the water had evaporated as dreams do in daylight.

He was no longer in the pool. He was now at the window.

His features became distorted as he pressed his face to the pane. His movements left a greasy trail on the glass. Joyce looked at his face and was offended by its slackness, by the way the eyes jittered beneath their drooping lids. Through the glass she could hear the wet flutter of the man's snore.

"Go away!" she pleaded, her voice waffling unpleasantly between a whisper and a shrill whine. She checked over her shoulder, fearing that Morgan had been woken, that she would see the shape that represented all Joyce had struggled to prevent herself from ever seeing. The house was still, which fed Joyce a sliver of relief. "Go!" She enforced her plea by waving her hands in a shooing motion.

Drool spilt from the man's hanging jaw, indicating just how deep in the nightmare he was.

Confident that the rear door was out of the somnambulist's reach, Joyce unlocked it and stepped out onto the patio. "Get the hell out of here—now!" she cried. The man's clothes were ragged. He pawed at the air as one love-starved, one desperate for an embrace. He was, Joyce knew, looking to pull her back into the living Dream.

The man shambled listlessly to his left, his right. His condition allowed Joyce to guide him on his way with relative ease. She steered him toward the open wooden gate. Pool water dripped from his clothing. Joyce hated the fact that she had to touch him.

Once he began shuffling down the driveway Joyce slammed and bolted the gate.

Her re-entry into the house had all the drama of a teen sneaking in after curfew. She broke from tiptoeing long enough to snap the deadbolt on the back door, then she moved to the living room and peered through the sheers of the large bay window.

The man was staggering like a drunkard down the centre of the street.

He'd managed to shuffle out of Joyce's view before the terrible squeal of tires, followed immediately by a thud.

Joyce backed away from the window, chilled by the sound of the panicked voices and cries from down the way.

"What's going on?"

The voice came from behind her. Joyce spun to see Morgan, who was rubbing her eyes with the heel of her left hand. Her tangled hair suggested a restless night.

"An accident," were the only two words Joyce managed to pronounce before she began to cry.

Morgan moved to her, wrapped her skinny arm around her, and asked repeatedly what was wrong. When Joyce was unable or unwilling to respond, all at once Morgan knew.

Her arm slipped off Joyce's quaking frame. "No," she said. Joyce looked at her, her eyes desperately assessing what, if anything, Morgan might have pieced together.

The girl's expression and demeanour were frustratingly blank. They prevented Joyce from any insights at all. Morgan made her way to the breakfast nook with melodramatic slowness. The padded bench huffed when she slumped down upon it. Joyce watched the girl as she sat like one mesmerized, lazily tracing the tabletop's grain pattern with one finger.

Resignedly, Joyce joined her, studying her from across the narrow nook.

"I want to ask you a question and I want you to answer me honestly. Morgan? Look at me, please. I need to ask you something."

Morgan kept her head against the crook of her elbow but did respond with "What?"

"Have you been doing something you're not supposed to?"

Morgan lifted her head at last. "What do you mean?"

"I mean have you been . . . curious."

Morgan's eyes slowly closed. Her chin rumpled and began to quiver. "I'm sorry," she squeaked.

"I told you never to go looking for her, didn't I? How many times did I say that if you start looking for a castaway, all you end up doing is calling attention to yourself, making the nightmare notice you?"

A thick wedge of tension was driven between them.

Joyce ultimately rose to collect the rudiments of breakfast. She peered out at the back yard. The birds had flown.

Morgan was unable even to consider eating the bowl of cold cereal that had been placed before her. Joyce smoked cigarettes over her own, allowing ash to darken the milk like polluted snow.

The telephone's ring jolted the pair of them—Morgan from the unexpectedness, Joyce from its kinship to her most recent nightmare. They let the answering machine take the call:

"Hello, Joyce? This is Alex from the store. I'm just checking to see if you were aware that you were scheduled to be our opening cashier this morning. Your shift started forty minutes ago, so if you could give me a call back as soon as you get this, that would be great."

The sing-song tone of her supervisor's voice both masked anger and betrayed an utter lack of concern for what might have prevented Joyce from fulfilling her retail duties.

Joyce rose and yanked the phone cord from its jack. She returned to the nook and lit a fresh cigarette.

"Can I have one of those?" Morgan asked. There was no longer any need of pretence.

Joyce flicked the pack across the table. Morgan felt herself being studied, as though she might be graded on her smoking skills. She cleared her throat and then confessed.

"I wanted to know . . . know who she was."

"I told you, you can't," Joyce barked. "Do I have to engrave it on your forehead? You can't and you won't."

"But you knew her."

Joyce sighed. "Yes," she said, "but I knew her *before* she fell into it."

"Well I wasn't around *before*."

"I know you weren't."

Smoking was evidently new to Morgan. Joyce noted the way her face was beginning to blanch.

"Let me ask you," Morgan began, "did you know *your* mother?"

Joyce cleared her throat. "Yes."

"Have lots of good memories of her, do you?" Morgan's voice was taking on a keen edge.

"Some."

"Oh? You weren't taken from her when you were still in diapers? How nice for you."

Joyce folded her hands before her. In her mind she counted the seconds until an appropriate pause was reached. "Did you know I once had two sons?"

Morgan did not know how to respond.

Joyce nodded. She was unaware of the fact that she'd begun to cry until she felt a tear splash upon her still-folded hands. "Isaac and Caleb. Well, to be accurate, Caleb hadn't been born yet, but I was in my ninth month. My husband Barry was a firefighter. Or maybe he still is. How can I know? Anyway, we'd just purchased our first house—a little place, a lot smaller than this house. Barry was working a lot, trying to pick up extra hours to pay for all the things we needed. I was trying to get as much unpacking done as I could, but Isaac was only three at that time, so trying to keep up with him and set up house while I was as big as a house myself, well, it tired me out. Plus, about that time Isaac had been suffering from . . . bad dreams. That must be how it got me. . ."

Joyce's voice dissipated like wind-scattered smoke. Several moments were spent on a vacant stare that made Morgan both heartsick and frightened.

"I remember," Joyce resumed, "I'd just put Isaac down for his afternoon nap. I was going to finish unboxing our kitchenware, but I was just so exhausted. I curled up right beside Isaac."

Morgan interjected with a rush of apologies. "You don't have to relive this," she told her.

Joyce's recollection was immune to protest. "We had an antique clock," she continued, "an heirloom. It was inside one of the open boxes in our bedroom. It was a pretty thing, with Roman numerals on the face and little brass chimes that rang on the hour. Anyway, the house was so quiet that day that all I could hear was the refrigerator buzzing in the kitchen and the ticking of that pretty little clock. As a matter of fact, I pulled that ticking sound into my dream.

"I must have dozed off fairly quickly, and the nightmare came right away. I was walking up a steep country road. The incline was so extreme that I could barely climb it. At one point my legs actually gave out. I fell down, but I still couldn't stop climbing. By then I'd begun to crawl, pulling myself along the asphalt, looking up to the top of the road.

"The sun was very white, blindingly bright. It hurt to look upward, but I could just make out that there was a silhouette at the top of the hill. It took what felt like forever before I was able to make out what it actually was—a stuffed chair, a wingback, very old-looking. The chair was turned away from me. When I got a bit closer I could see that something was sitting in that chair. There were spiky tufts of hair sticking up above the back. The upholstery was blue with a very ugly pattern of gold running through it, a zigzag thing that made me nauseous if I looked at it for too long.

"Standing next to the chair—and I'd forgotten all about it until just this very moment—was a little wooden table. There was a glass on the table, like a champagne flute. It was filled with this shining liquid. It was the colour of amethyst.

"I almost made it to the top when I suddenly froze. I can't remember exactly what it was sitting in that chair, waiting for me, but I was overcome with . . . awfulness. I tried to turn around, to get back to the bottom of the hill, but there was a magnetic pull that was forcing me closer to that chair.

"I tried to resist. I pressed my fingernails into the asphalt until they broke off. I even tried to bite down into the ground. Somehow it worked. I'd managed to stop moving forward.

"So the thing in the chair came to me.

"The chair came grinding down the sloping road. The sound was hideous, the shrill scraping sound of wood being dragged along the ground. I remember seeing the chair legs splintering and breaking apart. The closer it got, the worse it became. The upholstery was not patterned but stained with all these foul blotches. And I bet if you try really hard you can guess what the upholstery was made from.

"And then the chair was *right there.*" Joyce held her hand before her face to emphasize her point. "The magnetic pull came over me again. I felt my hand going toward the back of the chair. I knocked upon it. Three times I knocked. It was as firm and as cold as steel. My knocking was deafening.

"The thing in the chair stood up. That's how the little nightmare ended."

Morgan felt she should speak. She did not speak.

"When I woke up," Joyce added, "my babies were gone and I was in a little townhouse with a different lot in life. The stranger who insisted he was my husband got tired of my hysteria pretty quickly. It took him less than a day before he had me hospitalized. I was stuck inside there for weeks. But I got out of that situation too, eventually. Anyway, something good came out of it. I kept the name Joyce. I used to love James Joyce's story 'The Dead.' I really think I did . . . such a long time ago."

Morgan had reflexively positioned her hands as if wearing crisp white gloves. She envisioned a platter of fluted china that held cakes with all manner of luscious frosting. The reverie caused her mouth to hitch in a half-grin highly inappropriate in such a moment, but then again perhaps it was her oasis, a reflex of survival.

"I sent an email," Morgan confessed. "I found an online service that said they could track down lost relatives. It was that day we argued last week, remember? I was angry at you, and hurt, so I emailed them to ask for information. But I'll write them back and cancel, okay? I'll tell them to forget it."

"Don't bother."

"No really." She reached for her phone, which sat charging in the kitchen wall socket. "I'll do it right now."

"It won't change a thing."

Morgan withdrew her hand. "So what happens now?"

Joyce said nothing for a time, then: "What happens is that everything shifts."

"How can you be sure?" Morgan retorted. "Nothing's happened to us yet."

"Oh, it has. We just haven't seen it yet. Everything's always changing, in flux." Joyce crossed her arms across her chest, a posture that made Morgan uncomfortable, so great was its kinship to the dead in their eternal rest. "I don't know if there is a message in this whole thing, if there is any kind of lesson to be learned, but if there is, perhaps that's it: that nothing is ever stable, that we're never in control, no matter how much we believe ourselves to be."

Morgan was visibly deflated. Thinly, she asked, "Do you know how all this started?"

"No idea. But I think this . . . nightmare, vision, whatever you want to call it, has been around forever. I don't think we create the dream, we just experience it, get claimed by it. It takes from us, but weirdly enough, it gives to us too. I've had other children, other possessions. But I don't choose them. I just kind of . . . observe them."

"Like in a dream?" Morgan asked.

"Like in a dream. One thing I have figured out is that you actually had to have met someone in waking life before they can be pulled into this. Sort of like the way you dream about ordinary people, even the dead, when you dream. Your mother used to do my hair, as you know. That's how she got dragged in." Joyce's subsequent shudder was so violent that Morgan asked her what she was thinking. "That man, the one in the yard . . . I think I saw him panhandling in the alley behind the house last week. I even gave him a five. . ."

Despite her confusion, Morgan felt that further questions were futile.

The room donned silence like a garment, flaunted it for too long.

The doorbell's chiming broke the spell. Morgan flinched, gasped, and then rose to answer it.

Joyce reached across the table and gripped Morgan's arm. "Don't. It will be the police looking for witnesses to the accident. We're not getting involved."

There was a knock, then a stillness that lasted well into the afternoon. By then Morgan had migrated to the living room, where she stared at the television with its volume deliberately high. Joyce remained in the kitchen, smoking until the package was depleted.

Out of frustration and defiance Morgan rose from the sofa with a huff. She gathered her rolled mat and her petite gym bag.

"Where are you going?" Joyce asked her.

"Yoga. It's Wednesday."

"You can't."

Morgan shrugged. "I say I can."

The jangling of keys, the rattling of Joyce's nerves; she bolted toward the front door. "Wait! Don't go. It's not safe, you understand? It's not safe."

Morgan pretended that the woman's blubbering, her clinging grip, didn't faze her. "I'm not going to sit here and rot like some prisoner."

"Well then, I'm coming with you."

§

Joyce stationed herself upon a bench against the yoga studio's far wall. She was like a stoic bird watching emotionlessly as the women reached and twisted their bodies in mimicry of beasts, or, at a turn, as the holy that prostrate themselves on *sajadas* facing Mecca.

The studio was warm and the score that leaked from hidden speakers was a lullaby of chimes and babbling water. Joyce felt buoyant, cleansed. Her guard seduced, she allowed her heavy eyelids to draw shut.

But the nightmare didn't claim her until after she was

awoken. The yoga instructor who'd nudged her offered a warm smile and said something that Joyce didn't hear. The studio was empty.

Joyce rose and began asking about Morgan. The instructor's nonplussed expression spoke volumes. Numb, Joyce slipped out of the studio.

Dusk was thickening around her. The streets were a pale haze, the people mere moving props. Joyce found her way home by instinct. She fully expected her key to no longer fit the lock, but in the end she did not have to test it, for upon her arrival home she found the front door slightly ajar. She pushed it open and stood in the vacant frame.

To the uninitiated the disruption to the house would have been viewed as a robbery, but Joyce was keenly aware of the incongruous details: the thick coating of dust that suggested years of neglect despite the fact that she had left the house only hours earlier; the indentations in the carpet where a furnishing had once sat; the ceiling fan that dangled from its wires, as if something immense had stormed through the confining room.

Joyce ducked under the destroyed fixture. Chunks of plaster crunched beneath her soles. She followed the tracks in the carpet, which led her to the stairway.

The chair that was missing from the living room had been dragged to the top of the stairs. It was facing the top of the landing, its back to the steps.

Joyce felt herself moving backward. She pressed herself against the foyer window.

The figure that was seated in the chair was, Joyce reasoned, designed to seem familiar, much the way recognizable forms pass through dreams.

"Morgan. . ." Joyce whispered, knowing how desperate her guess was, how hopeless.

The shape in the chair rose, swelled. The chair was cast aside and went tumbling down the steps until it finally became wedged between the wall and the banister. Its upholstery was shimmering wet and reeked foully.

The shape that had once been seated now stood. It was colossal, tangled, yet it moved with a grace that defied its size and its anatomy. Every time it lowered one of its lumps onto the next carpeted step there sounded a thunderous knocking, metallic and deep and echoing endlessly. It began to contort itself, to flaunt its non-humanness by halting for a second or two so that Joyce could absorb each repulsive asana.

Joyce shut her eyes.

Weeping, she sputtered "Now I lay me down to sleep. . ."

THE WAKE

STEVE RASNIC TEM

Philip had not felt well for a very long time. He was fatigued and fell asleep frequently. His doctors—he switched habitually—said it was most likely some undiagnosed allergy, although they did not hesitate to prescribe new medications for what they could not diagnose. It seemed unlikely he would die from this, but he did not anticipate improvement.

He could not remember the last time he had sat through a movie, or an hour-long television show, without falling asleep. Often he would dream the endings of whatever he missed. He could have watched those shows again if he wanted, but he chose not to, thinking that the endings he dreamed were probably more than sufficient.

His father, that old drunk, would often fall asleep in front of the television when Philip was a boy. His father had an old dog, Duke, who would do the same. Duke would whimper and softly yip while sleeping, constantly moving his thin, white-haired legs. Philip's father said that meant Duke dreamed of hunting when he was just a pup. But how did his father know?

Philip always wondered if Duke had instead dreamed of being chased, terrified that he was about to be eaten by that vast mystery which pursues us all.

Philip remembered trying to watch TV while Duke slept and dreamed on the rug beside him, and his father slept in the recliner behind him, chewing at some unspoken distress, occasionally shouting at things he would never describe. Over time it seemed Duke and his father might be having the same dream, and if Philip fell asleep at that moment their dream might overtake him as well in a tidal hum of image and sound, which might not be entirely undesirable.

Today Philip had hoped he could just slip in and entomb himself in the crowd, but somebody had locked the front door, forcing him to ring the bell. When no one answered the bell—although he knew they were inside because he could hear them talking and, peculiarly, laughing—he was reduced to beating on the door. Which was humiliating—this was his family home, and the wake for his father was being held inside without him. He was considering breaking a window when his sister opened the door.

"Where have you been? You're hours late!" Her face was pale, but he was sure she hadn't been crying. Lisa hated their father.

"Are you actually considering not letting me in?" She didn't answer. "Sorry. I overslept."

She walked away, muttering about his lack of respect. She was appropriately dressed in a crisp black dress with a layer of black lace on top. Philip still wore the casual work clothes he had slept in.

The figure in the casket only vaguely resembled his father. It could very well have been a cleverly made-up mannequin. The old man's cheeks reminded him of painted plastic. The lips were much more defined than his dad's had been. The weight loss he expected—his dad had been ill all last year. The hair was perfect and nothing like his dad's characteristic and thinning, uncombed mop. He imagined Lisa preferred this approximation—a hopeful vision, closer to some unrealized ideal.

The only empty seat was a folding chair propped up by the foot of the casket. Philip supposed no one wanted to sit that close to the body. People would come by for a visit, gaze at the face inside, and half-smile or sad-smile or whatever those expressions were, but no one lingered for long. No one stayed. But he was the son, however troublesome their relationship might have been. So he took the chair and unfolded it and sat down.

The awkwardness was immediate. No one could come by for their near-obligatory visit to the deceased without dealing in some way with Philip. Perhaps they knew him and felt they should talk to him, but he remained sitting out of some vague sense of respect (or was he worried about losing his chair?) and they had to contend with speaking with someone whose mouth was navel-height. Or they didn't know who he was at all and had to maneuver around this stranger as they exited their visit.

Philip himself had to decide where to look. When there were people by the casket he was staring at a number of butts and crotches. He thought he should probably be gazing at his father's face—that was what a wake was for, wasn't it? Safeguarding the body, or at some point in history he supposed making sure the deceased was actually dead or that the body wouldn't be stolen for unspeakable purposes. Or perhaps he had misunderstood all that.

He could almost see over the edge of the casket's lid, but not quite. If he raised himself up a bit, straightening his spine, he could see much of his father's face, but he couldn't hold that position long without trembling. When he thought no one was looking he retrieved a couple of thick phonebooks from the corner cupboard and added them to his seat, perching himself on those. Now he could see his father perfectly. In fact there was something about the angle that made looking at his father almost compulsory.

But gaze at a still body long enough and you can't help imagining that it is moving, if ever so slightly. Philip had to look away finally, convinced that his father was preparing his enhanced mouth to speak to him.

It was chilly outside and apparently his mother, whom he hadn't yet seen, had turned up the heat. He was still wearing a lightweight jacket he hadn't hung up because the coat tree was missing from the front hall. He could not imagine where they had put the thing; perhaps for some reason it had pissed off the old man and he had chopped it up and fed it to the fire. The furnace, the crowded house, his jacket, his nervousness, all conspired to raise the temperature. When had his parents gotten to know so many people? Philip didn't recognize half of them.

He'd never been to a wake before. He hadn't even realized they still had such things, that you could have a body on display in the house like that without breaking some local ordinance. The heat was baking his head. He closed his eyes to escape it and nodded off.

Philip didn't know what the etiquette was for these affairs, but he presumed the deceased's son falling asleep was not acceptable behavior.

He opened his eyes and looked at his father again, who looked different. His father's head had tilted, had been tilted, approximately an inch to the left. His father's nose was at a different angle.

It wasn't a boisterous event. There was some drinking but not that much. And people largely avoided the casket when they weren't paying their respects. So Philip doubted anyone had bumped it.

He waited and watched, and noticed no other change. He wondered if he'd just slipped in his chair. He rearranged himself so that his father appeared at least somewhat closer to the way Philip had seen him before. And then he nodded off again. He couldn't help himself.

Even in sleep he was embarrassed. What would people think? What would his mother think? He made some attempts to wake himself up, but this had always been problematic— whatever happened in his dreams was always far more interesting, and truer, than anything that happened to him awake.

Philip snapped his head around. His father had rolled his head completely onto its side. The dead slept restlessly, Philip thought, especially in the dreams of their children. He glanced over the room to see if anyone else had noticed. He snapped his head around again and his father had rolled his entire body completely over onto his right side, messing up his carefully combed hair. Philip could see where his father's makeup had smeared across the white silk lining of the casket. "Dad, hey Dad," he said as softly as he could. "You really shouldn't be doing that. It isn't appropriate."

His father mumbled something, then cursed under his breath. "Don't turn the channel," he said. "I'm watching that."

Something warm and damp rubbed against Philip's pants leg. Duke was licking his right knee. The old dog looked up, revealing a cataract over his left eye. His right eye looked slightly cloudy. Philip wondered how much the dog could actually see.

"Philip," Lisa hissed from a few feet away. "Some men from the funeral home are at the front door. I haven't told Mom—you'd better handle it."

Philip got to his feet, told Duke to "stay!" Lisa had already disappeared. He jogged to the front door. Two men were standing there in their colorful prom tuxedos. He wondered if his mother had decided to go cheap with the services, and that was why the wake was being held at home.

"So sorry to bother you," the one in the lime-colored suit said. "We simply wanted to settle our bill, then we'll be on our way." He handed Philip a small slip of paper. "Due: $16,750" had been scribbled across it in red ink.

Philip supposed the amount was reasonable, but how could he know for sure? "I think I need this itemized. Not that I don't trust you, but when I show this to my mother, well, I'm sure she'll want it itemized. She's a specific sort of person."

The one in the peach-colored suit spoke up. "Well, this is highly irregular. We don't normally expose our internal paperwork."

Philip felt angry, although he wasn't sure why. Maybe because he didn't think it was his place to be handling this. He wasn't suited for it. "Well, that can't be helped. If you want to get paid." He handed the slip back and stared at the pair.

The one in the peach-colored suit pulled an envelope from his jacket pocket and handed it to Philip. Inside was an itemized list concerning his father.

Philip's finger flicked across one of the lines. "Music? What music?"

The lime-suited man replied, "We like to listen to music while we work."

Philip's finger stopped on another line. "Books?"

"We have books available for the bereaved. Self-help books,

I suppose you would call them. To help with the tricky emotions involved."

"You delivered these books to my mother?"

"She hasn't asked for them, but they're available."

But the bulk of the charges were under *embalming supplies*. "Molasses, sodium chloride, magnesium, glass cleaner, forty-weight motor oil, corn lotion, and there's more. You actually put these things inside my father's body?"

"Apparently. Those and more," the peach-suited man replied. "Formulations tend to vary with the individual, as one would expect."

"I don't believe you. We're not paying for half this."

"What is this?" A woman's frail voice behind him. Philip's mother squeezed in beside him and took the itemized bill out of his hand. She stared up at him. "I'm glad you came. Your father would have been pleased. But you have to wake up now. A son has to watch over his father's body. What if wolves try to eat it? You'll never forgive yourself, son, if wolves were to eat your father."

Philip turned and ran back toward the living room. They must have remodeled the house after he moved out, because the hallway leading into the living room was much longer than he remembered, and lined with such a standing crowd of people that he couldn't see any of the passing doors or mounted photographs or other familiar landmarks behind them, so he wasn't quite sure where he was in relation to his father's casket. Who were all these people and were they really his father's friends? His father had always been so unpleasant; Philip couldn't remember the old man as having more than one or two friends. In an earlier time they sometimes hired mourners. Was that what was happening here? Had his mother actually hired mourners to send the old bastard off?

He kept seeing these eyes among the forms—yellow eyes and red eyes, flickering like candle flames, moving rapidly in the shadows behind the standing mourners. These must be the wolves his mother was talking about, racing him to his father's casket.

And there was the casket, but a small child was climbing out of it, and now the wolves were chasing that poor child up the stairs. "Dad!" he called, because Philip thought he recognized the child from old photographs. Death had diminished his father, and now his father was being pursued by wolves.

The child, his father, didn't turn around—he was too busy being terrified. He disappeared around the turn of the staircase, three dark wolves nipping at his heels. Philip raced up the stairs after them.

But once he reached the top of the stairs there was nothing to be seen, the corridor was empty, and all the bedroom doors were closed. He listened carefully but could hear nothing except the loud noises coming from downstairs, the wake now in full swing. He realized he was foolish anyway for coming up here without a weapon to fend off the wolves, so he made his way back down looking for some kind of bludgeon.

His father was back in the casket, turned over, his hands over his eyes to block out the light. Philip went over to him and gently tapped him on the shoulder. "Dad, that's not the way you're supposed to be. Your clothes and hair, they're all messed up now—you don't want to look bad today of all days, do you? You should look your best at your wake. I'll comb your hair, okay? Just let me comb your hair."

He gently peeled his father's hands away, and there was Philip himself, hiding in his father's casket. "Get him out of there! Tell him he can't sleep there!" his sister Lisa said beside him. She reached into the casket and grabbed Philip by the hair and yanked. "Get out of here! You don't belong in here!" Philip wept and wailed back at her, his mouth impossibly wide and mobile.

Philip looked down at himself with shame. "Get out of there and back into your chair! You disgust me. Just get back in your chair and don't say a word—I'm going to go get Dad and try to talk him into getting back into his casket. Lisa is going to stay here and make sure you don't get into any more trouble."

He went into the hall closet and found one of his father's old golf clubs. His father had never played, but thought these were a bargain at some long-ago yard sale. Philip went back up the stairs, determined to kill the wolves and talk his father back downstairs.

The situation was relatively quiet upstairs, but Philip sensed a vague restlessness stirring behind the closed doors. He'd done this before, of course, gone to retrieve his father and get him to one place or another on time. His mother's birthday party. His sister's wedding. His own college graduation. Sometimes from this house, sometimes from other houses or rundown apartments when Mother had kicked his father out and Dad had increased his drinking as a kind of resentful or rebellious gesture. Philip was tired of it.

The first bedroom was empty. It was pristine, decorated in the floral patterns his mother loved so much. He figured this was either the guest room or his mother's room when Dad was away. Certainly his dad had never touched it.

The second bedroom was a bit more masculine—browns and reds and some wood paneling, but still quite tidy. That made Philip think his father had never used this room—or had his mother redone everything in the hours following his father's death?

But he found the missing coat tree. It was neatly tucked

under the covers, its bronze coat hooks elongated and reaching out from under the sheets and blanket, wriggling in dismay. One of his father's ball caps was jammed over the top of the spindle. Philip shut the door without saying anything.

He opened the third door and was immediately struck by the odor. The rooms his father lived in always smelled funny: cigarettes and beer, sweaty T-shirts and something that suggested chocolate but which probably wasn't. Philip entered and shut the door behind him. In the front room the wolves lay clumped together on a battered old sofa watching a rolling static pattern on a small TV with a coat-hanger antenna. Behind them white curtains stained with tobacco-yellow splotches blew out the window overlooking a raucous lower downtown. Trash layered everything except for a narrow, kicked-out path leading into the next room.

Philip crunched through the emptied beer cans and peered into the next room. The bed had a dirty white bottom sheet and matching flattened pillow but no other bedclothes. A variety of reading material including several romance novels was arranged in stacks between the bed and the dresser, whose clothes-strewn drawers had been pulled out at varying lengths on either side of a milk-clouded mirror.

He found his father sitting on the other side of the bed leaning against the wall under a window covered by a stiff brown shade. He had only his striped boxers on. His face showed several days' worth of stubble. He'd been crying.

"Dad, you have to get dressed."

His father turned his head and gazed at him rheumily. "Son. You found me."

"It's never that hard."

"What am I late for this time?"

Philip had no answer for this. "Do you have some clean

clothes? If so, where are they? I'll help you get dressed."

His father gestured vaguely toward the other side of the room. Philip walked over, examined the piles of clothing, and picked up the clothes hanging from the open drawers. He found a pair of pants and a shirt that appeared untouched, and more or less folded in the bottom of a drawer. He started with those and a pair of underwear that looked relatively fresh. All his father's socks were dirty and wadded up on various parts of the floor. He wondered if the old man could get by without socks. Philip could pull the pants down to cover the bare ankles. After all, all his father had to do was lie there and keep quiet.

"Did you hear that?" his father asked while Philip was dressing him.

"Hear what, Dad? I didn't hear anything."

"You'd know it if you heard it. Like a rhino charging right behind you, or absolutely the worst storm you can imagine. You think you've avoided it, but then you discover you've driven right into it. Like this dream, Son. You don't really want to be in this dream."

Philip paused and stared at him. "Let's just get you dressed, okay? We're holding everything up."

His father sighed and let himself go limp, allowing Philip to continue dressing him—not resisting, but not really helping either. Philip considered how it was a bit like dressing a dummy, or a dead body.

"I can't remember—did you ever get married, Son?"

"No, Dad. I didn't."

His father flopped over on his side. He'd become more stiff, and harder to dress. "You might consider it. It can help."

Philip pulled his father to his feet, wrapping one arm around his waist to support him, and started toward the door. "Are your wolves going to bother us?"

His father didn't reply, but they made it out into the corridor and back down the stairs with little trouble.

There was no sign of his sister, but everything seemed calm and unhurried downstairs. People continued to talk and drink as if nothing were amiss. Philip lifted his father as if he were a statue, or a rolled-up rug, and slipped him face up into the casket. Afterwards he arranged his hands and combed his hair.

He paused to study the effect: his father in the casket looked exactly as he had when Philip first entered the house. Then Philip awakened, sprawled on the floor, chair and phone books collapsed and scattered.

Lisa was kneeling beside him holding his hand. His mother was there too, crying. He tried to speak but could not. His father walked stealthily past his mother and sister, grinning, out of his box again. Philip tried to warn them, but there were no words, only this roar coming up out of the dream behind him, moving so fast, and sounding so loud, he couldn't hear, or think about anything else.

DEAD LETTER OFFICE

Caitlín R. Kiernan

A footfall easily as heavy as an eon here, here being this purportedly bounded territory of shadows. She has heard the lies and half-truths whispered by would-be explorers to wishful cartographers, that somewhere out beyond the black labyrinth there is more, that there is something that counters the darkness. Her name is not Dysnomia, but this is the only name she can recall ever having known. Names are generally unwelcome here, as they imply a state of individuality loathsome to the sameness of floors, walls, vaulted ceilings leading into nothingness, and faces. Not that all faces here are identical in their details and not that all walls are identical in their angles, but each and every one is precisely like every other. It is *perception* that spins *difference;* Werner Heisenberg would be pleased.

Once, long ago, in the Corridors of Reflection, Dysnomia glanced at herself, a most ill-advised course of action, and the woman she saw looking back at her had skin that seemed molded or carved from precisely the same hard, greasy black material as the pathways and chambers and presumably load-bearing pillars of the labyrinth. Skin that was not quite carbon nor graphite nor charcoal, but skin that, in its lividity and luster, exhibited qualities common to all those substances. Her eyes were good as oil, her teeth no more than pegs of lignite. Her hair was a hundred and fifty thousand shiny, slick, and writhing strands. She never looked again, and always since she has avoided the Corridors of Reflection.

Look with horror in your mirror at the eyes without curiosity; at the lips which never question.

Dysnomia—wearing her apostate's appellation—has sometimes listened hopefully to the myths of extraspacial geographies, and also to the heretics who imply that a veil lies over all which is perceived by those confined here. *If we could pull back the curtain, you would see. If we could but lift the veil.* And there's another heresy, that *here* is a prison, which leads some to posit that *here* is an underworld of the dead, a hell (and there may be many), that *here* is a garbage heap for discarded souls. But these heresies must, for their legitimacy, rely upon other heresies—that there is, for example, an Architect, or that there is at least a System. And most in these echoing plutonic spaces would find both ideas abhorrent. Such thoughts would long since have earned death sentences for those rare dissenters, if death were here a reality.

If we could pull back the veil, what would *you see, and, more to the point, what might see you?*

It hardly matters that there is no profit, here, in inquiry. Dysnomia may as well try to still her heart as try to push away the niggling questions spun by her consciousness. And added to the complexity of the equation of her thoughts are ghosts that must be memories, or memories that must be ghosts, of some time before *now* and of some other place before *here* and of some other *she* before her name was not Dysnomia. It isn't an uncommon psychosis, the belief in a beforeness, and it is one almost as pernicious in its persistence as the equally psychotic belief, by no few, that there must surely be a quality of afterness. These deniers of the eternal, of perpetuity, they exist like a canker sore beneath the tongue of Truth. So say the self-appointed priests and hierophants who have chosen to exist apart and alone in the nether corners of a nether world. Those men and women who have chosen to ruminate forevermore on their damnedness in a damned world. They have the pale eyes of blind fish, each and every one of them.

By damned, I mean the excluded.

But excluded from what and when?

Though there are no day times and no night times, there is undeniably time, which passes, like footfalls, one moment after the next, and within that framework exist the routines that define the rhythm of Dysnomnia's existence. She tends the mattresses in the ever-expanding event horizon above the quietly sloshing amoebic sea. She has heard rumors that the sea is composed of the remnants of the minds who tried too hard to reach those purported boundaries of this place, has heard that in the very act they were undone and became no more than the undifferentiated, unknowing slime that laps against the shore.

She tends the mattresses.

She watches over the sleepers.

No one has ever assigned Dysnomia this duty. Like her face and her name, it simply exists—even if some would argue otherwise. Perhaps it is hers because there are no others here willing to shoulder the weight. There might have been another before her to whom this task fell, but she can't say if that's true. She might have been watching over the sleepers as long as she has been, and she might have always been.

The mattresses lie upon the black floor of a room whose dimensions shift according to some unknown (and almost certainly unknowable) tectonic principle. Each is precisely the same size and has been sewn from worn goatskins stuffed with straw, cotton ticking, linen castoffs. There are sheets like shaved midnight, and granite pillows, and a disagreeable mustiness. There is about the mattresses not even the faintest hint of comfort, and the sleepers toss and turn and mutter, sometimes crying out in their dreams. They never wake, and, so far as is known to the scholars of *here,* they have never fallen asleep. Theirs is an uncaused, steady-state slumber. For them, no exploding singularity from which has followed these ever-expanding ultradian cycles. Behind her hydrocarbon eyes, Dysnomia has often wondered at the nature of her charges, locked inescapably in their waves and troughs of REM and NREM. All suppositions are futile, but they come anyway, and she lets them. Sometimes she sits beside this or that sleeper and listens to their unease, and other times she mutters gentle words to them, or she sings lullabies that she has no recollection of ever having learned. The songs come to her as readily as her next breath, as readily as her last. If the sleepers hear, they've never once shown any evidence that they do. Unless, she has thought, she is incapable of perceiving their responses; after all, she may not know that language. Rarely does this bother her. She's never expected recompense, nor even acknowledgment. All here have their unassigned roles—the mummers and penny-whistle pipers, the quantum clowns and geometricians, the whores and peddlers of hallucinogenic powders, the unseeing astronomers and faithless astrologers—all have their roles.

She leans near a golden-haired sleeper, skin as pale as hers is black, and Dysnomia's lips and tongue leak melody and lyrics:

Hush-a-by, don't you cry.
Go to sleep, you little baby.
When you wake you shall have
All the pretty little horses.

The music draws all-but-visible spirals in the air above the sleeper, weaving almost funnel clouds no larger than a thumbnail.

By the light of the moon
One could barely see
The pen was looked for,
The light was looked for.
With all that looking
But I do know that the door
Shut itself on them

Dust lies thickly on the sleepers' eyelids, and Dysnomia stops singing just long enough to blow it away. It accumulates too quickly, heavy and grey, ash from a fire that has never (and will never burn). She resumes her songs, which bleed imperceptibly one into the next.

Shule, shule, shularoo, sure and sure and he loves me.
When he comes back we'll married be.
Johnny has gone for a soldier.

Then she's interrupted by the thunderous clanging that comes sometimes, at no interval that has ever been discerned, from the perhaps not-emptiness high above the labyrinth. A cacophony as if all were constructed beneath a mighty cosmic bell, a galaxy for its uvula, clapping bronze and stars and vacuum. Dysnomia covers her ears, just as she always does, for there is some quality in the sound she finds dreadful beyond description, something that should turn her to stone, she thinks. It's Medusa's bell, and it should only be heard indistinctly through the precaution of a polished shield.

And something happens then that never has happened before. The sleeper with the golden hair and pale skin stirs just as the maybe bell's thunder begins to fade from the place where either a ceiling or the sky should be (but either likely isn't). At first, Dysnomia is certain she's suffering a delusion, shock inflicted by the clanging still rattling about inside her skull. They do not move, the sleepers. They do not ever move, except to draw the shallowest of breaths. In a million years, she's never before seen so much as the twitch of a muscle, no shift even by the slightest of degrees. But the golden-haired woman's eyelids flutter and her lips part enough that Dysnomia can see her teeth are emeralds set into ebony gums. The caretaker of the mattresses almost looks away, afraid this is some unimaginable blasphemy, worse even than the sight of herself in the mirrors.

A hoarse gasp escapes the sleeper's throat, or a rush of air near enough to a gasp.

If you can; go back to sleep, go back to your dreams from which your alarm will summon you to another day.. . .

She's waking, thinks Dysnomia, the thought more dreadful even than the bell. *They do not ever, ever wake, but here she is waking, all the same.*

The golden-haired woman's eyes open, slowly as the eons of a footfall, and her irises are the unhealthy violet-green of a bruise. Dysnomia almost gets to her feet. She almost runs, dashing pell-mell into the darkness that surrounds the place where the innumerable mattresses are laid out.

"I dreamt someone singing," says the golden-haired woman,

croaking out the words with a voice so clumsy it might never have been used before. A voice that is only guessing its way around the obstacle course of syllables. "I dreamt a singer."

Go back to sleep, thinks Dysnomia. *Go back to sleep this very minute, and don't you ever open your bruised eyes again. This is unseemly, waking. No, this is an atrocity.*

But what she says, instead, is, "That was me. I was singing to you. I come here, and I sing to all the sleepers."

"I was sleeping," replies the woman.

"You were," says Dysnomia, though the woman's words weren't phrased as a question. "Always and forever you've slept."

The golden-haired woman only stares up at her, her gaze clogged full with confusion, and then, as unexpectedly as her awakening, she lifts her left hand and rubs at her green-violet eyes. The small, disused bones in her wrist and the slender bones in her fingers creak very softly from the exertion.

"Do you have a name?" Dysnomia asks and immediately wishes that she hadn't. She certainly does not desire to know the answer. Names—even her own which is *not* her own—are anathema in the labyrinth. The woman on the mattress squeezes her eyes shut a moment, then opens them again. It seems to Dysnomia that her eyes are beginning to look less bruised, as if shedding the bludgeoning violence of sleep.

"Yes, I remember now that I had a name. I remember I was called Talia."

"Talia."

"I don't know that I *still* am her. But I believe I *was.*"

The woman coughs and asks for water.

"All the wells dried up long ago," Dysnomia tells her, which may be true and which may only be a myth. *Water,* thinks Dysnomia, *may only be a myth, like anywhere outside the labyrinth.*

Certainly, the sloshing, slopping sea is not made of water.

"There's no water here. I'm sorry."

The woman who might still be named Talia closes her eyes again.

"Why are you awake?" Dysnomia asks, hearing the tremble at the knife edges of her voice, and she quickly glances at the other sleepers on the other mattresses nearest her, terrified that possibly this woman is not the only one shaking off her slumber. What if she's heralded an epidemic? But they're all as still and silent as ever they have been.

"Isn't that a strange sort of question?" Talia asks in return, and then she opens her eyes (again), and now that sour tint of green is altogether gone, and her irises are the clearest shade of light violet.

"I wouldn't know. I've never spoken with someone who's awakened."

The woman begins to sit up, then looks ill and lies back down again. Dysnomia places a palm flat against her forehead, suspecting fever, but the skin above Talia's eyebrows is cool and dry.

"I dreamt music," Talia says again. And then she says, "I was dreaming of the navigator, and then a woman was singing to me."

Dysnomia hesitates, her head already dizzy with new and unwelcome knowledge. Even so, she whispers, "Navigator? I've never heard of a navigator. Not here. Not in this place. What would he or she navigate? I'm sure it was only a dream, a phantasm." And immediately it occurs to her that the golden-haired woman never implied it was anything more. Dysnomia takes her hand away from the woman's brow.

"How long has it been?" Talia asks, and Dysnomia is beginning to believe there's no end to the questions the awakened sleeper is going to put to her, same as there's said to be no bottom to the vast amoebic sea, same as the labyrinth is most assuredly infinite.

"I don't know how to answer that," Dysnomia replies. "Perhaps it would be best if you went back to sleep now. If word of this were to reach the priesthood, there could be trouble."

"I mean," the woman persists, "how long have I been sleeping."

"For always," Dysnomia tells her. "You should shut your eyes now, and you shouldn't say anything more. There are watchers everywhere." She doesn't know if that last part is true or only a wishful scrap of paranoia meant to push back against the loneliness, a thing more solid than the walls and floors and any flesh.

"No one has been asleep forever," the woman says and scowls. "I need to speak with the navigator. I need to get up and get water, and, as soon as it can be arranged, I need to speak with the navigator."

"Does he also have a name?" Dysnomia asks, hoping to distract the golden-haired woman from her insistence that she leave the mattress.

"Everyone has a name. For fuck's sake, even you were given a name." And then Talia shakes her head and closes her eyes a third time—which Dysnomia hopes truly is a charm—and Talia grows so still again that maybe she's fallen back asleep, and in a moment all the world will have returned to the banal normalcy of the labyrinth's night-bound existence. Hoping this is exactly so, Dysnomia begins once more to sing:

> No use pleading or praying
> For gone, gone is all hope of staying.
> Hush, hush, the anchor's a-weighing.

Don't cry in your sleep, bonny baby.

"Please," mutters the impossible golden-haired woman, the awakened, the former sleeper whose name might be Talia. "Stop that and go away now. Go away and let me rest, let me think. Come back later."

Wanting very much to be away from the woman, Dysnomia acquiesces, though for a long while she tarries in an alcove near the entrance to the mattress room. There is almost too much here to consider, much less make sense of, and the drawing of any conclusion seems, at this point, entirely beyond her grasp. There's also the nagging suspicion that this isn't something she ought try and ignore. What if Talia doesn't fall asleep again? What if she persists in this heresy that there is, somewhere, a navigator? What if she were to wake other sleepers? There is, above all, a way that the labyrinth seems always to have been, and that status quo seems preferable to the innumerable unknown variables of chaos that could be unleashed by Talia's insistence, should it spread beyond the well-tended sphere of Dysnomia's responsibility.

What if, she thinks, *it proved to be far worse than the deceits and deceptions tossed carelessly about by those would-be explorers and charlatan cartographers? How much damage might be done?*

It occurs to her that she should consult with another on this problem. Though that's nothing she's ever imagined she might do, might *need* to do, as her duties are simple and, until now, have presented no conundrums, not in all the apparently forever that they have *been* her duties. The very idea makes her apprehensive, but would it not be worse if she told no one and then this strange waking phenomenon were to spread?

So she decides.

There is a man of whom she's heard spoken, down the millennia, a man who keeps his own company in a chamber to be gained by a long walk through many rooms and winding passages and across an iron bridge that arcs above a shallow inlet of the slopping amoebic sea. She's heard, through those who have never met him, through those who have nothing to go on except myths and legends, that he's a wise man, and that he possesses knowledge lost to all others, if any others actually ever knew the secrets *this* man knows.

If he has, like her, the illusion of a name, that's a part of the story Dysnomia has never heard.

So she goes to seek him out, traveling farther and farther from the room with the goatskin mattresses and the sleepers, farther from them than she has ever known herself to have traveled. Memory must, of course, be taken with a grain of salt, but the mounting anxiety as she puts distance between herself and her charges would, she thinks, lend some credence to her suspicion. Her good-as-eons footfalls make no sound whatsoever, as though the hungry atmosphere devours whatever soft sound her bare feet make against the floors, catwalks, and stony byways.

I won't find him. I won't find him because he's never existed. And I've gone so far that I may never find my way back again.

Dysnomia remembers a fairy story of a boy and girl with breadcrumbs, and she wishes she'd devised some such clever way to mark her progress. Then again, she also recalls that flying monsters called *birds* came along and devoured the crumbs.

It surprises her when she actually arrives at the bridge, and she lingers, hesitant to step out onto its rusty, narrow span. The sea beneath it stinks of brine and filth, of unclean things she has no words for. But one doesn't need language to sense *unwholesomeness*. The bridge fords just that, unwholesomeness, and Dysnomia can't shake the sudden conviction that should she dare to cross it, she would be infected. Ahead of her, beneath the bridge, there's a splash, a heavy, wet, flopping noise, and then laughter from someone not very far behind her, back the way she's come, a taunting sort of laugh that seems to be daring her to turn back. Unless it's daring her to go on. It could be either, and how would she ever know?

After the splash, and after the laughter, there's a slithering sound, and the *unwholesome* smell grows stronger. This is enough, finally, to get her moving again, and she crosses the bridge as quickly as the physics of the labyrinth allow. She keeps her eyes downcast, glancing up only once, when she looks out over the inlet where it runs down to the amoebic sea. It's a living thing, as alive as the sleepers, as alive as she must be, its slow metabolism evident in high troughs and deep waves. Its surface is brilliantly iridescent.

There's a tall lancet doorway on the far side of the bridge—no walls to frame it, but a doorway all the same—and the crystalline knob is icy to the touch, almost cold enough to burn her graphite flesh. She turns it, steps across the threshold, and then quickly shuts it behind her. The world seems to shudder. Beneath her feet, the labyrinth shifts ever so slightly, and there's good cause to believe that if she opens the door the bridge will no longer be there.

I shouldn't have done this. I should never have come here.

And what would you have done instead?

Anything. I would have done anything else instead. Or I would have done nothing whatsoever and accepted the consequences.

When the labyrinth is still again, when the air no longer quivers with the echo of the closing door, Dysnomia turns away from the bridge and the inlet, away from the path leading back to the chamber of mattresses and sleepers, and she begins picking her way across a wide plain studded with the wrecks of shattered machineries. She imagines something vast falling from a high place, from the not sky, breaking apart as it fell, peppering this flat expanse with the debris of its calamitous descent. All the world must surely have shuddered in the instant of that disaster, all the unending miles of the labyrinth. She must have felt it, far away, and wondered what had happened, even if she has no such memory. Dysnomia glances upward, something she only rarely ever does, and then continues on her way. Twisted girders tower above her and form crooked archways through which she passes. Her bare feet are cut by diamond shards. Here and there, a viscous liquid drips and spatters; in places it has formed glistening pools. She's always careful to step around them, never through.

I shouldn't have done this. I should never have come here.

Before long, Dysnomia realizes that she isn't alone. There are others, huddled in the ruins, peering out with fearful or surprised or merely curious eyes as she passes them by. Occasionally, someone whispers, but she can never make out the words. She only catches the briefest half-glimpses of these muttering inhabitants; they all seem—like the broken machineries—twisted, warped, despoiled.

She leaves them all behind, and the wreckage becomes increasingly sparse until, finally, she's out of the debris field and has reached the bottom of a staircase spiraling up into the gloom. The rumors she's heard of the man she's seeking, they often suggested he is to be found at the top of just such a staircase, and she only pauses for a moment before she begins the climb. The steps are composed of some rubbery material that yields slightly under her weight.

At the top there's a hallway, no wider than the span of her arms.

And at the far end of the hallway is a small, perfectly round room with a low flat ceiling. There's a man sitting on the floor, near the center, and in his open palms he holds a ball of cold blue light. His skin is silver and reflects the glow of the sphere.

He's like a mirror. A man made of mirrors.

"Not many come here," he says, when Dysnomia crosses the threshold and steps into the room. His voice reminds her of the fallen, shattered machines. "Not many have ever found the way."

Her eyes settle on the ball of light, and for a while they remain there.

How, she thinks, *can anything be as bright as that? How can anything be as bright as that without searing a hole in the fabric of the world?*

"Something's happened," she says, at last, shutting her eyes tightly but still seeing the blue light shining there behind her lids.

"No one's come here in ages."

"I didn't know where else to go. I don't think I've ever before needed to speak with anyone, not that I can recall."

"You're the Singer," he says, and she almost tells him no, I'm the one who tends to the mattresses and the sleepers, because she's never before thought of herself that way.

But I am, aren't I? I'm the Singer.

"Someone woke up," she says, opening her eyes again.

The silver man's watching her, and his irises could be carved from chips of the blue light in his hands. He frowns very slightly.

"She claims that her name is Talia, and she's asked to speak with the navigator," adds Dysnomia. "I tried, of course, to explain to her that there is no navigator. But she wouldn't listen."

"If I ever dreamed," the man says, "I would dream of your songs. I hear them, sometimes. I listen to them, sometimes."

She wants to ask him how that's possible, how her voice could carry over so great a distance, but she doesn't. Instead, she glances down at her bare feet and the smooth black floor of the circular room.

Dysnomia tells the man, "She asked for a drink of water. I explained that there's no water left here, if, indeed, there ever has been water, here or anywhere. If water is anything more than a fancy."

"I'm the first one who ever heard your voice," he replies. "You sang to me long before you sang to the sleepers."

"Why do I have no recollection of that?" she asks.

"There's no water left," he answers. "Not *here*. Not anymore."

And then he calls her by a name that isn't Dysnomia, and he tells her to turn her attention back to the light cradled in his palms. She nods and does as instructed, realizing that either it has begun to emit a faint crackling sound or it was making that sound all along and she simply didn't notice. As she watches, the ball begins to rotate very slowly.

"What is that?" she asks, before she can think better of asking. But the man has begun to sing, and he doesn't answer the question. He's begun to sing one of her lullabies.

> *Such a pretty house*
> *And such a pretty garden.*
> *No alarms and no surprises,*
> *No alarms and no surprises, please.*

His voice was not made to soothe sleepers, she thinks, though it isn't precisely unpleasant to hear. She tries to remember ever having heard anyone else besides herself sing, but she can't, so perhaps she never has.

I wish, I wish, I wish in vain.
I wish I had my heart again,
And vainly think I'd not complain.

The blue sphere spins, hurried along by the mirror man's broken clockwork voice, and now Dysnomia sees something within the light that she hadn't seen before—a tiny planet, rocky and lifeless, frozen four and a half billion years, a world where the nearest star is only a pale dot in the black. And about it rotates four tiny moons.

Planet, moons, star, she thinks, playing the words over in her head, examining their heft and texture. She's always known them, but suspects that until this second they were little more than the most abstract concepts and possibly not even as substantial as the myth of water.

Or the myth of a labyrinth with boundaries.

The man is still singing, his songs spilling one into the next, same as her own are apt to do.

Angels watching, e'er around thee,
All through the night.
Midnight slumber close surround thee,
All through the night.

Planet, moons, star—and something else. Something only a fraction as large as the smallest of the moons, an ebony cube silhouetted sharply against the grey-brown silhouette of the largest of those orbs. The cube is but a speck inside the blue ball of light, lost and tumbling through a night without beginning and without end. Dysnomia is struck by a wave of vertigo, and she quickly looks away, even though the man hasn't told her that she can.

He's stopped singing.

"What do I tell her?" Dysnomia whispers, her voice seeming suddenly enormous in the small, round room. "The woman who awoke. The woman who's asking me for water and to speak with the navigator?"

"There is no navigator," the man replies, and he laughs a tired, dry laugh. "There is no one remaining here who can point the way. No one at all. You go back to her. You're the Singer. See that she sleeps."

"Does anyone else remember how this began?" she asks him. "Besides yourself, I mean. Is there anyone who knows whether—"

"Go *back*," he interrupts, and now there's a knife's edge to his voice, an impatient sharpness. "Do not trouble me with questions. You weren't fashioned with questions and answers in mind. You're the Singer. You're the Voice."

Dysnomia nods, slowly, and she waits to see if the mirror man is going to say anything more. When he doesn't, she turns and makes her way back along the narrow corridor leading to the stairway, then down the oddly yielding steps to the wide plain studded with the wrecks of shattered machineries. A second time, she ignores the murmurs of all those damned to cower in the devastation, hardly more than ghosts.

By damned, I mean the excluded.

A second time she crosses the iron bridge that spans an inlet of the vast amoebic sea, but this time she feels no apprehension, no trepidation, no fear of its slopping unwholesomeness or of the pitiless eyes that watch her from its depths.

If we could pull back the veil, what would *you see, and, more to the point, what might see you?*

Dysnomia walks the roads that lead her through the labyrinth and back to the room of uncertain, mutable dimension where the sleepers lie on goatskin mattresses and granite pillows. Only the one who calls herself Talia is awake, waiting, ready with more questions that the Singer was neither meant to hear nor answer.

"You should rest now," she tells the woman. Dysnomia sings for her, and when the song is not enough, she finds it is a very simple matter, pressing the woman back down flat against her bedding and clasping a hand across her face until she no longer struggles and there's no danger that she'll ever wake again.

> *I lost a world the other day.*
> *Has anybody found?*
> —Emily Dickinson

THE ART OF MEMORY

Donald Tyson

1

Alan Cartwright hurried across the immaculately mowed front court of King's College toward the library. The hallowed stone façades of the ancient university peered down at him in disapproval, but he had grown familiar enough with them that he no longer noticed their quiet dignity. He had been delayed, and resented having his daily routine disrupted. It was his habit to spend the free hours of his mornings at one of the library reading tables memorizing, or at least trying to memorize, the idiosyncratic verb constructions that were so common to classical Greek.

A group of gowned undergraduates clustered around one of those horseless carriage machines that were becoming so popular. They hooted and applauded as it coughed to life. He glanced at the shiny, shuddering contraption, but did not stop to watch. The future of science held little interest for him. The past was his obsession.

He adjusted his wire-framed glasses and wrinkled his long

nose in disgust at the smell of gasoline and the raw sound of the claxon horn that all such auto-mobiles, as they were called, were required to be fitted with to alert unwary riders of their coming.

"Mister Cartwright!"

The voice of his academic advisor made him pause reluctantly. Professor Mullen looked like an approaching steam locomotive as he strode along the gravel walk with energetic thrusts of his elbows beneath his tattered black gown. Puffs of smoke arose from the broad bowl of his briar pipe at each forceful step.

He withdrew the pipe stem from the bristle of gray whiskers that sprouted from his upper lip and chin like naked tree roots.

"I have something that may be of use to you. Now where has it gone?" Shoving his arm deep beneath his gown at the rear, he squinted at the blue sky. "Ah, here it is."

Cartwright eyed the book in Mullen's hand. It was a small, plain thing bound in dark leather, and appeared to be quite old.

"What do you know about the art of memory?"

Cartwright frowned. "Nothing at all."

"Nothing?"

"No."

"Well, no matter. The art of memory is the general name given to various systems for strengthening the memory that were popular during the Renaissance. It was quite the fad at the time. Almost as popular as these noisy auto-mobiles are today. I was in the library and happened to think of your problem. When I inquired after books on memory improvement, they gave me this."

The book was surprisingly heavy and the leather felt hard, as old book leather often does. He opened it with care and scanned its yellowed title page.

"It's in English," he said in surprise. "*The Art of Memory* by Marius D'Assigney. London, 1706."

The frontispiece was an elegant steel engraving that depicted the English Hercules standing with a club on a podium between armed Minerva and the three dancing Graces. Hercules seemed to be delivering an oration to a crowd below. Strings ran from his mouth to the heads of his audience.

"It's one of the later works on the subject, but it still teaches the classical methods of memory improvement, or so I was told."

"Thank you," the young man said. "It was very thoughtful of you."

Mullen shrugged with his pipe between his teeth.

"Well, look it over. Maybe you will see something in it that will give you an idea or two."

Cartwright met the old man's watery gaze.

"Look, tell me straight out. Are they going to expel me?"

"Not yet," Mullen said. "I don't need to remind you that you are here at Cambridge thanks to the legacy of your father. John Cartwright was an outstanding student and is still remembered with fondness by some of the old boys. When he made his success in the City, he bestowed upon the university a very generous gift, with the understanding that when you came of age, you should follow in his footsteps."

"I don't remember him," Cartwright admitted. "I was only four when my parents died."

"We know that. We've taken into account the difficult time you had, being sent to live with your uncle at so young an age."

"My uncle died when I was six. I don't even remember him very well."

"You were shunted around through a series of foster homes and institutions. It must have been difficult. Frankly, Mister

Cartwright, I'm surprised you turned out as well as you did."

2

Cartwright found his usual seat at one of the reading tables between the walls of bookshelves. He settled into it to read the little volume Mullen had given him. Not that he expected to find anything useful in it, but the art of memory was a subject from the past that was new to him. How he had missed reading about it, he could not imagine. It must be uncommonly obscure.

The book was not lengthy, really little more than an essay. Most of it concerned improving the memory for the purpose of delivering orations, a subject that had no direct bearing on his circumstances, but toward the end it got more interesting, when it began to describe artificial memory.

Natural memory was when you saw or heard something and remembered it. Artificial memory was when you deliberately created something in your imagination and remembered it. According to the book, artificial memories could be used to provoke natural memories.

Artificial memory consisted chiefly in the manipulation of places and images. The use of place in provoking remembrance rested on the observation of the ancient Greeks that memories were often associated with localities—that is, to enter a certain place would provoke a forgotten memory associated with that place. The use of images depended on the natural tendency of the human mind to remember visual objects or scenes more readily and more explicitly than artefacts of the other four senses.

The technique of artificial memory was sublimely simple. You created a memory space in your imagination which you subdivided into smaller places. Into these smaller places you put symbols or images that were designed to provoke a remembrance of the things you wished to imprint upon your mind. Then, at a later time when you desired to recollect the memory, you merely had to enter the memory space and walk through it until you came upon the image or scene that would trigger the memory, which it did by association.

One paragraph in particular impressed him. He read it over and over to himself.

Now some prescribe the Imagination of a fair and regular Building, divided into many Rooms and Galleries, with differing Colors and distinct Pillars, which the Party must fancy to stand before him as so many Repositories where he is to place the Things or Ideas which he designs to remember, ordering them according to their several Circumstances and Qualifications, for the better Assistance of Memory.

He decided that he would use a house for his memory gallery, and its various rooms for its repositories. It suddenly came to him that he knew just the house to use. For years he had experienced a recurring dream about an old country manor house. The dreams were always the same. He approached the house and entered it, only to find it deserted. He then wandered from room to room, examining their contents, before waking up. There was nothing sinister about the dream, but it was oddly evocative and melancholy in some way that he could never quite define.

The old manor of his dreams was perfect for his memory mansion. He already knew it in precise detail. He could place his various irregular Greek verb conjugations in its rooms and key them to the objects in those rooms. At any rate, it was worth a try.

There was another section of the little book that looked promising. It contained recipes for various potions, balms, pills, fumes, and ointments designed to strengthen the memory. Cartwright's heart fell when he read over their lists of ingredients. Some of them he didn't even recognize. Others, such as bear's fat, would be virtually impossible to come by. He decided to copy down what appeared to be the simplest recipe, which happened to be for a powdered incense, and present it to a chemist to see whether the ingredients could be found.

Take Lign-aloes, Frankincense, Gum-mastic, red Roses, Leave of Betony, Cinamon, Mace, Spice, Cloves, white Storax; and with all this make a Powder: cast it onto a Chafing Dish of Coals a morning, and it will wonderfully comfort the Brain, and help the Memory.

As he was finishing writing these things down on a sheet of paper, Tom Hobbs poked his head around the edge of the shelves.

"And how are you today, Mister Cartwright?"

Although Hobbs was at least thirty years his senior, his tone was obsequious and fawning, as though he were trying to make a favorable impression on a young child. Hobbs was a fixture of Cambridge. He did tasks and procured items for the students for small fees. It was generally agreed that he knew the library better than the head librarian, and he earned a large portion of his money by fetching books. Nobody seemed to know where he came from, but he had a working-class London accent. He was as thin as Cartwright and stood almost a head taller, a fact disguised by the habitual stoop of his shoulders. As much as Cartwright tried to think well of the man, he could not help being reminded of the Dickens character Uriah Heep.

"Can I get you anything? A book, perhaps?"

"No. Wait, yes, maybe you can." Cartwright passed him the list of ingredients for the incense. "Do you think you can find these things at the chemist in the town?"

Hobbs read the list over, squinting to see it. "Cinnamon, mace, spice, cloves? Seems more like you'll find these things in the kitchen."

"Do you think you can gather them all together? All, mind you. If there's one missing, it's no good to me."

After a moment, Hobbs nodded. "I know some people I can ask. I think I can find what you need." He looked knowingly at Cartwright. "It's to help your memory, is it?"

Cartwright nodded. Everyone in Cambridge knew of the problems he was having with his Greek. Or so it seemed.

"Your father would be proud to see you here, sitting in your scholar's gown, so prim and proper. He was quite the young man, was your father."

"Did you know my father?" Cartwright asked in surprise.

"Oh yes, we got on handsome, your father and me. Such a well-composed young man, so correct. Not like your uncle Edward. Now there was a wild one."

Cartwright suddenly found that he did not like to hear Hobbs speak of his family in such familiar terms.

"One other thing, Hobbs. See if you can find me some white frankincense as well, and keep it separate from the other ingredients."

Hobbs nodded but lingered. "I'll need some money in advance."

Cartwright passed over ten shillings. "Bring it to my chambers tonight."

He watched the rounded shoulders of the older man diminish down the aisle past the projecting bookshelves.

If anyone could get the ingredients it was Hobbs. Not that he seriously expected the incense to do any good, but it was something else to try and he had grown desperate enough to try almost anything. He could not bear the thought of being expelled from Cambridge. The only thing he knew about his father was that his father had intended him to take his degree here, and he could not endure the thought of failing.

3

When Hobbs knocked on the door of his private chambers, Cartwright already had a fire burning in the grate in anticipation of the success of his quest. He was not disappointed. Hobbs had managed to get all the ingredients for the incense, as well as the white frankincense for which Cartwright had another use. It had cost twice the ten shillings he had been given, Hobbs told him with a solemn face. The student paid without complaint, adding another five shillings for Hobbs's effort.

His own eagerness surprised him. His hands trembled slightly when he mixed the ingredients together in a mortar with a heavy marble pestle. When they were finely ground and thoroughly blended, he put them into a small bottle he had washed out and dried for the purpose.

The recipe for the incense said to burn it in the mornings, but he was too eager to wait. With the fireplace shovel he conveyed glowing embers to a small chafing dish that stood on his study table, then sprinkled some of the incense on top of the embers. White smoke rose up from the dish and the air filled with an exotic perfume that was sharp in the nose but not unpleasant.

One of the most important factors in building a successful house of memory was regular meditation upon the mental construction, so that it would remain clear in the mind.

Cartwright sat down in a plain wooden chair without arms that he had positioned to face a blank wall, and closed his eyes for the first meditation.

He began to visualize the manor house of his dreams. He imagined himself approaching the front of the house across a lawn of browning grass that had the appearance of neglect, as though it had not been mowed for a season.

The house was of red brick, but the corners were formed from decorative brown sandstone. The same sandstone ran in courses across the front at half-story intervals and framed the large double doors and high windows on either side.

The front doors were accessed by a flight of stone stairs that narrowed as it ascended. On either side of the doorstep, stone pillars supported an overhanging balcony with a wrought-iron railing. A beautiful full-length triple-window composed of three French doors opened onto the balcony. Above it was another window in the attic dormer. The house had four levels, including the attic.

The most quixotic feature of its architecture were two slender towers that ascended on either side of the balcony. They were capped with tall conical roofs that had the appearance of witches' hats. These towers were too narrow to serve any practical function, and appeared to have been added to the house as a romantic afterthought.

Cartwright climbed the stair and turned to survey the wild, bleak moorland that stretched away to the horizon, with only a scattering of stunted trees to break its monotony. In the distance, several grouse flew up with a flurry of wings, then settled again a dozen paces further on in the tall browning grass. It was a curious feature of his dream house that it always seemed to be late autumn when he visited it.

He turned and tried the right side of the doors. It opened

easily, as he expected. The doors were always unlocked. He entered a spacious entrance hall with a floor of polished pink marble tiles. A curving staircase on the right side ran up to a banistered landing. Above his head hung a handsome chandelier of cut crystal. Archways opened on his either hand, leading into other rooms, and the hall continued past the stairs toward the rear of the house.

The floor seemed to turn slowly beneath his feet. Was it the effect of the incense or only his excitement at walking into the house while still fully awake?

"Hello? Is anyone here?" His thin voice echoed from the high ceiling of the hall. He did not know if he had spoken aloud or only in his thoughts.

As always, he began to stroll through the rooms, beginning with the library to his right. The floor-to-ceiling walnut shelves were filled with old books, most of them from the eighteenth and early nineteenth centuries. In spite of the emptiness of the house, there was no dust on the shelves. He pulled out a leather-bound volume at random and discovered it to be Addison's essays from the *Spectator*.

Replacing the book, he moved through sliding pocket doors into a large room he took for a music room, since it contained a grand piano. The music book that rested open on the wooden rack above the keyboard displayed a German folk song titled "Der treue Husar." He sat on the piano bench and ran his fingers haltingly through the scales. This was the extent of his musical ability. As a boy he had taken piano for a few months, but had been forced to move to another foster home before he developed any proficiency.

In the rear corner of the house was a games room, dominated by a billiards table with a slate bed covered in blue felt. He picked up the white cue ball and rolled it across the table. It bounced from the cushion and came back to his hand. On the wall was a dart board. In a tall wooden cupboard with glass doors hung croquet mallets and badminton rackets.

Cartwright crossed the rear hall into the serving kitchen, which was accessed from the lower floor by a steep and narrow servants' staircase. He moved forward on the other side of the house into a paneled dining room with a long table of polished mahogany. An ornately carved serving board stood along one wall. On the center of the table was a flower arrangement in a crystal bowl. The flowers must have been made of silk or paper, given the late month of the year in this dream country, but they looked freshly cut.

He was passing from the dining room into the drawing room when he heard a footstep on the floor above him. He froze motionless, listening. It came again, the distinct sound of someone walking across the floor above his head. This wasn't supposed to happen. In his dreams the house was always empty.

"Hello?" His voice quavered like that of a child.

The footfalls stopped, then began to move more purposefully across the floor. They were moving toward the upper landing, he realized. He felt a wild panic and ran through the drawing room and the formal front parlor into the entrance hall. Above him, he heard the scuff of shoe leather on the landing. He could not turn his head. With the blood thundering in his ears, he grabbed the brass latch of the front door and yanked it open.

4

He found himself still sitting on the chair, facing the blank wall of his study. His entire body was drenched in sweat and trembling as though from fever. When he could gather enough of his wits to look over his shoulder at the wall clock, he saw that more than an hour had passed. In some way he didn't understand he had dreamed while awake, and had actually entered the house of his dreams. Which was not empty!

To settle his jangling nerves, he brewed a pot of tea on his hotplate and thought about why the footfalls had frightened him so much. There was nothing inherently terrifying about them, yet the prospect of actually glimpsing the person who made them—or worse still, coming face-to-face with that person, whoever it might be—made him break out in another cold sweat.

For a time he debated with himself whether he should simply abandon the memory mansion, but then the hot tea began to soothe his nerves. It would be foolish to give up before he had even made a serious attempt to use the technique, he decided. He spent another hour studying his Greek, then prepared himself for sleep.

Just before getting into bed, he took some of the powered white frankincense and stirred it into a glass of red wine, than drank it quickly before the powder had a chance to settle. According to the book, this was an aid to memory. He wanted to see if the study he had done for the past hour would stick in his head if he slept on it with the aid of the potion. One important aspect of the art of memory was to fix facts in the mind just prior to sleep, so that the sleeping mind could order and retain them.

Sleep came almost at once. He found himself inside the mansion in the entrance hall, standing beneath the crystal chandelier. With a part of his mind he knew he was dreaming; but as is often the case with dreams, there was no sense of urgency about it. He made his usual slow circuit of the house, pausing in each room to fix symbols representing the Greek verb conjugations to the walls or place them on the tables and chairs.

Everything was peaceful and orderly. He became wholly absorbed in what he was doing. When the footfalls sounded over his head as he stood in the drawing room, they caused surprise. It was a moment before he could remember that he had heard them before. Again they crossed the floor above, slow and deliberate as they moved toward the rear of the house. There was something in their regular thud that provoked a sense of menace. They had an inevitability that threatened some dire event.

Had he been awake, he might have fled from the house, but in the dream he felt himself impelled against his will to climb the curved staircase to the upper level and make his way down the broad hallway on the left along the carpet runner that extended its full length. The carpet was a deep red, almost a purple, and thick enough that it supported his feet for an instant before crushing softly beneath them. His shoes made no sound at all as he walked along it toward an open bedroom door near the end of the hall.

The strangest thing happened. He found his body shrinking. The nearer he drew to the open door, the smaller he became, until the crystal knob of the door was level with the top of his head. He reached up to grasp it and saw that his hand was tiny. Its little fingers would not encircle the faceted crystal ball. Slowly, he pushed the door wider.

The tableau revealed within the bedroom held no meaning for him. A man and a woman lay in a brass bed with the rumpled sheet pushed down so that it covered only their lower legs. They were naked. The man had a full, curly head of sand-blond hair and a huge sandy moustache. He lay on top of the woman, thrusting into her with animal grunts as the sweat dripped from the point of his long nose onto her face, which was twisted in a mixture of pain and ecstasy. The only sounds were the grunts from the red-faced man.

As the door swung a little wider, he saw another man who stood at the foot of the bed with his back to the doorway. He wore a dark wool suit of an old-fashioned cut. His hair was also dark, neatly brushed to the side of his head. The oil that had been used to hold it into place gleamed beneath the light from the ceiling fixture.

I need to wake up, Cartwright thought. I need to wake up right now, or I will see something I do not wish to remember.

But the dream continued with the inevitable flow of a great river, and his mounting terror was impotent against it.

He watched the clothed man extend his arm toward the bed, and realized that he held a revolver. The hammer was cocked. The sound of the shot was like the crash of thunder. For a moment it stunned the lovers motionless. A little red flower bud opened its petals in the forehead of the woman and spread down her dead face, while her blue eyes stared aslant at nothing. Some rivulets of red ran into her slackly open mouth.

The naked man leapt from the bed as though galvanized and grabbed a corner of the sheet with one hand to cover his groin.

"What have you done? My God, what have you done?"

The clothed man slowly redirected the muzzle of the gun at his chest. The naked man shrank back into the corner of the room. His wildly staring eyes met Cartwright's. He pointed at the door.

"Think what you do, John. Your four-year-old son is watching."

The clothed man slowly turned to look at the doorway. For Cartwright, it was like looking into time's mirror. He saw himself as he would appear in his early thirties.

"Is he my son, Edward, or is he yours? How am I ever to

know?"

The naked man cowered still lower and pulled up the corner of the sheet to cover his cringing face. Without taking his eyes off Cartwright, the clothed man redirected the gun to his own right temple and pulled the trigger. A spray of blood and brains erupted from the opposite side of his head and spattered across the rose-patterned wallpaper. He crumpled like an empty suit that had slipped from its hanger.

Suddenly the house was dark. Cartwright found himself running down the upper hall toward the stairs. His body was still small, but larger than when he had stood in the open doorway. Now he was six years old. Footfalls thudded behind him, too heavy for the thick runner to muffle.

"Where are you, you little bastard? Don't think you can hide from me."

The words were slurred with drink. It was his Uncle Edward who pursued him, as he had done many times in the two years since becoming his guardian.

"You can't get out of the house," his uncle said with a malicious glee that was almost childlike. "I've locked the doors."

Cartwright knew from bitter experience the futility of trying to open the front or back doors. They were always locked. He darted through the library and the music room into the games room, looking for a place to hide that he had not used before. One by one, the lights began to turn on in the rooms behind him.

"Take off your trousers," the drunken man roared. "I'm going to fuck you raw."

Cartwright's eyes fixed on one of the guns that rested in a rack on the wall. It was the shotgun his uncle used for hunting grouse on the moors. With nerveless, fumbling fingers, he lifted it down. It felt immensely heavy. As the overhead light snapped on, he lifted its barrel toward the man who stood in the doorway in a black-and-gold striped bathrobe. His blond hair was still wet from his bath, and the ends of his moustache drooped long on either side of his cruel mouth.

His face twisted in amusement when he saw what Cartwright held.

"You stupid little shit, that gun's not even loaded."

The blast of the shotgun knocked Cartwright off his feet. The gun flew out of his hands. With his ears ringing from the concussion, he realized that his uncle's face had disappeared. His eyes, nose, and upper lip were no more than a bloody pulp. He felt a sudden surge of relief and began to cry.

His uncle's body did not fall to the floor. It turned its faceless head toward him. One by one, the lights in the rooms behind the man went out. When the light in the games room failed, the entire house was dark, but in some strange way Cartwright could still see his uncle as he slowly advanced. His body became a black silhouette edged with flickering blue fire.

"You can't kill me again," the shadow told him. "I'm already dead."

Suddenly Cartwright remembered everything. He began to scream.

5

The specialist entered the hospital room, trailed by six interns in their freshly starched white coats. He stopped at the side of a bed surrounded by a curtain that hung from a track on the ceiling. The head nurse drew the curtain aside to reveal an emaciated man who lay in the bed with a sheet tucked neatly over his chest. His thin face had been freshly shaved and still showed a slight redness from the straight razor. His gray hair was trimmed short. The hollows of his pale cheeks made his long nose stand forth with startling prominence.

The nurse stood to the side with a slight smile, only half listening to the droning voice of the specialist. She had heard his discourse about this patient at least several dozen times and almost had it memorized.

"The patient's name is Alan Cartwright. At nineteen years of age, while he was an undergraduate of King's College, Cambridge, he lapsed into a catatonic state. All attempts to revive him have been futile. . ."

The interns made notes on their clipboards as he talked, their young male faces bright with interest. After ten minutes or so he turned on his heel, and the interns followed after him like ducklings after their mother, all but one of them. A young East Indian with compelling dark eyes lingered by the bedside to finish his notes.

He noticed the nurse and flushed with embarrassment. He was still intimidated by the older nurses, who had so much more practical experience in medicine than he had. He was afraid of saying something that would make him sound like a fool.

"It must be quite a chore, taking care of him day after day," he said in precise, clipped words that held only a trace of his original accent.

"We're quite proud of him around here, actually," she admitted. "It's been a challenge keeping him fit."

"How long has he been here?"

"This is his twenty-seventh year."

The young intern whistled.

"That must be a world record."

She shrugged. "It may be. I don't think anyone has ever bothered to look it up."

"Electroconvulsive therapy has had no positive effect?"

She shook her head. "Of course, we would never have managed to keep him alive were it not for the new treatment methods that came out after the Great War in response to all the catatonic veterans. Shell shock, you know."

The intern regarded the shriveled body in the bed. He glanced sideways at the nurse.

"Aren't you ever alarmed by him?"

"I'm not sure I know what you mean," she said with a frown.

"Well, look at his face. I didn't even know a human face could twist that way."

"It's the result of muscular rigor, nothing more."

"But late on the night shift, when you come in here to check on him, don't you ever get—"

Cartwright began to mutter. The young doctor stared at him, then at the nurse.

"Is he waking up?"

She shook her head.

"He does that all the time. As nearly as we can judge, he's talking in his dreams."

The intern's eyes widened as he considered this.

"I hope the dreams are pleasant."

"Pretty dull, I'd say."

"Why do you say that?"

She laughed.

"Years ago the doctors brought someone in from the university to translate what he's saying. All he ever does is conjugate Greek verbs."

WHAT YOU DO NOT BRING FORTH

John Langan

In the right circumstances, Pete's daughter, Lee, is fond of telling people that her father always has at least one knife on him at all times. Since these circumstances tend to arise at larger events—book signings, readings, dinner parties—there is never a shortage of raised eyebrows, furtive glances between guests, murmurs of disbelief. At Lee's prompting, Pete shoves one hand into the front right pocket of his khakis or slacks and retrieves a folding knife whose handle is paneled with dark cheery wood. He opens the knife with his left hand, disclosing a shining blade whose shape resembles a miniature scimitar. He's known for writing novels that feature serial killers, most of whom favor knives, and the audience for his display is unsure whether the weapon is produced ironically or in earnest. The majority deem it a piece of theater, though a few make reference to the perils of living in the City. None of them could guess the reason for this knife and the one like it Pete keeps in his other pocket. For the matter, neither could his charming daughter.

That reason wears a brown fedora pulled low over his

brow and a tan trenchcoat with the collar tugged up, as if in imitation of every private eye in every film noir since the form took shape. Pete has never seen enough of the man's face to be able to describe it to, say, a police sketch artist. Only the eyes, deep set, and the top of the nose, dented above the bridge, as if it were struck with a blunt instrument or the edge of a hand, and failed to heal properly. The man's hands have remained hidden from view—at least, Pete thinks they have. He has a confused memory of seeing them in heavy gloves, which he cannot place and therefore does not trust.

It must be noted, Pete carried some form of knife long before his first glimpse of the man he has christened Alan Ladd. It would be more accurate to say that, the moment his gaze settled on the trenchcoated figure standing at the back of one of his readings, he was overcome by a sensation of such distress, such dread, that he stopped reading. He reached for a cup of water with a hand trembling so severely he spilled the water all over his shirt. Mumbling apologies, he brought the event to an immediate conclusion, retreating to a bathroom in the bookstore's stock room, then slipping out the back door. Half expecting the man to be waiting for him, he had one knife out and opened, his free hand on the other. The alleyway was empty, but as he hurried to the nearest subway station he understood that it was for this man that he had been arming himself for years, since he was a teen, earlier.

He did not speak to his therapist about Alan Ladd (a name he had selected not for any overwhelming resemblance between this man and the actor, but because Pete's glimpse of him had brought to mind the actor's furtive, hunted air in *This Gun for Hire*). At the time, he and Dr. Mobley were discussing a dream Pete recorded in the dream journal she had instructed him to keep. In this dream, he was trying to climb a stepladder to reach a cord hanging from a door set in the ceiling of the room he was in—which he had the strong impression was in his aunt and uncle's house outside Chicago. With each step higher he took, the ladder grew less steady, swaying from side to side as if the bolts and screws holding it together were dropping out of it. He knew with absolute certainty that a) he was going to fall and b) the consequence of his fall would be severe, possibly fatal. Despite this foreknowledge, he continued his ascent, gripping metal less and less firm to the touch. When he was almost at the rope handle, the door in the ceiling flapped down, clanging against the stepladder and releasing a cloud of large, parchment-colored moths into the room. The insects filled the air around him; he swatted at them, lost his balance, and plummeted to what should have been his death, but was instead to his awakening in his bed, pulse racing, pajamas soaked in sweat.

While Dr. Mobley would not commit to a definitive interpretation of his dream, it was apparent she saw it as an expression of Pete's anxieties about his continuing success as a writer, of his concern that whatever critical status he had achieved was in danger of slipping away, and suddenly at that. Given the facts of his life, the analysis was reasonable, even compelling. Yet Pete remained unconvinced by it. Where the doctor focused on the detail of the ladder, he was drawn to the door in the ceiling that had crashed open, the moths whose wings had fluttered against the backs of his hands, his cheeks, his ears. He had been climbing toward something, reaching for admission to whatever lay on the other side of the ceiling. Had that been only the moths? Or was there something beyond them? Each night following that of the dream, he went to bed telling himself that this time his dreams would return him to the room in (maybe) his aunt and uncle's house, where he would discover what the door in the ceiling concealed. That space, though, remained closed to him.

When he saw Alan Ladd standing at the back of the bookstore, Pete immediately connected him to the dream. It wasn't that he was part of the dream—what was waiting behind the ceiling door—so much as it was that he seemed in some way to *be* the dream, made flesh through a process Pete could not guess and set loose on the world. This was lunacy, of course, but his recognition of the fact did little to alter his sense of the fundamental rightness of his impression. It helped, he fancied, to account for the terror that continued to grip him each time he spotted the fedora and trenchcoat toward the rear of whatever space he was delivering his current reading in. After all, dreams were inherently irrational, knots of image and action that stood in for emotions and experiences writhing deep within the brain's folds.

Though he has yet to discuss Alan Ladd with his therapist, Pete has had a brief exchange with his daughter about the man. This took place after they participated in a panel discussion at the CUNY Graduate Center on the one hundred and fifteenth anniversary of the publication of Freud's *Interpretation of Dreams*. Pete talked about the significance of psychoanalysis to the literature of crime and horror in general, and of his novels in particular. Lee compared Freud's ideas concerning the significance of dreams to those of Jung, about whom she had published a well-received popular study. One of the other panelists, a bearded man with glasses of whose credentials Pete was uncertain, pronounced it an essential quality of dreams that they retained a degree of opacity to the dreamer. Even in cases of lucid dreaming, the bearded man went on, he had never encountered an instance in which the dreamer fully understood what was happening. "A dream does not explain itself to you," he said.

"Neither does life," Lee said.

"Life is but a dream," Pete said, adding, "Oh, sorry: merrily, merrily, merrily, merrily," which drew a laugh from the audience.

Afterwards, before he descended from the stage on which the panel had been seated, Pete saw Alan Ladd lurking at the rear of the auditorium. With as much grace as he could muster on legs gone wobbly, Pete retreated to the table behind which he had spent the past hour and lowered himself onto the chair he had just vacated. Catching sight of him there, Lee ran up the short flight of stairs to the stairs and rushed to his side. "Dad," she said, crouching beside him. "Are you all right?"

"No," he said, too agitated to lie to her.

"What's wrong? Is it your heart?"

"My heart?" he said. "No, my heart's fine. No." He shook his head. How to phrase this to her? "There's a man who's been coming to my events for a little while, now. He wears a hat, a fedora, and a trenchcoat. He stands at the back of whatever venue I'm at."

"That guy?" Lee said. "I thought he was a fan."

"A fan?"

"Yeah. He dresses the way the hero of *The Cellar* does at the climax—what was his name?"

"Baggins, Fred Baggins."

"Remember, he even thinks he looks like something out an old film noir. And then he winds up in the cellar of that bar, where he has the showdown with the cop—"

"Pforzheimer."

"Who's wearing a trenchcoat and fedora, too, right? Jesus, Dad, you wrote it. I saw this guy the first time he showed up at one of your readings. I figured he was playing dress-up—

cosplay, right?"

"He isn't," Pete said. "He's . . . dangerous. . ."

"What do you mean?" His daughter's brow lowered. "Has he threatened you? Is he stalking you?"

"Yes. Not the threatening, but I believe he is stalking me."

"Has he said anything to you?"

"Not one word." Pete waved his hand. The strength had returned to his legs. He stood. "Maybe you're right. It could be—maybe this fellow is a fan, and that's all."

"Don't get me wrong," Lee said, rising, "some of your fans are pretty creepy."

"Never mind," he said. "It's probably all in my head."

As the words left his mouth, Pete could taste their dishonesty. It wasn't so much that he was protecting Lee from a potential threat—she had been taking *krav maga* classes for a couple of years and had successfully incapacitated a man who had made the mistake of attempting to mug her. Besides, Alan Ladd didn't seem the slightest bit interested in anyone but Pete. No, what he wanted to preserve was his freedom to pursue this matter in whatever way he judged best. His daughter narrowed her eyes, a sure sign she suspected Pete of dissembling to her, but she did not follow her critical look with the usual statement masquerading as a question.

Since that night, every time Alan Ladd has put in an appearance at one of Pete's events, if Lee is present, he has noticed her noticing the man. On a couple of occasions, she has attempted to navigate the room to him, only to have some woman or man stop Lee to talk to her. No matter how short she cuts their conversations, by the time they're done Alan Ladd has slipped away. Although Pete keeps an eye on her during these moments—one hand in his pocket, knife in his grasp—he has not said anything to his daughter about her efforts to confront

Alan Ladd. He isn't sure she is aware he's been watching her. Nor has she raised the matter with him.

If he has preserved his freedom of action in regard to Alan Ladd, Pete has not decided how best to use it. He could hire a private detective to watch for the man at his next reading, tail him when he ducks out, trail him to whatever address he calls home, and use that location to unearth information about him. He could talk to Dr. Mobley about the intense dread Alan Ladd's appearance continues to evoke in him, work at digging down to the reasons for this. He could focus on ignoring the man. He could take a break from public life, test whether his absence might cause Alan Ladd to lose interest in him. Each option has its drawbacks, but this is not what keeps Pete from choosing among them. Rather, it's because he has a sense that, when he arrives at his course of action, he will do so all at once, in the heat of the moment. He will lift the phone and punch in the number of the private detective he Googled. He will lean forward in his chair and say to Dr. Mobley, "I want to talk to you about something." He will avoid looking in Alan Ladd's direction. He will send a group email to every venue at which he is scheduled to speak for the next twelve months, explaining that circumstances beyond his control require that he withdraw from all such things for the foreseeable future. Dr. Mobley has warned him against impulsive behavior, which has not done him any favors in the past; but Pete feels, somewhere below the pit of his stomach, whatever he is to do must be done in this fashion.

That Alan Ladd might escalate their encounters drastically, dramatically, is a possibility Pete entertained a good deal the first times he saw the man but which, as time has slipped by, he has worried about less, on the principle that, if Alan Ladd were going to do anything more, he would have by now. Yet the next time Pete sees the man, this is exactly what he does. This happens in a small theater in Brooklyn, where Pete is part of a discussion of *Spellbound*. For the length of the panel—which includes Lee and a bearded man he recognizes from a previous event—the fedora and trenchcoat are absent from the audience. Nor does Alan Ladd put in an appearance during the question-and-answer period, which cheers Pete so much he remains in the theater to talk to a pair of young writers who have taken the train from Connecticut to attend the panel. After he has signed the copies of his books they have produced, posed for pictures with them, and sent them on their way, he climbs the stairs to the stage and the table where the panelists were seated, on which, he realized, he left his dream journal. He brought the book because some of its more bizarre imagery made a good fit with the film's famous sets, and while he has come to doubt the therapeutic usefulness of this record of his brain's nighttime activity, he thinks that a few of its scenarios might contain the germs of possible stories, even a short novel. As his fingertips brush the journal's leather cover, he hears footsteps hurrying up one of the theater's aisles. Lee, perhaps, coming to ask him what's taking so long. He turns, a quip at the ready, and sees Alan Ladd striding toward him.

Pete's response is immediate, automatic. He runs. Journal in one hand, he bolts for the back of the stage, where a red EXIT sign glows over a door. Pete slams into the pressure bar across the door, flinging it wide. He expected to emerge into an alley behind the theater; instead, he's at the top of a flight of wooden stairs. There's no other choice: he races down them. Overhead, the door booms as Alan Ladd heaves it open. At the foot of the stairs, a brick corridor stretches left and right. Pete chooses right, runs along a passageway barely wide enough to admit him, his flight lit by weak light bulbs caged every ten feet or so. Underfoot, the floor angles down. Behind him, Alan Ladd's shoes thwack one-two one-two.

The corridor empties into a large room. Thick brick pillars support a sagging ceiling. Wood crates stacked two and three high line the walls, their sides stenciled with words Pete cannot make out. His eyes dart around the room, searching for another way out of it. He must be under whatever building is next to the theater. (What is that? A bar?)

Coat flapping, Alan Ladd erupts into the room. Too late, Pete thinks that he should have used one of the pillars to conceal himself. He drops the dream journal, fumbles in his pocket for the knife there. Alan Ladd advances. There's something in his right hand. Black, snub-nosed—a pistol. He brings it up as he closes the distance to Pete, who has his knife out and is trying to open it with trembling fingers. The blade sweeps out and clicks into place. Alan Ladd is an arm's length away, pointing the muzzle of the gun at the center of Pete's chest. With a grace of which he would not have believed himself possessed, Pete steps forward and to the right, catching Alan Ladd's wrist with his left hand and sweeping the knife into the man's chest with his right hand. In quick succession, he stabs Alan Ladd half a dozen times, while twisting the man's wrist sharply, causing him to release the gun. Pete lets go of him, and Alan Ladd sits down hard. There is surprisingly little blood on the knife, which Pete holds in front of him as he sidesteps to where the pistol lies on the floor. He doesn't want to chance stooping to retrieve it, so he kicks it skittering to the side.

He is exuberant, exalted; he feels as if he could run a hundred miles, a thousand, skip across continents, seas. He should speak, say something to Alan Ladd, who sits hunched over, his head titled low, dark patches spreading across the breast of his trenchcoat. Now is the time to demand the man explain himself, account for his relentless presence. But his victory has placed Pete momentarily beyond language.

It is Alan Ladd who breaks the silence between them. In a voice that sits low in his mouth, he says, "I could not bring you forth."

"What?"

"If you cannot bring forth what is inside you," Alan Ladd says, "it will destroy you. So."

His words ring in Pete's head like the tolling of enormous bells, loosening his tongue. "What are you talking about? Who are you? Why have you been following me? What is it you want?"

"How many nights—" The man coughs, spraying blood over his coat. "I've sat in the diner, pen in hand, notebook open, trying the waitresses' patience with my endless cups of coffee."

"I don't—"

"Minotaur," Alan Ladd mumbles. "You were there, hiding between blue lines. I could feel you, roaming the long corridors." He sags forward, vents a liquid breath, and is still.

"Goddammit," Pete says. Suddenly he is deflated, exhausted. Nausea tightens his throat. He considers the blade in his hand. No doubt the police will want it. He crouches, sets the knife on the floor. He looks at Alan Ladd, whose face remains obscured by the fedora. Pete shifts into a half-kneel, reaching his hand to lift the hat's brim.

The instant his fingers brush its edge, the hat bursts into a cloud of fluttering insects, of moths, their furred bodies the color of antique paper. Alan Ladd is gone, the space in which he died full of the moths and their frantic motion. Pete scrambles backward, lurches to his feet, and flees along the passage that brought him here. Moths cling to his shirt, his hair.

For Fiona, and for Peter Straub

THE BARRIER BETWEEN

W. H. PUGMIRE

The ancient oak was a freakish thing of monstrous size and shape. Its trunk was of an inordinate breadth, and yet it seemed, seen from a distance, stunted, as if the thick and weighty limbs expanding over it had caused the trunk to shrink into yielding earth. In one place at the base of its trunk a gathering of bumps or small burls formed what resembled a weird crouching beast, and something in its form so disturbed onlookers that they were unwilling to approach the patriarch of wood. There were some few, however, who found the mammoth tree so compelling a sight that they mustered the courage to draw near and touch its bark; and they were puzzled by the litter of small animals' bones scattered around the trunk, remains of what might have been beasts brought as votive offerings. On this late afternoon, some few of those white bones had been strewn onto the small cot that had been set up beneath the tree and were being played with by the bending toes of the nude creature reclining on the mattress.

"I want your head hanging over the mattress and your hair

falling to the ground, as in Fuseli."

The reclining figure frowned. "I thought we were replicating Abildgaard—isn't that why I'm naked?"

"I'm combining the two—they studied together in Rome, you know. Fuseli's influence was profound; you can see it in Abilgaard's painting of Culmin's ghost, where the specter's pose is similar to the woman in Fuseli. Just a few more shots, Basil, while we have this light. That's an odd glaze up yonder, isn't it, shimmering just behind the sheen of muted sunlight?"

The lean fellow on the cot used his feet to push his body nearer to the rim of the mattress and combed fingers through long pale hair so that it billowed to the ground. Dashen Wilcott pressed his eye to the camera lens and studied his model, intrigued once more by the macabre image of the lounging figure that almost resembled a fresh cadaver. The camera clicked and whirred a few more times, and then Dashen stepped to the cot and bent to smooth his hands through the mass of hair. A whitish appendage reached for the photographer's face and stroked it. "Look how black your skin looks compared to my bleached hand—black as midnight. You smell strange."

"That's not me. There's something in the air, some piquant aroma that you can almost taste." Distant thunder sounded. "Damn, a storm is approaching. I wanted to change lens and try capturing you in shadow. Slip into your clothes and help me carry this cot to the pickup." They worked together, taking the lightweight cot and its small mattress to the bed of Dashen's dilapidated truck. By the time they were seated inside the vehicle the first heavy raindrops began to fall onto the windshield.

"What are you doing?" Basil asked as Dashen opened the door and climbed out of the truck. Not answering his friend's query, the photographer went to stand before the tree and study its sinister appeal. Below the long thick branches just above the width of trunk—limbs that were themselves of an uncommon width—was a cluster of very thin and long branches adorned with small bright auburn leaves. Dashen watched the leaves begin to tremble in the rising wind; and then he studied the lower section of the immense trunk, where the curious mass of bumps formed what seemed the semblance of a crouching beast. As he studied the thing it began to blur, like some form composed of coiling smoke and shadow. He became conscious of the figure that knelt beside him and watched as Basil rose to his feet with a small fragment of bone clamped between his lips. Behind the young model, the curious sheen of queer color that had earlier been noticed slowly rotated, like an image seen through a kaleidoscope. Dashen stepped backward, slowly, until he felt the heaviness of the freakish tree behind him. He pressed his back against the tree as the texture of its bark softened and allowed him entrance. Raising his arms, he watched the small red leaves that adhered to them twitch in moaning wind.

§

Dashen pushed through the crowded gallery until he was able to link arms with Arcadia Tallow, who stood before the gigantic print that was Dashen's contribution to the evening's exhibition.

"This is superb, my dear," the patron told him as she motioned to his work. "The rich antique brass tone of your tree is very fine, especially as it contrasts so absolutely with the deathlike tenor of your model's skin. Is the bone in your model's mouth an aesthetic nod to Ardois-Bonnot's series of 1928?"

"Who?"

"The French painter who did a series of canvases showing cadaverous females who all had human bones clamped between their lips. No? How strange. I do like how you've used Weisel's nightmarish imp there, with that queer hazy effect that makes the creature so indefinite. Oh dear, you're looking confused again. Have you been drinking? You know how that affects you." She moved nearer to the print and motioned to the figure composed of burls on the monstrous tree's trunk. "That's Mr. Shugoran, isn't it? I didn't know you two were acquainted. He's right over there, in the Hildegaard Alcove." Clutching his small hand, the woman tugged him to a long narrow room that was oddly bereft of people. "Not a very popular exhibit, eh?" she murmured to him. "But, oh, isn't it sublime!? It copies, of course, Thrivier's *Le Cauchemar*, although replacing white marble with black. Weisel's model here doesn't look *quite* as orgasmic as her French sibling—and his devil lacks wings, as does yours. Are you all right, dear? You look rather queer."

Dashen moved past three others who were looking at the sculpture and raised a hand, as if preparing to touch the female figure that reclined on its bed of ebony marble; but then he backed away from the sculpture and gazed in silence at the daemon depicted as squatting on the woman's stomach, and as he observed the thing he shuddered. Feeling eyes upon him, Dashen looked up to see two persons who were staring at him; and then the smaller of the two turned to Arcadia, acknowledging her with a smile as she stepped beside Dashen and placed a hand on his shoulder. With the assistance of a short cane of crimson wood, the figure hobbled toward them. Dashen, who was himself of small stature, felt his flesh chill at the sight of the runtish figure that limped nearer.

"Dashen, let me introduce you to Zaman Shugoran. Zaman, this is Dashen Wilcott, the photographer." Shugoran held out a limp hand, which Dashen clasped as he took in the full-length fur coat in which the dwarf had draped himself. Eyes of yellow tinge shimmered within deep sockets, and twisted teeth marred what was supposed to be a smile. The little hand suddenly tightened its hold, and Dashen winced as that hold became painful. Yet he could not force his hand away, for he was riveted by the cruel expression on the imp's hateful visage. Shugoran's lips curled in mirth, as if the fellow recognized Dashen's unease and delighted in it.

"Pleased to meet you," the tiny creature said in an accent that the photographer could not place. "You see what sly Weisel has done with me," and he indicated the sculpted fiend. "How like him to be late for this unveiling."

They were aware of some new person entering the small room, and Dashen quivered a little when he saw that it was Basil. Escaping Shugoran's grasp, he rushed to the model and guided him out of the room.

"That was rude, Dashen, not to introduce me to your friends. Wasn't that the wealthy patron Arcadia Scott?"

"Never mind that, I had to get away from that fiend. By god, it's like meeting Fuseli's devil in the flesh! That fur coat could have been his hide."

"What on earth are you muttering about? Gracious, you're rattled. Have you been drinking? Not wise, considering your past. Come on, I want you to introduce me to your friends."

"No friends of mine," the other answered; and then he stopped and gawked at Basil's hair. "What the devil have you done?"

"Don't you like it? I suppose you didn't notice me collecting some of those smaller bones near the tree at our shoot. I thought it would look rather goth to tie them into my hair. I've had any number of compliments."

"You look damn silly."

Basil's eyes narrowed in annoyance. "You're in a dreary mood." Sweeping past the photographer, he disappeared into the display room.

"Damn silly fool," Dashen muttered, and then he espied the refreshment table and went to grab a plastic cup of peach champagne. That first cup was drained too quickly, and so he picked up another and downed its contents. A couple came to greet him, and he mumbled replies as he reached for a third cup. Leaning against a wall, he watched the room's light fade to a soft blue glow that reminded him of a tinted print of *The Cabinet of Dr. Caligari* that he had screened at some art cinema house. He could easily be in such a film now, given how the walls around him were beginning to tilt. Carefully pressing one hand to the wall so as to secure his posture, Dashen made his way to the small chamber where he had encountered the outré dwarf. Yet he hesitated uncertainly; for there was a light oozing from the room, and it reminded him of the unearthly sheen of extraordinary color he had witnessed during the photo shoot at the monstrous tree. He moaned a little as the place before him began to gyrate.

Cautiously, Dashen crept back to the gallery where a few souls still gathered. At first he didn't recognize the indistinct figures before him, and the scene seemed more hallucination than sane reality. He had a hunch that his senses had been infected; indeed, the silence in the chamber felt like a heavy and oppressive weight inside his ear, causing his brain to ache. He nodded to two acquaintances whose features solidified before him, Gabryel and Isola, and thought that Gabe, with his hatchet face and red goatee, looked especially satanic in the queer illumination of the room. Turning to look at the figure reclining on the stone bed, he was confused to find that it was white, where before it was atramentous. The cloudy form that squatted on the pale figure's chest was dark indeed, and its face seemed to shift and coil. The eyes within that formless face contained the perplexing shimmering anti-color that seemed to be hunting Dashen. The fiend's tapered ears twitched a little as it bent to untie one of the bones attached to the reclining figure's mauve hair. The oppressive quietude became a spear of silence that stabbed into Dashen's brain, causing his quivering lips to part. His oppressive howling was but a momentary thing, for it was stopped when the dark devil pushed a glistening white bone into the mortal's wretched mouth.

§

Mild electric light greeted his opening eyes, and Dashen found himself in his own small bedroom, the walls of which had been painted dark red. Long green curtains before an opened window moved in silent breeze. Isola was perched beside him on the mattress, and Gabryel occupied a wooden chair that had been placed beside the bed. The young woman's gypsy face broke into a smile. "Ah, there you are, back with us." Dashen tried to speak, but his confused brain could find no language. The woman shook her head and ran a soft hand across his brow. "Just rest. We had the devil's own time maneuvering you to your apartment."

Gabe leaned forward a little. "I thought you'd given up the booze, my brother."

"No—it wasn't the champagne. It was that damn imp and that unwholesome wheel of light. God, my head is still spinning."

"You need to sleep a little more. We'll leave you alone, unless you feel the need for company."

"No, I'll be all right. Basil will probably show up eventually.

He always does."

"Who?"

"The boy I used as model in my photograph—there." Dashen pointed to one wall, the majority of which was taken up with an enlarged print of the photograph that had been his contribution to the gallery's current show.

"You mean the mannequin? The one you keep in your grandmother's wardrobe closet?"

Dashen frowned in confusion. Gabryel rose and walked to a tall cabinet that had been painted a pastel yellow and opened one of its slim doors, and the room's unnatural light reflected on the sleek plastic of the figure that leaned inside the armoire. Clutching at the figure's throat, Gabe shook it playfully and then lifted it out of the cabinet and waltzed with it around the room. Isola then helped him to place the thing beside their friend in his bed.

"When did you weave those bones into its hair?" Isola asked. "Looks rather macabre."

When they saw that Dashen could not reply, the girl patted his head and bent to kiss his brow. "We'll leave you with your plaything, dear. Get some rest." Reaching out, she took hold of Gabryel's hand, and Dashen watched as they backed into the shadows of the room and disappeared.

He moved his head a little and hated the nearness of the mannequin's face to his, the pale plastic of which seemed lurid in the unnatural light of the chamber. With jerky movement, Dashen covered the faux countenance with a hand and was about to push the object away from him when its surface seemed to ripple slightly beneath his palm. Something kissed his hand.

"Take away your hand, for pity's sake," spoke a muffled voice.

Oppressed with sudden fear, Dashen jumped from the room

and fled to the wall that was covered with his photographic art. Basil smiled, lifted himself from the bed, and floated to him. He touched one hand to the image of the monstrous tree. "Such a magnificent ancestor, lad. How fortunate for you to be numbered in its family."

"I have no family," Dashen moaned, turning away from the wall and noticing the dark mound that huddled on his cot. He whispered, "There's someone in my bed."

"Oh, don't disturb him," Basil responded. "He's dreaming."

The boy suddenly loomed before the photographer, so near that Dashen could see the wheels of strange color that gyrated in the youth's eyes. Dashen shut his own eyes as that unwholesome glow began to leak from Basil's eyes and permeate the place. There was a noise of clacking, and intoxicating fragrance that swam through nostrils. Lips touched his eyelids, which then lifted. They stood within a field, assaulted by windstorm that caused the bones in Basil's hair to swing against one another. The noise thus produced might have been some dainty danse macabre, and Basil, seeming to take his cue from the clattering, waltzed away from his companion, toward the monstrous tree and the dainty cot below it. Walking to that cot as Basil reclined upon it, Dashen saw that it was littered with bits of bone. Basil took up one shard of death and began to weave his hair around it.

The tree had altered, horribly, now being composed of what looked like the conjoined bodies of burnt corpses, each of which had one clean white bone clamped between its jaws. Dashen thought the thing resembled a ghastly cousin to Dali's *In Voluptas Mors,* one that was completely lacking voluptuousness. One lower section of the thing separated from the rest and crept onto Basil's chest, where it squatted and winked at Dashen.

"Good day, good sir," was Zaman Shugoran's greeting. "Come nearer, we have your gift." Dashen could not move at first, for his eyesight had become transfixed on the distant wheel of coiling light that coaxed him toward it. "Oh—the lurid light of reason," sneered Shugoran. "It so mars the madness of this place, don't you find? Ignore it. Here, let me give you this, and then you can find your place within the puzzle."

Dashen knelt beside the cot and leaned his head to the cloudy fiend, from which the rich perfume of the place seemed to emanate—that sweet stench of rot. The piece of bone looked unnaturally bright in the devil's dark hand, so bright that it hurt to look on it; and so Dashen shut his eyes as the black cloudy hand pushed the bone between his lips that did not protest. When something touched his face, Dashen parted his eyes once more and saw that the splintered hand of one of the corpses that composed the tree had fallen to him. Taking hold of that hand, the dark man allowed it to lift him into the company of carnage.

SLEEP HYGIENE

Gemma Files

Shut your eyes, let your breathing slow. Then follow the map, from any direction, and you will find you are there now, in that place—*your* place. Look to the horizon; something is coming.

A short list of things you may do when it comes:

Cry.

Scream.

Flinch.

Shut your eyes again.

Find yourself unable to shut your eyes.

Find yourself short of breath, or unable to breathe entirely.

Hear your own heart in your ears.

Hear absolutely nothing.

See absolutely nothing.

Feel your face go blank.

Feel your mind go blank.

Watch everything cloud over, then go black.

Find yourself elsewhere, discovering you've lost time.

Think: "I must have fainted." Have no proof this is true.

Have no proof otherwise.

Wake up. Fall asleep once more. Dream. Lose yourself. Wake up. Repeat.

Repeat, repeat, repeat. . .

. . . until, one night, you never wake up again.

§

"I need you to make a map of whatever landscape you find yourself in, next time you're there," Gracie Hollander told me, to which I frowned. "Keep a dream diary, you mean," I replied. But she just shook her head.

"No, I don't," she said. "I mean—do that too, obviously. But this is something different."

It was only our second consultation, officially. My regular GP had recommended her to me, after I finally admitted I'd gone a month and a half without sleeping more than a third or quarter of the night: fallen asleep at three, or four, or five, always knowing I'd have to be up again before eight. Sometimes I'd steal a nap in the afternoon, then pay for it—get the bulk of my day's work done between seven and eleven, feel mounting fatigue suddenly permeate me like a drug injection and brown the fuck out, sleep from noon to two before waking again with groggy surprise to my iPhone's warbling alarm tone, mouth gummed and cheek sheet-printed, hair sweat-stuck up in horns. And when midnight finally rolled around, I'd start the cycle all over again: take a bath, brush my teeth, lie down whether I wanted to or not, and force myself to keep my eyes damn well shut while I took long, slow breaths through the nose, willing my monkey-mind silent: *let go, let go, let GO.* Could count on one hand the times that worked as a strategy, but it didn't ever seem to stop me trying.

At least I live alone, I often caught myself thinking. *Nobody but myself to inconvenience with this sad, stupid shit.* Still, this was no sort of comfort at all in the long run; the way I lived—endured, existed—probably wasn't that different from the way anyone else around me did, except for the fact that they might be dealing with it better. Because loneliness is this century's true disease, with every other problem just a symptom of the same.

Anyhow. My doctor had told me I couldn't go on much longer this way without damaging myself irreparably, and I agreed, having no other option. So off to Gracie I was sent, for lessons in what her employers at the Sleep Habits Clinic apparently called sleep hygiene.

"Think of sleep as a destination," she said, sketching freehand with a soft charcoal pencil on the paper she'd placed between us, after already ticking off the usual checklist of pro-somnolence habits to cultivate: don't eat after six P.M., drink nothing caffeinated, start a wind-down routine that involved turning off all my devices, taking a bath, making sure my bedroom was light-tight. "A place securely located in time and space, with fixed coordinates. As if you could only find your way back there twice in a row, you could retrace your steps the same way forever and never get lost again."

"Program it into my mental GPS," I suggested, not actually trying to be facetious. But she shot me a pointed glance, so I fell silent.

The resultant map was divided into quarters and the path she drew meandered through all four in roughly circular fashion, spiral-form, like the world's easiest-to-beat maze. The terrain itself was intentionally generic—upside-down Vs for mountains, looping scribbles for forests, a dashed white space for grasslands with wandering lines for rivers, a tiny shaded-in lake and a wooded island in the middle—but came out with a weird vividness nonetheless; either Gracie was a born artist or she'd done this so often she had it down to a formula, an idea I found somewhat troubling.

I was no stranger, after all, to the concept of lending supposedly important tasks only a portion of my full attention. Though that was less a choice on my part, by this time, than a simple necessity: the only way I knew of to preserve what was left of my mind as the wall between waking and sleep grew ever more flexible, bulging darkly with the shadows of things that might lie beyond and stretching my life out recklessly around the damage that was left behind, like some slow-forming, paratemporal bruise.. . . .

"—based mine on Strawberry Island, up in Lake Simcoe," Gracie said, indicating the central island with her eraser, as I belatedly forced myself to focus in on her voice once more, recalled to myself from yet another one of those increasingly-too-frequent microsleep episodes, apparently by the sharpening ring of her tone alone. "I used to go there as a kid, so it's extra-easy to summon, a great little anchor. You might want to use someplace closer, a point on the Toronto Islands maybe, or whatever works for you. The key is, it has to be a location that's an overall *pleasant* memory, yet has some clear element of separation from your normal life. What kind of places do you normally dream about?"

I shrugged. "Honestly, I don't remember. When I sleep at all, I'm *out*—completely inert. Maybe I don't see anything."

"Unlikely. You'd have other symptoms if you really didn't dream." Gracie tapped her pencil against her teeth. "Can you remember faces?"

"What? Yeah, sure. Of course."

"Okay, good, then your brain probably isn't damaged."

Probably? I furrowed my brow at her as she went on. "True complete dream loss is associated with focal, acute-onset cerebral harm—hemorrhage, thrombosis, trauma. Charcot-Wilbrand syndrome, specifically characterised by visual agnosia and loss of ability to mentally recall or 'revisualize' images: face-blindness, in other words, which can be triggered by lesions in the parietal lobe or the right fusiform gyrus. What you have sounds more like being so tired overall you just forget your dreams as soon as you wake up, which is a far better deal, because we can fix that."

"How?"

"Oh, by using memory tricks to build you a personal dreamland, one worth the exploration; the more attractive we make sleep as a process, the longer you'll want to spent there, so we make it into a reward, not a chore." She gave me a smile. "I know it sounds like mumbo-jumbo, but trust me, it really does work—so long as you don't use scepticism as an excuse to be half-assed about it, that is."

"I have no plans in that direction," I said dryly.

"Excellent." She scribbled something on her prescription pad. "I'm also prescribing a drug regimen, short but sweet, just to help kick things off—a mild sedative combined with a *very* mild hallucinogen, so you won't have to work too hard. Stop by the pharmacy on your way out."

Me being who I am—born and raised in a paved-over former Paradise turned current parking lot, Br'er Fox—I opted to make my own dream map strictly urban, not rural. I picked the quarters of Toronto I knew best, then strung them along a mental subway-loop, from least to most interesting: Rosedale, the Yonge-Dundas downtown core, Distillery District, Queen West Village, the Annex. A favourite used bookstore became my anchor-point, the end of my quest; it was the place where I felt most relaxed and comfortable in real life, so why not? Good as any other.

Remember, this was all theoretical at this point. Remember, too, how I didn't really expect that to change anytime soon.

Gracie studied my map for a moment, frowning slightly. "You may not end up where you want to, following this," she told me, at last. I shrugged again.

"I'm not sure I expect to end up anywhere, to tell the complete truth," I replied. To which she eventually simply quirked an eyebrow and smiled.

"We'll see, I suppose," she said.

§

That night, I lay down after taking my first pill (one nightly and no more, thirty minutes before bed, absolutely *no* mixing with alcohol) and shut my eyes, expecting nothing but the usual: a shallow handful of hours spent knotted in on myself, teeth grinding, hands fisted. Light leaking in from outside, gradually bleaching my eyelid-darkness red. Morning's familiar despair.

Before Gracie, my idea of "good sleep" had been simple darkness at worst, nothing at best—a glitch, a blink, lost time. Followed, if God was good, by a refreshing sense of physical renewal: laxness without lassitude, no aches or pains, no hangover. I had some vague idea that once upon a time, long ago in distant childhood, I'd almost always woken up happy, sharp, ready to jump up and get at it, whatever it might be. That that had once been my *natural state,* the rule, not the exception. But it seemed so frankly impossible these days, I barely spared the matter a thought anymore. Just composed myself yet again, ready to suffer.

Instead, without any clear sense of how it even might have

happened, I found myself abruptly . . . elsewhere.

People I'd overheard talking about their dreams always claimed that half the time they couldn't tell they'd been having one, except in hindsight. Interactions with dead relatives, talking animals and singing flowers, surreal landscapes, ordinary objects suddenly converted to starkly awesome fear-totems, flying while falling, falling while flying—it all just got taken in stride somehow; the abnormal normalised. Some put it down to simple neurology, a side effect of their brain's effort to protect itself proactively against a wholesale invasion of the uncanny, installing filters, building walls. The mental flinch before the equally mental bruise, unprovably skull-shrouded, invisible even on MRI or X-ray.

Whatever you see behind your shut lids must still come from you, though, right? I mean, where else? And that's why it always seems so familiar, even when it's anything but.

Suddenly snapping conscious—or seeming to—and finding myself footsore yet upright, Achilles tendons stretched out and calves trembling slightly, wavering heavy-ankled in the centre of an open, roughly circular, eerily quiet block of wilderness: thick grass, scattered trees (elm, birch, maple), hummocks, hills, and ivy-draped cliffs. Nothing unnatural, literally, yet all of it strangely regular, as though laid out on a grid. All of it with a very slight touch of design.

Above, the sky hung striated, red and green and grey. The air smelled of ash, furze underfoot coarse as hair, dew-greasy. I wasn't wearing any shoes in the dream, so when I stepped forward I felt something hidden jut up under my toes—hard, uneven. The submerged cobbles of a long-dead street, thrust apart by dirt and overlaid with mulch, then furred over yet once more by crop after fallow crop of wind-blown seeds.

Peering around, eyes narrowed; feeling the sun on my face,

the wind at my back, a fresh cool breeze with the mounting chill of deeper shadow barely hidden underneath. And thinking, while I did: *I know* this place, *though I very palpably do* not *know this place, not in any way, shape, or form . . . feel deep in my soul that I've been here before, even as I know for a fact that I've never been here at all.*

Ridiculous. No one had ever been there, I realised later on, back in the waking world. Because that place didn't exist, had never existed. I was—

—almost sure.

Some people claim they can make themselves wake up the moment they understand they must be dreaming, but I hadn't been aware of my nighttime explorations anything like long enough to learn *that* trick. The only viable alternative plan, I decided, was to pick a random direction and simply start walking until something stopped me, so that's exactly what I did: vaguely right, sort of diagonal, possibly south. I followed the dead road's corkscrew track wherever I found it, trying not to trip, as the cartoon sky roiled above me.

No insects. No animals. No human noises, however distant.

Eventually, after who knows how long, a particularly sharp turn snagged me and I stumbled, almost going down on one knee; my hand met the largest chunk thus far palm-first, wetting itself with what I thought at first was blood, until I wiped it on my pants—too dark, too shiny. Oily asphalt and gravel with a forked line of white paint scored down one side, like the broken pieces of roadway you see around every pothole in Toronto during the summer roadwork season. And with that, the whole scene snapped into . . . not focus exactly, but clarity, the picture hidden inside the illusion.

This *was* my city, it turned out. Or it had been.

That flat green square off to my right, great mounds of grass-covered rubble on every other side, intersected by waving, urine-coloured stands and sprays of weeds: it was Yonge Street and Dundas, the junction, but reduced to long-empty wreck and ruin, digested by wilderness. I turned slowly in place, three hundred and sixty degrees, overlaying Toronto's downtown on top of this wasteland and seeing it match, point for point. Even then, I don't remember feeling horror, grief, or any of the other things you'd expect, simply a vague confusion. Senseless; no sense. Nonsense.

I only saw the temple once I'd completed my full circuit.

Set in the far corner of the flat sward that had once been Yonge-Dundas Square—and I was absolutely certain it hadn't been there when I'd first looked around—it looked more like an amphitheatre than anything else, a sunken cup surrounded by concentric walls with an empty space down in the middle. There was nothing like an altar: no signs or images, no ikons, only a circular hole in the centre like a beehive turned inside out. But by the time I was standing in it—

(*And when the hell had I done that? Walked over, stepped in? Why was I there now?*)

—the silence became even deeper: cathedral, funereal. A low grey hum. Cold air breathed from that black gap at my feet, whispering up the broken steps I saw spiralling down into it; discoloured wine-vomit splotches ringed it, sunk deep into the stone, the stains round a dead drunk's mouth. And here I felt my stomach clench for the first time, coldly filing in with fear, or its dimmest echo. Thinking dully: *Please. Not down there.*

Of course, I went. Trudging down the steps, into the cold, the black. Down, and down, and down, until I was too exhausted even to imagine turning around to climb back up. Which might well have been why I didn't scream when the stone vanished under my feet, when I fell face-first into the dark. Why I only screamed when I dimly began, at long last, to see exactly what I was falling *towards*. . .

. . . but here I lost it, memory falling from my mind to shatter like a dropped dish, as I jackknifed awake with hammering heart, burning eyes, and raw-rasping throat. I clenched my hands before me, pressed to my breastbone, gulping down air, hunched amid twisted, sodden sheets. The awful colour of the light that had swelled around me—some horrid, poisonous shade of yellow-green—lingered on my retinas like the after-flash of a strobe.

Thinking: *Something, coming. Something is. Coming.*

(*What?*)

"Jesus," I croaked aloud, half wanting to weep. Yet not able to, not then.

Not now either.

§

Gracie was silent for more than a few seconds after I told her all this the next day.

"Well," she said at last, "let's focus on the positive. Even with the interruption, you got a total of eight hours sleep last night, for the first time in . . . how long?"

"That was the *antithesis* of 'restful,' Gracie," I said flatly.

"Yes, but it's an amazing improvement for your first night. And it means we can write off the possibility of brain injury."

"Really? 'Cause if this is the cure, I think I'd rather have the damage." I leant forward, prodding the map between us with my finger. "I don't ever want to go back there, map or no map. I *won't*."

"Then you don't have to." Gracie held up her hands, palms out. "Don't like this map? Draw another." She shuffled it into a nearby file folder, grabbed her pad, and scribbled a few notes. "I'll tweak your 'scrip, too—we may not need the hallucinogen as much as I thought."

"That's it?" I demanded. "Aren't we supposed to, like, go over the dream? Figure out what it means?"

Gracie shrugged. "We could if you want, but . . . honestly, that strikes me as a distraction." She closed the pad and leaned forward again, looking earnest. "Alex, I know this is difficult. But believe me, it'll all be worth it in the end."

I let out my breath in a sigh. "Fine," I said, picking up the sketchpad and another pencil, and turned to a blank page.

§

This time, the map had been chronological rather than geographical: I'd sketched out all the houses I'd ever lived in, from a tiny apartment out in Brampton with my father through various Torontonian townhouses and converted, semi-detached units, to the current condo. When I shut my eyes and found myself standing in the marble-tiled lobby of my own building, I folded my arms—the mental semblance of them, anyhow—in deep satisfaction.

It was only when I passed by the open door of the building's coffee lounge that I caught a glimpse of grass with a telltale flash of stone hidden under it, heard the low grey sound of a hollow wind. The shock hit me in right in my stomach like a punch; I actually wobbled on my feet, then turned and ran.

Maybe if I'd had more experience dreaming, I'd have known not to expect that tactic to work. Or maybe not—people do seem to keep on trying to extricate themselves from repetitive nightmares, however useless it always proves. One way or the other, the effort proved fruitless: after what felt like a quarter of an hour spent crossing the lobby, I hauled open the main double doors and staggered out, only to find myself right back onto that flat plain, which looked even wider this time, stretching from horizon to horizon like images of the prairies in winter. Yellowish-grey corn stalks, harvest's detritus, whipping in the wind; gangrene-coloured clouds racing by overhead.

I spun, and my building was gone. But the temple was there instead, of course, slap-bang in the middle of the flatland. Ring of grey stone, a black crater at its heart, cold air perceptibly welling up from the dark, the cup, the well. And the stairs, going down.

Oh, God.

Don't know if I said it or thought it; didn't help, either way. Tried to run once more in the other direction, till I was gasping and dizzy, only to look up and find the temple back in front of me again. Tried yet one more time, closing my eyes, not stopping until I stumbled over that gap and nearly fell down the stairs, clinging to the side with both hands. At which point it frankly just didn't seem worth fighting any more.

Muscle memory led the way, unprompted and unwanted, as I tested each step with my feet, just barely able to pull back from the point where the stairs vanished, plastered against the stone wall as I stared down into the abyss; a tiny speck of light glimmered some unimaginable distance below me, the same nauseating yellow-green as before, gut-wrenching even at a distance. My grip was uncertain. The stone felt soapy under my fingers, slippery, as if fat-coated.

Far away, in the back of my head, I could almost hear a woman's voice singing some fragment of a plaintive miner's lament, Appalachian style: *I'm down ... in a hole ... I'm down ... in a hole ... I'm down ... in a deep, dark hole...*

I don't know how long I stood there, if that even means

anything. All I remember is that sick, spine-shaking jerk of my foot slipping on the stone, shooting out from under me as I tried to the very last not to move, cold air burning my face as I fell. That ghastly light coming at me like a hammer, throat bursting with screams, as I finally saw what was in it: there, then gone, an empty space. A hole inside a hole inside a hole.

For all that forgetting should have been a good thing, surely, I shook awake feeling as if I'd just witnessed a death foretold — my own, maybe. And knowing, now, *knowing*. . .

. . . there was no way on earth it wouldn't happen again.

§

Something coming.

§

A week, then two; seven nights, fourteen, more. Eight hours a night, sometimes more, but when I looked in the mirror, all I saw was the blue-grey shadows under my eyes, steadily deepening. Hygienic as my sleep cycle might have seemed from the outside, I was still *tired*, to my very bones, in a way that only looked likely to get worse. I felt caught in a loop, a snare. I couldn't see my way out.

Before you ask: yes, I stopped taking the drug. I stopped taking the drug about five nights in. And no, it didn't help.

(I woke up in yet another field, in a ravine, in a crevasse. The first time I thought it was a hangover, prescription still making its way out my system. But there I was, following the crevasse along, tracing a trickle of muddy river, only to turn a sharp corner and find myself at the place where the temple's door should be, the very threshold. The very next night, meanwhile,

I started off inside what looked to have been a parking garage, two floors below street-level, so I deliberately turned and went down instead of up, found a door, opened it—right into the temple's stairway, the grim fading light, those steps leading down, down, down. Into the Well.

And yes, again: the name came to me there and then, in the dream. I've never since thought of it as anything else.)

"This shit is worse than homeopathy!" I complained to my GP two and a half weeks in, not feeling like facing Gracie again; I was slumped back against the wall, still in my paper gown, too exhausted to stand. "I mean, at least that doesn't do *anything*; Gracie's map-drawing crap is actually making a bad situation *worse*."

She'd just given me an all-over exam, entering the initial results as she sat there nodding, one eyebrow cocked. And: "Not according to your numbers," was all she had to say in return, at last, angling the page towards me so I could see for myself, as if she really thought that proved anything. The only good part of which, I guess, was that it at least made me mad enough to force myself back upright again.

"Yeah, okay," I managed, grabbing for my clothes. "But riddle me this: what do you really know about Gracie Hollander, anyhow—what can you *attest* to? Professionally?"

My GP thought that over. "Well," she said, at last, "I know her methods work."

"Always? For *everybody*?"

As if it were gospel: "Always."

"...better start working *soon*, then," I muttered, momentarily defused.

Sometimes, all I can think is that nobody believes in the assumed social contract between and doctor and patient quite as much as doctors themselves do. Which is good, I suppose;

really, they sort of have to. Seeing how it's all that keeps them from abusing their authority till it bleeds.

So, yeah: I don't know whether I thought Gracie was mishandling my case deliberately, or what. By that point, frankly, I could have been thinking all sorts of crap. I *was*. On paper, physically, I was well rested and firmly on my way to recovery, but my *mind* didn't feel that way at all. Even if that *was* happening with my body, provably, there's no way my mind believed it.

Three days on, though, I sat in Gracie's office once more, my own file open in front of me. I'd spread the sheaf of discarded maps out in front of me first, then had the strange impulse to lay them on top of each other, stacking them clockwise; the paper was thin enough you could see them form what looked like one huge, circular chart.

"Like a whole other world," Gracie remarked, her tone oddly admiring. As she stared down, eyes never leaving the map-made-from-maps, studying its multiple-choice fan-shaped destiny of paths for all the world as though, on some level, she was beginning to recognise them.

Each route made a sliver of a quadrant, filling the whole thing in. I pointed to the result, and she studied it, eyes narrowing—because done this way, it seemed fairly undeniable how, no matter where they might have begun, all roads did indeed lead to Rome: the fallow field, the temple, the hole. The Well.

"What made you choose to call it that, you think?" Gracie asked, gaze still held fast, doodling a series of unintelligible notes in her scratch-pad's margins.

"No idea," I replied. "But you do see it, right? The pattern?"

"I see what looks to *you* like a pattern, yes."

I snorted. "Then look again, goddammit." Tapping the papers, as she did: "No matter where I start out, I always end up *there,* every time. Does that seem . . . normal, to you?"

She smiled, eyes crinkling adorably. Pointing out: "Normal's a fairly negotiable concept, Alex."

I shook my head sharply, neck sparking, impatience fierce as rage.

"No, but seriously: 'distraction' or not, why would I keep on *doing* that to myself? Why the temple, the Weh—the *hole?* Why those endless fucking stairs? All night, every night. What's the goddamn point of it all, exactly?"

She was frowning slightly now, pen still going, a veritable mile a minute. "In dream language, the well is a very primal image," she allowed, at last. "Basic shorthand, the place where Jung and Freud meet; it can symbolise change under pressure, sometimes forcible, beyond your control. More shallowly, it could stand for anything that opens inwards: a mouth, a door, a grave . . . your own vagina, even—"

"Pretty sure it's not *that,*" I snapped back, annoyed.

"—but my *point* is," she continued, as though I hadn't even spoken, "*most* people in general dream of wells, even repeatedly; it's not just you. A lot of my other clients do it, too."

"Wells, or *well?*"

"I don't know what you mean by that, Alex."

I tapped the ream of paper between us. "Like, *this* well? That's what I mean. Do most of your other clients also dream of *this* well, maybe?"

"That's . . . ridiculous."

I could hear the words coming out of my mouth, but didn't seem able to stop them; it was as if I'd finally been pushed beyond my limits, so far that my internal censor had popped a fuse. As if something inside me had simply burnt out, leaving me as naked in daylight as I felt during the dark, down the Well, clinging to my unreliable perch as I teetered in the bare instant before the fall. Forever hovering between fear of the unknown and whatever unknown thing I feared.

"Oh, yeah, I'm sure," I snapped back, before adding, far too brightly: "But could I really trust you to tell me if they did?"

§

This is where my research phase would surely have started, if this was another sort of story—plunged myself into the Internet, found myself some sort of magic keyhole giving me access to other people's medical records. Where I would have waited until Gracie went home and broken into her office using my mad lock-picking skills, the ones I'd picked up osmotically by watching an ass-load of *CSI: Crime Scene Investigation* holiday marathon instalments; where I would have been able to find exactly what I was looking for on the first try, just by glancing through her filing system. Some sort of paper trail, or pixel trail. Some patient—or colleague—who'd bonded hard with Gracie, volunteered to prove her theories correct, then disappeared up her own repetitive dream cycle forever, leaving no forwarding address. Some Case Zero that would prove I was right in my frankly demented suspicions about Gracie's methodology, about the reasoning behind her continually pushing me to keep doing exactly what I'd been doing thus far yet acting as though I truly expected a different result, however many times I might have had to try before that happened, like some goddamn crazy person.

(Which I probably was, by now. True sleep-deprived, hallucinating . . . yeah, I can see it, from the outside, the way I couldn't back then, when I was in it neck-deep. The way no one ever can in similar situations.)

In hindsight, the only sort of sight I have to reckon by, this is what I realised afterwards I must have been looking for. But no, that's not the way it went. Because when it comes to solving your own dreams' puzzle, the only investigative tool available to a person in my position is a willingness to do things personally, confrontationally; take a leap of faith, however potentially damning. Take the challenge between your mental teeth and run.

I went home, took a bath, lay down, closed my eyes. Let the nightmare enfold me yet one more time. Welcomed it with open arms.

Just lie down in the dark and let whatever was going to happen . . . happen.

§

Something is coming, the voice whispered once more, under that cold wind, but the Well itself didn't move, ever. Remained the fulcrum, the still point at the centre of this otherwise fluid world. And: *Am I the thing that's coming, then?* I wondered, before finally relinquishing that last step—plunging downwards into darkness, voluntarily, for once. *Was that always me?*

Only one way to find out.

The green light came at me bullet-fast this time, as I felt a wrench that cracked my whole dream's spine. Felt things around me splinter, split, and branch, cracks extending fractally in every possible direction, like roots from some invisible tree. They reached upwards, spiking into the shimmering shadows of what seemed like a hundred brains at once, scattered countrywide yet all asleep and dreaming the same dream; a hundred other sleepers, presumably linked by Gracie's therapy and/or prescriptions, all making their slow way across a hundred different landscapes towards the exact same destination. Not a habit, not a chore: a ritual pilgrimage, infinitely shared, bleak and black though it might be. A method of worship.

Around me, the Well flipped itself front to back to inside-out, becoming a tower—a beacon. Descent into ascent, stairs down into stairs up, though still hammered haphazardly together from the same crumbling, greasy stone, each cobble a puzzle-piece only lightly intertwined, a relic from some age before mortar. And at the top—

—at the top, laid open to that glaring, gangrene-coloured sky whose stars were nothing like the stars we see from Earth, someone waited.

(Who?)

I didn't know their name, even now, even here. I never expected to. But . . . I knew that voice.

(. . . *in a hole . . . I'm down . . . in a deep, dark hole.*)

Cast herself down the Well, just like me, I thought, not knowing why. Then: Just *like me, oh God, oh God. Oh Jesus fucking* God.

(*Just like me.*)

And here it spoke, that same too-familiar voice, skull-resonant even masked under the Well's low grey din. The ruin-echoed blood-slosh of some long-dead ocean, on some long-empty world.

Gracie? it asked, apparently to the empty air. *Is that you? Did you come back for me . . . to find me? Has this been long enough?*

I drew you a map, but I went too far. I lost it.

Can I finally come home?

Oh, what the hell.

I swallowed, hard enough something seemed to scrape, suddenly dry from lips to esophagus. My tongue felt numb, stinging. And: "I'm not Gracie," I finally told it, wincing at how weak my voice sounded in that unhallowed place.

As I spoke, the person—more a thing, really; greenish-black

on greenish-purple-red, more an absence where someone once used to be, an echo rather than the actual person—shifted its attention onto me fully, or appeared to. Stood watching me from afar, but not quite far enough. And though I couldn't see its eyes, not even at that distance, I *knew* somehow . . . it recognised me.

Could almost feel the words graze me all over, like snakeskin, or a poison tongue: a lack of voice, almost too alien to organise itself into words. Yet hearing them nonetheless, if only in some highly primitive way—tasting, *smelling* their most basic meaning, borne on a burnt-skin stink-wave. Reading them out loud and translating from a foreign language, even as they carved themselves, stroke by cauterised stroke, into my mind's soft meat.

Oh, oh yes. So it's you, *finally.*

(At last.)

Did Gracie send you after me? it asked after an aeon.

"Not . . . as such."

Then why are you here? How did you—?

I shrugged, helpless.

"I don't know," was all I could say.

We stood there a minute more—several, crawling like fossils, like erosion, shale tectonically crushed against shale. All the slowest moments of the earth.

I was someone before I got here, the thing told me, almost sadly. *Now I'm something else. No one can stay who they are here, not for long.*

I nodded, trying not to breathe. Not that it seemed to need my agreement, exactly.

If I let you leave, it began again slyly, *will you go see her, Gracie, when you—wake up? Will you tell her what you found?*

If? Jesus Christ; my stomach clenched against the very idea, knotted itself off like a bag, burning bile. But I wouldn't let the implications faze me, not for long. I couldn't.

"If you do, then . . . yes," I replied carefully.

Of course I will, then. No sense not. Neither of us get what we want if I don't.

I agreed, not trusting my words any longer, in silent dumb-show; bowed my head, spread my hands. Pinched a helpless smile and felt—rather than saw—it bare broken teeth at the spectacle, half amused but all angry, colder than death and twice as raw.

Thank me for that, Alex, it suggested.

". . . thank you."

Tell her I want to go home, but I don't know the way. Tell her . . . I need a map, the *map.*

I nodded. "The one you drew. Right?"

No. The one she *drew for me. She knows which.*

"All right."

Be very sure to tell her, Alex. Or we'll see each other again.

Another clutch, bodywide this time, running me like a gauntlet from top to toe. I had to wait just a few more beats to have any hope of self-control, let alone avoid dying of sheer, existential terror before I got the chance to answer.

"I don't think either of us want that," I said, at last. And felt the thing give something not at all like a laugh in return, resonant with the universe's anti-rotation, so awful on a cosmic level that simply acknowledging it risked madness.

Just the touch of that laugh killed something inside me, some capacity I hadn't known I had until then. But by that point, frankly, I was glad to feel it go.

§

When you ask me where Gracie Hollander can possibly have disappeared to, officers, you must therefore take the preceding as my very poor stab at an explanation. Or not. I'd absolutely understand if you didn't.

You tell me she had a partner once, long ago, and I nod. You tell me that partner helped her develop her methods, as well as the drug regime that bolsters them. That this woman disappeared as well, years back, with similarly little trace left behind; it was as though she slid off the world's surface, slipped through a crack, to somewhere underneath. As if she'd tripped, unseen by anyone else in her life, and fallen down a deep, dark hole.

You say this, and I nod, as I've said. No other response seems suitable; it all sounds extremely plausible to me. But I don't have anything else to tell you, unfortunately, beyond what you've already heard. I simply can't remember.

I'm not capable of it.

I'm back to not dreaming at all, thank Christ, though I maintain the hygiene of my sleep habits zealously. Of course, the brain damage has a lot to do with the former, if not the latter. My GP thinks it might have been a series of small strokes brought on by stress in the wake of my insomnia. All I know is that since I woke that last time, I've basically been unable to picture anything visually inside my head at all; if I didn't have this document to remind me I'd once been able to, I'd be tempted to assume everyone around me is lying or joking whenever they claim they *can*. Not classic prosopagnosia per se, but I do have a lot of trouble telling one person from another, unless I use certain tricks—recognising voices, or knowing where people are likely to be at any given time, or categorising people by their accessories, their favourite T-shirts, the colour of their hair, eyes, skin.

It sounds bad to say, for example, but because there are only so many black people I *know*, if somebody with dark skin comes up to me using my first name and acting as if we're friends, I'll always give them the benefit of the doubt. I actually thought one of *you* might be a friend of mine when you first walked in, but by now I've certainly spoken with you long enough to understand I must have been mistaken. The minute you leave, however, my ability to remember you will go straight back down to zero. I'll reset like a bad alarm system, waiting for the next person to set me off.

The worst part is my family—they can't understand why I can't tell, say, my own mother from any other woman on the street, and I can't blame them for that. But there's nothing to be done, and by now I'm used to it.

My nights are neither long nor dark anymore. They pass in a blink. I wake refreshed, remembering nothing. If something still lurks behind my eyes, buried deep into that interior landscape I can no longer map, then it's invisible to me—completely, utterly, safely so. I'll never see it coming.

I prefer it that way.

If you'd been where I have, you would, too.

PURGING MOM

JONATHAN THOMAS

Had a typical nightmare on dozing off after two of Holly's Ambiens, as soon as the red-eye to London cleared the runway out of JFK. In my dream I was home, that is, the home whose mortgage Holly and I had paid off with the inheritance from Mom, but all our furnishings had been usurped by those of the maternal homestead where I'd grown up. I rode a wooden rocking horse that hadn't supported my weight since kindergarten. I was slapping its polka-dotted rump, urging it toward the edge of second-floor landing.

How I'd proceed from there was moot because the curio cabinet that had tottered in ruthless pursuit down the hall planted its stubby walnut clawfeet squarely behind me and swung one of its vitrine doors wide open. To the tune of smashing glass it smacked me and my painted pony down the stairs. I woke up gasping, mostly in chagrin that Mom's furniture had tracked me 200-plus miles from her address.

Had I jinxed myself with positive thinking? Shouldn't I have crossed psychic borderlands already, miles safer each second from oneiric outlash? I did have to hand it to myself, arranging to be an ocean away for the grand purge. Leaving Holly in charge sat fine with my conscience, as she'd suffered no nightmares, no pushback whatsoever, while helping dispose of Mom's effects. I was the bad son for busting up the place, whereas during and after Mom's life Holly was a cipher, a negligible bystander at best. This may have come of reciting our courthouse vows amidst the onset of Mom's dementia. She was never necessarily aware Holly existed.

Or maybe Holly was immune to paranormality by virtue of a wholesomely secular upbringing, exempt from church, superstition, folklore. She had no credulity whereon occult influence could gain a toehold. I, meanwhile, was more broadminded, receptive, giving bogies from poltergeists to yeti my principled benefit of the doubt, a sitting duck for the occult. Fortunately for me, Holly and I constitute a case of opposites attracting. She keeps me grounded more often than not.

That said, I gather she encouraged me to skip the country, sticking her with the heavy lifting at Mom's, in preference to humoring my delusions, as she presumably dismissed them, of defunct mother haunting my dreams. Still, what's my alternative, going animist, alleging the souls of grungy furniture were ganging up on me for quashing their decades of domestic stability, consigning them to junkmen and the landfill? A desperate ghost sounded relatively plausible.

What's more, I'd crossed my fingers that spirit residue wouldn't cling stubbornly to the earthly plane. But under the most schematic definition of a ghost as a "force of attachment," Mom's unquiet afterlife had been predictable in light of her aversion to change, her truculence about keeping every blessed household article in its assigned place forever. She'd eschewed renovations, redecorating, in an unconscious bid, perhaps, at stopping time, erecting barricades of outdated calendars and soy-sauce packets between herself and death, hiding bulwarks of catalogs and chipped dishware in cellar or attic to avoid accusations of hoarding. And as infirmity advanced, change only became more hateful: upholding selfhood meant killing talk of downsizing or assisted living.

Nonetheless, at age ninety-four a pelvic fracture triggered tailspin to the grave, whereupon I wagered mere extinction wasn't about to evict headstrong psyche from the environs on which its integrity depended more than ever. But once her monumental inventory began dispersing, theoretically so would she, and damned if she'd submit to that with good graces.

Before a certain tipping point in that dispersal, I reckoned Mom was the invisible helper who deposited missing keys, stock certificates, pearl necklaces on the kitchen table. But thereafter, she became the spiteful gremlin that popped a valve off the furnace to flood the cellar, among other fluke mishaps. Then again, from Holly's healthier perspective, "shit happens." I owe her big time for keeping it together, unlike myself.

Even as I peered out the porthole into starless void, Holly was, if I knew her, sound asleep, well en route to racking up eight dreamless hours as usual. A pettier husband might chafe envious. Instead, thanks to Ambien, I just floated through wine service, midnight dinner, postprandial decaf, all of it good at least for inhibiting my relapse into dreamland.

And thumbing through the balky small-screen "entertainment system," I hit upon a docudrama semi-relevant to this trip, not that the lowdown on Stonehenge was of practical value to me as the location scout enlisted to earmark the ideal terrain for the heroic fantasy *Dolmen Wizards: Blades of Bronze*. Stonehenge, right off the bat, was too obvious, too recognizable, and getting permits was next to impossible.

Tinny screaming and minor chords steered my unsteady attention to a writhing, fur-clad re-enactor squashed from midriff down by a mock 20-ton slab in a Neolithic construction accident. Or was I dreaming this, a scene right at home in *Dolmen Wizards*? Was this the stuff of reputable historiography or my groggy mash-up of infotainment with barbarian-epic hogwash? Whatever, it beat visions of vindictive dining-room sets. When next I realized, the lights came up for breakfast, and I sighed, strung out but grateful at eluding phantom apron strings at last.

The wife and I observe an unmodish rule that might have saved many a less rock-solid marriage. In this age of Skype and iPhones, when I'm away, I'm away, we're on break from each other's little peeves and tribulations, we solve our problems solo. Hence Holly went about her business blissfully ignorant of trains and buses I caught or missed by minutes, to fetch up toward noon, half-delirious with fatigue, at the charming Aubrey B&B from which I'd recon Wiltshire, first of several promising regions on British soil.

She'd have most appreciated hearing nothing of the looniness I dreamed after belly-flopping into bed for a wee nap and waking up four hours later. For once I was aquiver with anxiety at Mom's house and not mine. My ass was pressing grimly against the edge of her mahogany desk in the upstairs office, and surrounding me were even more green metal filing cabinets than used to congest the floorspace.

As if to give my dread some *raison d'être,* drawers of random cabinets burst open with the erratic timing of popcorn kernels, and their endless contents spumed to the ceiling like gushers from punctured arteries. Vintage utility bills, sales receipts, insurance policies, medical records, bank statements spilled out of airborne folders and rained around me. None of them had to pelt me to exert an impact, for here, unmistakably, was Mom's stockpiled past diffusing as her house emptied out, a callous assault upon her ectoplasm.

Still, despite the chaos, this doubtless wasn't her ghostly protest; it too neatly symbolized my own upwelling guilt at expunging her remnant identity one wastebasket at a time, at recruiting Holly to do my dirty work, as I gallivanted with impunity 3,500 miles away. Dozens of drawers had yet to erupt when my *Tubular Bells* ringtone jarred me awake, and my arm lunged toward the cell on my nightstand as if doing the breaststroke toward a rescue boat.

I first feared Holly was suspending our code of silence due to some grisly emergency, but no, it was my Brit contact Stephanie, an intern in effect who worked for food, and I was late for the afternoon feeding. Luckily, to join her at the Waggon and Horses, I had only to comb my bedhead hair and cross the road, which, she reminded me, was busy, "so take extra care you look to your right, yeah?"

We'd met across opposite sides of the cordon during a shoot in the carny bazaar labyrinth of Camden Markets, London, where she stood out among the rubbernecks by tapping my shoulder and lauding my choice of locale for its fidelity to the filmscript's literary source. Further dialogues ensued. Beneath the blue meringue coif and tatty apricot leggings of her punkette image beat the heart of a film savant who professed an incorrigible longing to get a foot in the industry's door.

In the years since that initial chat, however, she'd apparently done nothing to advance her career beyond sporadic research for me. Not that she ever spoke of family or relationships or means of support; cinematic art in general and whatever job of mine she was abetting bracketed the range of her conversation.

For that matter, I never got around to learning how she knew I was a location scout. Her personal feelings toward me also remain enigmatic and off-limits to broaching aloud.

If she was perturbed at having to nurse a pint in my absence, it didn't impinge on her flirty welcome, her perennial breezy cheer, unless her British social norms were unreadably different from mine. She'd been an angel to arrange our rendezvous here, a literal stone's throw from the Aubrey. And all the better, for as Steph imparted, this pub, replete with thatch roof and sarsen walls, dated to the seventeenth century, sheltered not one but two celebrated spooks, and had served steak pie and ale to Charles Dickens.

Steph had also assembled a printout of prehistoric monuments, and she must have striven mightily to shortlist the candidates, as antiquities were as plentiful here as cowflaps in a pasture. Right out the window above our booth was Silbury Hill, an earthwork on the scale of Egypt's pyramids, built by hundreds of subsistence farmers 4,500 years ago using antler picks, shoulder-bone shovels, and bucket brigades of soil and chalkstone. From the vantage of my oaken pew it resembled a colossal green gumdrop, which I declined mentioning, lest it smack of insult to English heritage.

After our palaver about *Dolmen Wizards* played out, she channeled the talk, as always, into moviedom, on the recent spate of Argentine thrillers, on the underrated noir lighting of Nick Musuraca. This saw us through boar burgers and bland stouts, and then Steph had to nip back to London. She didn't explain why, and only muddied our boundaries further with a clingy hug and gratuitously wet kiss on the cheek. Delectable, sure, but what mixed transcultural signals, to keep me up and wondering despite persistent jetlag! On the upside, when I did doze off, my subconscious was too abashed to fabricate bad dreams.

The kid's enthusiastic, absolutely, but she can lose track of basic priorities. I could have avoided miles of wasted motion had I done my own online research. The quest, of course, was for the most camera-ready landscapes, and Ivor my homegrown Uber driver had the air of tussling with his conscience about everywhere I sent us. Must have been a no-brainer to him that "Marden henge," however renowned for its extraordinary breadth and myriad artifacts, retained nothing aboveground, hardly enough gradient to trip over. Nothing to film here!

Likewise, instead of monoliths, a stubby circular arrangement like half-submerged wharf pilings was all that marked the dismantled majesty of Durrington Walls. More dubious yet were the cement nubs that outlined the hilltop Sanctuary. Maybe Steph misapprehended how much CG was in the budget to recreate primitive splendor. I wished that contemplating my cute, effervescent intern didn't prompt the reflection, *Well, you get what you pay for.*

Ivor, meanwhile, perked up when we headed for Avebury. His indoorsy complexion waxed ruddy through butterball cheeks like a lingering case of the mumps, through five o'clock shadow uniformly stippling his chin and shaven scalp, which with silver ear studs insinuated nostalgia for the heyday of "Oi!" What was it about me that attracted England's unregenerate punks? Yet his formidable husk disguised a mellow temper. Had his bonhomie rebounded because he approved of our destination, or because I was springing for lunch at the Red Lion before surveying stone circles?

Regardless, I was uncommonly comfortable around him on short acquaintance. No sooner was the Sanctuary behind us than sleep deficit kicked in and I nodded off, keeling into another loopy dream. I was still in a speeding vehicle, except it was the Plymouth station wagon of my boyhood. At the wheel was Holly, and it was unnerving only in retrospect that she doubled as Mom. I was in the backseat making out with Steph, while we traversed a patchwork world of my grubby hometown and Bedrock from *The Flintstones* and blasted plains where squalid cavemen skulked about towering menhirs like African termite nests.

But not even the balderdash of stone-age dinosaurs would have pried me off Steph; nor did Holly when she yoohooed, *Everything okay back there?* I wasn't cognizant she'd turned around, though she slammed on the brakes as if trouble ahead had caught her unawares. The frightful jolt that finally extricated me from Steph landed me in the passenger seat of waking reality again, no less alarmed than in the dream. Was this "dream a wish my heart made," to paraphrase some Disney guff or other? Yikes!

"All right, brother? We're here. Red Lion." I nodded, which helped defog me as I blinked around at a parking lot and, across the road, hurray, a smattering of megaliths in a pasture, albeit none half as tall as those I'd glimpsed while smooching. Still, they were big enough to rate a smile, which I shared to reassure Ivor of my well-being as I bumbled from his Ford Fiesta. And incredibly, our bistro, in fact the village, sat amidst the stone alignments.

Harking to Steph's notes, I gathered the seventeenth had been a grand century for pubs, for the Lion was contemporary with the Waggon. Moreover, discounting the rows of picnic tables out front, it agreeably looked its age, half-timbered, whitewashed walls under a beetling roof of black thatch and shaggy splotches of moss. Inside, we nabbed a table next to a masonry well, around which the inn must have been built. The well had a transparent lid bolted on, and the rank, fuzzy flora within amounted to a belowground terrarium; fascinating, but it did tarnish the appeal of my "Avebury Well-Water" ale.

"I like it here," Ivor declared as we tucked into gammon steaks. He flourished his knife toward the window to affirm he meant more than the dining room. He went on about a lot of childhood daytrips to these precincts, how he'd acquired a certain local-color expertise, if he did say so. By way of example, he launched into rumors of hauntings at this very tavern, and it did me no credit, sleep-deprived or not, that my attention drifted to the well, and from there to broodings on how often I'd used my career to skip out on onerous filial duty. Ordinarily I'd have hung on a native storyteller's every gruesome detail.

What was that Yardbirds lyric, "sinking deep into the well of time"? Yeah, thanks to job-related travel, I'd dodged a good decade of eldercare bullets: ER visits for slip-and-fall treatments, flareups of bedsores and diverticulitis, hospital stints for recurrent pneumonia, tiffs with neighbors and health aides over imaginary pilfering.

But why be guilty today when I, after all, had been scrambling to support Holly and myself, when it felt as if Mom would always rebound and live forever? Not as if she had an expiration date stamped on her person, and let's not forget, some judicious distance was needful to safeguard my embattled sanity. Those senior incidents, anyhow, were better handled by professionals.

Something about "the oldest scissors in the world" wrenched my vision from the well and toward Ivor expounding, his eyes earnestly seeking mine, with no evident umbrage when I hemmed, "Come again?"

He patiently recapped, "They're in the museum down the street. They've shifted only a couple hundred yards since the thirteen-hundreds from where they'd been. I ought to show you." He was no doubt inured to the fickle attention of flaky tourists. He came closest to remonstrative when I added a 20% tip to the check. "You don't have to do that here!" he admonished, unlike Steph at the Waggon. But my arbitrary conscience demanded that much appeasement and more.

Ivor had begun lumbering toward the museum; he had to understand, though, I had business to conduct before the afternoon sun dimmed. I grabbed my Nikon from his car and in a half-cocked gesture of compromise asked to see where the scissors had lain since the 1300s. Like a caring parent, he barred me with an outstretched arm on the verge between the parking lot and an amazingly active road, led me across the corner of a megalith-dotted field, and repeated the procedure on another verge.

Tromping along, he recounted, "When some fallen stones were being stood up again, during the thirties, a medieval skeleton was discovered beneath one, and the theory goes he was an itinerant barber, because of the scissors on him, and that he was helping pious villagers pull down the pagan circle and bury it, till a slab happened to fall on him. They had no way to get him out, so there he stayed, and them too spooked to carry on tempting evil spirits. Or else the people murdered him and tipped the rock on top of his body. Perfect crime, eh? And here we are."

I'd been snapping away as we followed an arc of megaliths, some over twice my height and frankly more imposing than this ten-footer, but ever the completist, I documented the killer slab, its contours like an art-brut apostrophe or incipient bust in profile. After I lowered the camera, Ivor anticlimactically disclosed, "This is called the barber stone." We moseyed on, as he yammered about one megalith almost crushing a cobbler who'd been fixing a shoe in its shade, another that lightning had shattered right after a deacon had sheltered under it from a downpour.

With every word my punchiness mounted as we zigzagged between alleged outer and inner rings inside the henge's thousand-foot diameter. The overall form, so clear in aerial view, was summarily lost on me: none of the circles had survived the millennia halfway intact, and intervening trees and houses further obscured the site's coherence. Efforts to pinpoint our position within the complex set my head swimming, not unlike my recurring vertigo when Mom's had been partly gutted, furniture, books, and tchotchkes in unnatural huddles, and spaces bare where they shouldn't have been.

The terrain and Ivor's narrative flowed along as a commingled blur, while I went through shutterbug motions on autopilot, till Ivor escorted me by the elbow through more traffic and identified a gargantuan, diamond-shaped, symbolically female boulder as the "Swindon stone" because it flanked the road to that town. "Witnesses report these here sixty tons have pirouetted right around at midnight, or skipped across the highway searching for a long-gone consort, an equally enormous phallic sarsen." I dutifully converted "Swindon stone" to digital pixels, and followed suit with this fourth quadrant's crescent of monoliths fringing their segment of precipitous ditch around the collective stoneworks.

Aha, and there across this section of lawn, beyond a klatch of blasé sheep, was the Red Lion again. My thirst had grown terrible ever since Ivor's malarkey about menhirs strolling around and dancing. That malarkey rang a bell, may have echoed archetypal folklore, except it resonated ominously, tied in somehow with my broader circumstances, flustered me into neurotic red alert. Imperative that I detune my high-strung nerves, and the balm of alcohol couldn't have been handier.

Ivor, however, bowed out, citing family commitments, and cajoled me into repairing to the Aubrey to "relax and regroup." I could have imbibed on my own at the Lion, which, it developed, was under a mile from the B&B, as Ivor probably knew full well. Was I so visibly overwrought that he wanted me in safe harbor, or anyway in someone else's bailiwick?

Though I couldn't articulate why, I paced my cozy chamber leerier than ever about relaxing, dozing off, reentering dreamland. At any rate, I'd have been too wired to nap without a fistful of Ambiens. Pleasantries I exchanged with my diffident host passed for normal, I supposed, en route through the hall to an early-bird repast at the Waggon.

I, sole customer, reoccupied that booth overlooking the colossal gumdrop of Silbury Hill. The strongest ale on tap had an unfortunate aftertaste of burnt rubber, which didn't stop me from downing three and pretending they grew on me. I cushioned it with a savory pie-du-jour, figuring if it's good enough for Dickens . . . The beverages hadn't tasted so insipid in Steph's company, had they? Pairs and more of diners filtered in, and their sidelong glances seemed to question whether I, a loner, was fitter to be pitied or censured. Neither townsman nor proper vacationer fared solo; what was my game exactly?

Not that their opinions were of value, especially as I embarked tomorrow on the next leg of my mission, to Cornwall. I hauled out my phone, speed-dialed Steph, got her voicemail, and encouraged her to join me in Truro, citing my need for a savvy colleague, for her finely honed insights and judgment, and in my heart, none of this just then was a tissue of lies. Sick of evil-eye pinpricks of disapproval, I paid up and skedaddled, and with the exaggerated prudence of mild intoxication, scurried across the road unscathed.

In my warmish quarters I threw open the window, flinched at how each vehicle thundered by in the nocturnal quietude, and resigned myself, restless with ale and angst, to lying awake indefinitely. Ambiens and alcohol would certainly breed nightmares or worse. I pulled out my phone for companionship. Nothing from Steph, *quelle surprise*. And no stateside news was good news, the maternal haunts presumably stripped to the bones, according to schedule. That should have been a load off my mind, a dose of satisfaction, however little I'd earned it. But no, pronouncing "mission accomplished" sent pangs of remorse through me, like multiple jabs of emotional pitchforks.

What faults in my mental bedrock made me indict myself as hypocritical, traitorous? I had to liquidate Mom's estate, period. Yet a malaise of blame oppressed me, as if simply walking away from the house should have been okay. What easier to do, for the sake of Mom's happiness, than nothing? Off the point that she was defunct, her phantom influence really my imagination, right? I was a heel to the same extent I acted in self-interest.

But if dreams of volatile furniture were pleas from Mom for benign neglect, to spare her dwindling identity, her belongings were, in one sense, of a piece with Neolithic monuments. Did ectoplasmic tribesmen abide on their home turf, like Mom on hers? My overheating thoughts raced on, though their feet were miring in exhaustion. Mightn't those Wiltshire ancestors, like Mom, want nothing more of posterity than to leave their towering "furniture" alone, such that they'd been riled by too much vandalism into tripping a medieval barber into the path of a toppling sarsen? My sprinting thoughts must have hit a patch of quicksand about then, for that's when they went under.

I picked up sprinting, breathless as if this strenuous dream were *in medias res*, along the floor of the formidable ditch around Avebury's rock circles, till the urge possessed me to bound up the steep incline, impetuously, as if catching defenders off-guard. Directly above, the barber stone, poised on the precipice, flipped through midair like a flyswatter, rushed downslope like a toboggan. I hopped aside within inches of being flattened and skittered back to the bottom. Behind me the slab crashed with a din like a tone cluster octaves below middle C.

A brief dash onward and I involuntarily sprang uphill again, to confront the barber stone's twin up top, prefatory to another round of playing chicken with tons of geology, another hairsbreadth escape, another discordant crash. I was philosophical about exercising the volition of a needle on an LP, about prospects of reeling on forever in steady-state fatigue. I worried only on beholding the symbolically female Swindon stone around the bend, balancing on the bottom of the trench, utterly blocking it, like the palm of an upheld hand. My lack of bodily control was now cause for alarm.

As I careened toward the boulder, it rocked minutely like a sea-fan in a gentle current. In those final paces it loomed much grander than laws of optics could explain, and it quaked as in anticipation, and its shadow cast me in darkness as it slammed down like the bar of a mousetrap.

In the microsecond before contact, the sarsen's grating deadfall became the racket of a monstrous truck rocketing by out front, extremely overdue for a tune-up, new muffler, new transmission. I, lightheaded with hyperventilation, was staring agog at the ceiling. As the ruckus faded, the chiming of *Tubular Bells* sent me groping around the nightstand. It had to be Steph, better late than never, and if she had a compulsion to return calls at whatever hour she checked her voicemail, fine, we had that in common.

Confusingly, a stranger, and an American at that, was on the line. It's much earlier stateside, I remembered, maybe broad daylight in California, was this my employers at *Dolmen Wizards*? Nope! The caller made officious noises about confirming he had the correct party, and then broke stunning news in a monotone, or else American accents registered as flat, affectless, after two scant days of British English. His nasal droning, by design or not, did tamp down any unbridled reaction, aside from basic shock.

A tinge of annoyance was the closest he came to modulation, in remarking his difficulties reaching me. The accident occurred midafternoon sometime. My wife had overseen laborers hauling a piano up some cellar stairs and through a bulkhead when the cords slipped or snapped. The piano slid to the foot of the steps and did a "backflip," as witnesses put it, onto Holly. She'd sustained spinal and internal injuries. Efforts to save her were unsuccessful. Sorry for your loss. I hung up then and switched off the phone.

Good Lord, the last thing Holly heard must have been a godawful tone cluster. Bad as I felt, I was unable to cry yet, perhaps because transatlantic distance rendered the tidings less immediate, less vivid. My wife is dead, my wife is dead, I repeated aloud till it made me borderline giddy, and worse, I blanked out to resurface chanting the specious litany of every survivor, It's my fault, I've failed her, if I'd been there this wouldn't have happened; but it also wouldn't if one of umpteen circumstances had differed, say, she'd stood somewhat to the left.

Still and all, the room was devolving into claustrophobia, dejection, like the bottom of a well filling with guilt, and damned if I'd lie there and drown. What rank injustice that would be, when my mental processes, without my conscious interference, were feverishly building a case for blaming Mom, constructing a ladder out of this toxic groundwater.

Yes, Mom had been as oblivious to Holly in death as in life. But as we denuded room after room, from attic to cellar, less and less context remained to harness her atomizing selfhood.

Reduced to mad smithereens, she'd have lashed out at anyone orchestrating the *coup de grâce* as if it were me. If I had to be guilty of anything, how about casting Holly in the role of Judas goat?

The way forward was both limpid and murky, or rather I had every idea what to do, and no idea what I was in for. I had to surmise the worst: Mom had killed Holly and, if I returned, would kill me. Her domicile contained nothing to die for. As for the balance of my "adult responsibilities," Holly was no more; the household that was ours was gone with her. And if I did go home, how to refuse driving the ten minutes to Mom's from there?

Let Holly's punctilious kin handle funeral arrangements, et cetera. It might even solace them. They're like that. And what, they will cavil, about the marital assets? Binoculars couldn't see that many eventualities ahead. My livelihood, meanwhile, was doable from anywhere. The phone was my office; a fixed address was a virtual albatross. The more I rambled, the better I prospered.

I switched on the phone, sat up against the headboard, and redialed Steph, foreseeing euphoria, then disgrace, every other second, but ready at least with a spiel for voicemail. Don't go to Truro, I'll be in London bright and early, we can take the train together. Much to discuss. Call if you can, please, though my phone won't be on.

Hated to admit, one topic for discussion was her mode of transport. Car, moped, neither? How woefully unacquainted we were; I'd no clue what she'd make of my message, or what I honestly made of it myself. Whatever her response, I decided I was, without libido, as good as dead. But beyond me to hash out if I was leveling with or glamorizing myself.

This non-issue I shelved, and rolled over into a few hours of the serene sleep usually bestowed on problem-solvers. At dawn my eyes popped open. I bounced out of bed, awaited breakfast downstairs, and informed my host and hostess of urgent work-related summons to London. I must have acted impressively frazzled, for my host-cum-cook doffed his apron and drove me to Swindon, where I made the 9:31 to Paddington.

On the train, I played at weighing whether each earthen bump along the hilltops was or wasn't a Bronze Age barrow, but this proved the equivalent of counting sheep. I'd racked up inadequate sleep last night, hadn't I, despite my buoyant start? The on-and-off vibrations of the cool window were soothing against my temple. I conked out.

Then I had the damnedest misperception I was awake, on my feet and oddly anxious about a tunnel toward which the train was hurtling. But I had to be dreaming because I wasn't on a moving locomotive anymore, and never subject to tunnel vision in reality. And if I'd had my druthers, this lowering, ominous black chute would have been a hundredfold longer, such that Mom at the far end would have been infinitesimal.

I had nowhere to look except at her, and as I did, my field of view around her expanded. She was, at rough estimate, the length of a train car away, and I readily discerned her osteoporosis and hunching shoulders, arthritic knuckles and general emaciation. Gray sweatshirt, pink sweatpants, and beige slippers were of major consolation, covering as they did more than bedsores and other dermal insults, since decay had been underway for months, and grisly enough to behold how it had gorged on face and scalp and hands.

Her features were too wormholed for me to decipher her expression as she beckoned, though lidless, fishy eyes smoldered with no inviting warmth. By now the space around her had ballooned to a Cinemascope vista and clarified into a coliseum of the sofas, TVs, porcelain, coffee tables, toiletries, winter coats, vases, rolled-up rugs, meds, bodice-rippers, costume jewelry, washer-drier units, and infinitely more that had been her life. They shuddered like a packed crowd of jostling onlookers, like a projection of her jumbled memory bank, massing for one last stand. Or onslaught?

What the hell was she hoping I'd do? If my behavioral norms weren't altogether lost on her, she'd have realized I'd do nothing, rooted to this dream ground of no specific color or manufacture till the proverbial chickens came to roost. But what was my passive-aggressive defiance against her tenacity, her unholy acumen for sniffing out family blood across the ocean? I didn't know the half of it when I used to say it was orneriness that kept her going.

She let drop her arm, and I grimaced, expecting it to detach. Her jaw, after twitching side to side, dropped too, like a gallows trapdoor, and my queasiness escalated unbearably. Her mushy larynx fought to eke out words and expelled only bubbling, malformed groans. From the oral cavity at that instant also flowed a clammy, acrid miasma of highly distilled death. I jounced awake, bumping my forehead sharply against the window.

I had a leaden misgiving the dream wasn't over, or at best this was an intermission, because the shaky tonnage of Mom's possessions hadn't yet collapsed into an avalanche and pulverized me. Plus, the miasma still infested my nostrils, doubly thick after I tried snorting it out and inhaling fresh oxygen. Was it me, I winced, peeking around for signs I'd incommoded fellow riders. But neither I nor any single offender could have triggered the uproar spreading throughout the carriage.

Passengers were coughing, cursing, squawking in disgust, robustly putting the lie to vaunted British reserve. Some were hustling fore and aft into other cars before I'd drawn my tentative, and even fuggier, next breath. Speculations volleyed to and fro about a toxic spill outside, a ventilation breakdown, a blockage in the lavatory, terrorism. The sole island of calm, the one passenger unperturbed as if her sinuses were incurably clogged, as if she were deaf, sat way up front. From my seat I could just about distinguish the sparse, frowzy white coif straggling from her scalp—and were those multiple port-wine marks showing through?

A fat fly, likewise unperturbed by the bedlam, lazily swooped in and met with no reaction as it lit on the apparently insensate head. With that, the source of the effluvium became as obvious here as in dreamland. The quiescent passenger's hairstyle, albeit from the back and pathetically wispy, had been damnably familiar, and denying I knew to whom it belonged amounted to self-delusion.

Pretending indifference would be especially foolhardy now that she and I were alone in the carriage. Of course, I might yet be dreaming, and if not, well, my first step would be the same, to join the ill-humored exodus. I lurched up and dragged my cumbersome satchel from the overhead rack, frantic to exit quietly, despising myself for every unavoidable bump and scrape. Sneaking off was no solution, but I was thankful for the wherewithal, just barely, to do that, to go with what I knew.

I had to get to Steph, her image wavery like the mirage of a welcoming shore that receded as I swam gasping toward it. My baggage and I had caromed half a dozen rows toward the rear, and my free arm was outstretched to punch the panel that opened the door, when the phone rang. Unbelievable! What the hell had inspired Steph to call now? But the phone was off, wasn't it? I dug it out and checked the number. It was Holly's, not Steph's. I stuffed the phone back into hip pocket.

Lunging forth, I did grasp how unfair I'd be to impose on Steph when two ghosts, in dreams or not, were simultaneously hounding me. But alternatives, I was certain, I had none, not that England equaled safe haven. This was how broadmindedness, receptivity to occult realms had repaid me, though Holly's skepticism had served her even worse.

My sweaty fingertips poked the panel, the door whooshed aside, cleaner air rushed in, and I dared a backward glance. Mom wasn't there, or at least not where I could see her, and on my person *Tubular Bells* had desisted. My overwound nerves slackened, maybe in purely organic response to breathing easier. And tricky to say, down to semantics perhaps, whether my relief was real or not. I had no means, and might well never again, to verify if I were dreaming or awake.

Before I'd crossed the threshold, three conductors in black jackets and blue ties bustled through the passage and forced a retreat. They were overtly displeased with me, quite understandable if they had instructions to detain me in this car for questioning. "Can you tell us what you're doing in here, when everyone else has fled from this awful pong?" demanded the senior, pockiest guard. "Do you know something the rest of us don't?"

Yes, I did, but wisdom dictated I mutely shake my head.

"Nice opportunity, wasn't it, to go through people's baggage?" piped up the shortest, scrawniest inquisitor in an outwardly chummy tone, as if he envied my pluck.

Tubular Bells emanated from my pocket again. Nobody spoke or moved till my inaction goaded the third conductor, with nigh-albino complexion and pencil mustache, to carp, "Aren't you going to answer that?"

When I shook my head once more, the senior guard archly asserted, "Would you mind passing it to me then?"

I complied, despite my arm's reluctance to cooperate. The conductor dourly squinted from the screen to me. "Someone named Holly. Who might that be?" He pushed the Talk button and raised the device to his clamshell of an ear, which muffled the caller's voice after he barked, "Hello?" He tendered me the phone and gratuitously explained, "For you, right?" I accepted the phone and perfunctorily hit End Call.

I had to say something. The truth was manifestly off limits, so I went with the first words that floated up as in a Magic 8-Ball. "You're right, I set off the chemical agent, and I needn't harp on its success. I also guarantee there's nothing in here you could analyze. I'll go quietly."

They frowned as if it were a shame about my sanity. The senior guard produced handcuffs, and I presented my wrists. Sorry, *Dolmen Wizards,* I guess we're on hold. The Brits, like anyone, seem inclined to deal more harshly with foreign than homegrown terrorists, but my relative innocence will inevitably come to light, with my confession chalked up to gas-induced delirium.

Or else I'm still dreaming, and if I am, let the cuffs chafe, where's the harm? And if not, fine! For all that I'm the "bad son," Mom would never dream of finding her own flesh and blood in jail.

THE FIFTH STONE

SIMON STRANTZAS

My first memory was of grasshoppers trapped in my tiny cupped hands. The image remains stuck in my memory, untethered from time or place, and I remember nothing else but the feel of their skittering wings against my skin.

Outside that void of infancy, my first true memory is of finding the first stone. I was at most five years old, and because I fully awoke on discovering it in my family's back yard, the stone became one of my most treasured possessions. Flecked with glittering minerals between layers of the deepest emerald, it vibrated as I held it, a feeling not dissimilar to those imprisoned grasshoppers. I remember dancing with glee in my little rubber shoes while my oblivious mother stood above, lost in distraction and intense garden-party conversation. Even then I knew better than to tell her what I'd found. Some discoveries were meant to be kept secret from everyone. I took the stone and placed it in the folds of my dress for protection until I found a place where I could study it better. It felt warm against my skin. The stone was the most wondrous thing in the universe, and I knew that

I would never find its equal. Until, of course, I did.

The second stone called to me as soon as I spotted it in the dirt during a weekend visit to the cottage, and when I smuggled it back home and compared it to the first, the two sparkled in unison. I kept them beneath my mattress, careful to look at them only while the house was asleep. When I discovered the third a year or so later, I had to find a different place to store them. Leaving the three together beneath my bed gave me nightmares.

It was when I found the fourth stone that I experienced my first grand mal seizure. I wasn't older than nine, but already I was straining at the yoke childhood had put on me. While my mother walked along the woodland path in Millbrook Park, I stayed on its edges, existing between trees and steep hills. My mother kept her eye on me, but I did my best to melt into the woods, become one with the shadows and bark. As soon as she was distracted and looked away, I stopped to investigate the fauna and take in the sight of Rogue Creek trickling over the fenced-in rocks. I knew the park was nothing like a real forest— especially with the asphalt path leading through its center— but it was as close as I'd ever been. Seed pods and leaves rained down on us like a winter storm.

No one understood how consumed my life was by the stones. In private, I would arrange my collection in various patterns on the bedroom floor, looking for a configuration my intuition suggested was correct. Then I would delicately commit the shape to paper. I did this in an attempt to understand the stones and their incongruous presence in the world. But also to understand my own feelings of disconnectedness from those who claimed to love me, and my desperation to be any place that didn't tie me down. Drawing the stones made me as they were—immutable, permanent. But despite my attempts at capturing the stones' mystery, none of the drawings felt accurate. All were approximations—impressions devoid of both power and something else I couldn't define.

I scoured the sides of the path through Millbrook Park, looking beneath fallen tress and amid flower beds. My mother was distracted with caring for my younger brother, which allowed me to stray farther than I was allowed. The stones I'd found until then had been accidental discoveries, but I was determined to purposely uncover another, and couldn't do so under her suspicious gaze. Time crept slowly on, and when she finally realized I was gone, she frantically called out for me to return. But I didn't. Instead, I hid in the bushes and plotted my next action. It was my first brush with freedom, and I was invigorated. I shifted my weight to find a more comfortable vantage point, and my foot caught something hard. It was as though someone had reached up through the dirt and grabbed hold. I pitched forward before my arms knew enough to protect my face.

I landed hard and it pushed the air out of me, scrambling my thoughts. When the haze cleared, I made sure my mother hadn't witnessed my fall, then looked to see what had caused it. Another stone. It remained in the dirt, half exposed, and was unlike any of the others. I couldn't describe it; I could hardly look at it—it refused to sit still in my hand long enough, vibrating at such an extreme frequency it hummed. As I held the stone, my little nine-year-old hand numb from the vibrations, the world around the stone vibrated too, accelerating until the two were in sync. Then, the world overtook it, shaking faster, and from the stone ripples expanded outward as through reality were only the surface of a pond. Light ceased to behave, glowing and pulsing and flashing, and though I remember shocks dance across my limbs and skull, they were so far distant that

I saw them erupting outside the blurry haze. The memory of what transpired next vanished, and I returned to groggy consciousness in my hysterical mother's arms as she sobbed. My brother's tiny lungs commiserated a few feet away.

It took time for my mother to calm down and realize I wasn't in immediate danger. If anything, the only threat I faced was from her arms as they tightened around me. I was terrified of what had happened, the experience of losing control over everything I was. How could I go on when it was clear the barrier that keeps chaos at bay was thinner than rice paper? But I kept it hidden, worried she might squeeze me so tight I'd stop breathing.

We were in a cab to the hospital as soon as we emerged from the park, and when we arrived my father was there to retrieve my brother and ensure I was okay. I wasn't—I still felt weak and shaken and disconnected from myself—but I remained quiet and smiled nonetheless, nodding and answering politely, all the while secretly hoping everyone would leave me to my panicked thoughts.

While waiting for the Emergency Room doctor to call us, I remembered the stone I'd found. It still wriggled in my brain and made my shoulder blades and stomach twitch. I was convinced I'd slipped it into my pocket as the seizure struck, and the idea I might still have it made me want to retch. I rose and frantically patted down my pockets, two at a time, as though putting out a fire.

"Elizabeth, sit," my mother ordered, her manic voice wavering. I ignored her and continued searching until I was sure I hadn't pocketed the stone, then I slumped back into the plastic waiting room chair. It was gone, and when I returned home the others would follow.

"You really scared me today, kid. I hope you know that."

"I'm sorry, Mom."

"What were you looking for?"

How could I explain it to her? How could I tell her about the stone and the visions it brought? Especially when it was the reason we were at the hospital?

"I found something in the park. I thought I'd kept it."

She gave me a queer look, then opened her bag and pulled out that terrible vibrating stone. She held it up for me to see. The world dropped away, leaving behind faint chirping.

"You mean this?"

I nodded.

"You were squeezing it in your hand when you—when you got sick. Do you want it?"

I reached out then stopped. The hairs along my arms stood. Quivering found the recesses of my back. A flash of spines, the echo of screeches. What would the stone do to me if I touched it?

A nurse materialized before I found out. She ushered us along. By the time my mother and I were settled and awaiting the doctor my Emergency Room dance was forgotten.

The doctor was unconcerned, explaining that sometimes children simply have seizures. There's no discernible reason, and they outgrow it quickly. Still, she made some recommendations and gave us referrals for more intensive tests. My mother wrestled me over the course of weeks and months to attend them, but at the end of the process none of the doctors found anything wrong. My family was told to wait and see if the seizures returned. My mother cursed that answer, but it was clear it relieved her. She stopped asking me how I was doing, at least. She also made me promise to tell her if anything like that should happen again. I agreed, despite having already suffered three more seizures by then. And all remained a secret.

They occurred each time I touched the stone. My mother had left it on my study desk as I slept off my adventure, unknowingly providing me with the key to inducing what most worried her. I was filled with dread on seeing it, but was either too young or too old to trust my suspicions. It seemed so impossible, but I learned quickly that bringing the stones close together was not worth the cost. Once I awoke bleeding from the back of my head, no doubt having slammed it on the ground during an episode; another time my lip was bitten almost clean through and had to be blamed on a bicycle accident. The stones were destroying me, each seizure a rope thrown around my neck and staked to the ground. I didn't understand what was happening, but I refused to succumb. Instead, I did what any sane, rational girl would do: I gathered the four stones into a burlap sack, and when my parents' attention was elsewhere I found a spot behind our garden shed to bury it. As each shovel of dirt rained down, the pressure on my soul eased.

The fifth stone literally hit me out of the blue. Once I buried that burlap sack I left my seizures and childhood behind. Puberty struck soon afterward, changing my body and diverting my thoughts, and my urge to flee my home and what was buried there only grew stronger. I stayed away as much as I could, and when I couldn't I locked myself away from my parents' prying and my brother's incessant neediness. I never thought of myself as unhappy, but being at home, under rule and responsibility, pulled at my being. I wanted to abandon it all and escape.

The stone changed everything. I was walking home from school, books pressed against my burgeoning chest, passing by the local baseball diamond. It was early enough in the school year that gym classes were still being held outdoors, yet late enough that I was wearing a sweater and the sky was already painted with shadows. My attention was elsewhere as I daydreamed about how different my life would be once I left for college, and how no force in the universe could ever make me return home. The taste of freedom was so close my mouth watered, and when I closed my eyes to savor it, I was struck. Pain interrupted my thoughts, so sharp I thought my head had exploded. I buckled in agony, fell to the ground, the pain eliciting the strangest images in my head. It was all too fleeting to comprehend, but it lasted long enough to fill me with terror. Harsh chirping echoed and screeched in my head. I rolled on the ground writhing in pain, hand pressed to my throbbing temple, grass staining my new sweater as I sobbed. Someone grabbed me, tried to comfort me and ensure I was all right, but it took an eternity before the pain ebbed and I could pry my eyes open. I lowered my hand from my temple and saw the blood waiting there for me. It ran over my fingers, down my palm, into the cuff of my filthy sweater. It was sickening. I turned into the blinding light silhouetting the face hanging there, eclipsing the world, as he asked if I was all right.

"No, I'm not," I spat. "What happened?"

"I don't know," the boy said. He wore a baseball cap, but the rest of his features were concealed in backlit shadow. "You fell down screaming. Then you just started—I don't know. Shaking. Do you need to go to the hospital?"

"I think something hit me," I said. "It was hard." I looked again at the blood on my hand. "Is it bad? It feels bad."

He ran his fingers over my bleeding head, pushing apart either my hair or my flesh. His fingers were rough but warm.

"It's still bleeding. You need to go the hospital. I'll get my car. It's just over there."

He snapped his fingers.

"Did you hear me? You look spaced."

"Did you see what hit me?"

He shook his head. The remaining afternoon light illuminated the side of his face. I didn't recognize him, but he smiled and my heart beat with so much wondrous terror I had to turn away. I concentrated on pawing through the grass.

"What are you looking for?"

"Whatever hit me. It's got to be around here somewhere."

I dare a glanced at him. His shadow shrugged.

"Why?"

I stopped and looked at my dirty bloodied hands, my stained clothes, my books strewn on the ground. He was right. What was I doing? I didn't know. I just knew I had to do it.

"I won't be able to rest if I don't."

I returned to searching, running my hands through the blades. I sensed him standing behind me, but he didn't leave and I didn't stop no matter how embarrassed I felt. We stayed that way—me pawing the grass like a blind woman, him watching—until I realized I wasn't well. The world was slowly rocking, and losing volume. My limbs were getting heavier.

Then my hand grazed the stone lying in the grass. Those screams I'd cried when it hit me paled in comparison to the agony of touching it. Every inch of my body twitched alive, and I was engulfed by a seizure unlike any I'd experienced. I screamed and screamed and wondered if I'd ever stop screaming.

I was in my house. The edges of my vision sizzled and popped like a stuck film strip. Beyond it, a slowly collapsing star. Everything was rotten and decrepit—cobwebs hung from corners, the floor uneven as dirt pushed through it. There was a horrible pulsing screech, a low frequency that hurt my ears and eyes. I found myself at the foot of an incongruous staircase, and at the top, beyond a slowly twisting corridor, a foreign second floor waited, guarded by a single closed door.

That door, I knew, must never be opened.

I climbed, the staircase twisting with each step. The screeching resumed, long and deep, and the edge of a shadow appeared on the surface of the door beyond. It grew larger. Larger. And whatever cast it followed close behind.

Then the world smelled of dirt.

I opened my eyes and saw blinding pale sky, my limbs heavy, shackled to reality. I tasted dry metal, and every word I tried to speak was random vowels whispered from across the room. There were other noises, but I ignored them, too lost in my skull to make sense of what was happening. When the tumblers in my brain fell into place, I wanted to sit up, terrified and humiliated by what had happened. The boy in the baseball cap held me back.

"You're going to the hospital."

And that led to a lifetime of medication. Pills of various sizes, shapes, and colors, all designed to do a single thing: stop the seizures. Epilepsy wasn't the curse it once was, they assured me. I could live a normal life without worry. That was the promise. But a switch had been flipped, and I lived in terror of it. What if the grand mal seizures returned? What if what had happened to me on the grass was the first volley in a lifelong war my brain was waging against me? I needed to avoid it at all cost, so I made the bargain with the doctors, with my mother, with myself, and took their pills. Took their counseling and their therapy and everything they prescribed, even as it dismantled and dulled every desire for freedom I once had. Each chained me down one at a time, deadening my dreams and leaving me as everyone wanted me to be: safe and sound and free from suffering. But I got what I wanted; my seizures were gone. And as the years piled on one another, I eventually forgot it had ever been different.

During those years the boy in the baseball cap never left me. The hats changed, the clothes changed, but his smile never did. One day I found myself married to him, another holding the first of our three daughters, and I was never quite certain when each new rope had been tied. By the time those children moved away and left him to me alone, the seizures were so far distant they were forgotten. The pills were merely my pills, and my dreamless nights merely the way I slept. Those years were peaceful, at least. Everything buzzed with ordinariness.

When my husband died, things were not so peaceful. Our daughters were spread across the globe, two unreachable and the third unable to stay beyond the funeral. I was left to clean our house alone, a single old woman who moved slower than ever, who thought slower than ever, trying to piece together what remained of her life. I was afraid to leave the safety of our home, and yet every room reminded me of him—every chair and plate and pillow and photograph. They all once belonged to both of us, and overnight they became only his. I spent my days going through his belongings again and again, not knowing what else to do. Occasionally, I would stop to smell what was left of him on an old sweater, or touch his jacket and pretend he was still in it. The house was an empty prison without him.

It was in the bottom drawer of his dresser, pressed against the back and wrapped inside an old sock. I didn't know what it was when I removed the bundle, grabbed the toe, and shook the contents free. It fell onto the bed with a dull thud and confronted me—a flat quartz surface, light reflecting oddly. My suffering prevented me from immediately recognizing it. Then, when I did, I was overcome by fear.

He'd kept that fifth rock. The one that had appeared out of the blue, the one without which he and I might never have met. I knew him, his sentimentality—he had kept it because it was the spark of our beginning, and yet when I saw it I also knew it spelled my end. It was a chunk of suppressed nightmare dropped without ceremony into my waking life, and after so many years without suffering dreams of any kind I didn't want it anywhere near me. I left it on the bed and closed the door to the room I'd shared with my husband, perhaps forever. I doubted I would ever be brave enough to step through the door again.

Yet I couldn't forget the stone waited for me, as it had for more than sixty years. My obsession with it grew until all other thoughts were pushed out of my mind. It didn't take long before I was forgetting to take my medications, and once I was off that handful of tiny pills the murky patina cleared from my eyes and revealed the prison I'd let fear drive me into. My dreams flooded back, and in those dreams I was a child again, unburdened by love's or life's hardships, seated in my childhood home with the fifth stone in my hand. I placed it on the ground with the other stones I'd collected—five stones in a circle, equidistant from one another. I drew invisible lines between them with my finger, and as I did my dream-self's eyes grew larger, her mouth wider, and a colossal force pressed against her. I woke into the dark of the real world. Or what I thought was the real world. I wasn't all together convinced.

I returned to our old bedroom and stood over the stone. The house was silent—everything vanished as I gazed deep into the quartz surface. Could I see ripples emanating from it? Some strange force pulsing? I extended my shaking hand, wanting to touch it but afraid. The stones had evoked visions of a future inevitability I didn't want to admit, and though it had been decades since I last touched one, its warnings of something approaching were as vivid as if they'd happened only minutes before. The visions and dreams, despite being long abandoned and blocked, were nevertheless trying to explain something to me, and it had taken my entire life until then to realize what. I was being prepared. But for what would only be clear once I gathered the five stones together.

My daughters had put my husband's Chrysler up for auction, but it still sat in the garage, waiting for a buyer, and I still had the key. Getting behind the wheel and out onto the street was an unexpected challenge—the baseball cap atop the dashboard was a painful reminder of my loss—but once the car was on the highway a renewed sense of freedom washed over me. It was fleeting, though, lasting only until I remembered I was anything but free. I drove as fast as my nerves would allow, hurtling back to the house I'd once wanted so desperately to escape, back to where the rest of the stones patiently awaited my return. On the passenger's seat was a small bag weighted with so many questions.

An hour later I was driving down a narrow street I hadn't seen in a lifetime. The car moved slowly over the asphalt and beneath rows of overgrown trees, while the sound of the highway faded into the background. I barely recognized where I was, despite having spent so many years riding my bicycle through the web of neighborhood streets. Like a dream, everything was both familiar and foreign. The bushes and trees were trying to overtake the road, and I wondered if the houses I passed had been abandoned. Branches hung low enough to scratch against the car windows and over the hood and trunk, fingernails trying to claw me back. The few street signs that hadn't yet been consumed were inexplicably blacked out. Only my vague childhood memories kept me from getting lost in the labyrinth, steered me through suffocating trees and past blackened signs. Eventually, the branches were forced to surrender to the inevitable and let me pass. My old family home emerged from the foliage and into view.

I took some time to ease out of my husband's car, my muscles aching from sitting for so long. The house watched as I did so, wanting me to look at it, but I refused. I wasn't ready yet to face what was waiting for me. Instead, I walked slowly around the side, opened the small wooden gate, and proceeded into the back yard where our old shed stood.

As impossible as it seemed, the foliage there was more overgrown than what I'd already driven though. I waded into the long grass gone to seed, insects leaping out of my way as I made my way to the shed. There I eased myself down onto my swollen knees, and with only my crooked fingers dug at the dirt. And continued to dig until I found the burlap sack.

I reached down into the hole and pulled it up. The bundle was heavier than I expected, as though the four stones within had swollen over the years, absorbing the thoughts and dreams of those in the vicinity. But I knew it was only my newly rediscovered imagination exploring its surroundings and testing it limits.

Being so close to the stones after so long was like a waking dream, and the world shook and vibrated out of step around me. I carried the sack back to the car and opened the door. On the seat was the fifth stone in its own bag, and I felt a pull toward it—all five stones eager to be reunited. I reached into the bag on the passenger's seat, and on touching the stone's surface my fingers went numb from shock. I drew back, but forced myself to suffer through the pain long enough to transfer the fifth stone into the burlap sack with the others. All five radiated heat as though on fire.

My knees were still swollen and I had troubling walking, but I made it to the front door of the house. It wasn't locked, and when I walked through I realized my once-home had been uninhabited for too many years. Memories of holding my mother's hand, sitting in my father's lap, chasing my brother, all flooded back, and I cried at what had become of them. Everything of my childhood gone to ruin and rot. Why hadn't I sold the house after my mother's death and let some other family try to find the happiness that had evaded us? I couldn't remember the answer, too distraught over the house's state. Or perhaps my memories of the time were too garbled. All I'd wanted was to escape the prison of that life, and I managed it only under the yoke of medication. I'd traded a cell for a prison, and returning to the house was like stepping behind the bars once again.

My old bedroom waited at the top of the stairs. It beckoned me, but I hesitated. Something was wrong, and if I listened, I could hear whatever it was faintly humming in the background. I put my hand on the banister and the world shifted, vibrated ever so slightly. I watched that second floor and waited for something to happen, for something to appear from around the corner. I waited. And when nothing came I started to climb.

My old legs grew shakier with each step, the world around following suit. The vertigo increased until, out of breath, I reached the second floor and saw the door to my old room. It looked just as I'd remembered it. Just as I'd dreamed it.

The air smelled of ozone. Everything shifted, vibrated. The stones, too, out of sync with the rest of the world, then slowly catching up. Faster and faster, the vibrations eventually found their balance, started to resonate in harmony. My gut twisted, the blood rushed from my face, my teeth gnashed.

I put my hand against the door to keep either it or myself steady, and the vibrations ran up my arm. There was a noise, a low droning chirp from behind the door that I recognized, and that filled my stomach with dread. That pressure I'd dreamed about arrived, pushing down on me as if the walls were closing in, and though I saw daylight out the landing window, I felt submerged in the deepest earth. The air stank of it.

Scratching, pounding, came from my old room. Something was in there. Something large and powerful and angry. Something penetrating from another place, a weak spot I'd felt throughout my childhood. My nightmares were flesh, were real, and they were coming forth. The world rippled from the bag at my side, concentric circles warping the air around me.

My dreams returned then—images of me sitting before the vibrating door, of me placing the five stones on the ground, equidistant from one another, of me drawing invisible lines from one stone to the next. Then my visions went further, memories of my dreams resurfacing. I saw the door shut with the stones piled against it, saw the determination in my eyes, saw the exhaustion of keeping what was behind that door at bay at all cost.

I looked at the sack of stones in my hand, vibrating with potential as the door in front of me shook from the pounding buzz on the other side, and I realized that my entire life had led me there. That I had not found the stones, but they had found me. They sought me for this task, to be the one to keep everything at bay, to hold the line between this world and the next at all costs. I had been given a burden no one else could bear, and would hold it for the rest of what remained of my life. I was finally awake from my lifetime of dreams—awake and aware of what needed to be done.

I reached into the bag, took a stone in my arthritic hand. It jumped, full of charge, and the shocks ran up my arm. I took hold of that stone tight, tighter than I had ever held my husband or my children or my parents or brother. I took hold of that stone and I turned and hurled it at the landing window with all my might. The shattered glass filled the air like snow, and the stone disappeared from view. The pounding at the door beside me grew stronger.

I did the same with the next stone, and the next, each time the pounding, the wailing, the screaming increased, until the frame buckled and pieces of wood flew and all the stones in the sack were gone, scattered on the ground outside. I collapsed on the floor, unable to hold at bay what was inevitable.

I would let it come. I would let it enter this world from wherever, let it do what it wanted. I was not a prisoner. I was not born to carry a burden. I was meant for freedom. I was meant to be free. I would no longer accept a prison. I would let the world suffer, let it bleed for a million years, as long as I was free.

The door trembled, broke. From behind it first emerged a long slender leg, covered in spines. A chirp, then another, then a narrow head with eyes as large as my skull pushed through, mandibles clenching, opening. It pushed its chitinous body through, and I recognized it. I recognized it from my earliest memory, from before I had any real memories. I recognized it as it looked at me, cocked its inhuman head, and leapt through the broken window into the dying afternoon sky. And behind it another followed. Then another. Then another. And more still. Until the sky was full of them, a plague escaping into the world through a door left unguarded, a plague carried forth on clear membranous wings.

IN THE CITY OF SHARP EDGES

Stephen Woodworth

"So the dream is always the same?" Dr. Ingalls asked. Paper rustled, pen-point scratched.

"It always *starts* the same," Alan amended. "In the same place."

"Do you recognize this place? Have you ever been there before?"

Alan grimaced. "I don't think anyone has been there before."

"Why do you say that?"

"Because it makes no sense. Doorways that end in stone walls, hallways that seem to go on forever and lead nowhere, vast rooms with no floor."

"And you are the only one there?"

Alan shifted in his chair, grateful that Ingalls let him sit upright. He'd never been to a psychiatrist before and had feared the indignity of having to lie on a couch.

"No other people are there," he said. "But I'm not alone. Another . . . being is with me."

"Have you seen—" Ingalls paused to rephrase the question.

"Can you describe this being?"

"It changes. Sometimes it's so cold, it burns, like dry ice. Sometimes it crackles and sparks, hot and stinging, like the static on clothes fresh from the dryer. Sometimes it has skin; sometimes, scales."

"Then how do you know it's the same being?"

"Its smell." Alan's nose twitched. The overly masculine musk of the psychiatrist's cologne nettled his nasal membrane. "I've never encountered anything like it."

"Hmm." Ingalls's tone was noncommittal, even uninterested. "And you feel this being is pursuing you?"

"Yes."

"Is anything troubling you at the moment? Work? Family? Depression?"

"No."

"How about issues from your past? Any childhood trauma?"

With his index finger, Alan absently rubbed the lower lid of his right eye beneath his glasses. "There was some bullying, as you might imagine. But that ended ages ago."

"Granted. But sometimes these suppressed conflicts can manifest themselves years after the fact. If you continue to have the dream, perhaps you should try confronting the beast rather than fleeing it. You might find out what it truly represents."

Alan swallowed saliva to ease his parched throat. "Wouldn't that make the dreams worse?"

"Only until you wake up. And, contrary to old wives' tales, a dream can't kill you."

"How do you know that if all the people who've died from dreams never wake up?"

Dr. Ingalls chuckled but did not answer the question. More scribbling, followed by rustling and tearing. A chair creaked, and the psychiatrist placed a scrap of paper in Alan's hand.

"I'm prescribing a mild sedative. With any luck, it'll knock you out all night, and if you have any dreams, you won't even remember them in the morning. If you do dream, however, try taking control of the dream, as I suggested. At the very least, it will give us more to talk about the next time you come."

"Thanks," Alan said, although he wasn't sure what he had to be grateful for. He placed the scrap of paper in his wallet, then took the folded cane from the pocket of his tweed jacket and, with a single shake, snapped it to full-length. He had been told the cane was white, just as he had been told his glasses were black. The names of these colors meant nothing to him, but they signaled his condition to those with vision. Indeed, he wore the glasses strictly for the benefit of others, for his eyes were as opaque as the lenses that hid them.

He tapped his way out of Ingalls's office to the elevator, pushed the appropriate Braille-marked button, and descended to the building's foyer. As he exited, the street greeted him with the bracing aroma of exhaust, the air brisk with the first nip of autumn.

On his way home, Alan dutifully had the cab driver stop at a pharmacy so he could submit the paper Ingalls had given him to collect his prescription. Afterwards, when the taxi dropped him at his apartment, Alan pulled a bird and a dog—a twenty and a ten—from his wallet and handed them to the cabbie.

"Keep the change," he said with a grin. There were other ways of distinguishing one denomination from the other—the engraved ridges on Andrew Jackson's portrait differed from those of Alexander Hamilton's, for example—but the whimsy of the folded origami amused him.

As Alan entered his second-floor walk-up, he sighed with relief and collapsed his cane. Here he could maneuver by memory alone, for everything was in the exact place where he'd put it. Five paces forward and two to the right would take him to his desk, upon which rested a computer with a Braille display instead of a monitor. Nine paces straight ahead sat his workbench with its rack of apothecary flasks. The living room had no lamps, and although the apartment management insisted that the overhead lighting fixture have functional bulbs in case of emergencies, Alan never turned them on. Darkness was the medium in which he lived, and he thought no more about it than a fish noticed the water in which it swam.

He shoved the folded cane in his jacket pocket, then shed the coat and hung it on a rack beside the door. Six paces to the left took him into the apartment's kitchenette, the soft tread of carpet beneath his feet giving way to the squeaky smoothness of linoleum. Lightly pawing the air before him until his fingertips contacted the metallic monolith of the refrigerator, he gathered ingredients for his supper with impulsive haste. It was early for dinner, but he felt a need to drown his senses in stimulation: the grassy tang of fresh basil pesto, the whirr of the food processor that sliced mushrooms into pliable, earth-scented cross-sections, the burble of garlic and sun-dried tomatoes sautéed in olive oil.

He turned on his stereo and listened to Vivaldi as he listlessly dined alone. It was no use: the memory of the dream-sensations seeped into his consciousness like leaking gas, smothering the humble comforts with which he tried to distract himself. A crackling shriek as shrill as feedback warped the harmony of strings he heard, and the food went sour in his mouth. And the smell—indefinable yet noxious.

Alan retrieved the plastic vial of sedatives from the pocket of his coat, twisted off the childproof cap, and shook two of the slick capsules onto his palm. He popped them onto his tongue, but before he could wash them down with water, he reconsidered. What if the medication didn't prevent the dreams, but merely prolonged them by keeping him asleep? Captive in that hive of senseless halls, unable to wake. . .

He spat out the pills and dumped them into the kitchen garbage basket with the uneaten remains of his dinner. Maybe Ingalls was right. He ought to grapple with the dream-demon and overcome it, or else he would never be rid of it.

It was early still, and Alan did not feel the least bit sleepy. He tried reading a book, but his finger skidded over the pinpricks on the page without interpreting them. Having resolved to endure the nightmare, he became impatient to get on with it.

Without light to demarcate the division between day and night, Alan often suffered the plague of insomnia, which he attempted to combat by adhering to a strict schedule of rising and retiring. Tonight, however, he reclined on his bed in his pajamas and tried to drift off, even though the position of the exposed hands on his old-fashioned electric alarm clock told him it was barely past eight o'clock. Thoughts of the nightmares so preoccupied him as he lay there that he believed he must already be dreaming, but the scent and feel of laundered sheets affirmed he was still awake.

At some uncertain point in the night, he slid into oblivion in a seamless transition of unvarying darkness.

Alan gradually became aware his body had changed position. He felt himself to be standing upright, his arms hanging at his sides, though he had no memory of having risen from his bed. He had been stripped of the linen cocoon of pajamas and bedsheets, and clammy air stippled his naked skin with gooseflesh. Textured stone abraded the soles of his bare feet, confirming to Alan that he had arrived in the dream city.

With no cane to tap, he put out his arms to full length in front of him, then swung them in a semicircular arc to the left and right. His fingers contacted nothing.

"Hello!" he called, not expecting a response. Rather, he gauged the echo of his voice; it reverberated back to him from either side, but rolled away distantly in front of him. He deduced that he must be in a narrow corridor.

Alan pivoted to the right and toed the floor with his right foot. He gingerly planted the foot and ventured forward, swiping the space before him to sense any hazards. Although he realized that he was merely dreaming, his childhood fear of falling made each step feel as if he were seesawing on a high wire.

His fingertips touched hard stone. A wall. Fashioned from the same material as the floor, it felt like carved glass, with the smooth whorls and sharp ridges of an obsidian arrowhead.

Relieved to have the wall to guide him, Alan crept along the rough plane as if clinging to the ledge of a skyscraper. As he felt the way ahead of him, his right hand reached a sudden, jagged end to the rock. He folded his fingers around the corner, and the razor keenness of the stone slashed his palm.

Chuffing breath at the sudden pain, Alan jerked his hand back. Liquid trickled down his wrist. He licked his palm and tasted the salt and iron of blood.

From somewhere in the cavern came a screech that made the glassy walls ring like fine crystal. Alan slapped his hands over his ears, yet the sound hummed in his molars, throbbed in his skull. He wanted to run, but didn't know which way to flee. It was difficult to tell whence the cry emanated, for the bizarre architecture of the place seemed to share the deceptive acoustics of a cathedral dome's whispering gallery, causing the shriek to come at him from every direction at once.

A humid draft whisked through the passageway—in and out, to and fro, as if the entire cavern were respiring. Its warm breath carried that stench that Alan had come to know so well yet still could not identify: not animal, nor vegetable, nor mineral, but with hints of all three, as of a stalagmite encrusted with guano and fungus.

The odor inspired an irrational revulsion in him, and he groped his way back to the serrated corner where the stone wall had cut his hand. He followed the wall as it continued at an acute angle into what proved to be an adjacent passage. The shrill and the smell swelled in intensity until they fused into a revolting synesthesia—an odor that grated, a sound that stank.

Alan shuffled faster, the soles of his bare feet chafing on the stone floor.

Then the wall abruptly ended again. His right hand fluttered, seeking solidity. In his haste to relocate the spearhead of rock where the wall branched off, Alan became careless in choosing his steps. Only when he felt his toes curling in empty air did he realize he teetered on the shard-sharp brink of some unknown precipice.

The shock of the discovery unbalanced him, and he pinwheeled his arms to keep from pitching forward into the crevasse. He overcompensated and fell onto the floor behind him, his whole body throbbing with the smack of hard stone.

The humidity thickened around him like gelatin, congealing the ineffable stink into a tactile putrescence on his skin. The thin treble shriek slid down several registers to a deep-bass howl, yet the sound grew louder—nearer—as if the Doppler shift of a passing train whistle were played in reverse.

It was coming.

Alan rolled over and frantically fingered the edge of the pit, seeking a way around it, but the ledge extended from one wall of the tunnel to the other. He extended his right arm down into the depression to gauge its depth and could not feel the bottom.

With no way forward, Alan considered backtracking to the

junction of the previous hallway. For all he knew, the thing was already there, or would overtake him as soon as he reentered its path.

This is nothing but a dream, he reminded himself. At worst, falling into a chasm or being devoured by a bogeyman would only wake him up, and he desperately wanted to wake up.

Alan decided to take his chances with the pit. Perhaps, he thought, it was not as deep as he feared, and he could jump down and continue fleeing on foot.

Belly-down, he snaked his body until his feet stuck out past the ledge. Gripping every handhold he could find on the chiseled floor, Alan gradually lowered himself until his chest and waist draped against the cliff. His toes brushed the sheer rock face without finding purchase. He inched downward until only his forearms clung to the ledge, yet his feet still hadn't landed on anything solid.

The tunnel above him belched a hot, gaseous roar like dragon's breath.

None of this is real, Alan told himself again, and let go of the ledge.

Nothing happened. Rather than falling, he remained impossibly pasted to the cliff wall.

Alan stretched an arm up to the ledge again to make sure it was still within reach. Yes, it was there—he hadn't moved at all. The space around him seemed to tilt, inverting the directions of up and down, and he had the dizzying impression that the stone plane he lay against was now the floor of a tunnel, and that the ledge he touched was the edge of a pit below him. Had he somehow imagined lowering himself into the hole? But the sound—and the smell—continued to emanate from the opening, so it *had* to be the passageway he'd just left.

Skittish about moving, he pushed himself onto his knees,

then got to his feet with coltish uncertainty. If he was correct, he now stood at right angles to where he'd been a minute before.

He had no time to marvel at this miracle. The reek flooded this new passageway, a fetor of commingled species, like a pet store full of unclean cages. Alan staggered to the right until he contacted another stone wall. He spun around and fled in the opposite direction, his left hand tracing the wall, his right slicing the air in front of him.

He'd barely managed fifty paces forward when he ran into another wall in front of him. Alan moved along it, feeling for another opening, but only came to another corner on the right. A dead end.

He turned to retrace his steps, but the onrush of fetid air stopped him. If the thing was right behind him, it now blocked his retreat.

Intuitively, Alan pressed up against the wall at the end of the passage and strove to convince himself that it was now the floor. Then he scrabbled forward, gecko-like, up the plane of graven rock.

Again, the bizarre dream-gravity of the place rotated. The fluid in Alan's inner ears shifted and settled like the bubble in a carpenter's level, adjusting to the new frame of reference. He soon lost all internal sense of direction, for it felt as if he were crawling in place while the universe revolved around him.

When he reached the cut corner where the wall joined the roof, something brushed the bare skin of his left leg: a membrane as soft and slippery as the underbelly of a fish. It squeezed his calf—the liquid lap of a giant tongue—and he recoiled so violently that he pushed himself onto the ceiling of the corridor. He now lay upside-down, provided that such a relative position had any meaning in this directionless abyss.

Although it no longer touched him, he could sense the

beast seething beneath him. Its unimaginable bulk filled the tunnel until it deadened the echo of the stone, and every ripple of its form shivered the thin current of air that separated it from Alan. Yet it made no move to capture or consume him.

"What are you?" Alan shouted. *"What do you want?"*

In response, the creature emitted a nerve-shredding vibrato, a dog-whistle amplified to excruciation. But that was not what made Alan grab his head and convulse in apoplectic agony. Clashing sense-memories inundated his brain, as if it were an antenna receiving interfering broadcasts from a thousand different transmitters. He guessed that some of the impressions were visual images, such as sighted people had attempted to describe to him throughout his life, but the other perceptions were of senses he was certain no human possessed: frequencies and wavelengths of energies beyond the receptivity of eyes and ears, chemical syntheses too rarefied for nose or tongue, tactile stimulation that would lacerate mere skin.

The creature was evidently trying to answer him—to tell him what it was and whence it came.

Alan howled. Unable to process the onslaught of alien perception, his mind imploded, collapsed into the catatonia of the insensate.

The transition out of nightmare remained ill-defined. As consciousness returned, only the presence of the familiar—sheets and pajamas damp with rank-smelling sweat—reassured Alan that he had awakened. Reflexively, he touched the fingers of his left hand to the palm of his right, but did not feel any gash or dried blood. It still stung, though, as if sliced by finely honed rock.

For hours Alan lay in bed in a state of anxious enervation, too fretful to sleep, too exhausted to rise. He had no idea what time it was and did not care enough to touch the exposed hands of his alarm clock to find out. Finally, the fear of accidentally dozing off prodded him to get up and get on with his day, if only to keep his mind from relentlessly turning over the imponderable remnants of the dream.

He dressed, shaved, and picked at a meal he couldn't bring himself to finish, vainly trying to submerge himself in the tangible and mundane. Seating himself at the table in his living room with its rack of small vials, Alan strove to embroil himself in his work. Ordinarily, he savored the olfactory challenge of blending scents, a skill that enabled him to operate a successful aromatherapy business. Today, however, every aroma he uncorked—sage, vanilla, jasmine, cardamom, lavender, patchouli, lemon grass—struck him as dulled and flat, as though he'd contracted a head cold. He waved an open bottle of fragrant oil beneath his nose, but his thoughts wandered to that other smell, the mutable odor that evoked so many terrestrial scents, yet transcended them all.

Alan stoppered the flask, stood, and ambled from the workbench to his desk. If he couldn't think of anything but the cursed dream, then he might as well do something about it.

Seating himself at his computer, he aligned his fingers with the Braille-marked keys of the keyboard. In front of the keyboard sat the long, narrow, rectangular box of the Braille display. Alan typed in the Web address of his usual search engine, which his "screen reader" software repeated in a pleasant artificial voice that came from the speakers on either side of the desk. He then entered his search terms.

"Blind," the screen reader said calmly. "Dreams. Nightmare."

It listed a variety of pertinent articles for him. He selected the first and moved his right hand to the Braille display. He could read the text faster and more accurately than the screen reader could drone it. At first smooth, the row of touchpads on the display sprouted tiny pinpoint-sized bumps to form the Braille letters of the first line of text. Alan ran his right index finger across the display, then pushed a button to scroll to the next line. The dots of Braille danced beneath his touch, forming new words. As he worked his way through the article, his finger began to twitch so badly that it became difficult to read, yet he steadied his hand and finished the piece.

Several hours and dozens of articles later, Alan sank back in his chair, his index finger rubbed raw. Absurd, half-formed theories battered the inside of his skull, clamoring for release. Having spent the better part of the day convincing himself of the impossible, he now wanted someone to tell him it was all nonsense.

Alan took out his voice-activated cell phone, but before he could speak Dr. Ingalls's name, he paused. No . . . Ingalls would never understand. Alan needed to speak to someone who shared *his* world.

He only hoped she still had the same number.

"Call . . . Stacey," he enunciated, and the phone dialed.

§

The following afternoon, Alan sat at a wrought-iron table on the patio of his favorite café, trying to think of nothing but the autumnal sun on his face. He had to be careful about such exposure: As a boy, ignorant of the sun and its power, he'd once gotten so sunburned his skin blistered. Though he now wore a broad-brimmed Panama hat to shade his brow, he could not resist reclining his head every so often to bask his cheeks and forehead. The warmth enveloped him in lulling nullity, numbing body and mind like ether. . .

Alan shook himself and hunched forward, swilling the cold

dregs of his fourth triple-espresso from the cup in his hands. He hadn't allowed himself to sleep since the night before last and had drunk so much coffee to stay alert that its acid burned his throat in a backwash of bile.

Then he sensed her presence. Perhaps it was the light ticking of the tip of her cane or the distinctive clop of her low-heeled shoes, but he recognized her even before she said "Thank you" to the hostess who'd led her to his table.

"Alan?"

He stood. Her hand squeezed his upper arm, and he wrapped her in an embrace. "I'm sorry to drag you out like this."

"No, it's fine," she insisted, the voice a soft balm to his ear. Everything about her was just as he remembered from their days as kids at the Institute: the tender roundness of her cheek, the faint citrus of her perfume, the frizzy ringlets of hair at her temple that tickled his nose. She may have been a bit thicker at the waist than when they'd last hugged, but so was he.

"I must admit, you scared the crap out of me, calling when you did." She pulled away and he reluctantly released her. The scrape of the chair opposite him cued him to retake his own seat.

"Yeah, sorry about that. I didn't realize how late it was." He cleared his throat. "So how have you been?"

"You didn't drag me all the way across town for the first time in four years just to catch up," she chided. "What's wrong?"

His face warmed, and not from the sun. Alan had always hated admitting he needed anyone—it smacked of dependency, which he despised. This was the primary reason he'd allowed Stacey to drift away from him once they'd finished school. But he needed her now.

"You ever have dreams, Stace?" he asked.

"Sure. Doesn't everyone?"

"Bad ones?"

"Yeah. So?" Her tone of annoyance indicated she thought he was still making small talk, dodging the real issue.

"Can you describe them? The bad ones, I mean."

"I don't know . . . I'm usually in an unfamiliar place and I'm lost."

"Are you alone?"

She hesitated. "There aren't any other *people* around, but there are all these weird sounds. . ."

"And a smell?"

Her sudden silence answered his question. "I don't get what this has to do—"

"Did you know that congenitally blind people have nearly four times as many nightmares as sighted people or those who became blind later in life?"

Stacey sighed. "And why are we talking about this?"

Her dismissive tone made it even harder for him to begin. "Tell me if any of this sounds familiar," he said, and recounted his repeated sojourns in the strange stone labyrinth.

Stacey did not respond immediately when he'd finished, and Alan fretted that he sounded crazy. When she finally spoke, however, it was with a more thoughtful voice.

"It's not really like my nightmare place. Mine is a vast, dusty plain. There's nothing to hold onto, so I always have to crawl on my hands and knees. There are plants with prickers sharp as pins. And every so often, I feel indentations in the dirt, like the footprints of—" She either couldn't or wouldn't describe what made the tracks. "But isn't all that just an expression of our anxieties? We have a lot more dangers to deal with than sighted people."

"*Is* that all the dreams are?" Alan asked.

"What else would they be? Have you talked to a psychiatrist about them?"

He recalled the consultation with Ingalls. "Yes, and he's useless."

"So what do *you* think they mean?"

He tried to moisten his lips, but the excess of coffee had left his mouth dry. "You know the old saw that being blind sharpens your other senses?"

"Yeah. Which is kinda true."

"Well, maybe it sharpens senses most people don't even know exist. Maybe we can perceive worlds beyond the physical one we live in, particularly when our conscious mind isn't interfering. Maybe we even project ourselves to these places in astral form."

Before Stacey could reply, a male voice intruded. "Hi! Can I get you folks anything?"

Alan was chagrined to think the waiter might have overheard his delusional theory.

Flustered, Stacey ordered a latte. "You think they're real?" she whispered when they were alone again. "Those things—"

"If I can convince myself they're all in my head, maybe the dreams will stop. Until then, they're real to me."

"What are you going to do?" Stacey asked softly.

"I'm going to find out as much as I can about this place I go to, and everything in it. Real or imaginary, I'll figure out how to escape it."

The waiter delivered Stacey's coffee, but Alan did not hear her lift the cup from its saucer. "Do you want me to stay?" she offered.

He considered the invitation. For once, it was not pride that made him decline her. Rather, he did not want to expose Stacey to possible contagion from whatever unearthly perceptions he'd been receiving. She had her own nightmare world to cope with.

"No." Alan slid his right hand along the surface of the patio table until it found where Stacey's hand lightly rested on the porcelain of her latte cup. "Just sit with me a while."

She let him take her thin, soft fingers in his grasp, and they sat that way until the clink of china around them dwindled and the waning radiance of the sun let the world go cold.

§

That night, the atmosphere in the tunnel felt frigid and stagnant. Alan ran his hand over the glassy, rough-hewn wall to his right, verifying that he had returned to the same dream-labyrinth. This time, he would not wait for the beast to find him.

"Where are you?" His cry echoed away into hollow vacancy. "Come and get me!"

He padded forward, bolder than before now that he knew he would not plunge to his death if he walked into one of those gravity-defying pits. *"Do you hear me?"*

Nothing answered but his own reverberating voice. Alan did not expect the creature to understand his words, but he thought the sound alone would draw it out. Was it gone?

Tracing the wall with his right hand to guide him, he advanced to what seemed to be another intersection of passageways. The edge of another cliff nicked his toes, and when he let out a yell, the sound rebounded to him from a half-dozen different directions.

From above, Alan heard a faint, yawning roar. This time, the draft that misted his face felt cold, redolent of mold, chalk dust, and offal.

Alan leaned against the wall closest to him until his bearings shifted to reorient the world around him. Then he scrabbled upward toward the source of the sound.

When he crawled into the passage that had once been directly above him, the roar had scaled up to a batlike chittering, and Alan wondered if the thing were using echolocation to find him just as he was trying to find it. The headwind of its odor blew stronger now; it was closing the distance between them.

Alan pushed himself to his feet again and searched for a wall to hold onto. Although he expected more of the flinty ridges and whorls, his hand glided over a surface as smooth as polished granite. Only a series of perfectly rounded indentations, some circular, others oblong, pocked the stone. Their irregular yet deliberate domino patterns were so teasingly similar to Braille that Alan traced the lines of incomprehensible dots and furrows as though he could interpret the inscriptions. They reminded him of when his mother had let him touch the grave marker after his father's funeral. Who had written this unfathomable text? Did the petroglyphs tell what this place was . . . and what inhabited it? If only he could read them. . .

A fusillade of percussive popping noises, like a million suction cups being peeled loose in sequence, accelerated toward him from the corridor to the right. Clinging to the wall, Alan instinctively staggered a few steps in the opposite direction before deciding to stand his ground. He'd intended to face the thing, after all. Why not here?

The popping sounds ceased, and the beast emitted a saurian bellow whose force knocked Alan back against the wall. He pushed himself upright, turned, and put out his hand. His fingers brushed over a thicket of wriggling, chitinous spines, as if the legs of a millipede had been magnified to the size of cattails.

The creature screeched as he touched it, and Alan nearly

collapsed as another onslaught of incomprehensible sense-images infiltrated his brain. Still, the being did not attack; rather, it seemed to await some action from him.

Alan sidled along the wall and into the passageway on his left. He heard a squishing and slurping as the thing trailed him; the air at his back seethed with its presence. When he paused, it stopped. When he advanced, it followed.

For the first time, Alan suspected the thing might be imprisoned here just as he was. Maybe it was blind in its own way and dogged him in hopes he could lead it out of the labyrinth. Perhaps, if he freed it, the dreams would end.

But how could he release it when the maze seemed to have no physical exit? The only way Alan himself escaped each night was by waking up.

That might be the key, he realized. If the prison was a mental one, then maybe the only exit was psychic as well. For whatever reason, the trapped creature could not "wake up" on its own as he did. If he could establish a connection with it, then maybe he could pull it out of the labyrinth, setting it free.

Alan halted and reached toward the thing again. Where the spines had quivered a minute before, his hand now sank to the wrist in a mass as viscid as aspic and as frigid as liquid nitrogen. Like water in a vacuum, the flesh felt as if it existed at the triple-point: solid, liquid, and gas all at once, it froze and boiled simultaneously.

Alan howled in agony, yet did not pull his hand away. He fought to concentrate as the being, in attempting to communicate, again barraged him with fragmentary conceptions of impossible shapes and places.

With their minds thus conjoined, Alan focused his mental energy on a single aim.

Wake up!

The compressed enclosure of the tunnel seemed to dissolve. Alan's cries no longer echoed but instead drifted away to infinity. The floor beneath his bare feet fell away, leaving him tumbling in a bottomless maw. Where the creature went, he could not tell, for this pit seemed to have no gravity at all, nor walls to fall upon. Alan flailed in a void, deprived of touch, taste, smell, and sound.

Then he heard himself gasp and gulp air, and felt the trampoline bounce of his bed's box-spring beneath him as he flopped about on the mattress like a tuna on the deck of a fishing trawler.

Alan sagged into stillness, trying to deconstruct the nightmare. He'd bonded with the dream-creature in a deeper way, sensed he was close to understanding it fully, yet now that he tried to reconcile his recollections of it, he could not assemble the parts into a whole. He was like the blind men in the parable, unable to conjure the image of a complete elephant from the feel of tusk and tail and leathery skin. Insectile spines, membranous flesh, vocalizations that ran from a rumble to a squeak—and that unclassifiable reek. . .

Alan's nose squirmed. Just recalling the odor made him feel as if it still clung to him. He wanted to shower to cleanse himself of it.

Before he could rise, the smell clotted around him. Alan grabbed at the sheets beneath him, afraid he might still be dreaming. But no—he was in his bed, swathed in its comforting cotton reality.

A dank draft billowed over him, and something permeated the thin material of his pajamas to brush the bare skin beneath. The touch was coarse and hairy—gelatinous and sticky—prickly and caustic, all at once.

Only then did it occur to Alan that the cryptic inscription

he'd discovered in the dream-city might have been a warning.

Like a stray pet, the being had followed Alan out of its prison of nightmare and into the freedom of his waking world. Alan's rarefied senses instantly grew even more acute, and an Eye opened in his mind, endowing him with a new and terrible Vision that had nothing to do with light.

As the creature enfolded him, Alan at last saw it in its totality and screamed for blindness.

AN ACTOR'S NIGHTMARE

REGGIE OLIVER

I think I am now the only person who can tell the astonishing story of Laurence Hamlet, because, in a sense, he no longer exists. I apologise if that sounds cryptic, but I hope you will come to understand if you read on. I tell the story only because I feel I must, and "Laurence" never will. I have a certain responsibility, and, besides, it is likely to be the strangest story you have ever heard. Even if you believe it to be a fantasy and completely untrue, you must believe that *I* believe it, and that is possibly the strangest thing of all.

The first thing you need to know is that his name was not Laurence Hamlet at all but Kevin Piddick, and that may have been at the root of the problem. He had changed his name by deed poll shortly before he went to drama school.

I had known him at the Irving Academy of Speech and Drama, where he had a certain reputation. He was not exactly disliked, but people tended to avoid him and laugh at him behind his back. In that competitive atmosphere he somehow acquired the taint of being a potential loser, which can make things difficult. Actors are notoriously superstitious and easily make themselves believe that failure is contagious. Laurence was not without all talent, but his performances always had something strained about them, as if too much time had been expended on calculating their effect and spontaneity had been extinguished. In that vivid French phrase they "smelled of the lamp." This artificiality was also evident in his personal dealings: he seemed unable to let himself go in the company of others, with the result that he gave off an impression of detachment, even deviousness.

You may ask at this point whether he was gay or straight. It is a valid question, but I am afraid even now I can give you no clear answer. Certainly I never heard of him having any kind of close relationship either with a man or a woman. (He was, I believe, strongly attached to his mother, but that is a separate issue.) He was physically a man, and not a notably effeminate one, but there was something curiously sexless about him. Perhaps that was one of the reasons why people found him off-putting, even though he did nothing obvious to cause offence.

After I had left the Irving I did not see him for another five years until he unexpectedly appeared again on my horizon. Following the success of *Nicholas Nickleby*, someone had made a rather pedestrian stage version of Charles Dickens's *A Tale of Two Cities* for the Royal Shakespeare Company, which thanks to some good acting and accomplished direction had become immensely successful. It had caught the public's perennial desire for romance and sentiment, I suppose. While the RSC was with it in the States, Victory Productions had been licensed to take out a national tour of the same show. Victor Kean (currently famous for being the last Dr. Who) took the starring role of Sydney Carton, and the rest of the cast consisted of cheap, reliable, unknown actors like myself. I had been offered the decent minor role of Barsad, the spy. When I arrived at the church hall in Fulham for the first day of rehearsals

I was somewhat surprised to find that Laurence Hamlet was also in the cast.

The first day in a new company can be an awkward occasion, particularly if it is a large one. Actors gather in an impersonal space and eye one another. Old friends, even old enemies, are greeted effusively; shy introductions are made. The stage management, if efficient, offers you a cup of tea. The stars and the director make later, grander entrances.

I noticed Laurence as soon as I came in to the hall but made no effort to renew the acquaintance. He had obviously come early and was sitting on his own sipping a cup of tea with a deliberation that seemed to suggest that tea drinking was a necessary part of the actor's work schedule. I greeted a few casual acquaintances. One of them, an actor called Tony Mawson who was playing Stryver, was looking at one of the cast lists that were on offer.

"Good God," he said. "Laurence Hamlet. Do you think that's his real name?"

"I believe not."

"You know him, then."

"Not really. We were at the same drama school, that's all."

I felt slightly ashamed of myself for not acknowledging and pointing him out, but some of the old superstition we had about him at drama school welled up within me.

"Well, he doesn't seem to have a very exalted status in our little company. According to this, he is playing a citizen and a peasant and is understudying; though it doesn't say whom." Tony had his pedantic side.

Just then we were approached by Laurence.

"Hello, George," he said to me. "Fancy seeing you here." Then turning to Tony, he said: "I'm Laurence Hamlet."

Tony put on a satirical expression. "Ah! The man himself. Well, George, I'll leave you and young Laurence here to reminisce about drama school days." And he left us. I felt vaguely diminished by this little episode and irritated that I was now saddled with my tiresome former acquaintance. The fact that he had called me by my Christian name was another irritant: it implied a familiarity that was unwarranted. Yes, I now feel ashamed at the snobbery of my reaction, but I cannot deny it.

Laurence, always a stocky figure, had put on some weight since I last saw him and seemed to me to be well cast as a French peasant. He was dark with regular but rather blunt features. Perhaps his greatest asset was his eyes, which were large, liquid, and brown with long eyelashes, like a cow's. On a woman they might have been seen as a rather attractive feature; they had a wistful quality, a dreaminess that I noticed for the first time while recognising that it had always been there. We exchanged some information about ourselves. Laurence was quite obviously delighted to find himself in the company. He had made the best of his acting career since drama school, but it had obviously been sporadic and undistinguished, or, as he put it, "mainly Theatre in Education." He appeared, however, to be confident of himself and his abilities, but it was a confidence which I was pretty sure was put on for effect. "Assertive" might have been a better way to describe it.

As he was talking to me I noticed that his eyes occasionally flicked away to other corners of the rehearsal room. Then, as I was saying something to him about the play, I noticed as that his attention was distracted.

"Right, yes. Will you excuse . . . ?" he said and walked straight past me without further acknowledgment. I turned round and saw that Victor Kean had entered the room with the director. Laurence went up to him and spoke a few words. Kean listened politely with his head on one side and a faint ambiguous smile on his handsome features (a familiar attitude), said something briefly, perfunctorily shook hands with him, and moved on. The director, Ken Savage, a young meteor fresh out of Cambridge, who stood beside him looked annoyed by Laurence's intrusion. I watched the scene with the calculating interest of the actor. Trivial though it was, there was something characteristic about the actions of all three of them.

And so rehearsals began. It is perhaps only in retrospect that Laurence loomed large. At the time I had my own concerns, mainly to do with getting my own part right and making it memorable—a traditional actor's concern—but I did notice Laurence. It was again that streak of cold observation which is part of the equipment of most actors that kept my attention on him. He was one of those people who, without doing anything outright offensive, make themselves shunned by other members of the company.

He attended all rehearsals, even the scenes he was not in. I noticed him anxiously taking notes and writing in his script. When I asked about this he answered that he was there as understudy. I asked him whose parts he was covering, but he was vague, though I understood that at least two of them were Charles Darnay and Defarge. It seemed improbable, but perhaps the management couldn't find anyone else to take on the task, a thankless one. Though I never overheard any conversations between them I noticed that he occasionally talked with Victor Kean, who responded always, as befitted a star (of sorts), with distant politeness. When given the opportunity Laurence would bring Kean his tea in the breaks which several of the company noticed and disliked. "Brown-nosing the stars," was the phrase used about him. "What the fuck is he up to?" Tony asked me once. It was a rhetorical question.

There was something needy and over-anxious about him which made one want to avoid Laurence. His evident desire to please was regarded, as it so often is, with suspicion, especially as it was focused on the more prominent members of the company, in particular Victor Kean. Laurence would often quote some remark of Kean's, prefaced by the words: "Victor said..." As Kean's obiter dicta were neither unusual nor intelligent enough to merit such attention, Laurence began to be regarded with ridicule if not active dislike.

None of this excuses what happened, though I myself took no active part in it. I am and was a mere spectator: that is what makes it so unfair.

It began, I suppose, one night in a dressing room of the Empire Hartlepool, our second week of the tour. The allocation of dressing rooms was always somewhat haphazard and, after the stars had been catered for, paid little heed to any order of precedence or seniority. Laurence had been put in a dressing room with myself, Tony Mawson, and a couple of others, Jock Raven and Arthur Bullard. The rest of us were getting on well, but Laurence, because we thought he was not one of us, was casting a slight shadow over our camaraderie.

A dressing room is the place on tour where you keep a few tokens of your life outside the theatre: photographs of loved ones, postcards of people and places that have taken your fancy, the odd mascot or ornament. Far more than your "digs," the dressing room is your home away from home, in spite of the fact that it can be crowded, stuffy, and reek of sweat and face powder. The bright bulbs round the mirrors, the cream-coloured walls intensify the atmosphere and turn one's own space before the mirror with its cards and personal memorabilia into something like a shrine.

I take an interest in these shrines because they reveal character, aspirations, and dreams. I was not sure whether Laurence's shrine revealed or concealed his nature. Aside from the small array of good-luck cards, several photographs—clearly taken by an amateur—were stuck into the frame of his mirror. They were of theatres both interior and exterior. All were of late nineteenth- or early twentieth-century design, municipal temples to the Muses: their interiors all red plush and gilded putti, the exteriors red brick with decorative marble courses and ornate canopied entrances. When I asked him about them he told me that he had taken the photographs himself in theatres where he had performed, and that he had worked in some "modern" theatres but they did not interest him. Frank Matcham, the great theatre architect at the turn of the last century, was his idol, and he was evidently something of an expert on the subject. However, the information that he offered about Matcham, though detailed, was not in itself of great interest, being largely a matter of dates, names, and places. I have noticed that when men conceive a passion for some subject, they usually express their obsession in the most prosaic, factual terms. Laurence, to add to all his other insufficiencies, was a nerd, but he did say one thing of interest. Apropos of very little, he suddenly said to me: "Even when I'm not in the theatre I try to imagine I'm in one. I'm in them in my dreams all the time, aren't you?" Yes, all actors have theatre dreams and nightmares, but "all the time"? Not me.

The pictures he had taken of his theatres were not inspired. Though in colour, they were often underexposed or taken in poor light; and there was one further aspect of them which slightly disconcerted me. In none of the pictures was there a single human figure. This gave the pictures a feeling of desolate expectancy. All, buildings, but theatres especially, require vibrant human occupancy; but this was excluded from Laurence's pictures, deliberately it seemed to me. Empty seats, empty boxes, and empty foyers, empty stages all uttered a mute appeal for human presence, bustle, and applause.

I was thinking of this while Laurence was talking to me. It was during the interval of the Saturday matinee of the play. Tony,

Jock, and Arthur were also there, drinking tea and consulting their mobiles.

"Victor said he would sit in and watch me," he was saying.

"I'm sorry?"

"Victor Kean. He said he'd sit in and watch me in the understudy rehearsals."

"You must be joking!"

"No. He did. In fact, I might be taking over from Stu who understudies him."

Tony looked up from his mobile and asked why.

"Well, I don't know, but he hasn't learned the lines. I know the lines."

"In your dreams, darling!" Tony said. By this time Jock and Arthur were also paying attention. This made Laurence a little nervous but no more.

"Getting on, aren't we?" said Jock.

"Any objections?"

"No, not at all," said Tony with a quick glance at Jock and Arthur. "But you want to watch that Victor Kean."

"Why?"

"Jealousy. If he comes to rehearsals and sees you giving a better performance than him, he could get nasty."

"You're not serious!"

"Deadly serious." Arthur and Jock were finding it difficult by this time to suppress laughter. "V. K. is a tricky customer. Very tricky. How do you think he got Dr. Who?"

"How?"

"I'd better not say. You never know who might be listening. But suffice it to say, there was dirty work at the crossroads."

"What do you mean? You're winding me up."

"Believe what you like, young Laurence, but don't say I didn't warn you."

It was on our first day in Newcastle that I was approached by the director Ken and asked as a great favour if I would understudy Victor Kean as Sydney Carton. I declined, telling him firmly that my understudying days were over. I asked what was wrong with the previous candidate, Stu. Ken made a face and said that there had been some trouble with the police and that when Victor had heard of it he had objected strongly to the possibility of his role being taken by Stu; he even wanted him out of the company. I didn't ask what the trouble was, but I discovered subsequently that boys in public lavatories were involved, and that he would shortly be making a discreet exit from the company.

"What beats me," said Ken, "is how Vic got to hear of it in the first place. I thought I'd managed to hush it up quite successfully. I thought nobody knew except me and Stu, and the police of course."

"How little you know about theatre companies on tour," I said. "They are like God. You know, 'to whom all hearts be open and from whom no secrets are hid.'" For some reason Ken found the liturgical allusion in rather poor taste. He grimaced. "Anyway," I said, "I thought young Laurence was going to shoulder the burden."

Ken found this remark even more distressing. "Where on earth did you get that idea?"

I decided it would be tactful to be vague. "As I said, a company on tour is a hotbed of gossip and rumour, misleading or otherwise. Anyway, why not poor Laurence?"

"Look, all I wanted to ask you was whether you would help me out by covering Victor in the unlikely eventuality of his being off for some reason; but as you're not prepared to be of any assistance I see no reason why I should prolong this conversation."

Ken was a lucky young man, not long out of Cambridge, where it is still possible to make a name for yourself. Such people, unaware that their youthful success is very ephemeral, can give themselves airs. On the other hand Peter Hall, Trevor Nunn, and other influential names had come from Cambridge. I decided to give him the benefit of the doubt and relented, though I insisted that this new responsibility should be reflected in my salary. Ken said he would see what he could do, but I rang my agent to make sure.

That evening I came into the theatre early. An empty theatre is a place of shadows and sinister excitement; it appeals to me. I was glad that nobody seemed to be around. Quietly, as if unwilling to disturb the silence and solitude, I pushed through the pass door and crept into the wings. The curtain was up and a faint light came from the auditorium where the fire exit signs were still illuminated. One of the features of our set design was a rostrum upstage centre on which stood a guillotine—a permanent reminder of the spectre of the fate awaiting enemies of the revolution, you see. On this rostrum just in front of the guillotine stood a figure in silhouette. It gave me a shock because I was expecting no one. I heard it mutter something. The words were repeated, and then I recognised them as the last lines of the play.

"It is a far, far better thing that I do than I have ever done. It is a far, far better rest that I go to than I have ever known."

He was speaking in a drugged voice, as if from a sleep. The tone was muffled and not at first recognisable. Then he spoke again with a slightly different emphasis:

"It is a far, far *better* thing that I do than I have ever done. It is a far, *far* better rest that I go to than I have ever known."

It was Laurence. The voice was just distinguishable; the solid stocky figure, still only a black shape in the dimness, recognisable. I could think of nothing to say, so I coughed. Laurence uttered a sharp cry and jumped. Then I heard heavy breathing.

"Sorry to disturb," I said. It was inadequate.

"Oh, hi!" His voice was shrill and slightly shaky. He seemed unnaturally perturbed about having been caught out in an act of routine theatrical narcissism.

"Victor's last lines," I said. "You do know that Stu has been replaced as his understudy."

"Well, I thought—"

"By me." That is how it came out. I may have intended to shock him, I don't remember, but if I did it had the desired effect.

"Bloody hell! What the hell are you doing getting in on the act?"

"I didn't want to. Ken insisted."

"What's Ken got to do with it? It's Victor's decision, isn't it?"

"Don't ask me. I'm only obeying orders."

The dark figure, still barely visible, gave a sort of gasp and strode off stage. Just as he was vanishing into the blackness of the wings I heard him trip over a stage weight. He stumbled off screaming obscenities. It startled me that such a small change of circumstance should have aroused such passion, but I have to admit that it also gave me a kind of thrill. I stepped onto the rostrum and my voice rang out.

"It is a far, far better thing that I do than I have ever done. It is a far, far better rest that I go to than I have ever known."

Then I laughed. I don't know why, but I almost frightened myself. Still, it sounded lovely in that empty theatre.

Laurence shared our dressing room again that week. He was even more solitary and divided from the rest of us than he had been before.

"Everything all right, Laurence?" said Tony that night before the performance. Laurence ignored Tony, who glanced round at the rest of us, smiling. Arthur and Jock sniggered. Perhaps they also knew. During the interval I saw Laurence earnestly engaging Victor Kean in conversation in the corridor outside the "star" dressing room. Victor's handsome features wore a distant, bored look. When he saw me he nodded in acknowledgment of my presence, a thing he had not done before.

Understudy rehearsals are tedious, uninspiring events, even at the best of times. Those for *A Tale of Two Cities* were peculiarly unrewarding. They were conducted, as was the custom, by the Company Stage Manager, a woman called Karen who made it plain that she had many better ways to occupy her time than to listen to actors and actresses in parts for which they were not intended. She took us meticulously through lines and moves and that was all. I cannot say that the other performers, myself included, showed any greater enthusiasm. The exception to this was Laurence: he entered into his parts with gusto and even offered suggestions to Karen and the other actors as to how things might be improved. This did not find favour with any of us. After one such outburst from Laurence we heard Karen from the back of the auditorium say in tones of extreme weariness:

"Can we just get on with it, please?" It was a sentiment with which the rest of us, Laurence excluded, completely concurred.

I found it tiresome—no more than that—that Laurence attached himself to me during these dreary sessions. I paid very little attention to what he said, but I was conscious of something being wrong about him. I will say no more than that; but the feeling grew. He seemed preoccupied by the fact that various members of the company, as he put it, "had it in for" him. "They don't want me to succeed," he said. I did not encourage these delusions but neither, I must admit, did I try to dispel them. Several times what he said suggested that his mental state was infected by something more serious than a routine professional paranoia.

We had finished a listless session of understudy rehearsals one afternoon and were beginning to disperse. I had, I admit, moved rather quickly towards the pass door, partly out of an anxiety not to be caught by Laurence, but he was too quick for me. I felt my arm seized from behind.

"This is the problem," he said, as if he was in the middle of a conversation and I had intruded on it. "There are some people who have been chosen. Something in them is meant and they have no choice in the matter. Every night I dream I am in the theatre, and every time I am in a theatre I know that is where I am meant to be. I have been given the road to stardom, because this is the world that has been chosen for me, I had nothing to do with it. The theatre is my cathedral. But when you get chosen there is always an enemy who stands in your way. Where there is a chosen race, there is also anti-Semitism. Where there is Christ, there is the Antichrist. Do you understand? I know who my enemies are in this company; but I don't know about you. I can't work you out. Whose side are you on?"

"Do I have to be on anybody's side?"

"Oh, yes. You'll go mad if you're not."

"I see. There's just time for a swift drink before the half. Coming?"

"I never drink before a show."

I noticed how deliberately he was being shunned by the other members of the company. I remember when we were in Blackpool, walking down the Golden Mile one night after the show. It had been raining and I was hurrying over wet pavements that glittered with a thousand gaudy reflected lights. I was destined for an Indian restaurant where I had arranged to meet other members of the company for a late-night curry. I had reached the point where, outside an amusement arcade, there used to stand in a glass case an animated dummy of a sailor boy who periodically rocks to and fro letting out screams of maniacal laughter, his toothy mechanical jaws gnashing up and down, locked in a death's-head grin. Is he still there? I rather hope not. I had paused briefly to contemplate this monstrosity when I saw Victor Kean coming towards me, bound in the opposite direction. There was as usual a look of dreamy abstraction on his face. Suddenly he stopped and his expression froze as he stared past me; then he darted down a side street. Behind me I heard a voice say: "Did you see that?"

I turned and saw that it was Laurence carrying an open umbrella above his head even though it had stopped raining. The top of his face shadowed by the umbrella, the lower part lit from below by reds and greens and yellows of Blackpool illuminations reflected in the shining pavement, made him look like the villain in a melodrama, looming over the footlights.

"What?"

"Victor. Did you see? He deliberately avoided me."

"Oh?"

"I know why. So do you."

"Ah. Excuse me. Must dash." And I too deliberately escaped him, just as the sailor boy began once more to rock and scream.

Was it from this moment that I noticed an atmosphere of malice and venom enter the company? Or is this just retrospective imagination? At our next date, which was Leeds, I noted that for some reason Laurence had a small dressing room to himself at the top of the theatre. I shared again with Tony, Arthur, and Jock, and there was some talk of him, though I suspected that they were keeping a secret plan from me. I had by this time learnt my understudy part and was almost beginning to hope that Victor would have an accident and give me the opportunity to play Sydney Carton, but I kept these thoughts to himself. It was on the Wednesday evening after the matinee that Tony sidled up to me after the performance and asked me if I would like to see something amusing the following day. He told me that he had arranged what he called a "special understudy" rehearsal in which Laurence would read Victor's part and he, Arthur, and Jock would read the other parts. They had even secured the use of the theatre in the afternoon for that purpose.

"But why?" I asked.

"For a laugh. Because Laurence is always saying he ought to be playing Victor's part and you stole his understudy role."

"Did he say that?"

"We're going to hold this rehearsal and put a stop to all the shit he's been coming out with. We're going to put an end to his dreams. We're sick of them, and him. Are you game?"

I said, "I don't want anything to do with it." I walked away and that's what makes it so unfair. I still feel guilty about it. I doubt very much if anyone else does.

What happened next I gathered from various sources, including, with much difficulty, Laurence himself.

I heard about the so-called "special understudy rehearsal" afterwards from various sources including Laurence himself, though his account for obvious reasons was sketchier than the rest. What all are agreed on is that it took some considerable time before Laurence realised that he was being comprehensively mocked, or that it was, as his tormentors put it, "a wind-up." Even they began to feel uneasy when he started to put vehement passion into his portrayal of Sydney Carton. Perhaps it was this unexpected animation that stifled their laughter and prolonged the agony. When Laurence finally realised that he was being had, he was performing Carton's final speech on the scaffold: "It is a far, far better thing. . ." By that time the sniggers of his persecutors could no longer be stifled.

Laurence stopped mid-speech and went white; then he screamed so loud and long that his tormentors began to fear for his safety, or at the very least his sanity. They came up on stage and tried to restrain him, but by this time Laurence had lost all control and his strength was considerable. Four of them, not without considerable injury to themselves, finally managed to restrain him, and it was then that the accident happened.

In order to restrain him better they had laid him out on the guillotine that formed the central stage prop of the production, and they had the back of his neck directly under the blade. Now of course, it was not a real blade; it was light and made out of some kind of resin painted to look like metal, and its edge was blunt. Nevertheless, it was, as they say on the stage, "practical" and could descend on the release of a handle. Well, somehow the handle was released and the "blade" came down with considerable force onto the back of Laurence's unprotected neck. Laurence was knocked unconscious, and when he failed to come round his fellow actors began to be uneasy.

Finally an ambulance was summoned and Laurence was taken off to hospital, where he spent several days in a coma in intensive care. The tour limped on for a few weeks and I, feeling oddly guilty about the whole wretched business, visited him when I could.

It was only after the tour had come to an end that Laurence became fully conscious again. I began to visit him regularly. He looked very much the same, except for one thing: his hair was white. He was sitting up in bed and taking food and drink by mouth, but his hand movements were still severely limited. He expressed neither pleasure nor surprise at my appearance, but he wanted to talk. I say he wanted to talk, but this was merely an intuition of mine because at first he seemed incapable of initiating a conversation.

It was only on my third visit that he began to talk fluently about his experiences, and then it was difficult to stop him. The first thing of importance was that he said he had nearly died, but they had got to him in time. There was a long pause before he added: "Or did they? Perhaps he did really die." From then onwards, as he talked, Laurence referred to himself purely in the third person. My account now is all in his own words, but taken from several sessions with me in which he obsessively went over the details of his "experience," as he called it.

After the being held down on the guillotine and feeling a heavy blow on the back of his neck, the next thing Laurence remembered was a feeling of surprise that all was now well. He was back in his dressing room at the theatre, or, at least, a dressing room very like his. He was seated at a dressing table, before a mirror surrounded by bright bulbs.

Laurence looked into the mirror and adjusted his makeup with a little brush. It was never going to be perfect, but it would do. His costume was magnificent, though—one he had always dreamed of. It was of tight-fitting black velvet encrusted with sequins and paste diamonds—tastefully though—and it made the best of his still slightly podgy figure. Over his dressing-room speaker he could hear a faint but voluminous sound like an ocean moving restlessly under an infinite sky. It was the rustle of a thousand dresses, the murmur of a thousand barely audible voices: it was the noise of an audience coming into a theatre. Laurence wondered why he was not more excited. Here he was, for the first time in his life, in a dressing room of his own, encased in a splendid costume, looking his best (such as it was) and obviously about to perform a major role. But what?

The murmur from the speaker ceased and was replaced by a voice, metallic and impersonal.

"Overture and beginners. Mr. Laurence Hamlet to the stage, please! Mr. Laurence Hamlet to the stage, please!"

For all its mechanical intonations it was a gratifying speech to his ears. Laurence rose with the luxurious stealth of a practiced performer. He permitted himself a turn in the full-length mirror with which he had been thoughtfully provided and then opened the door into the passage.

Here he was confronted with a problem: which way to the stage? There was no one about whom he could ask. There were other doors in the passage, but when knocked on they yielded no answer from beyond, and they were locked. He would have to follow his instinct, so he turned left, knowing that the main entrance to the stage was usually "prompt side" or stage left.

He turned a corner and—yes!—he had been right. There was a pair of dark red swing doors with the word STAGE written in bold white paint across them. Imperiously Laurence pushed them both open and entered. With a reverential whisper the dark red doors closed behind him.

He was now in the wings of the theatre. He noticed shadowy figures moving about in the gloom and nodded to them with distant friendliness. The only light came from a single "worker" which shone down from a space high above the curtain, behind which he could hear the muffled tumult of his audience. He looked up into the fly tower, hung with cloths and pieces of scenery, but there was no roof, only an infinite regression of theatrical paraphernalia. It was all very impressive, and at this moment perhaps he should have been feeling fear, but he did not, at least not predominantly. It was all too exciting.

Presently he became aware that a shadowy figure in the prompt corner was gesturing to him. He should take his place on stage for the opening of the show. He walked on and found himself in a set that looked like the courtyard of a castle. It was detailed and heavily ornamented with Gothic crockets and finials, ogival arches, turrets, and stairs. It was a fine thing and if he found it a little oppressive, that was only natural. The one feature of the set that seemed a little out of place was a vast structure, about as high as the castle walls, which stood on one of the rostra. It was a guillotine.

Laurence placed himself on a landing from which a flight of

steps led down to the stage level. Behind him was a Gothic portal, the keystone of which was carved in the shape of a grinning mask with prominent teeth. Laurence approved the workmanship, even though the whole effect was a little disconcerting. He could not rid himself of the impression that the jaws were slowly moving, and that he could have heard words if the muttering of the audience and the tuning of an orchestra beyond the curtain had been softer.

He might have begun to think what he was doing there, but just then from beyond the curtain he heard the crackle of applause. Then, after a brief silence, the overture began. He recognised the music as mid-nineteenth-century Romantic—by Weber perhaps or Marschner? It was one of those, but perhaps neither, all crashing chords, rushing climaxes, and shivering string arpeggios. There seemed to be no discernible melody; however, it was exciting enough and almost alarmingly consonant with the thrilling terror in his head. Then the working light snapped off and he was left for a moment in complete darkness until he saw that the curtain was slowly rising and the lights beyond were being revealed.

For several seconds all he saw was lights, concentrated as they were, gratifyingly, on himself, but as the orchestra came to its crashing conclusion his eyes became accustomed to the scene. The auditorium before him was vast, far vaster than any he had ever been in before. It was not a theatre, it was an opera house, and an opera house greater than any he had ever seen: a giant red plush and gilt stadium, palatial in its grandeur. Above the stalls which stretched back into obscurity, there was a grand tier, full of gilded boxes, every inch decorated with writhing plaster putti, swags of flowers, tritons, sea monsters, and other opulent mythical beasts. Above the grand tier was a royal circle, above that another and another, one above the other encircling the stalls into infinity, and every seat was occupied. The men were in white tie and tails; the women, gowned and jewelled, coruscated faintly in the dimness.

Laurence was facing the greatest audience he had ever seen. He did not at that moment know what he felt; his emotions were so conflicted. Trying to compose himself, he looked at the faces of his public. They were all white, it seemed to him, and curiously nondescript. He tried to concentrate on one. It looked as if it had been made of dough, with two holes punched in it for eyes and a lipless maw for a mouth. The nose was little more than a blobby protuberance, but, even as he stared at it, the features changed, stretched, expanded, and contracted into a different set of features, equally vague and nondescript.

The overture concluded with a great swish from the cymbals and a monumental chord on the brass. After a spattering of applause there was a silence, and Laurence knew that it was his turn: all eyes were on him. For a brief moment he wondered what on earth he was going to do or say, then he opened his mouth and the words came rolling out.

> *Round the wide earth's unhindered mindless crust*
> *I seek the regions of my boneless life*
> *Passing through miles of incandescent dust*
> *Onto the plains of fire-encircled strife. . .*

The words seemed to come out of him from nowhere. He could hear the faint echo of his voice as it resounded through that boundless auditorium. His utterance soared through the edifice. He was exhilarated; he had achieved the pinnacle of theatrical magnificence, and yet—what on earth was he saying? What play was he in? What part was he playing? What the hell did it all mean? Still the words came—

> *Moons that have been and stars that burgeon still*
> *Extinguish all but my undented soul*

Hopeless and sad, I grind the bitter pill
And still the wind that blows from pole to pole. . .

The absolute silence that had greeted his first four lines were now being punctuated by little ripples of laughter from odd corners of the auditorium. Coughs and snorts, like tiny gunshots, indicated that some people were beginning to lose control of themselves. A part of Laurence began to despair, but he continued to speak, raising his voice, trying to assume greater authority over the words that seemed to him to mean even less than they did to his public. . .

A piece of elsewhere, parsnip-trousered now
Pervades old songs that whisper in the gloom
I sport a peacock on my furrowed brow
As boldly I invade my punctured tomb. . .

By this time the titters had expanded into laughter, which was coming from all quarters of that vast and limitless theatre, drowning any sound of his own voice. Laurence could no longer hear himself speak. He stared at the millions of faces whose mouths, grinning, almost retching with mocking merriment, now obscured every other aspect of their elastic faces. They were just grinning maws on top of boiled shirtfronts and jewel-encrusted necks. That great golden opera house was alive with laughter, and all of it directed at him.

I rest and yet I rest not. Winter burns,
And summer shuts up mice in golden urns.

The words were barely coming out. Laurence's heart was pounding. The horror of it was building. Words came to him, as if he had learned them, but they made no sense and the laughter built and built until it became a deafening roar. Then, with a great effort, he stopped himself from speaking and all at once a silence fell as piercing and terrible as the roar. He had to speak; anything, even derision, was better than this silence, in which the embarrassment of failure was magnified by a thousand. But now, no words, not even gibberish, came up to him from his subconscious. He cast around for something to say and then he remembered one speech, one only, so he spoke it:

"It is a far, far better thing that I do than I have ever done. It is a far, far better rest that I go to than I have ever known."

A great roar of derision went up, accompanied by a thunder of feet upon the ground. The noise became intolerable. Laurence covered his ears with his hands and ran from the stage. Now where would he go? For what seemed like an age he was blundering about in the wings. The stage was still brightly lit, but very little of the illumination penetrated beyond it. At last he found the pass door and was in to the backstage corridors. Which seemed to stretch a very long way in both directions.

Laurence considered his position. He needed to escape from the theatre, and to do so he must find the stage door. He had no idea where to find it or even whether the corridor he was in was at ground level. As he emerged from the stage from a pass door roughly situated in the middle of the back wall, there was no obvious direction in which to go. He turned to his left.

Along the corridor were several doors, and on each was a gleaming brass plate on which had been incised in italicised capitals: *LAURENCE HAMLET.* He tried one of the doors, but it was locked. Something told him that he should not try to enter. He walked along the corridor until he found some stairs which went up. He ascended them and found, not as he had hoped, an exit via the stage door but another corridor with a blank wall on one side and a row of doors on the other. On each of the doors was a brass plate or a card affixed by adhesive, or a mere piece of paper attached by a drawing pin. All bore the same two-word legend: LAURENCE HAMLET. Laurence tried one of the doors, but it would not open, and his reluctance to try again overwhelmed his now desperate need to escape. Laurence tried to describe what he was feeling. Was it fear? Not exactly. It was more a deep feeling that something in this world was wrong and there was no remedy for it. "I felt hopeless . . . helpless . . . one or the other. Perhaps both," he told me once. That was his most succinct description. He listened at one of the doors and heard a kind of chanting sound which at first he did not understand, then he recognised the tune. It was the *galop* from Rossini's overture to William Tell, to which words had been put.

> *"Many men, many men, many men, men, men!*
> *Many men, many men, many men, men, men!*
> *Many men, many men, many men, men, men!*
> *Many men!*
> *Many men, men, men . . . !"*

A long time ago—it seemed to him—when he had been an actor on the stage he used to say that in the dressing room as a vocal warm-up, to aid articulation. It sounded . . . it sounded horribly like his own voice. He began to run down the corridor almost blindly in search of some way out. He came to another flight of stone steps. They led upwards and he took them.

There were more corridors, more stone steps leading upwards. He must be high now, high above the stage almost at the level of one of the higher circles, but it was a vast theatre. He was in a corridor with a glass roof through which a white light filtered. There was no sun, just an even distribution of bland daylight. One side of the corridor was, as usual, blank, and painted with the same glossy cream paint as all the other corridors; on the other side were a number of doors, but less frequently distributed than on the lower levels.

From one there came a murmur of several voices. Reluctantly, but with desperation now prevailing, he tried the door and it opened. Within was what he recognised as a chorus dressing room, long, almost infinitely long, with dressing tables and mirrors surrounded by bulbs all along one wall. Against the corridor wall were racks of costumes, and within the body of this room were a crowd of men, all chattering, all in various stages of dress or undress, and all of them had the face of Laurence Hamlet. He was looking at upwards of a hundred replicas of himself.

The conversation died, the room fell silent, and Laurence stood looking at a staring crowd of men who were him. One was completely naked except for one white silk stocking which he was in the act of putting on. Above the panic and confusion of this still moment what Laurence felt most of all was mounting rage. He was him. There must be nobody else who was him except himself, Laurence. The silence and the stillness continued. The almost naked man, the only one who was not motionless, began to put on a second white stocking, still making no effort to cover himself. There was something defiant, almost aggressive, in his exposure.

It began to feel like a test of nerve. Whose would break first? The naked man bared his teeth in a grin and a kind of laugh began to come from him, though as his face and jaw made no further movement it was hard to tell. Laurence could stand it no longer. He broke and made for the door. There were a few hideous moments when his sweat-slicked hands could find no purchase on the round brass doorknob—and then he was through, back into the corridor. A shout came from behind him and a thunder of feet.

Laurence did not look behind him, but he knew now as he ran

that he was being pursued by a hundred half-dressed men who all looked like him. Some objective element within him recognised the absurdity, the impossibility of the situation, but terror was sweeping all aside. In his panic he missed, or thought he missed, the stairs which were his only certain means of escape.

At the end of the corridor there was a door on the stage side. Laurence opened it without considering where it might lead, anxious only to get away from his pursuers. He closed the door heavily behind him. It clanged shut and he leaned against it breathing heavily.

At first he thought he had stepped into complete darkness, as the light in the passageway from the windows had been brilliant if not warming. He listened at the door but heard nothing beyond it and no one was trying to open it. Small patches of light began to manifest themselves. He stamped on the ground and felt around him and discovered he was on a metal walkway high up in the theatre's fly tower. His hand reached out to grasp an iron railing.

Now far below him through a latticework of gantries and forests of dangling ropes he could see the stage, deserted, but still lit with a golden glow. Music rose from the orchestra pit, full of scurrying strings and elaborate arpeggios. Like music in a dream, it gestured and struck attitudes but never resolved itself into a melody or a developing sequence. The door behind him began to rattle. Laurence's pursuers were on to him.

Laurence ran along the walkway, his boots clanging loudly so that the whole upper part of the theatre seemed to echo with his stride. Then he came to some steps down to a lower level, and he took them. There was no other way but down. Through the pierced metal of the steps and walkway he could see the stage below slowly coming closer. There was no way for it: he would have to brave the stage again.

As he clattered down the steps towards the stage he could hear the orchestra getting closer, and its stuttering rhythms appeared to be in exact timing with his own rushing feet. When he halted for breath, the music halted; when he ran on, so did the music. From above there was a faint hubbub. He looked up and saw that the creatures with his face were in pursuit, albeit clumsily, stumbling along the walkways and down the stairs, sometimes tripping over one another and falling together in a heap at the bottom of a flight. It was almost comic. This meant, at least, that they were not gaining on Laurence.

He was returning to the stage from which he had fled so ignominiously, but there was no alternative. Down the clanging metal flights he came, fleeing from the multiplications of himself. It was the sense of what he was that was under attack, that sense which, in spite of everything, had been so strong through the years. Had it been too strong? Was that why he was now in hell?

He did not feel like a disembodied spirit—not that he knew what a disembodied spirit should feel like. His body ached with physical exertion and his legs felt rubbery and uncertain from fear. He even touched his cheek to see if his sensations were authentic. They were all too real. In fact, he had never been more conscious of his physical being. There were moments when he thought he could feel the blood pulsing through his veins. Above him the crowd of his own clones—or "clowns" he called them in a moment of wild, spontaneous wit—were making their way down towards him, all now murmuring in chorus:

> *"Many men, many men, many men, men, men!*
> *Many men, many men, many men, men, men . . . !"*

And the orchestra seemed to be accompanying them.

Laurence at last reached the stage where he paused to gasp for breath, not caring a jot now for the audience or its derision.

He stared out. Beyond the orchestra pit, where the musicians were busy sawing away at *William Tell,* and all of them for some reason in white clown masks and Pierrot costumes, he saw again the audience. But something had happened to it. Those grinning elastic faces in their thousands, rank upon rank of them, tier upon tier, had begun to merge. In twos and threes their faces began to glue together and the faces became more and more amorphous, mere stretches of undifferentiated flesh, creased and striated with lines of senseless mockery. The sound of laughter had turned into a series of crackles and wheezes, barely human, barely even animal. The bodies merged too into corpulent bulges of black cloth, like elderly opera singers in the last stages of their obese celebrity. Now the whole of the stalls wobbled and crepitated as one. And in the higher reaches of the theatre, the circle, the gallery, the gods, the upper gods and beyond the crowds of onlookers were congealing and merging. Laurence's mind spun, but a centre somewhere kept its reluctant control.

Behind him the chorus of clones, still babbling, had reached the stage level. He saw himself trapped and in a world that surely must be an extension of his own troubled mind. And at that moment the urge merely to give in to his own madness, to renounce any strength he had left and curl inwards into a closed dark space of oblivious regret, was almost overwhelming. Something within him held out.

He saw no way back, but now that the audience had merged into a disabled blob he saw a way past it. Behind him the clones were preparing to charge him to seize him and carry him away into themselves.

Laurence took one step back and then ran at full tilt towards the edge of the stage, taking a leap which took him almost over the heads of the clown orchestra. His right foot clipped the brass rail that separated the conductor's podium from the auditorium, and he fell sprawling onto the front row of the stalls.

As he was getting to his feet he touched the mass of amorphous flesh that now composed the audience. It was damp and sticky and smelt of decaying fish. He reeled with horror against the conductor's rail, and his throat was seized by a violinist whose red-lipped mask grinned into his face. With the strength of desperation Laurence twisted himself round and broke free. There were two narrow aisles between the centre block of seats and the blocks to the left and right. Laurence took the left-hand aisle and began to run. His heart was now pounding, his rubbery legs threatening to collapse at any moment, but he pounded on. Behind him the whole theatre was roaring. The sound felt like a great wind at his back.

At the back wall of the auditorium, red as the inside of a flayed body, Laurence saw a set of double doors with two panels of bevelled glass set in them through which he could see a flicker of yellow light.

In another moment he was through the double doors and into a glittering hall. Onyx columns with gilded Corinthian capitals supported painted vaults from which hung crystal chandeliers and on which painted putti played fatuously among shining clouds.

Laurence stood on a balconied landing carpeted in scarlet spangled with silver stars. Before him a flight of marble steps which led down to a vast floor in chequered black and white marble. Behind him the double doors groaned and he saw something vast and fleshy trying to burst its way through.

He took to the stairs rapidly and did not look behind him, but by the time he had gone down twenty steps and was on a second carpeted landing he heard a noise behind him halfway between an explosion and the sound of a bag full of offal bursting on a stone floor. He took the second flight, and as he did so he noticed something oozing down the marble stairs beside him, a viscous semi-transparent fluid in which floated grey rags of flesh and gristle. He tried not to rush his descent in case he fell, but something monstrous was behind him, unseen because he did not dare to look.

Now he was at the bottom of the steps, of which there had been scores, hundreds. There was no time to admire the chandeliers, the onyx columns, nor the ten-foot-high marble statue of—Athena was it? It looked like a man in a dress and the features of the face were curiously familiar. They were his own. But there was no time. The thing that he dared not turn round to see was behind him. Something sticky lapped at his heels. He took a plunge towards the double glass doors in front of him, and the next moment he was outside.

Only then did he look back. Laurence stood in an empty grey street, and behind him reared a vast structure that he had never seen before but which reminded him of so many buildings he had seen except that it was bigger by an almost infinite factor. It was slightly yellowish in colour but with infinite, if rather limited, variations on this shade. The even grey light in which he stood did not add lustre to it. It rose in tiers of colonnades, architraves, courses of rusticated masonry, Doric friezes. Rows of pedimented windows and blind arcades were full of niches holding gesturing statuary. Some miles, it seemed to him, above him, was a dome, gilded evidently but not glittering because the grey light was too evenly distributed to be the sun.

He stood on an empty grey pavement among tall buildings every one of which, apart from the theatre, was made from the same grey stone on which he stood. It took him a few moments to recognise what was strange about these structures. It was odd that they had no windows, but what was even more curious was the fact that their façades did not resemble ordinary exteriors but rather casts taken of the inside walls of the rooms and passages of which they were composed. Thus the interior of a fireplace stuck outwards while its overmantel was a dark, oblong recess in the wall of the building.

Why this troubled Laurence so much he could not say, but it disturbed his sensibilities deeply and stole his attention as he stood panting from his exertions in the street. It preoccupied him so much that he failed to notice, or at first only dimly perceived, the thing that was emerging from the theatre.

It was something like a bulbous cloud of blue-grey smoke that was forcing its way out of the great double doors of the theatre and into the street. It was not quite like smoke because it seemed more solid, and yet not quite as solid as flesh or stone — something between, like the gently yielding exterior of a vast jelly. Laurence began to retreat before it.

Slowly, as more and more of the grey matter began to emerge from the theatre, it began to congregate and build itself up into a form, starting with a pair of ill-shaped feet. Then a pair of bare legs reared up, followed by a torso, then a head. Only the genital area remained undefined: Laurence was obscurely grateful for that. The whole was as grey as a storm cloud and utterly innocent of colour. It might have been a statue except that it seemed less substantial and it moved. Laurence was briefly reminded of an opera his mother had taken him to in his youth. Most of it had passed him by, but when at the end the stone statue of the Commendatore had come to life Laurence had been mesmerised. It had come on with great heavy steps and when it had seized Don Giovanni in its granite grip Laurence knew that the hero was doomed. Then a trapdoor opened in the stage, alive with red light, and the demons had dragged him below.

Laurence stared up at his own Commendatore, except that this one was unclothed, if not exactly naked. The face too was odd. It seemed to be undergoing all kinds of subtle transformations. At one point it was the head of a baby, then of a very old man, then of an intermediary state between these extremes. Because of these quite rapid changes it was some time before he could identify the features as his own. Then he knew he must run.

He fled him down the grey streets, not looking to see if the Commendatore—as he called him, for fear of something more precise—was pursuing, but knowing he was. He heard a ground-shaking tread behind him. He was in a maze of streets, all grey, all the same, all with grey buildings rearing up on either side of him. Sometimes he would come upon a cul-de-sac at the end of which was a building on which hung a banner, or sometimes an advertising hoarding on each of which was a vast image of himself, well delineated but always grey. Sometimes they were old, and sometimes young, the features of the face clearer than other parts of the body.

Whenever he came upon these, there always seemed to be a side-street down which he could dart, but then he would always emerge on the other side into another great grey street and the pursuit would continue. He only caught glimpses of his giant follower, but he never failed to hear the great heavy footsteps that seemed to him like the footsteps of time.

He found that each time he turned away from a cul-de-sac into a side street, the way was darker and narrower. Then he found himself squeezing sideways down a passage so dark and high that he could barely see the grey light above and to either side. Halfway down he found himself stuck, unable to move to one side or the other, and it seemed to him that the walls of this deep dark alley were closing in on him. There was a heavy pressure on his chest. With great difficulty, and knowing that he was near extinction, he slid his hands upwards and inwards so that, with barely enough room, he managed to cover his face with them.

It was then, Laurence told me, that he faced complete

annihilation. Well, if he ceased to be, then he ceased to be; that would be it. There would be nobody to have regrets or feel guilt: what would be wrong with that? This is what reason told him, but something within rebelled violently against the idea. The prospect of non-being sickened him. But why? There would be nothing to be sick about. Some inner force, quite outside all logic and sense, strove to remain conscious and alive, even within this hideous dream or vision of his. Until that moment, if it can be called a moment, he had not known how strong was the will to live. It was, he said, the one small light in this world of surreal misery that he was enduring.

Turning the palms of his hands away from his face, he began to push with all his strength. At first he thought of it as a vain gesture, a mere act of defiance against the inevitable, but slowly he felt the wall opposite him—dark and clammy and covered with some kind of viscous substance, possibly tar—yield a little. He pushed harder until he could get his feet up against the wall and push with his back and feet.

Suddenly he felt and heard something crack and splinter against his feet, and the next moment they encountered vacancy. Scrambling painfully to a standing position, he found himself half in and half out of some kind of opening in the wall opposite. Both walls of his passage were now inexorably beginning to close again, so there was nothing for it but to enter the hole he had created.

He was in the dark. He felt no roof above him nor walls on either side. There was only a floor, solid enough but covered with a kind of grit that crackled when he walked. Strangely enough, though he could see nothing, he felt safer, less threatened than he had been for some time. He walked forward, knowing no direction, caring for none, pleased only that he made conscious progress, of a sort. It was a long while before he thought he saw a light, albeit a grey one. As he moved forward, the light resolved itself into a figure that was walking towards him, still too dim and distant to identify. When he stopped it stopped too. He tried raising an arm; it raised a mirror image of his arm. Was he walking towards a looking glass, then? He shouted, but his voice met a dead acoustic, so that he could barely hear himself speak. He began to run towards it, and it ran too. The next moment his head crashed into glass. It was a mirror, but a thin one, because he was now walking through it and found himself in a dimly lit space, surrounded by images of himself.

Behind and before him to his left and right his reflections stretched away into a dull green distance. He began to feel trapped once more, but there must be a way out. If there had been a way in, then there must be a way out. Indeed there was. As he was feeling his way around this hall of mirrors, which were on the floor and the ceiling as well, he found a break in the long smooth surface. Here was a passageway, but it too was walled and floored and ceilinged with glass reflections of himself. The atmosphere in it was even more oppressive than the hall, but he resolved to walk down it, because it might lead somewhere.

He thought it was strange that he could see all these reflections of himself and yet he could detect no source of light. He paused to consider this, studying himself closely.

His hands and extremities were visible, but the main part of his body was a mere dark shape. The most visible part of him was his face, and he came to the conclusion that whatever light there was in this strange environment was coming from his own head.

The passage led to more halls of mirrors, more passages, some long, some short, some vast, others confined. He walked a long time in a wilderness of mirrors until he began to notice something strange. It was hard at first, Laurence told me, to recognise strangeness in a world that was, from an objective point of view, all strangeness. But there were times when he could see no reflection of himself in the glass, and there were other times when he could see himself reflected, and yet not reflected. He saw another being, like him in some respects, and yet not in others. For one thing, he appeared to be wearing a long dress, like the Greek chiton worn by the statue of Athena, and he had breasts. Though the figure he saw was not exactly voluptuous, it certainly had more curves than his own. The hair was white and silvery, longer than he knew it to be.

As he wandered he encountered this apparition more and more. The reflection of his female self mirrored his movements exactly. Only the costume and the shape was not his. Turning a mirrored corridor, he found himself in a new hall of mirrors vaster than all the others in which every image of himself that he encountered was dressed as a woman.

He stopped, he tried to keep silence, but found that the beat of his heart had filled the chamber with monstrous echoes. Where else might he go now, surrounded at last by these travesties of himself? Long moments passed while the beat of his heart slowed to the reverberation of a great funeral drum.

Then came the decision. He retreated to one wall of the great reflecting chamber and, running as fast as his legs and his heart would allow him, charged down the hall straight at one of his images while she, picking up the folds of her skirt, ran like a fury to meet him. They collided in a crash of broken glass, and a million starry shards shattered across him as he fell through the fractured mirror and into space. Down he went, down a tunnel towards a light, bright and clinical and uninspiring, but a light nonetheless. Then with a convulsive leap as it seemed to him he landed on an operating table, gasped, vomited, opened his eyes and found himself surrounded by masked medical men and women. He tasted the sourness in his mouth and was almost blinded by a shaft of pain in his head, but he knew for the first time in his life that he was alive again. Someone said fatuously, "Hi, Laurence!" He gasped for breath and vomited again. He felt safe and matter-of-fact once more.

§

All this Laurence told me while recovering in hospital after the accident. I visited him there several times and, at first, he seemed pleased to see me and to provide me with the elaborate details of his extraordinary adventures; but on the last occasion I called on him, he was listless and abstracted. When I next called at the hospital three days later, he had left. The nurse told me that he had discharged himself and had gone abroad "to have an operation." When I asked the nature of the operation the nurse merely smiled and shook her head. She said that his mother had just died and he had come into some money which enabled him to make the journey.

It was more than a year before I came across Laurence again, quite by accident at the Covent Garden offices of Equity, the actors' trade union. By this time, he was no longer Laurence.

Vivien Piddick, as he—or rather she—now calls herself, works for Equity in some sort of administrative capacity. Her hands are rather large and coarse for a woman's, but otherwise you would take her for just another dumpy, undistinguished, middle-aged female with sparse, lank hair dyed henna red. Her only really attractive features are her eyes, which are large, liquid, and brown with long eyelashes, like a cow's. She smiles much and seems to get on well with her colleagues, but on the few occasions that I have tried to engage her in conversation, she pretends that she doesn't know me. Perhaps she genuinely doesn't.

DREAM-LAND

EDGAR ALLAN POE

By a route obscure and lonely,
Haunted by ill angels only,
Where an Eidolon, named Night,
On a black throne reigns upright,
I have reached these lands but newly
From an ultimate dim Thule—
From a wild weird clime that lieth, sublime,
　　　Out of Space—out of Time.

Bottomless vales and boundless floods,
And chasms, and caves, and Titan woods,
With forms that no man can discover
For the dews that drip all over;
Mountains toppling evermore
Into seas without a shore;
Seas that restlessly aspire,
Surging, unto skies of fire;
Lakes that endlessly outspread

Their lone waters—lone and dead,—
Their still waters—still and chilly
With the snows of the lolling lily.

By the lakes that thus outspread
Their lone waters, lone and dead,—
Their sad waters, sad and chilly
With the snows of the lolling lily,—
By the mountains— near the river
Murmuring lowly, murmuring ever,—
By the grey woods,—by the swamp
Where the toad and the newt encamp,—
By the dismal tarns and pools
  Where dwell the Ghouls,—
By each spot the most unholy—
In each nook most melancholy,—
There the traveller meets aghast
Sheeted Memories of the Past—
Shrouded forms that start and sigh
As they pass the wanderer by—
White-robed forms of friends long given,
In agony, to the Earth—and Heaven.

For the heart whose woes are legion
'Tis a peaceful, soothing region—
For the spirit that walks in shadow
O! it is an Eldorado!
But the traveller, travelling through it,
May not—dare not openly view it;
Never its mysteries are exposed
To the weak human eye unclosed;
So wills its King, who hath forbid

The uplifting of the fringed lid;
And thus the sad Soul that here passes
Beholds it but through darkened glasses.

By a route obscure and lonely,
Haunted by ill angels only,
Where an Eidolon, name NIGHT,
On a black throne reigns upright,
I have wandered home but newly
From this ultimate dim Thule.

NOTES ON CONTRIBUTORS

The Editor

S. T. Joshi is the author of *The Weird Tale* (University of Texas Press, 1990), *I Am Providence: The Life and Times of H. P. Lovecraft* (Hippocampus Press, 2010), *Unutterable Horror: A History of Supernatural Fiction* (PS Publishing, 2012), and other critical and biographical works. He has edited the complete fiction, poetry, and essays of H. P. Lovecraft and has prepared editions of the work of Lord Dunsany, Arthur Machen, Ambrose Bierce, and many other writers of weird fiction. Among his anthologies are *American Supernatural Tales* (Penguin, 2007), the *Black Wings* series (PS Publishing, 2010f.), and *Searchers After Horror* (Fedogan & Bremer, 2014). He has won the the British Fantasy Award, the Bram Stoker Award, and the International Horror Guild Award.

The Contributors

David Barker is, in collaboration with W. H. Pugmire, the author of two works of horror fiction: *The Revenant of Rebecca Pascal* (2014) and *In the Gulfs of Dream and Other Lovecraftian Tales* (2015). A collaborative novel, *Witches in Dreamland*, is forthcoming from Dark Regions Press. *Little Gray Bastards*, his nonfiction book on alien abduction written with Jordan Hofer, appeared in 2016.

Jason V Brock is an award-winning writer, editor, filmmaker, and artist whose work has been widely published in a variety of media (*Weird Fiction Review* print, S. T. Joshi's *Black Wings* series, *Fangoria*, others). He describes his work as Dark Magical Realism. He is also the founder of a website and digest called *[NameL3ss]*; his books include *A Darke Phantastique*, *Disorders of Magnitude*, and *Simulacrum and Other Possible Realities*. His filmic efforts are *Charles Beaumont: The Life of Twilight Zone's Magic Man*, *The AckerMonster Chronicles!*, and *Image, Reflection, Shadow: Artists of the Fantastic*.

The *Oxford Companion to English Literature* describes **Ramsey Campbell** as "Britain's most respected living horror writer." He has been given more awards than any other writer in the field, including the Grand Master Award of the World Horror Convention, the Lifetime Achievement Award of the Horror Writers Association, and the Living Legend Award of the International Horror Guild. In 2015 he was awarded an honorary fellowship by Liverpool John Moores University for outstanding services to literature.

Probably best known for her Weird Western Hexslinger series (*A Book of Tongues*, *A Rope of Thorns*, and *A Tree of Bones* [all from ChiZine]), **Gemma Files** has been an award-winning horror author for more than twenty years, as well as a film critic, journalist, and teacher. Her most recent novel is *Experimental Film* (ChiZine).

Richard Gavin's work explores the realm where dread and the sublime intersect. He has written five collections of supernatural fiction, including *At Fear's Altar* (Hippocampus Press, 2012) and *Sylvan Dread* (Three Hands Press, 2016). His esoteric writings include *The Benighted Path* (Theion Publishing, 2016). He lives in Ontario, Canada.

Caitlín R. Kiernan is a two-time recipient of both the World Fantasy and Bram Stoker Awards, and the *New York Times* has declared her "one of our essential writers of dark fiction." Her recent novels include *The Red Tree* and *The Drowning Girl: A Memoir*, and, to date, her short stories have been collected in thirteen volumes, including *Tales of Pain and Wonder, A Is for Alien, The Ammonite Violin & Others*, the World Fantasy Award–winning *The Ape's Wife and Other Stories*, and *Beneath an Oil-Dark Sea: The Best of Caitlín R. Kiernan (Volume 2)*. Currently she is editing her fourteenth collection, *Houses under the Sea: Mythos Tales*, for Centipede Press. She is working on her next novel, *Interstate Love Song*, based on "Interstate Love Song (Murder Ballad #8)." She lives in Providence, Rhode Island.

Award-winning author **Nancy Kilpatrick** has published eighteen novels and more than 220 short stories, and has edited fifteen anthologies, including *nEvermore! Tales of Murder, Mystery & the Macabre*, a finalist for both a Bram Stoker Award and an Aurora Award. Recent short work includes: *Black Wings 5; Searchers After Horror; The Darke Phantastique; Zombie Apoclaypse: Endgame!; Blood Sisters: Vampire Stories by Women; The Madness of Cthulhu 2; Innsmouth Nightmares; Stone Skin Bestiary*. Her graphic novel *Nancy Kilpatrick's Vampyre Theater* has just been released.

John Langan is aht euathor of two novels, *House of Windows* (Night Shade, 2009) and *The Fisherman* (Word Horde, 2016), and thee collections of short fiction, *Mr. Gaunt and Other Uneasy Encounters* (Prime, 2008), *The Wide, Carnivorous Sky and Other Monstrous Geographies* (Hippocampus Press, 2013), and *Sefira and Other Betrayals* (Hippocampus Press, forthcoming). With Paul Tremblay, he has coedited *Creatures: Thirty Years* *of Monsters* (Prime, 2011). One of the founders of the Shirley Jackson Awards, he served as a juror for the awards during their first three years. He lives in New York's Hudson Valley with his family and a metal owl.

Reggie Oliver has been a professional playwright, actor, and theatre director. Besides plays, his publications include the authorized biography of Stella Gibbons, *Out of the Woodshed* (Bloomsbury 1998), and six collections of stories of supernatural terror, of which the fifth, *Mrs Midnight* (Tartarus Press, 2011) won the Children of the Night Award. His novel, *The Dracula Papers I—The Scholar's Tale* (Chomu Press, 2011), is the first of a projected four. Another novel, *Virtue in Danger*, was published in 2013 by Zagava Books, and a new novel, *The Boke of the Divill*, is due from Dark Renaissance Books. His stories have appeared in more than fifty anthologies.

W. H. Pugmire writes fiction so as to be identified with his literary hero, H. P. Lovecraft. He is the creator of Sesqua Valley, and for the past few years has delighted in setting his tales in the mythical towns invented by E'ch-Pi-El. His most recent books are *In the Gulfs of Dream and Other Lovecraftian Tales* (Dark Renaissance Books, 2015), coauthored with David Barker, and *Monstrous Aftermath* (Hippocampus Press, 2015). His collaborative novel (with David Barker) set in Lovecraft's dreamland, *Witches in Dreamland*, is forthcoming from Dark Regions Press, and he is writing new stories for his second book from Centipede Press. He dreams in Seattle.

Darrell Schweitzer is the author of three novels, *The White Isle*, *The Shattered Goddess*, and *The Mask of the Sorcerer*, and about 300 short stories. A collection of his Lovecraftian fiction, *Awaiting*

Strange Gods, recently appeared from Fedogan & Bremer. He is a four-time World Fantasy Award finalist and one-time winner. He was co-editor of *Weird Tales* from 1988 to 2007.

John Shirley is a novelist, screenwriter, television writer, songwriter, and author of numerous story collections. He is a past Guest of Honor at the World Horror Convention and won the Bram Stoker Award for his story collection *Black Butterflies* (Ziesing, 1998). His screenplays include *The Crow.* He has written teleplays for *Poltergeist: The Legacy, Deep Space Nine,* and other shows. His novels include *Demons* (Del Rey, 2002), the *A Song Called Youth* trilogy (1985–90), *Wetbones* (Ziesing, 1992), *Bleak History* (Simon & Schuster, 2009), and *Everything Is Broken* (Prime Books, 2012). His newest books are *New Taboos* (PM Press, 2013) and *Doyle After Death* (HarperCollins, 2013). His latest story collection is *In Extremis: The Most Extreme Stories of John Shirley* (Underland Press, 2012).

Simon Strantzas resides with his wife in Toronto, Canada, and is the author of four short story collections, including *Burnt Black Suns* (Hippocampus Press, 2014). His fiction has been reprinted in *Best New Horror, The Best Horror of the Year,* and *The Year's Best Dark Fantasy & Horror,* and has been a finalist for both the British Fantasy and Shirley Jackson Awards.

Steve Rasnic Tem's last novel, *Blood Kin,* won the Bram Stoker Award. His new novel from Solaris, *Ubo,* a science fictional exploration of violence told through the viewpoints of some of history's most dangerous figures, is due out in January 2017. Also appearing in 2017 from Apex Books is a writing guide, *Yours to Tell: Dialogues on the Art and Practice of Writing* (cowritten with Melanie Tem).

Real doozies of nightmares were a staple of **Jonathan Thomas**'s childhood, possibly thanks to permissive parents indulging his taste for movies such as *Angry Red Planet,* TV fare such as *Thriller,* and their horror-comics equivalents, under the pretext of "developing his imagination" (and really, should his mother have read him *Island of Dr. Moreau* as a bedtime story?). Decades later, these dreams have informed numerous of his stories and lyrics, and he takes it as the highest praise when his work inflicts nightmares on others. His newest collection is *Dreams of Ys and Other Invisible Worlds* (Hippocampus Press, 2015).

Donald Tyson was born in Halifax, Nova Scotia. His horror stories have appeared in numerous anthologies, such as *Searchers After Horror* (Fedogan & Bremer, 2014), *A Mountain Walked* (Centipede Press, 2014), and *Innsmouth Nightmares* (PS Publishing, 2015). In 2015 his short novel *The Lovecraft Coven* was published by Hippocampus Press, and his collection of Abdul Alhazred stories, *Tales of Alhazred,* by Dark Renaissance Books. Currently, he is a regular contributor to *Dark Discoveries* magazine.

Stephen Woodworth is the author of the *New York Times* bestselling Violet series of paranormal thrillers, including *Through Violet Eyes, With Red Hands, In Golden Blood,* and *From Black Rooms* (Random House, 2004–06). His short fiction has appeared in such publications as *Black Wings IV* and *V, Weird Tales, Realms of Fantasy, Fantasy & Science Fiction, The Year's Best Fantasy,* and *Midian Unmade.* He is currently at work on a new novel.